Praise for L.A. Witt's *Conduct Unbecoming*

"I really enjoyed these two guys and their struggles with being gay in the military. L.A. Witt writes a really hot book and her voice is one that I can't get enough of. I'll definitely be hitting her back list."

~ *USA TODAY*

"A wonderful story about two lonely men stationed overseas who find love and companionship with each other."

~ *Reviews by Jessewave*

"Between Ms. Witt's descriptive words and wonderfully flawed, but sexy heroes, I really enjoyed every minute of it and hated to see it come to an end."

~ *Top 2 Bottom Reviews*

Look for these titles by *L.A. Witt*

Now Available:

Nine-tenths of the Law
The Distance Between Us
A.J.'s Angel
Out of Focus
The Closer You Get
Meet Me in the Middle

Tooth & Claw
The Given & the Taken
The Healing & the Dying
The United & the Divided

As Lauren Gallagher:

Who's Your Daddy?
All the King's Horses
The Princess and the Porn Star

Conduct Unbecoming

L.A. Witt

Samhain Publishing, Ltd.
11821 Mason Montgomery Road, 4B
Cincinnati, OH 45249
www.samhainpublishing.com

Conduct Unbecoming

Print ISBN: 978-1-61921-405-7
Digital ISBN: 978-1-61921-160-5

Editing by Linda Ingmanson
Cover by Angela Waters

First Samhain Publishing, Ltd. electronic publication: October 2012
First Samhain Publishing, Ltd. print publication: December 2013

Dedication

To my husband, Eddie, for helping me with all the military references in this book.

To my editor, Linda, for putting up with me on all my Samhain books.

Thank you for everything.☺

L.A. Witt

Chapter One

Eric

"Dude, Okinawa is a fucking shit-hole."

My cousin Jim's words repeated over and over in the back of my mind, but I couldn't bring myself to give a fuck. Yeah, yeah, yeah, maybe the place was a shit-hole like he said. Maybe it was worse. Fine. Whatever.

Wedged into an uncomfortable seat in coach, equal parts physically and emotionally drained, I watched the map on the screen document every mile the plane had traveled. I couldn't have cared less about the tiny green dot that was my destination. After nearly twenty-four hours of sitting in airports and flying, with that green dot rapidly approaching, all I could think about was the person I'd left behind.

How the fuck was I supposed to get through three years living this far from my daughter? The year in Iraq and the other in Afghanistan hadn't even been this daunting. *Three* years?

When she'd dropped me at the airport this morning—yesterday?—and we'd said good-bye, Marie hadn't cried like she had when I left for Iraq or Afghanistan, but she'd had tears in her eyes. Sure, she was excited that I'd given her my car, but that didn't soften the blow by much. The girl could handle a lot, and she could keep herself together better than most people I knew. Like anyone, though, she had her limits. If I knew her, she *just* made it out of the airport parking garage before she had to pull over and cry. If she made it that far, she did better than me.

We could do this somehow. I'd just try not to think about the fact that by the time we lived on the same landmass again, she'd be twenty. I was leaving during her junior year in high school, and I'd be back with just a few months to spare before I could buy her that first beer.

I sniffed sharply and swallowed the ache in my throat. Taking a deep breath, I looked at my watch. It was a few minutes shy of 2300, and my ears had popped twice, so we must have been descending. About fucking time too. My flight had been delayed a couple of times, and my 2145 arrival was now scheduled for 2315. Didn't really matter, though. My body clock was so fucked up from almost an entire day of traveling, I couldn't figure out what time it was or what time I thought it should be. Every time I looked at a clock, my mind went "Really? I thought it was...fuck, I don't know what time I thought it was."

Out of curiosity, I opened the window shade and peered outside.

Darkness obscured most of the island that would be home for the next three years. City lights glittered with considerably less intensity than those of Tokyo or San Diego. Scattered headlights wound between buildings just beyond the airport, and the occasional tiny, bobbing light indicated a boat out in the ink-black water. Distant pinpricks of light suggested power lines and cell towers along uneven, maybe mountainous terrain, and faintly glowing areas implied cities and towns extending much farther into the distance than I'd have expected on such a small island.

"Trust me, man," Jim's voice echoed in my head. *"That place blows. Everything's so Americanized, it barely even counts as living in a foreign country. The people fucking hate us, they can't fucking drive, and oh my God, there is* nothing *to do."*

Great. Yet another reason I'd probably finish out this tour just like everyone else who came here: bored out of my mind, itching to go back to the States, and with a substantially higher alcohol tolerance than I'd ever imagined possible. As if two combat tours and my last stateside command hadn't already ratcheted up my alcohol tolerance to unhealthy levels.

I exhaled and pulled down the window shade. Didn't really matter what the island or the command were like. This could be the shittiest command in the Navy on the shittiest piece of dirt in the world, and I still wouldn't feel any worse than I did now. Three years without my kid? It hadn't even been twenty-four hours, and the distance already hurt like hell.

The plane touched down as gently as planes ever do. Smoother than the three-bounce landing in Narita, anyway. Hell, we could have come in sideways and rolled a few times for all I cared. I was just happy to be on the ground, even if this was the last place in the world I wanted to be.

I followed the other passengers off the plane into the airport. In the terminal, most of the brightly colored signs were in both English and Japanese, but I couldn't comprehend them anyway, so they may as well have been in Swahili. Or Martian, for as far from home as I felt.

I trudged down the walkway with the other passengers, hoping they weren't quite so aimless. Someone must have had half a clue, because at some point we were in baggage claim.

Within minutes, the belt started, and one by one, bags appeared from behind the black rubber flaps. It hadn't been a crowded flight, so it didn't take long for my luggage to show up.

I picked up my seabag and slung it over my aching shoulders. With that and my laptop case, I shuffled after the slowly moving crowd of passengers. We'd already cleared customs at Narita, so I went straight from baggage claim to the automatic glass doors that divided arriving passengers from the crowds of people waiting to meet us. I scanned the crowd for my sponsor, the person my new command had assigned to pick me up at the airport and help me get to where I needed to be. Over the next two weeks, his job was to help me find a car, get a cell phone, learn my way around the various bases, and check into our command.

A guy in civvies and sporting a sandy-blond high-and-tight stepped out of the crowd. "MA1 Randall?"

I extended my hand. "You must be MA2 Dawson."

He nodded and shook my hand. "We're off duty, so call me Chris."

"In that case, I'm Eric."

"Well, welcome to Okinawa, Eric." He gestured at my bags.

"Need a hand with this stuff?"

"Think I've got it. Thanks, though."

"No problem." He nodded toward the exit. "This way."

I followed him to another set of automatic glass doors, and when they slid open, we stepped outside.

My first breath of Okinawa was so thick it almost choked me. I coughed and swore.

Chris laughed. "The humidity takes some getting used to."

"I'm sure."

He led me into a fluorescent-lit parking garage and stopped behind a beat-up silver Toyota. Obviously, he hadn't been kidding when he'd told me about buying a beater instead of dropping serious money on a car.

"You're only here for one tour," he'd said via e-mail a few days ago. *"Just buy a piece-of-shit hoopty ride that runs. It's all you need unless you're into drifting or something."* Evidently, he practiced what he preached, because I was pretty sure the rust and salt were the only things holding the car together.

He popped the trunk, and the lid squealed on its corroded hinges as he raised it all the way. We loaded my luggage into the trunk, and after he'd slammed the lid, I started toward the passenger side, but Chris stopped me.

"Other side," he said.

Fatigue and jet lag conspired to keep me from understanding him for a few long seconds. Then I remembered cars were right-hand drive here.

I got in on the other side, and as Chris started the car, he said, "You want me to stop so you can get a bite to eat or anything? Or just get you back to the barracks?"

"Barracks," I said. "I ate something in Tokyo, and I'm about ready to fucking collapse."

He chuckled and turned around to back the car out of the parking space. "I've made that trip a few times myself. I know exactly what you mean." As he shifted into Drive and started out of the garage, he added, "Just wait until you go back stateside. The jet lag going that way is fucking brutal."

"I could think of worse things," I said, more to myself than him.

By the time he pulled out of the garage and onto the road, I was already mentally writing up a leave chit so I could fly home. As if they'd grant leave when I was barely feet dry on the island. It'd be months before I could accrue enough leave time to go home, unless there was some kind of emergency. I didn't even qualify for that once-a-year free flight back to the States until I'd been here six months, and then it was still a matter of getting leave approved. Leave which I'd burned like it was going out of style when I thought I was staying in San Diego for three more years. Leave which would take months to accrue again so I—

Whoa.

The curving road suddenly dumped us on a highway with a view of the city, and... This was not the Okinawa I expected.

The city of Naha was nothing short of sensory overload. Bright neon signs, most of which were in Japanese, lit up windows and storefronts. Casinos rivaled those on the Las Vegas strip for their ostentatiously colorful displays advertising huge jackpots, slot machines, and something called Pachinko. Buildings didn't quite qualify as skyscrapers, but they cut an impressive profile along either side of Highway 58, suggesting Naha was much more cosmopolitan than I'd anticipated seeing anywhere on Okinawa.

And much more...alien. The vast majority of signs were in Japanese kanji, which flew right in the face of my cousin's accusation that Okinawa was heavily Americanized. I had taken his comments at face value and hadn't prepared myself for this. Not that I'd had the opportunity, since I'd gotten slam orders and barely had time to get my shit together to move, but this? This was all so bizarre and weird, and I was completely...lost. Dropped in the middle of a place that was a lot more Japanese than it was American, when I'd expected the polar opposite, and unable to shake the feeling that I was more alone than I'd ever been in my life.

As Chris continued driving, the occasional familiar symbol emerged from the scenery, but even they were alien here. Traffic signals were horizontal instead of vertical. A giant bowling pin was all that gave away the purpose of one brightly lit, kanji-inscribed building, and the golden arches gleamed above some more kanji that presumably spelled out *McDonald's*. A few blocks later, the red-and-white likeness of Colonel Sanders stood out from a bunch of incomprehensible signs, though the text on the Kentucky Fried Chicken sign was in Japanese. Even the familiar...wasn't.

God, this was weird. It was like an alternate universe where everything I knew was skewed and warped into something I didn't recognize, underscoring how lost I felt. How far I was from home. From anything. From any*one*.

It wasn't my first time in a foreign country—hell, I'd been to two war zones—but every light and every sign in a language not my own drove it home that I was nowhere near Kansas anymore. A million miles from everything I knew, surrounded by an alien landscape, I was keenly aware that I was the alien and I wasn't going home anytime soon.

I rubbed my eyes and sighed, then focused again on the strange world around me. Maybe it was an exercise in futility, but I was hell-bent on adapting to this place. Getting used to it. Making sense of it.

And maybe I was just tired, but I could swear I had never seen so many vending machines in my life. Of course, they stood out—while the rest of a particular block might have been dark, the alternately red and white machines glowed with rows of colorful drinks. And sometimes there would be a cluster of four or five machines. Then half a block later, another one. Or another cluster.

Am I losing my mind?

"Am I imagining all these vending machines?" I asked.

Chris laughed. "Nope. They're everywhere. Just wait until you see one out in the sticks. I've seen them next to sugarcane fields, in cemeteries, all over the place." He gestured at what appeared to be a convenience store with a green, white and blue sign that read *Family Mart*. "You'll see shitloads of those too."

Well, at least I wasn't losing my mind.

Yet.

After a while, the scenery changed. The flashing, glittering lights faded. Buildings weren't as tall—maybe two to three stories at most—and weren't packed together quite so tightly. Along the right side of the road, a chain-link fence with three strands of barbed wire across the top lined the sidewalk. A base, I guessed.

"We here already?" Already? Jesus, I'd been traveling for at least the better part of twenty-four hours. Already, my ass.

Chris shook his head. "Nope, Kadena's further up. This is Camp Foster. Next base is Lester, then after *that* is Kadena."

Great. I hoped when he said "further up," he didn't mean more than a few miles. Then again, this island was the size of a potato chip crumb. If we drove much farther, we'd wind up on the mainland or something.

Scanning as much of my surroundings as I could see, though, it occurred to me that while the island looked tiny on a map, it was a good-size chunk of land in person. I wasn't sure how small I'd expected the place to be, but I couldn't help thinking it was bigger than I thought it would be.

Big, small, didn't matter. I was stuck here. No turning back, no early parole. There might as well have been a fence all the way around the island's perimeter, keeping me here until the Navy was damn good and ready to let me out. Who knew a landmass could be so fucking claustrophobic?

"This is Kadena." Chris drew me out of my thoughts as he turned off the highway and pulled up to a base gate. "You'll be staying on this base until you find permanent housing."

"How far is this from White Beach?"

He shrugged. "Ten or fifteen clicks."

I raised an eyebrow. "And I'm staying here even while I don't have a car?"

"I'll be driving you until you get your car and license," he said. "Don't worry about it." He rolled down the window. The sentry took our IDs, looked them over, then handed them back and wordlessly waved us through.

At the barracks, I checked in, and we took my bags up to

my room. Then Chris left for the evening, and I could finally settle into something that wasn't a hard plastic chair in a terminal or a sardine-can seat on a plane.

It was oppressively hot outside, and the air conditioning in my room was like an icy slap in the face. Naturally, there was no adjusting the A/C. It was either on or it was off, and with the heat outside, I didn't dare switch off the cold air.

Lovely. I'd have to bundle up in my room and strip down to shorts and a T-shirt whenever I went outside. It was only temporary, though. When I finally found a more permanent place, it would damn well have adjustable A/C, or I'd install it my fucking self.

As for tonight, sleep. Sweet, sweet, no-longer-crammed-into-a-damned-plane *sleep*.

I had just energy enough left for a desperately needed shower. Once I'd dried off, I turned on my laptop long enough to tap into the barracks Wi-Fi and send e-mails to my daughter, ex-wife, and ex-boyfriend to let them know I'd made it safely.

Then I closed my laptop and left it next to my seabag on one of the beds. As I did, a couple of travel brochures that had been fanned across the table caught my eye. Though I was so exhausted I could barely see straight, curiosity got the best of me, and I picked them up. Golf. Hiking. Boating.

Snorkeling?

Well, that was promising. At least there was *something* here I enjoyed. If the snorkeling was anything like Hawaii or Guam, then maybe I could get through this three-year tour without completely losing my mind.

I tried not to think about that number, but it just kept banging around in my head. Three years in this foreign place where I didn't even know how to drive or how to speak the language. Three years without my daughter. Three fucking years.

I tossed the brochures aside. Only I could find a reason to be depressed after looking through pictures of turquoise water and colorful fish, but the promise of snorkeling didn't quite make up for everything else on my mind.

Lying back on the hard barracks bed, fingers laced behind my head, I should have fallen asleep in seconds. I should have been out cold before I even hit the pillow.

But I was exhausted to the point of restlessness. I teetered on the brink of thinking myself into insomnia or crying myself to sleep. Again.

It didn't help that my options were limited when it came to making friends on this island. Even finding someone to go snorkeling with once in a while promised to be a challenge because the military was ridiculously restrictive about fraternization. As an E-6, I couldn't hang out with E-5s or below without risking disciplinary action, and the E-7s and above had to be careful spending time with my paygrade or below. That and if the chiefs were anything like the ones at my last three commands, I could pretty much rule out the E-7s and above anyway, unless I wanted to go to the brig for kicking someone's ass. So it was E-6s or nothing. E-6s who were usually married, which meant family get-togethers instead of hanging out with single guys. Well, unless they were golfing. And of course, I didn't golf.

If making friends would take an Act of Congress, I had a sneaking suspicion it would also be three years before I could get laid on a regular basis either. And fucking *forget* any kind of relationship. Most Americans on Okinawa were military, which meant if I wanted to date, casually or otherwise, I had to fish off the company pier. Even with the repeal of DADT, that was never a wise career move, but unless I learned to speak Japanese, I didn't have much choice.

I was a single, gay E-6 on an island where nearly every American was military. I didn't golf. I wasn't a huge drinker. I didn't speak a lick of Japanese. My kid was an ocean away.

Reality started sinking its teeth in. I tried to blink away the sting in my eyes, tried to ignore that pressing ache in my throat, but with each passing moment, the scales tipped more and more in favor of crying myself to sleep—again.

No two ways about it, Eric. The next three years are going to be very, very *lonely.*

The next two weeks were occupied with the delightful process of finding my sea legs in a new command. There was the usual endless stream of paperwork, headache and more paperwork. My favorite part of the military. I was assigned a duty section of about a dozen other masters-at-arms—Navy police, like me—and was made watch commander. By the end of it all, I was settled in at work, had a piece-of-shit car and a nice apartment a few kilometers off base, and still missed my daughter so bad I couldn't see straight.

Day in, day out, getting to know strangers at a professional arm's length. Then I'd go home to an apartment building full of people who were lovely and polite, but there was a mile-wide language barrier between me and every one of my neighbors. Fifteen minutes here and five minutes there, talking on the webcam with my ex-wife or my parents. An hour every couple of days with Marie. My plane had long since landed, but the distance just kept growing the more I realized I was here and she was there and that wasn't changing anytime soon.

My skin crawled from the lack of human contact. Real, genuine human contact. Something that wasn't filtered by regulations and geography.

On my third Friday night in town, Chris offered to take me out to dinner with his wife and some guys from work, but I bowed out. All my things had arrived yesterday, I'd told him, and I still needed to unpack.

Forget unpacking. I was itching to find something to do.

Who was I kidding? I didn't want something to do. I wanted some*one* to do. I couldn't think of anything else to alleviate this craving, or at least distract me from it for a while.

Sitting on my couch with my feet up on a box of something I hadn't bothered unpacking, I balanced my laptop on my knee and opened up my browser.

More than once while I'd lived in temporary lodging, I'd been tempted to look up certain aspects of Okinawa's nightlife, but—rational or not—I was terrified someone would find out.

Not that I was one of those tin-foil-hat wearers who was convinced Big Brother was constantly peering over my shoulder, but my time in the military had given me a healthy respect for the need to be extra, extra, no-measure-is-too-paranoid discreet about some parts of my personal life, especially in a place like this where any man I fucked probably carried a military ID.

Safely on my own off-base Wi-Fi, I searched. The search engine brought up a few places that didn't pique my interest. One catered almost exclusively to locals, and I wasn't familiar enough with Okinawan customs to venture into that realm yet. Another was on the off-limits list because the bartenders had been busted selling spice, a synthetic form of marijuana that was a huge problem here. A third had some attractive photos and looked like it was easy to find, but a few people had posted reviews saying it was more of a hangout for members of the Yakuza crime syndicates than a place to meet other guys. Not a good place for a cop to show his face, never mind try to get laid.

Ah, but what was this? Palace Habu.

It was down an alley off Gate Two Street. Of course it was. I'd heard that the majority of the nightlife for Americans on this island existed along that several-block stretch of clubs, shops and restaurants just outside Kadena's Gate Two. And being down an alley wasn't unusual either, apparently, the alleys and side streets here were not only safe but brimming with places to eat, shop and party.

For that matter, dangerous or not, the fact that the Palace Habu was down an alley meant it was harder to see from the main road. Always a bonus when I didn't want anyone I worked with to know where I was spending my evening.

I printed the directions, then looked up the number for a taxi to take me from my apartment out by White Beach, which was the base I was attached to, to the legendary Gate Two Street.

Half an hour later, I was in a cab and on my way.

Gate Two Street certainly lived up to its reputation as party central. The street was choked with cabs, and nearly everyone on the sidewalks was obviously American and military. Bright neon signs blazed above shops, clubs and tattoo parlors, trying to draw people in to spend their freshly deposited paychecks. Signs advertised the beers on tap, especially Orion, a local beer that was wildly popular among Americans and Okinawans alike.

Maybe one of these days I'd go exploring and check out the rest of this street, but not tonight. I had a destination, something I needed, and that was final.

In front of a clothing store, which the website had said to use as a landmark, the cabbie let me out into the sticky, humid night. From there, according to the directions in my hand, I was supposed to face the store, then turn to my left until I saw a sign with a cartoon monkey on it.

What is this? A scavenger hunt?

Certain I was about to end up on some form of *Candid Camera—Hey, look! Another clueless new guy fell for it!*—I faced the store and turned to my left. Sure enough, on the corner of another building about twenty feet away was a weather-beaten sign with a cartoon monkey.

The directions indicated I was to go down that alley. I paused at its entrance, looking down the narrow, mostly empty gap between the two buildings. Everyone had said Okinawa had little to no violent crime, so it was reasonably safe to go to places like this, but instinct is instinct, especially when that instinct has been fine-tuned by sixteen years as a cop.

I checked the directions one more time. Then I glanced around the street and sidewalk in search of any familiar faces that might recognize mine. If any of my guys were here, looking for the booze and tail that drew everyone to Gate Two Street on Friday nights, I didn't see them. Hopefully that meant they didn't see me either.

Taking a deep breath, I started down the alley.

Numerous doors lined the brick walls, and thumping music came from behind several of them, adding an irregular, echoing heartbeat to the otherwise quiet alley. About forty feet from the street, I found the door I was looking for, the one marked *Palace Habu*. I went inside and followed a dark stairwell up to a windowless, black-painted door with a similar sign.

I put my hand on the doorknob, which vibrated with the music on the other side, and closed my eyes. Going into a gay establishment in a new city was always unnerving, especially if there was a significant military population. It didn't matter how often I told myself that if someone saw me in this place, that meant they were there for the same reason and thus wouldn't be inclined to rat me out. And even if they did, I couldn't get kicked out for being gay now. Still, I didn't want people to know. Bad for the career, shitty for the work environment.

But no one would know. They wouldn't know I was here, they wouldn't know how badly I needed to share a bed with someone tonight, and what they didn't know wouldn't hurt me.

A glance to the left, a glance to the right, another deep breath, and I pushed open the door.

Chapter Two

Shane

When he walked into Palace Habu, I sat up so suddenly, I almost choked on my beer.

He'd never been here before; that much was immediately obvious. Maybe he was new to the island, maybe he was just new to the club, but he had that bewildered, fish-out-of-water look on his face of someone venturing into someplace unfamiliar.

Couldn't really blame him. I'd given the place the same sweeping, disbelieving look when I stepped through that door a little over six months ago. Palace Habu was pretty much designed for sensory overload: flickering lights, bright colors, music videos playing on six different flat-screen televisions. A fog machine kept the air opaque on one side of the room, but an industrial-strength air conditioner prevented the place from getting too humid.

Whether or not it was deliberate, the gaudy, retina-searing sensory overload made it difficult for newcomers to make out those of us who were already in the bar, whereas a strategically placed spotlight made sure we all got a good, clear view of every man as he came through that door. In other words, if my commanding officer came waltzing in, I had a chance to make myself scarce before he saw me.

Which meant this new guy couldn't pick me out of the onslaught of flicker-shadow-flicker, but I could see him. Oh God, could I see him.

He was obviously military. Of course he was. The vast majority of Americans on this island were, but he wore it even in civvies. The high-and-tight haircut was neat, but his dark hair was grown out enough on top to suggest he knew how far he could push the regulations. Even as out of place as he was, he didn't give off much of a nervous vibe. He just looked like someone processing unfamiliar surroundings. He still had confident shoulders and fearless eyes, still carried himself like the kind of man who didn't get intimidated but would look another man square in the eye even if he *was* intimidated.

He was the perfect combination of squared away and arrogant. Not enough of the former to be uptight, just enough of the latter to be irresistibly attractive. He must have been a pilot. They always carried themselves like that, and pilots were, as a rule, hot as hell.

I moistened my lips.

God, please don't be meeting someone here.

That wasn't likely. Men didn't come here to meet someone with whom they'd already crossed paths. No one came here just to hang out, and no one came here on dates. This wasn't a watering hole; it was a hunting ground, and on an island where out, attractive gay men were difficult to find, a man had to move quickly if he saw something he wanted. My head wasn't the only one that had turned when he walked in, and I'd be damned if anyone else got to him first, so when he started through the crowd toward the bar, I flagged down the bartender.

Gesturing toward the newcomer, I said, *"Kono hito no bun wa ore no ogori."* Loosely translated, *Whatever he's drinking, it's on me.*

The bartender, a balding local in a red Hawaiian shirt, grinned and said something I didn't catch over the music. Then he smiled and sidled down the bar toward the newcomer.

Over my drink, I watched, pretending the moisture on my palm was from the ice-cold glass of Orion in my hand.

At the bar, the newcomer stopped, probably poised to order a drink, but then did a double take and looked past the bartender. His lips parted. Yep, he was new to the island. Everyone had the same "what the fuck" reaction when they saw Habu sake for the first time. It was, after all, a little unusual to walk into a bar and see a row of jars containing equal parts transparent amber liquid and angry-looking coiled snake.

He shook his head and returned his attention to the bartender. He placed his order, and while he waited for his drink, let his gaze drift to the Habu sake again. Grinning to myself, I wondered what he'd say if I suggested doing a couple shots of the stuff.

No, Connelly, don't get ahead of yourself. Meet the guy first, then see what kinds of shots he's willing to do.

The bartender slid the glass across the bar, and I held my breath as he put up his hand to reject the thousand-yen bill that came his way. He gestured toward me, and the newcomer's head slowly turned. Through the fog-thickened air and the crazy lights, our eyes met. He raised his glass and inclined his head, a vague smile forming on his lips. I returned the gesture.

He broke eye contact as he took a drink, and I loosed a couple of curses that just got lost in the music anyway. But then he set the glass down, collected the yen he'd tried to use and slipped the bill back into his wallet. After he'd put his wallet in the pocket of his khaki shorts, he picked up his drink and started toward me.

Blood pounding in my ears, I casually hooked my foot around the leg of my barstool just to anchor myself in place. As he neared me, his features sharpened and came into focus like a developing Polaroid. High, smooth cheekbones. Disarming blue eyes. Lips that were probably always *just* on the verge of either a smirk or a devilish grin.

And just like that, some motherfucker with a death wish stepped into the five-foot gap between us and cock-blocked me.

I ground my teeth, glaring at the guy's back. They both made a few small, casual gestures, as people do when making conversation, so I swore into my drink and turned back toward the bar. I wasn't the type to give up easily, especially when I saw someone who intrigued me like this, but there was just enough of a wobble in the intruder's posture to suggest he'd had a hell of a lot to drink. I was in the mood to get laid, not get into a bar brawl, and I had more than enough experience with rowdy drunks to leave well enough alone. No one in this place needed the JPs—Japanese Police—breaking up a fight and calling all our chains of command.

Oh, but for a man that attractive, I had to admit, it *was* tempting.

I took another drink and looked up at the backlit jars of Habu sake. The flickering strobes and wild disco lights rippled over the motionless, coiled snakes, which at least gave me something to look at besides someone else moving in on the guy who'd caught my attention like no man had in I didn't know how long. Shit, maybe I was just way too horny for my own good tonight. It had been a while, after all. Maybe it was just that relentless itch to let some willing stranger distract me from how long it had been since the last willing stranger.

But...no, it was definitely him. Those eyes. That face. That bold I'm-completely-in-control way he carried himself in spite of being someplace unfamiliar. That...that...every fucking thing about him. Even from halfway across the room, the man didn't just radiate sex, he radiated the kind of sex I'd been *dying* to have. Fuck my life.

Probably just as well someone had intercepted him. A man that hot, after I hadn't slept with anyone in months, we were liable to break furn—

Movement beside me turned my head, and in a heartbeat, I couldn't breathe.

From just inches away, so close he could touch me if he wanted to, he shot me a mouthwatering, asymmetrical grin. "Hi."

I cleared my throat and managed a strangled, "Um, hi." Up close, he was even more attractive. His features were sharp in all the right places, smooth in all the others, and the flickering and flashing lights didn't even try to take the edge off the intensity of his blue eyes.

"I, um..." He paused, then set his glass on the bar beside mine. "Thanks for the drink." He extended his now-free hand. "I'm Eric."

"Shane." Holding his gaze, I shook his hand, and *oh my God, I want you.* Heat rushed into my cheeks, and I was thankful for the club's lighting, which hopefully hid any new color in my face. Desperate for some sort of conversation, I said, "You new to the island?"

He laughed, which did all kinds of weird shit to my blood pressure. With an expression that was probably as close to shy as he was capable, he looked at me through his lashes. "Is it that obvious?"

I smiled. "Nothing to be embarrassed about. Culture shock's just part of the experience."

"Yeah." He looked around the bar, then sniffed as he raised his drink almost to his lips. "So much for the whole place being all Americanized and shit."

"Someone fed you that crap too?" I shook my head and laughed, pretending I wasn't holding on to my glass and the edge of the bar for dear life. "For all the bullshit people told me before I came here, you'd think we were talking about two different places."

He eyed me. "So, the things people say, they're not true?"

"If they told you the place was boring, Americanized or a dump? Then no, they're not true."

"Interesting," he said, more to himself than to me.

"Trust me," I said. "This place is awesome. You just have to, you know, get off the fucking bases and go check it out."

"Is that right?" He rested his elbow on the bar. "So what else haven't I been told about this island?"

"I don't suppose anyone mentioned the castles?"

His eyebrows shot up. "Castles? No, I can't say they did."

I chuckled. "Didn't you do any homework before you came out here?"

He rolled his eyes and gave me a good-humored scowl. "I got slam orders. Forget researching the place. I barely had time to schedule a pack-out."

I grimaced. "Oh, ouch."

"Yeah." He took a drink, holding my gaze over the rim of his glass. As he set it down, he said, "So. Castles? Do tell."

Thank God for that easy conversation piece. Nothing like a bunch of fourteenth-century castles to give us something to talk about while I tried to get used to just being this close to him.

My heart pounded all the way through the stories of exploring the ruins of Katsuren, Nakagusuku, Shuri, and Nakijin Castles. When he asked about some of the hiking trails, the legendary aquarium, and the Japanese Navy Underground Headquarters, I had to ask him to repeat himself. I blamed it on the loud music, which was a convenient enough excuse. He didn't need to know I was too distracted by thoughts of what he could do with his mouth to understand the words those perfect lips formed.

All through the conversation, one thing neither of us brought up was work. We both had the posture and haircuts, and we were both Americans on Okinawa. The vast majority of men who came to the island were military, and Palace Habu may as well have been a gay officers' club. That answered any questions either of us might have cared to ask about what we did, and the less we knew about each other's jobs, the less anyone here might overhear anything. In fact, right now, I didn't give a shit what he did for a living, and I'd have bet money he didn't care what I did. If I wanted to talk about work, I'd be out with my buddies from work.

And all the while, as we talked about the island and everything it had to offer, I still couldn't quite find my equilibrium. The things this man did to my head were unreal. Especially since I was right about one thing: Eric didn't shy away from eye contact. Not at all. And the more he held my gaze, the harder it was for me to hold his. Captains and admirals couldn't get a flinch out of me, but he had me seeking refuge in my drink like a nervous kid.

After a while, as they often do, the conversation reached a lull. One of those moments when neither of us was in any hurry to leave, but we didn't know each other well enough to know which direction to take the conversation.

I surreptitiously tapped my fingers on my knee beneath the bar, trying to figure out my next move. Some guys liked dancing. Me, I preferred to wait on breaking a sweat until the clothes had come off. Eric threw a few glances toward the dance floor, but most guys who were itching to dance couldn't help keeping time with the music. Tapping a foot, drumming fingers, nodding to the beat. Not Eric. Wherever we went from here, the dance floor wasn't it.

Eric gestured at my drink, which was almost empty. "Refill?"

"Yeah, sure."

He smiled. "It's on me this time." He flagged down the bartender and ordered us a couple of drinks.

Silence once again set in, and it didn't help that the music was getting progressively louder. This place never got extremely crowded, but more guys had arrived since Eric showed up, and there would probably still be more. More people, more music, more noise. I glanced at Eric. Maybe out here in the loud, wild open wasn't the place to continue this conversation.

With a sharp but subtle nod, I indicated the other side of the room. "Want to grab a booth? It's quieter over on that side of the club."

"Sure." He picked up his drink. "Lead the way."

Most of the booths were occupied, but we found an empty one near the back. I slid onto the bench, and Eric followed. Though we were still in public, the high walls on three sides of us offered the appearance of complete privacy. We may as well have been alone now, and if not for the murmur of voices straining to be heard over the thumping music, I might have convinced myself we were.

"You're right," he said. "It *is* quieter back here."

"Thank God," I said.

"You know this club pretty well, I'm guessing?" he asked.

"Well enough."

"You come here a lot?"

I laughed. "At the risk of sounding like a complete whore, probably more than I should."

An unreadable thought narrowed Eric's eyes and raised one corner of his mouth. "So you probably know all the little games people play between buying the first drink and getting into bed, don't you?"

I gulped. He was certainly...direct. "I, um, yeah. You could say I've played them a few times." I reached for my beer because my mouth had suddenly gone dry. After I'd taken enough of a drink to moisten my parched tongue, I set the glass on the tiny table. These booths were more bench than table; I wondered if the designers had the same idea I did for how to put such a booth to good use. I wondered if Eric had the same idea. Meeting his eyes, I said, "You know those games pretty well yourself, then?"

"I do." He absently swirled his drink, ice cubes clinking against the sides of the glass. "And to be honest, I hate playing them."

So much for my mouth not being dry. I coughed into my fist. "Do you, now?"

He nodded and held absolutely rock-solid, unwavering eye contact as he said, "Let's just say, when it comes to things like this, I'm more of a shortest-distance-between-two-points kind of guy." A quiet laugh parted his lips and sent my pulse into the stratosphere. Higher still when he added, "Leaves more time and energy to enjoy the destination, don't you think?"

God *damn*, but he was aggressive. Usually, I was the forward one. I was the one who bought a drink for a guy before he even made it to the damned bar. I sure as fuck wasn't the one who broke eye contact first or waited for the other guy to make a move. I was never caught off guard when someone all but brazenly suggested we go someplace else and fuck, because I was usually the one who said it. I wasn't used to someone who was easily as aggressive as I was, almost to the point of intimidating.

I wasn't used to it, but I liked it.

I moved closer to him and draped my arm across the back of the bench. Before I could even speak, Eric's eyes flicked toward my arm, then met my own, and the grin on his lips said nothing if not, *That the best you got?*

Oh, so it's gonna be like that, is it?

In one smooth motion, my arm was around his shoulders. He broke eye contact long enough to watch his own hand deposit his glass on the table, and as he looked at me again, his now-free hand went to my leg.

I cleared my throat just to get some air moving. "So are you suggesting you prefer to skip everything between point A and point B, and go directly to point B?"

His hand drifted farther up my thigh. "Abso-fucking-lutely." If I thought his eyes were intense when they locked on my own, they damn near liquefied my spine when they flicked to my lips, then met mine again. It didn't take a genius to figure out what he was thinking, and I didn't doubt I wore the exact same thoughts on my sleeve. We both knew where this was going, and now we stared each other down, our eyes issuing silent dares to make the next move.

I let my gaze flick to his lips. The corner of his mouth rose slightly, bringing that almost-there grin to life and sending a shiver right through me. Then we made eye contact, and we both moved in for the kill.

Our lips met, and everything was still. The club pulsed and flickered around us, but here in this booth, nothing moved except my pounding heart.

Slowly, we eased into motion, wrapping our arms around each other as I dragged my lower lip across his. Eric's hand continued up my inner thigh, and I was sure he intended to tease my painfully hard cock through my shorts. Instead, though, he lifted his hand, then let his fingers drift up the front of my shirt, catching every button on the way up like a silent countdown to making contact with my neck.

Three...

His fingers snagged just below my collar.

Two...

Eric parted my lips with his tongue.

One.

Warm skin grazed the side of my throat.

I closed my eyes and shivered, and Eric took advantage of my being off guard just long enough for him to shove me up against the back of the booth. His kiss went from still and calm to desperate and violent, and I raked my fingers through his hair, returning his kiss with equal ferocity. We both drew sharp, rapid breaths that hissed over the music.

God damn, I wanted to take him someplace private, but I didn't want to stop. Not long enough to stand up, get a cab, go somewhere else and start all over again. I was hard-pressed to think coherently right now, never mind to stop kissing Eric.

His mouth was vaguely sweet with the drink I'd bought him. It was something strong; that much was for certain, though I couldn't identify it. I didn't imagine a man like him needed much liquid courage, but if he did, he certainly used it well.

He held the back of my neck with an unforgiving hand, pressing his fingers in just enough to order me to banish any thoughts of pulling away. As if pulling away was an option. His deep, demanding kiss was fucking addictive.

I slid my hand over the front of his shorts, and he whimpered into my kiss, pushing his erection against my palm. His hand materialized over the back of mine, pressing it even harder against his cock as he kissed me hungrily. Goose bumps prickled every inch of my skin as blood pounded in my ears.

I grabbed his hair and pulled his head back. He groaned, then gasped when my lips met the hot flesh of his throat. He dug his fingers into my back, and we both pressed against each other as I kissed up and down the side of his neck.

He wore some kind of spicy cologne, and it overwhelmed my senses. On some visceral level, I recognized it. I'd smelled it before. Whatever association I might have had with that cologne and some other memory was erased, though, at least for now. All it said to me now was *Eric. I'm breathing Eric.*

The thought of inhaling that spicy, Eric-cologne while I was deep inside him drove me out of my mind. I couldn't wait. Not another goddamned minute. We had to get out of here, or we were going to end up fucking in the men's room.

I was used to men who balked at my aggression, not someone who saw my offer of a drink and raised me a blatant comment about skipping the games and cutting to the chase. I usually had to rein it back to keep from scaring a guy away. Not Eric. He gave as well as he took. Hell if I knew if he was a bottom, a top, or if he—please, please, God, *please*—switched, but I didn't really fucking care. I *had* to get this man into bed.

I brought my head up and, just before our lips brushed, said, "What do you say we get the fuck out of here and get to point B?"

Chapter Three

Eric

I couldn't say if it was Shane's breath warming my skin, his hand over my erection or the blatant acknowledgment this night wasn't ending until we fucked, but as soon as he suggested leaving, I damn near came. The hot guys were *never* aggressive enough for my taste, but Shane was both sexy and brazen. And for tonight? Mine.

I kissed him harder. He gripped my hair tighter and pulled me closer. This wasn't like me. Not even close. I could be almost businesslike in my pursuit of a one-night stand. Buy a drink, exchange some small talk, flirt enough to test the water, then get the fuck out of there. That all went to hell right about the time I found out what Shane's kiss tasted like, and I couldn't let him go even while my mind tried to tell me the only way I'd get him naked was if I pried myself off him long enough to get the fuck out of here. Just...just one more kiss. One more minute. Maybe two.

It must have been at least ten minutes before we finally pulled ourselves apart enough to make an effort to leave the club. Maybe longer than that. The ice had melted in my neglected drink, but for all I knew, that was just from being in such close proximity to the two of us.

Panting just as much as I was, he asked, "Ready to get out of here?"

"Definitely."

We stayed at the booth for a couple more minutes, catching our breath and calming down so we could walk out of here without being too obvious about where we were going or why. My drink was appallingly watered down, thanks to the melted ice, but I didn't care. At least it was cool. Sort of.

We'd already paid our tabs, so we shouldered our way through the crowd and the fog to the exit. We stepped out of the club into the hallway that would take us to the stairwell. Before we reached the stairs, Shane stopped and pulled out his phone.

"I'll get us a cab," he said and speed-dialed a number that presumably connected to a taxi company. He spoke to the person on the other end in impressively fluent Japanese, and a moment later hung up and slid his phone into his back pocket. "Ready?"

"Very."

We started down the stairs, but another thought crossed my mind: if we got into a cab on Gate Two Street, someone might see us. It was way too visible out there.

"Wait." I touched his arm. He stopped and looked back at me, eyebrows up. I gestured down the stairs past us. "We, um... Isn't Gate Two Street a little out in the open for us to leave together?"

He smiled. "Don't worry about it. We're not going out that way."

I hesitated. "Which way are we going?"

"There are tons of back roads and alleys through here. No one will see us." He put a hand on the railing and pushed himself up to kiss me lightly. "Trust me. I've done this before, and I don't want to be seen any more than you do."

After another moment's hesitation, I nodded. "All right, let's go."

At the bottom of the stairwell, we stepped out into the muggy evening air. Instead of turning right to go back to Gate Two Street, we went left. The alley narrowed and zigzagged between oddly shaped buildings.

"I guess before we get in the cab," he said as we walked, his voice low even though the alley was pretty much a ghost town. "We should figure out where we're going."

I glanced at him in the low light. "Well, your place or mine?"

"I'm only a few clicks from here," he said. "Maybe ten or fifteen minutes by cab."

"I live out by Awase and White Beach," I said. "Which is..." I hesitated. "Um, well, I guess you'd know better than I would. I'm still learning the area, but, twenty or thirty minutes, maybe?"

He smiled. "My place, then. If that's all right with you?"

"Fine by me."

My heart beat faster. We both walked a little faster. Christ, we couldn't get to his place fast enough. Some of the shadowy corners in this alley were starting to look really tempting, and to hell with the consequences if someone caught us. Tempting. Very tempting.

As we walked, I struggled to keep my feet under me and not steal too many glances at him. I'd hoped to find someone for a night, but he was more than I'd bargained for. Thank God I'd had the bar to casually lean on earlier when the bartender had pointed out the guy who'd bought my drink, because Shane was fucking gorgeous. His hard, angular features made my mouth water, the cockiness in his posture screamed the kind of confident boldness that melted me in bed, and his piercing green eyes weakened my knees. Good thing he'd bought me a drink, because my mouth went dry the instant I looked his direction.

So I'd taken a drink just to moisten my tongue and started toward him. Then, of course, another jackass had stepped in between us. The room was just crowded enough, I couldn't body-swerve him as easily as I would have liked, and he was insistent as all hell in spite of my polite attempts to exit the conversation. Well, at least until I told him I was a power top with a couple of "questionable" fetishes. Bullshit, of course, but he quickly lost interest, got the fuck out of my way and left me to introduce myself to the gorgeous man who now walked beside me down an alley to meet a taxi.

Okinawa was more than welcome to be a complete shit-hole as long as there were men here like Shane. It had been several minutes since we'd kissed, and my lips still tingled. He was what my ex would have called a Goldilocks kisser: not too forceful, not too timid, but *just* right. Was he ever. I was used to men who either kissed so gently they tickled my mouth, or those who almost bruised my lips. Shane was bold and assertive without overdoing it, and he didn't balk at my own boldness or assertiveness.

God, I *had* to find out what he was like in bed.

Soon, Randall. Soon.

The alley bent once more and spilled out onto a mostly deserted street. Pale streetlights illuminated immaculate flower planters and signs above nail salons, travel agencies, and shops I couldn't identify, thanks to metal doors that had been rolled down over their windows. There were a few cars parked here and there, but otherwise, the place was empty. By day, it was probably as alive with activity as Gate Two Street was after dark. Not now, though.

"There's our ride." Shane nodded down the street, and two headlights approached. On top of the car was a glowing yellow dome with something written in kanji, and when the taxi stopped beside us with a muffled squeak of aging brakes, the green-and-white sign on the door read *Taxi—On-Base Allowed.*

That gave me pause. With the number of people having affairs and fucking around, base housing was a rumor mill if there ever was one. Two men coming home late in the evening could go unnoticed, or it could be very, very noticed. Not good.

When Shane opened the car door and gestured for me to get in, I hesitated.

"You do live off base, right?"

He shot me a toothy grin. "You think I'm crazy enough to bring a guy home in base housing?"

I chuckled. "Just checking."

Our eyes met again. We exchanged grins; then I got into the cab ahead of him. He slid in beside me and said something to the driver in Japanese. The driver responded in the same language, and the car lurched into motion.

For the entire ride, Shane and I didn't look at each other. I didn't look at him, anyway, and I was sure the hairs on my neck would have stood on end if he so much as glanced in my direction. Whether he looked my way or not, the only way I was staying anywhere close to sane was to stare intently through the windshield. There'd be plenty of time to look at each other when we made it to his place.

At Shane's direction, the cab stopped in front of a four-story apartment building. I handed the driver two thousand-yen bills, and he passed back a few coins worth of change. He could have shortchanged me for all I knew, but whatever.

As the cab drove off, Shane led me to the stairs in front of the building. The stairwell was partly open-air, partly enclosed. At every landing, the high concrete wall curved around us like a shell, and I was tempted to grab him and pull him up against me. God damn, I wanted him, and I only barely convinced myself I wouldn't burst into flames if we made ourselves get all the way into his apartment and into his bed before we finally got out of these clothes.

On the third floor, Shane gestured toward the door instead of continuing up the next flight of stairs. Oh, thank God. That meant we were almost—

Shane grabbed me and kissed me. Without missing a beat, I seized fistfuls of his shirt and hauled him to me, hoping he saw it as an aggressive move, not a bid to use him for balance before my legs gave out. Then he shoved me up against the door and pinned my arms beside my head. His kiss was so deliciously aggressive, and with his cock pressed against mine, his hands gripping my wrists painfully tight, and his mouth demanding access to mine, I was sure I'd come if I so much as moved.

He dipped his head and kissed my neck, and I fought to stay in control.

"I suppose I should have asked earlier," he murmured, his breath hot against my throat, "but are you a top or bottom?"

"Either. Both." I licked my lips. "I don't fucking care, just—"

He cut me off with another violent kiss. Then he released one of my hands. I grabbed on to his shoulder for balance, and not a moment too soon, because a second later, his hand was over the front of my shorts, and my knees damn near buckled.

"Fuck," he growled, squeezing gently with his hand as his

lips descended on my neck again. "I've wanted you so damned bad since you walked into the club."

I bit my lip and closed my eyes. I wanted to tell him the feeling was mutual and had been since I first laid eyes on him, but as he stroked me through my clothes and let his lightly stubbled chin brush over my neck, speech was impossible.

Then his fingertips found my zipper pull, and my eyes flew open, but the air in my throat refused to move. His other hand released mine, and with both hands, he unbuckled my belt and unbuttoned the top of my shorts. All the while, his mouth explored the sides of my neck and the underside of my jaw, and I squirmed between him and the door.

His fingers closed around my cock, and that delicious, warm contact made me gasp, which got my breath moving enough so that I could finally speak.

I licked my lips. "Shouldn't we...in the house..."

"Yeah, we should." But he dropped to his knees right there on the welcome mat, and before I could think of a reason to protest, his mouth was around my cock. One flick of his tongue, and my vision blurred. One stroke of his hand, and my spine turned to liquid. I pressed my palms against either side of the doorframe, bracing myself as my knees threatened to go slack. I gasped but forced my eyes to stay open because I wasn't about to miss this.

The dim light from a single overhead bulb rippled across his dark blond hair as his head moved in time with his hand's rapid strokes. It had been too long since I'd experienced a man who sucked cock like he wanted to, not like it was just an obligatory step toward getting what he wanted. Jesus Christ, he was enthusiastic.

I didn't hear him make a sound, but I damn sure felt his voice vibrate against my skin, and I thought I'd go out of my fucking mind. Every stroke, every circle his tongue made around the head of my cock, every groan I felt but didn't hear, drove me insane. I took one hand off the doorframe and dug my teeth into my second knuckle, fighting to stay quiet. I didn't have to ask if he was just doing this to turn me on or if he intended to get me off. Nothing about this said I was going anywhere without coming, and I didn't fight him. Probably couldn't have if I wanted to. Maybe I was just that horny, maybe he was just that good, but holy fuck, there was no holding back.

My back arched off the door, and my knees shook so bad I didn't even bother hoping he didn't notice. My palm slammed against the doorframe again, and I let go of a groan that might have made me panic if I'd given a flying fuck about anything other than coming, and coming, and coming.

Shane stood, and I put my arms around his neck just to stay upright. We kissed breathlessly like we had at the club, except this time, there was salt on his tongue, and my head spun faster with every heartbeat as we made out against his door. I just couldn't get enough of him.

What had gotten into me, I had no idea. Usually once I'd come, I at least slowed down. Backed off a little, long enough to catch my breath, if nothing else. Not now. My need for release was sated for the moment, but my need for him? Not even close.

Hope you can keep up, Shane. I dug my fingers into his shoulders. *Because this is going to be a long night.*

Shane broke the kiss, and between gasps for air, whispered, "Okay, *now* we should get in the house." He pressed his hard-on against my hip. As if I wasn't dizzy enough already, he added, "My neighbors probably wouldn't appreciate it if I fucked you out here."

I just whimpered and pulled him into another kiss. He didn't let it last long, though. Using the door for leverage, he pushed himself off me. Our eyes met in the dim light, and he swept his tongue across his lower lip.

"Bedroom," he said and reached into his pocket. The jingle of his keys made me shiver, and while I fixed my clothes, Shane unlocked the front door.

Inside his apartment, he led me down the dark hall into his bedroom. There, he flicked on the light, and our eyes met. Judging by the hunger in his expression, I suspected we were both very much on the same page: screw making out and slowly getting out of these clothes. Forget being coy and lovingly removing everything one piece at a time like either of us had any doubt about where this was going.

He confirmed that suspicion when he went for the top button of his shirt. I took the hint and started on my own. The more clothing he lost, the more I struggled to navigate simple things like my belt buckle and the buttons on my shirt, because he was even sexier naked. He had the physique of a man who didn't pass his Physical Readiness Tests by the skin of his teeth. If his powerful arms and perfectly flat abs were anything to go by, Shane's gym routine probably made the PRT look like a leisurely stroll down the beach. And, I realized as he kicked off his shorts and briefs, I *had* to have that cock in me sooner than later. Oh my God.

Once we'd stripped out of our clothes, we grabbed on to each other and kissed again with nothing between us. Hot flesh against hot flesh. Fingers digging into bare skin. Shane's very hard cock pressed against my hip. I had to have him. Right now. Foreplay, yeah, yeah, yeah, whatever, fuck me *now*.

I forced myself to break the kiss. "You do have condoms, right?"

"You'd better believe it." He drew me back a step toward the bed. "I wouldn't have brought you back here if I didn't have condoms *and* lube."

"Good. Put 'em on."

He laughed softly and kissed me again. "Eager, are we?"

I wrapped my fingers around his cock, grinning against his lips when he gasped. "Aren't you?" I stroked him slowly, squeezing and releasing just enough to make him squirm.

He grabbed my wrist, exhaling sharply when my hand stopped. "Let me get a condom."

I let him go, and he reached for the nightstand. He pulled out a box of condoms, freed one, and tossed the box next to the bedside lamp.

As he tore the wrapper and rolled on the condom, I wondered what the best position would be to enjoy the hell out of him. If I was on my knees, he could fuck me hard and fast.

On my back with him on top, we could keep on kissing like we had all night while he drove himself into me.

No, no. I knew how I wanted him.

Condom in place, Shane reached for the lube and nodded toward the bed. “Turn around.”

“Nuh-uh.” I grinned. “Get on your back.”

Stroking lube onto his cock, he said, “And what if I want to put you on your knees?”

Oh, it was tempting. Especially with the growl in his voice. Tempting, but no. I wanted him on his back and at my mercy.

I put my hands on his waist and leaned in to kiss him but pulled back at the very last second. “Maybe I want you to do things my way.”

He grinned. “All right. We’ll do things your way.”

He got on the bed on his back, and I sat over him, begging my knees not to shake. It was all I could do to maintain this illusion of being in perfect, unwavering control. Usually, I *was* in total control, and the more Shane rattled my foundations, the more he threw me off balance, the more he intrigued me. The more I wanted him.

He put some lube on his fingers and, eyes locked on mine, reached between us. I sucked in a breath and closed my eyes as he pressed his cool fingertips against my ass. He pressed one in. After a few slow, easy strokes, he added the second. White light flickered at the corners of my vision, and I gritted my teeth every time he withdrew his fingers. Maybe he was just being careful, maybe he was a motherfucking tease; either way, I lost a little more of my mind every time his fingers slipped almost all the way out.

He did withdraw them all the way, and I was about to protest, but then he closed his hand around his cock. *Finally.*

He steadied his cock with one hand and my hip with the other, and he bit his lip as I lowered myself onto him. We both exhaled hard when I took the head of his cock, and Shane closed his eyes and moaned as I took him deeper. No more teasing or being careful. I was in control now, and I wanted every inch of him, fast and hard, and I fucking *took* it.

"Oh my *God*," he groaned, gripping my hips. "Oh, fuck. Faster, Eric."

I slowed down, rising and falling so slowly I could feel every inch of his cock moving in and out of me. He tightened his grasp on my hips and thrust up, trying to urge me into a faster rhythm.

Oh, but I was having none of that. I grabbed one wrist, then the other, and pinned them to the bed like he'd pinned mine to the door.

He smirked. "Like being in control, do—ooh God." He squirmed under me, thrusting up again when I tried to rise off him. "God *damn*, you feel good."

"So do you," I breathed. "You feel amazing."

"I can usually..." His voice trailed off into a moan. "I can usually go on for a while, but you..." He bit his lip, closing his eyes and lifting his hips in search of mine. "Fuck..."

Leaning on his wrists to keep him immobile as well as give me some leverage, I rode him faster, and he rewarded me with the most delicious moans and whimpers.

His fingers curled around empty air, and his wrists twitched in my hands. When I gave him a little more, his eyes flew open. "Jesus..."

"I hope you have more condoms left in that box," I whispered.

Confusion furrowed his brow momentarily like he couldn't even comprehend what I'd said. Then he made the connection. "Ooh, yeah. We have plenty."

"Good." I leaned down and let my lips brush his. "Because I fully intend to fuck you before tonight's over."

Shane groaned, and I couldn't be sure if it was because of what I'd said or because I'd picked up a little more speed.

"God, don't stop, Eric," he moaned. "Don't..." He stared up at the ceiling with unfocused eyes. His lips parted. He closed his eyes and shuddered as he murmured, "Oh God, Eric. Oh God..." His back arched off the bed, and with a soft, helpless sound, Shane completely unraveled. Brow furrowed, fists clenched, lips apart, he lost it, and I kept riding him hard and fast until he pleaded with me to stop.

I leaned down again and kissed him. Like me, even in the wake of an orgasm, he still kissed like a desperate man, and I knew without a shadow of a doubt this night was far from over.

He freed one arm and gripped the back of my neck with a shaking hand. “Hope you’re not ready to call a cab yet.”

Even as I laughed, I shivered. “Not a fucking chance.”

Chapter Four
Shane

Why the fuck *didn't I get Eric's phone number?*

I rested my elbow on my desk and rubbed my eyes with my thumb and forefinger. All I'd wanted was a one-night stand. Even two nights could get too complicated for my taste, especially with men—especially with *military* men—and from the get-go, I hadn't intended to see him again. I hadn't intended to want to see him again.

That was, until the taillights of Eric's taxi had disappeared from my apartment's parking lot around sunrise on Saturday morning. From that moment on, I'd been kicking myself for not getting his number. The last thing I wanted or needed right now was a relationship, but I wanted another taste of him. Sex like that was too good to end with a one-night stand.

But with no way to contact him, that was how it had to end.

Now if I could just stop thinking about him, I'd be in good shape. That wasn't happening anytime soon, though. I hadn't had sex like that in ages, and my mind kept going back for more. God, I was usually so focused at work. I never daydreamed. I didn't get distracted.

I also didn't usually get laid by men like him. He was...he just...*why* weren't there more men out there like Eric? One minute he was demanding I fuck him harder; the next he was begging me to come for him. I swore to God my sheets were still smoldering long after he left.

Concentrate, Connelly. I exhaled and stared up at my office ceiling. For a one-night stand, Eric had certainly parked himself in my consciousness. After another day or two, I supposed I'd probably shake him completely so I could get on with my life without thinking about how much I wanted to have him naked and panting in my bed again. Not today, though.

My e-mail pinged, drawing me back into the present. When I looked at my in-box, I gritted my teeth at the sight of my ex-wife's name. Now wasn't that just a cold bucket of water over a good, if *slightly* distracted, mood?

Great. How much do you need this *time?*

Taking a breath, I clicked on the e-mail.

Shane,

My hours got cut again. Any chance I could get part of this month's child support early?

Best,

K.

It was just as well she couldn't see me roll my eyes or hear my profane muttering as I logged into my bank account. Four years after our divorce, we maintained one joint account so that I could transfer money if the kids needed something. When I was stationed this far from home, it was the fastest, simplest way for me to get money to her. She knew I'd never say no, and sometimes I wondered if she really needed the money, or if she just...knew I'd never say no. Whatever the case, the end result was the same.

"Being a single parent isn't cheap, you know," she'd reminded me in an e-mail a few months ago.

Yeah, I know it isn't cheap, I'd wanted to reply. *And it wouldn't be an issue at all if you'd been a little more faithful.*

Grumbling to myself, I shifted some money around between our accounts, then replied to her e-mail.

Katie,

I transferred $250 into the account. Let me know if it's enough. Won't take it out of the child support check. Hope it helps.

Shane

Reading over my bland, to-the-point message, it was hard to believe there was ever a time when she and I passed our workdays exchanging carefully worded and subtly racy e-mails. *"Checkbook's balanced"* used to mean she really, really wished I could duck out of work, like, right now. *"I'm taking the car to the dealership"* meant she'd be waiting in bed when I got home. And, after the twins came along, *"Kids are at my parents' house"* meant it was going to be one *long* night.

I read my e-mail one more time, then sent it. Sighing, I minimized my e-mail program. Those playful, suggestive e-mails were long gone. If the kids weren't in the picture, she and I wouldn't be in contact anymore at all. And, oh, wouldn't *that* just break my fucking heart?

"Commander?"

I looked up to see Lieutenant Commander Gonzales leaning in my open office door. For the life of me, I couldn't say how long she'd been there.

She looked at me with an expression that was equal parts concerned and amused. "Rough weekend, space cadet?" Like some of the other officers in this group, we knew each other well enough to drop the customary formality when we spoke one-on-one.

I coughed, hoping my cheeks weren't *too* red. "No, sorry. Was just running some numbers in my head." *Good save, Connelly. Good save.* "Anyway, what's up?"

She eyed me skeptically but then came in and handed me a stack of file folders. "Just a few things I need you to sign and pass on to the skipper."

I flipped through them. Nothing out of the ordinary; just the usual endless stream of paperwork to dump on the captain's desk. "All right, I'll have a look and give them to him before I leave. And while you're here..."

We exchanged forms, files and folders, and she left me to my lack of concentration. I could focus enough to work, just as I always could, but there was a distinct, niggling tension in the back of my mind that kept me fidgeting and irritated. Short, terse e-mail exchanges with Katie always left me in a foul mood, but I was distinctly aware of something else tugging at my consciousness. Something that had been occupying my mind before her message came through.

When I leaned down to get a folder out of a file drawer, a twinge in my back reminded me— Eric. Goose bumps prickled the length of my spine. It had been a long time since anyone, male or female, had distracted me like this. And the night we spent together was a hell of a lot more pleasant a distraction than my ex-wife's e-mail, so I didn't fight it this time.

He'd had me wrapped around his finger from the first kiss. A lot of men didn't like to kiss when it was something casual, but Eric loved it. In my apartment, we'd barely spoken to each other because even when we weren't fucking, we were too busy making out.

I shivered and flipped open one of the folders Gonzales had given me. I perused the forms, but what was left of my concentration had jumped ship, and the words on the pages didn't make any sense. Not when my hips and back still ached from slamming my cock into Eric until I lost it. Or when the A/C's cold air brushed the back of my neck and reminded me of Eric releasing a cool, sharp breath just before he swore in my ear and came.

Or when I remembered, for the hundredth time, that I'd neglected to get his phone number.

Damn it.

Eventually, I managed to read and sign everything from Gonzales. I took all of that, along with another stack of similar paperwork from others in the department, to the captain. Then there was a meeting I attended physically but checked out of mentally. More paperwork. More signatures. More wondering what I was thinking when I didn't make damn sure I'd have the chance to see Eric again.

Commander Damien Mays, my closest friend on the island, leaned into my office's open doorway. "Want to bust out of here before the skipper gets back?"

"Already?" I looked at my watch. *Quarter after five? Holy shit, really?* Christ. The man had even scrambled my internal clock.

Pushing my chair back, I said, "Sounds good to me. Who's DD tonight?"

"Gonzales," he said. "She's waiting for us."

"Thank God, because I need a beer."

He laughed. "You and me both."

"Yeah, you'd better enjoy your freedom while it lasts."

"Hey, shut up," he said, chuckling.

I closed up my office, and we started down the hall.

"How's Noriko doing?" I asked.

He smiled. "Almost there."

"How long does she have left, anyway? Like a month?"

"About three weeks, according to her OB." His smile faded a little. "She's getting pretty uncomfortable, though."

"Poor girl," I said. "Katie was miserable the last month or two."

"Yeah, well, thank God Noriko's not having twins." He chuckled. "She'd probably have killed me by now for doing that to her."

I laughed. "Trust me, Katie was ready to strangle me the second they found two on the ultrasound."

"I can only imagine. But as tiny as Noriko is, she might as well be having two." He grimaced. "The fact that she's handled it this well for this long? Girl's a better man than I am."

"Yeah, just wait until the day—"

"Don't." He glared at me. "I don't want to think about that any more than she does."

I just chuckled, and we kept walking.

"So how was your weekend?" I asked.

"Not bad," he said. "Setting up baby stuff, mostly. And my mother-in-law came by to make sure I knew every way I'd screwed up."

I laughed. "Good thing you don't understand a word she says, right?"

Mays snickered. He spoke more Japanese than I did, but he and his wife very carefully kept that fact from her mother.

Apparently, that kept his mother-in-law's direct criticism to dirty looks and sharp gestures instead of lengthy tirades. When she bitched about him to Noriko, he just tuned her out. I wondered how she'd react if she ever found out we both knew exactly what she was saying whenever he and I were drinking beers on the couch while she loudly ranted about him to Noriko.

"So what about your weekend?" Mays asked. "Do anything interesting?"

Oh, you could say that.

I cleared my throat. "Oh, I just relaxed a bit. Did laundry, that sort of thing."

"What?" He scoffed. "Since when do *you* stay home on the weekend?"

"Whatever," I said. "I'm not out and about every damned weekend."

Under his breath, Mays said, "So what's his name?"

I almost tripped over my own feet. He just laughed but didn't press the issue as we continued into the lobby where Gonzales waited for us. Mays was the only one in the command who knew I was into men, but around coworkers, he didn't ask and I didn't tell.

Gonzales folded her arms across her chest and rolled her eyes. "Would you two hurry up? It's bad enough I don't get to drink tonight, but don't keep me waiting."

"Is that any way to speak to a superior officer?" Mays asked with mock offense.

"Define superior," she said.

"Oh, you're funny."

Laughing, I pushed open the door, and all three of us winced at the rush of hot, humid air as we stepped out of the air-conditioned building. Then we put on our covers and walked across the parking lot to Gonzales's car. Mays and I left our cars here, and his wife would give us a ride into work in the morning. It wasn't like any of us ever got drunk on a work night—this was just a beer or two to unwind—but we always had a designated driver. The maximum blood alcohol content in

Japan was obscenely low, and it was better to have a DD after two beers than kiss a career good-bye over a DUI. Especially a DUI that counted as an international incident.

And tonight, Gonzales had drawn the short straw, so as she pulled up to the O'Club, I could barely wait to get into the club and dive into my first cold beer. On the way in from the car, though, I swore at the sight of a familiar red sedan a few spaces over.

"Oh, lovely," I said. "Morris is joining us?"

Gonzales laughed humorlessly. "And this surprises you?"

"Surprised isn't the word I'd use," I grumbled on the way into the club. Morris was one of our coworkers, and where an after-hours beer was a once or twice a week thing for the rest of us, it was a nightly occurrence for him. I couldn't stand the son of a bitch. I didn't like him sober, I liked him even less drunk, but there was an unspoken expectation that we'd keep an eye on him. If he got in trouble because of his drinking, that meant a headache and a half for the rest of us, particularly if we all knew he had a problem and let him go boozing on his own. In the military, we are our brother's keeper, no matter how much of a loudmouthed, alcoholic, trouble-making asshole he is.

Morris and a few other guys from work had taken over a couple of tables near the bar, so Mays, Gonzales, and I ordered our drinks at the bar, hid our distaste for our colleague and joined them.

I took a drink and had to suppress a groan as the flavor hit my tongue. Without even thinking about it, I'd made the mistake of ordering an Orion. It was my preferred beer, but this beer wasn't going to help me unwind when it tasted like the other night. After all, I had *just* taken a drink when Eric walked into Palace Habu, and in an attempt to cool myself off, I'd taken another long swig. A long swig that tasted just like this.

Jesus, Connelly. What is the matter with you?

Good thing I had my dickwad of a coworker around to, just by speaking, put a bad taste in my mouth and drag me right into the irritating present.

"I don't like that new kid," Morris muttered into his beer.

"Who?" Mays cocked his head. "Ensign Lange?"

"Lange is great," Pickering said. "Kid should've gone to Annapolis, I'm telling you. I'd bet beer for a year he'll have his star before he retires."

"No kidding," Mays said. "Come promotion time, I'd bet half my paycheck he makes Lieutenant JG. He's as good as a shoo-in."

"Yeah, well." Morris wrinkled his nose. "He's a little light in his loafers, if you ask me."

"Good thing no one asked you, then," I growled.

He glared at me. "Well, maybe he should come work in your office, because—"

Mays slammed his palm on the table. "Okay, both of you. You see this?" He picked up his beer bottle and gestured so emphatically with it, he almost unloaded half its contents on the rest of us. "This is my first beer of the night. I'm not even halfway through it. Can I get through *one* fucking beer before the two of you start in on this DADT bullshit again?"

Morris threw him a sidelong glance. "Sorry, man. Forgot you only have so much time before you have to route a request chit to go out for a beer."

"Very funny," Mays said.

"It's true," Morris said with a shrug. "All women do that. Once they crap out a kid, they keep you on a fucking choke chain. *Especially* Japanese women."

"Oh, knock it the fuck off," Mays snarled with enough venom to persuade anyone else to shut the fuck up.

Not Morris, though. "Hey, look, I'm just saying. I've been there, so—"

"Morris. For fuck's sake." Gonzales set her drink down. "Can we go one evening without you ranting and raving about everyone on the damned planet? Just, you know, shut up and drink your beer."

Morris started to say something else, but a warning look from Mays shut him the fuck up. Maybe the idiot was smarter than I thought.

I ground my teeth. I swore, one of these days Morris and I

were getting dragged out of this place in cuffs. I wasn't violent by nature, but Morris had a serious anger problem, especially when he was drunk. That was part of the reason he'd only just put on commander after seventeen years. Man never quite knew when to close his damned mouth, which hadn't done good things to his career. Put a few beers in him, get him spun up over something, and everybody watch out. The only reason we even drank with him was because we could usually settle him down before he got stupid. When he drank alone, especially after his divorce six months ago, an alcohol-related incident was inevitable. Good thing the fucker had never been to the Middle East like everyone else at this table. Combat fucked us all up to a degree, and Morris was enough of a loose cannon without a little PTSD on top of it.

True to form, it wasn't long before he started off on another tangent about God only cared what, and I tuned him out. The less I heard, the less likely I was to mouth off myself, and the less likely we were to end up going toe to toe.

The rest of the group carried on around me, laughing about something and bitching about work in between listening to Morris rant, but I drifted off into my thoughts. The e-mail exchange with my ex-wife still bugged me, even hours later. I hated how cold, terse and businesslike we were these days, and I deeply resented her for that. It takes two to make a marriage work but only took one to make it crash and fucking burn. Well, no, I guess it did take two to make our marriage fail. Maybe three, or four. I never did find out if he was the only one. Didn't really want to know. I'd made my mistakes in our marriage, but the fatal blow? That was hers. Theirs. Whatever.

Jesus, I was supposed to be having a relaxing drink after work, and what was I thinking about? My ex? Fuck this. I was here to unwind, not get more pissed off.

I took a long swallow of beer. Oh, wasn't that convenient? A less infuriating diversion at the ready, right there in my glass?

With cold Orion on my tongue once again, my mind wandered back to Friday night.

As soon as we'd left the club, I'd had a sneaking suspicion

Eric and I wouldn't make it to my bedroom. In fact, I was surprised we made it as far as we did. It had taken every bit of restraint I possessed not to pounce on him in the taxi. Getting up the stairs, knowing we were away from prying eyes, I couldn't take it. I couldn't wait another second. Holy fuck, pinned against my door and falling apart while I sucked his cock, Eric was almost unbearably sexy. And when we finally got into bed, and he begged me to—

Morris slammed his beer down with enough force to snap me out of my pleasant haze. "Fucking president. Motherfucker just wants to fuck us all over."

"All right," Mays said. "I think you've had enough. You stopped making sense about fourteen *fucks* ago."

"Fuck you," Morris said.

"He's right," Gonzales said. "It's only Monday, man. You have to work tomorrow. Quit drinking like it's Friday."

Morris made a clumsy, flippant gesture. "You sound like my fucking wife."

"Yeah, well," Gonzales said through clenched teeth. "At least she had the option to divorce your idiot ass. I'm cutting you off." She shoved her chair back, stood and stomped off to the bar, undoubtedly to ask the bartender to *please* cut Morris off.

About damned time, as far as I was concerned. He was up for orders in a few months, and I hoped to God the Navy sent him to some base in Bumfuck Nowhere so he could be someone else's problem. I didn't know how much more I could take before he wore my beer.

Mays waved a hand in front of my face. "You all right, man?"

"Yeah, yeah, I'm fine." I cleared my throat, then forced a smile as I shifted in my chair. "You know, just shit with the ex-wife." I immediately regretted playing that card within earshot of Morris.

Morris laughed bitterly and made a sweeping gesture with his beer bottle, nearly dropping it in Mays's lap in the process. "That's about all they're good for, am I right?"

I rolled my eyes and drained my beer. I hated having a bad divorce in common with him. My shitty relationship with my ex-wife kind of took the wind out of my sails whenever I tried to argue with him about ex-spouses and how they weren't *all* the spawn of Satan. So I just didn't argue with him this time. The mood I was in, much more of his mouth and we were going to blows.

I just ordered another Orion and let myself get lost in the taste of Friday night.

Chapter Five

Eric

Come on, Eric. Pay attention.

Muttering a string of profanity only a Sailor could muster, I pulled down a side street so I could turn around. I could kind of say I was still getting used to navigating Okinawa's confusing tangle of roads, not to mention driving on the left, but the fact was, I'd missed my turn because I flat-out wasn't paying attention.

It's been almost two weeks. It was a one-night stand. Get over it and move on.

Once I was back on the road, I very carefully pushed all thoughts of a certain one-night stand out of my head until I had made the turn and was on my way into Camp Shields, the Seabee base a few kilometers down the road from Kadena. I'd already been here three times today, and this was the second time I'd missed the turn. Neither time did it have anything to do with not knowing my way around.

I pulled up to the guard shack at the gate, and the sentry—MA3 Royal—waved me through without checking my ID. I was his watch commander and I was in a government vehicle, so there was no need for him to stop me.

Part of my job entailed doing post checks: driving to all the places where my guys were on post, making sure everyone was doing their job, shit like that. I'd already been to White Beach, Awase, and Tengan Pier, and now was checking on the boys at the gate here at Shields again. Of course, my visit had *nothing* to do with the fact that it was well past lunch thirty, and the Enlisted Club was about two blocks from the gate.

I parked my vehicle in the parking lot across the street, then walked to the office that was thirty feet or so behind the guard shack.

Inside, MA3 Diego fucked off on his iPhone, MA3 Grant typed away at the computer at one of the two desks, and MA2 Colburn was just coming back in from, I guessed, a smoke break.

"Hey, MA1," Colburn said.

"Hey, guys." I took off my cover. "Anything new and exciting over here?"

"Besides Grant writing tickets to anyone who comes near the gate?" Diego muttered.

Grant put up his hands and shrugged. "Not my fault they keep running the stop sign or forgetting to signal."

"Whatever." Diego rolled his eyes. "I swear, you're the only MA in this section that gets wood from writing tickets."

Grant flipped him the bird.

I laughed. To Diego, I said, "You do know that's your job, right?"

He shrugged. "Yeah, but it's not like the tickets actually do anything. If we fined people and shit, then I'd be writing them left and right."

"Dude," Colburn said. "It's not like you'd get a commission if we fined people."

"No, but they might slow down and stop breaking the law."

"They do when I give them tickets," Grant said. "I almost never write the same person two tickets."

"That's because you're an utter dick when you make a stop," Colburn said. "I wouldn't want to be pulled over by you either."

"See?" Grant beamed. "Result."

"He's got a point, guys," I said.

Diego quirked an eyebrow. "So you're saying we should be assholes when we stop speeders?"

I shrugged. "Well, don't make it a felony stop or anything, but you don't have to act like their best friend either."

Colburn snorted. "Yeah, we've seen how *you* make stops."

"What?" I chuckled. "Oh, come on. I was totally polite to

that lady."

"Sure you were. Would you talk to your mom like that?"

I shrugged again. "If my mom suggested I shove my ticket book up my ass and then go fuck myself, yeah, I might."

Diego laughed. "That chick really said that to you?"

"In not so many words, yes." I looked at Grant. "You have the logbook over there?"

"Yep." He picked up the binder and handed it to me.

While I perused it, making sure entries were done correctly and nothing had happened that I should have been notified about, Diego said, "You ever going to get out and party, MA1?"

"With you guys?" I eyed him. "Yeah, sure. Let me just add 'get strung up for fraternization' to my to-do list for the week."

"What do you do, though?" Grant asked. "Just sit at home with your dick in your hand?"

Diego snickered. "Or someone else's?"

"Oh, very funny," I said in spite of the chill running down my spine. "No, I usually just spend the evenings on the webcam with your mom."

"Dude," Grant said. "Have you *seen* Diego's mom?"

Diego flipped him off while Colburn, Grant and I cracked up.

I skimmed over the watch bill. "Harris and Jansen out on patrol?"

Colburn nodded. "They'll probably be back in ten or fifteen."

"All right." I set the watch bill and logbook on the desk. "Looks like you boys have this all under control, so I'm going to go get some—" The radio on my hip crackled to life.

"Whiskey Charlie, White Beach."

I cursed. White Beach dispatch looking for me, the watch commander, as they always did when I wanted to eat. "Well, I *was* going to go get something to eat." I pulled my radio off my gun belt and pressed the button. "Send it for Whiskey Charlie."

"Respond to a domestic, O'Donnell Gardens."

I grabbed a notepad off the desk. "Building and unit

numbers?"

The dispatcher gave me the address, which I jotted down. I confirmed it over the radio and told her to show me responding. Then I grumbled, "So much for lunch."

Diego laughed. "Don't you know, man? That's when the radio always goes off. Right when you're gonna eat."

Grant chuckled. "If that were true, you'd be getting calls every five fucking minutes."

"Man, fuck you."

I looked at Colburn. "You been to any domestics, MA2?"

He nodded. "Tons."

"Good. You're with me." To Diego and Grant, I said, "When Harris and Jansen come back from their rounds, have them stand by in case I need backup."

With my stomach still growling, I left with Colburn. He knew the base better than I did, so he directed me as we left the gate and headed toward housing.

As I turned down the road that led into officer housing, Colburn shook his head. "I think this is the tenth domestic I've been to over here in the last six months."

"At Shields?" I said. "Or the officer side?"

"Officers. Trust me, on the enlisted side, there's—oh, look, a cheater's house." He gestured out the window.

I pulled up to a stop sign, then looked at the house he'd indicated. "What? How can you tell?"

He shot me an incredulous look. "You don't know this shit?"

"Well, on my last base, the my-husband-isn't-home signal was a mop next to the front door." I craned my neck but didn't see the incriminating mop propped up next to the door.

"Not here. All the husbands found out about that one. Here, it's a detergent box in the dining room window."

I glanced up just before I pulled through the intersection, and sure enough, peeking down from the window of one unit's dining room, was a box of Tide.

I shook my head. "Every fucking base."

"Yeah, get used to it," he said. "It's way worse out here than it is in the States."

"I can imagine."

"Fucking people, man. It's like fucking Groundhog Day out here sometimes." He pointed to the left. "Turn here."

I made the turn, and didn't need any further directions after that. The couple was on the sidewalk, gesturing sharply and shouting at each other. He was in his white working uniform, though he'd taken off his cover.

At least they were out in the open. There were few things scarier in this job than barging in on a domestic in progress. It was just impossible to know what was happening on the other side of the door until it was open.

That was a moot point with these two, though. As I pulled up to the curb, they didn't even notice us. Even as we stepped out of the truck and started toward them, they were too caught up in screaming over the top of each other to notice until the husband happened to glance in my direction.

He stabbed a finger at me. "This is none of your fucking business."

"Yeah, well, your neighbors beg to differ," I said. "So, I'm going to—"

"Hey," he said. "Anyone ever taught you to salute an officer?"

I resisted the urge to roll my eyes. "Sir, I'm going to need you to sit down."

"Fuck you."

"Sir, I'm going—"

"I said fuck you." He stepped toward me, eyes narrow and lips tight across his teeth. "This is a private matter." He had easily six inches on me, but I didn't back down.

I took a step toward him. "You have two choices, *Sir*," I growled. "You can sit down and shut up, or you can sit down and shut up with a face full of pepper spray."

His eyes flicked downward, and his eyebrows jumped slightly, probably at the sight of my hand resting on the canister of OC spray on my belt. Then he looked back at me, and I narrowed my eyes.

That's right, Sir. Do not *fuck with me.*

Apparently, he was capable of seeing reason, because he quietly took a seat on the bumper of a car. While I'd dealt with the husband, Colburn had calmed the wife, and she had taken a seat on the porch steps.

"We're going to take this in the house," I said. "I'm going to take statements from both of you, and I don't want either of you looking at each other or speaking to each other unless you want Petty Officer Colburn or me to put you in cuffs. Am I clear?"

The wife nodded.

The husband—Lieutenant Commander Sorenson, I gathered from the rectangular plastic tag on his chest—glared at me. I returned the look, and he dropped his gaze, nodding.

"There any children in the home?" I asked.

"Our son," the woman said quietly.

"How old?"

"Three."

"Is there anyone else in the home with him?"

"No," she said.

I gritted my teeth. How nice. At least they weren't fighting like this in front of their kid, but leaving him unsupervised while they duked it out on the lawn? Fucking idiots. I had a hard enough time staying emotionally detached when kids weren't involved, and this guy was just asking for me to fuck up his world.

To Colburn, I said, "Radio for Main Gate to send someone up here to—"

"You're taking my son away?" Mrs. Sorenson asked, a mix of panic and rage in her tone.

I put up a hand. "No, ma'am, I'm not taking your son away. I'm making sure someone is keeping an eye on him while we sort this out."

"We don't need you to sort it out," the husband snapped.

I shot him a warning look, and he didn't push it.

To his wife, I said, "Your son can either go with another officer, or if there's a friend or neighbor who can take him..." I let my raised eyebrows finish the question.

She chewed her lip. "Our next-door neighbor."

"Do you have a phone out here you can use?"

She tentatively reached for her pocket but paused, glancing up at Colburn. He nodded, and she slid her hand into her pocket to get her phone.

Her husband fidgeted impatiently while she called the neighbor to come get the little boy. A moment later, a blonde woman came out of the apartment opposite the Sorensons' place. She and Mrs. Sorenson exchanged a few words, and the blonde went in to get the boy.

Once their child was safely away from the situation, Colburn and I took the Sorensons into their apartment. Inside, the dining room and living room were connected, separated only by a waist-high wall. Perfect.

"Take her in there," I said to Colburn.

He guided Mrs. Sorenson into the dining room and had her face the wall in the chair farthest from her husband and me. At my instruction, Lieutenant Commander Sorenson took a seat near the opposite wall in the living room, also with his back to his wife. He muttered something about being treated like misbehaving children, but tough shit for him. It would have been less tense if I could have separated them completely and taken them into different rooms, but that would have left both Colburn and me vulnerable. We had to stay within each other's sight for officer safety. The Sorensons could just suck it up and deal with it.

With everyone situated and reasonably calm, I glanced from one spouse to the other.

Sorenson obviously had a temper. The wife seemed to give as good as she took, and there were no signs of physical violence on the surface. That said, I'd been to domestic calls where a battered spouse took the fight outside for his or her own safety. Rare was the spouse who'd get violent outside where others could see it, and if that was the case here, no one would admit to it while the other was within earshot.

I beckoned to Colburn. Each keeping an eye on our respective halves of the dysfunctional marriage, we met at the waist-high wall between the two rooms.

"I want to get statements from them separately," I said, keeping my voice low. "Gut feeling, but I want to separate them. Completely."

He nodded. "Want me to radio for backup?"

"Please do."

"What the fuck is going on?" Sorenson demanded. "We just going to sit here all fucking night?"

I reminded myself to stay calm, no matter how much I wanted to pistol-whip the guy just for the hell of it. "Sir, I need you to just stay quiet until I can take your statement."

"What the hell are you waiting for?" he asked. "An engraved invitation?"

Neither Colburn nor I spoke. Fortunately, Sorenson just muttered to himself but otherwise shut up.

Harris and Jansen arrived a few minutes later. When they came in, I turned to the sullenly quiet couple.

"This is Petty Officer Harris and Petty Officer Jansen," I said. "I need one of the two of you to step outside with them, so they can—"

"What the fuck is this?" Sorenson snapped. "You never seen people get in an argument before?"

"Sir," I said coolly. "I'm not going to ask you again."

"I'll go outside," his wife said. "I need a cigarette anyway." She followed Harris and Jansen outside.

Once she was gone, I had her husband move to the couch so I wasn't backed up against a sliding glass door. Colburn stayed off to the side, leaning against the wall that divided the two rooms. Close enough to intervene if something happened, far enough away to keep from agitating the man any further.

"I need you to tell me what happened," I said quietly. "Start from the beginning, and take your time."

"You married?" He glanced at my left hand, probably looking for a ring.

"I'm divorced." I kept my voice even in spite of my impatience.

"You know how it is, then." He gestured at the door

through which his wife had gone.

"I can't say I ever had the police called to settle a dispute," I said. "So, no, I *don't* know how it is."

I thought he'd get pissed off and defensive, but his posture deflated a little. The lieutenant commander exhaled and ran a hand through his hair. "Look, I got home a little bit late, and she lit into me as soon as I came through the door. Just, you know, one thing after another. And we, I guess...I guess we got carried away, and we took it outside. Then you guys showed up."

"Have either of you been drinking?"

He narrowed his eyes. "I'm in uniform, Petty Officer," he spat.

"Have either of you been drinking?" I asked again, this time with enough force to suggest he cut the crap and answer my fucking question.

He swallowed. "No. Neither of us have been drinking."

"Was there any physical contact or was anything thrown?"

"No, we were just yelling at each other." He paused. "With a lot of enthusiasm, if someone called the cops." His cheeks colored, and his black-and-gold shoulder boards went from flat to sharply declined as his shoulders sank. He looked up at me. "Listen, I'm sorry they called you guys out here tonight. We got carried away, but I'd never lay a hand on her. We're both just...stressed." Sighing he rubbed the back of his neck with both hands. "I'm leaving on an IA tour soon, and it's been rough on her. On both of us."

That much I could understand. Iraq and Afghanistan tours were stressful for everyone involved. My ex and I had already divorced when I went to the Sandbox the first time, and we'd *still* squabbled like nobody's business in the weeks before I left on both tours.

"Anything else I need to know before I go have this conversation with your wife?" I asked.

I was less concerned with his answer and more with his body language. When he shook his head and quietly replied with a negative, there was no sudden tension, no defensive posturing, not even a glance toward the door.

Satisfied with his responses, I called Harris in to switch places with me. He and Colburn stayed with Sorenson while I stepped outside to talk to the wife.

Jansen and Harris had already taken a statement from her, but I still wanted to talk to her myself.

I asked her the same questions. She calmly repeated everything she'd already told them, and she corroborated her husband's story: no drinking, nothing physical, just a stress-fueled dispute that got out of hand.

"Any history of violence or alcohol abuse?" I asked.

She shook her head. "No. This is...pretty unusual for us." She dropped her gaze, and some color rushed into her cheeks. She struck me as more embarrassed than anything, not nervous or scared. Judging by her body language and her tone, she was upset, but not scared. Didn't sound like anyone was covering for anyone. Nothing in the house looked like it had been thrown or struck, and neither spouse had any indications of giving or receiving any kind of violence. Everything checked out that this was just an overly heated argument.

After talking to both spouses, I made the call to let them both go. I hated being the one to make that decision. Every time I arrested someone on suspicion of domestic violence, I was afraid I had made a bad call and needlessly fucked someone's career. Worse, whenever I left without making an arrest, I was certain we'd be called back after things got a *lot* worse.

But in this case, I was as close to confident as I could be that I wasn't putting either spouse—or their child—in danger by leaving.

We brought the couple into the living room. As Harris and Jansen left, Lieutenant Commander Sorenson put an arm around his wife's shoulders.

"I'm sorry, babe," he said and kissed her cheek.

"Me too." She wrapped her arms around his waist and rested her head against his chest. He gently stroked her hair and kissed the top of her head.

"All right," I said. "We're going to leave. We've got both your statements on file. Your chain of command will be notified of our visit, but I'm not arresting anyone, and no charges will be filed."

They both exhaled and glanced at each other. His expression turned mildly sheepish, and so did hers.

"I have to come back out here tonight or any other night," I said, "we're sorting this out someplace else. Am I clear?"

"Yes," they both said.

"Thank you," Mrs. Sorenson said quietly, and a ghost of a smile flickered across her lips.

Sorenson picked up his cover and showed us out while his wife went to get their son. Now that things were settled, we were outdoors, and he had his cover on again, Colburn and I both saluted the lieutenant commander. He returned it, then shook our hands, and we left.

On the way out of the neighborhood, Colburn radioed dispatch to let them know we'd taken care of the call and were on our way out. Then he put his boot up on the dash and lounged back in the seat. "That has to be one of the cleanest domestics I've been on in a while."

"No shit," I said. "I've been to some nasty ones."

"Me too. Man, last year?" He whistled and shook his head. "We had to arrest a Marine, his wife, her boyfriend and his wife. Well, after we took the Marine to get stitches."

I glanced at him. "Seriously?"

"Yeah, it was ugly."

"So which one cut him up?"

"Oh, fuck, who knows? They were all shit-faced, and I guess someone let it out that someone was cheating on someone, and..." He waved a hand. "Shit hit the fan. Fuckin' looked like they'd been throwing bottles, throwing punches, you name it. They were all cut the fuck up, but only the Marine needed to be sewn up."

"Bet he had fun explaining that to his chain of command."

Colburn laughed. "Yeah, really. Man, I've had some crazy fights with my wife, but that shit? No way."

"Life's too short for that," I said. "I can see why they do it, though, honestly. This life, it isn't easy."

"No," he said with a sigh, "it definitely isn't."

On the way past a row of houses, I glanced up and noticed an innocent-looking box of laundry detergent in the window of one dining room. Shaking my head, I turned my attention back to the road. This was why I lived off base. Well, that, and being single, I'd have been stuck in the barracks if I lived on base, but I'd refused to live in housing for my entire career. *Desperate Housewives* didn't have the drama base housing did, and from what I'd been hearing, overseas was even worse. The isolation of being thousands of miles from friends and family stressed people out. Cheating was rampant, and it worsened before, during and after deployments. People drank, people fought, and people got stupid.

Okinawa was peaceful in terms of murders and burglary. The only violent crime we dealt with on a regular basis was domestic violence, and there was plenty of that, thanks to stress, booze and infidelity.

I would have liked to believe it wasn't that bad, but I was a cop. I saw it all firsthand.

And there was another house with a box of Tide in the window.

When I got home, I dropped onto the couch and picked up my laptop. I wanted nothing more than to strip out of this uniform and grab a shower, but it was early enough in the day back home that I might catch my daughter online before she went to school.

I shrugged off my blouse—the blue digicam jacket that went over my dark blue T-shirt—and draped it over the armrest. Then I logged on, and sure enough, her instant-message icon was set to Available, so I sent a request for a video chat. The request showed pending for a good thirty seconds. I thought she might have left her computer logged on, but then the Request Accepted message came up.

The chat window opened up. When the video came on, I

expected to see Marie, but it was Sara, my ex-wife.

"Oh, hey," I said. "I thought Marie was on."

"She just stepped away to get ready for school," Sara said. "She'll be back down in a minute. Guess you're stuck with me until then."

I laughed. "Oh, I'll manage. How are things?"

She shrugged. "Not too bad. Same old, same old. How's Japan?" Her lips twisted into a sympathetic grimace, and her eyebrows rose.

"Actually, it's not bad," I said. "I'm not quite sure what Jim was smoking when he was here, but it's pretty nice."

"Really? Well, that's good."

"Yeah, tell me about it. I'm still figuring things out, but it's not a bad place to live."

"How is it driving on the other side of the road?"

I gestured dismissively. "Oh, that took, like, a day to get used to. And I didn't hit anyone or anything, so I'll call that a win."

She laughed. "With the way you drive? Absolutely."

"Very funny." I chuckled, then, more serious, asked, "How's Marie doing with all of this?"

Sara bit her lip and glanced over her shoulder. When she looked at me again, she lowered her voice. "I'll be honest. It's been rough on her. You know how she is. She's a strong kid, but..." Sara paused, glancing back again before shaking her head. "I think it's a little overwhelming, knowing you're going to be gone for three years."

I barely kept myself from visibly flinching. "Yeah, I understand that. Believe me, I'm still not happy about the arrangement myself."

"She'll be fine, though," Sara said. "And so will you. I hope you're at least doing everything you can to enjoy the island, instead of moping about the fact that Marie can't be there."

"I am, don't worry." *Especially when I manage to find some company.*

"What's wrong?" Sara furrowed her brow. "Eric Randall, are you blushing?"

"What? No, not at all."

She gave me a knowing look. "Don't tell me you've met someone already."

"I..." *Kind of did. Sort of. Except he was just a one-night stand. And I'm never going to see him again. But oh God, I want to. And—*

Sara laughed. "Well, look at you. So is he cute?"

I snorted. "Are you suggesting I ever date men who aren't?"

"So you *have* met someone."

I shrugged. "Maybe."

"And he's cute?"

"Of course."

"You know," she said with a failed attempt at a stern look, "with you living so far away, it's really hard for me to ogle the men you date."

I put a hand to my chest. "Oh, I am *so* sorry."

"You should be." She snickered, then glanced off-camera. "Oh, here comes Marie." Turning back to me, she said, "I'll give the computer to her. It was nice talking to you."

"You too." We exchanged smiles. Then the camera shifted as Sara passed the computer to my daughter. Seeing Marie brought an instant smile to my face, even as my throat ached. God, it sucked being this far from her, and seeing her now just reminded me how much I hadn't seen her recently.

She smiled. "Hey, Dad."

"Hey, kiddo. How are you doing?"

"Okay," she said with a shrug. "Up to my face in homework."

I laughed. "Well, get used to it. That pile of homework's just going to get bigger in college."

"Ugh, don't remind me."

"Oh, you'll be fine," I said. "So is my car running okay for you?"

"Well, it was until I wrapped it around a telephone pole."

I rolled my eyes. "Very funny."

She laughed. "Yeah, it's running fine." Her smile fell. "So, um, how do you like Japan?"

I didn't miss the note of sadness in her voice, and I couldn't quite keep one out of mine. "It's better than I thought it would be. Still kind of learning my way around, but..." I shrugged. "It's pretty cool."

"Good," she said without much enthusiasm. "Glad you're enjoying it." This time, bitterness joined sadness.

"Listen, baby," I said. "I know this is rough on you. It is for me too. But you can always message me or e-mail me."

She nodded. "I know. It just sucks having you that far away."

"It does," I said. "But maybe after school's out, you can come stay with me for a while."

Her expression brightened. "Really?"

"Sure. You work out the details with your mother, and I'll take leave."

"Cool." She grinned. "I finally get to see Japan." Then she glanced at her watch. "Crap, I should get to school. Guess I'd better let you go."

"Yeah, don't be late. And I'm counting on you to keep your mother out of trouble, so—"

"I heard that," Sara said from off-camera.

Marie and I laughed.

"All right," I said. "Off to school with you."

"Okay, I'll see you later."

"I love you, kiddo," I said.

"I love you too."

The screen went dark.

Sighing, I shut down the IM program. Then I closed my laptop and leaned back, clasping my hands behind my head and staring up at the ceiling. I knew when I signed up for the military that there would be stress and there would be separations from my family. That sort of thing isn't exactly a big secret. But signing on the dotted line and agreeing to occasionally be a few thousand miles away, possibly even having people shoot at me, was very different from the reality of stepping onto a plane and leaving. There was a reason I'd seriously considered getting out after my last contract was up.

But I'd been in too long. Had too many years invested to quit before I retired. I needed the income, the benefits, the GI bill for both myself and my kid. So I'd stayed in, and now I was here, with a laptop screen as my only face-to-face contact with Marie. The benefits were great, but the loneliness... God. The distance. Watching my kid grow up via webcam.

My mind wandered to that domestic call Colburn and I had responded to a few hours ago. It was fucked up what this life did to people. A lot of us ended up separated from our families, and for those who didn't, the stress tore them apart anyway. And some of us even got the added bonus of being a million miles from our families *and* playing mediator when the people still living together couldn't get along.

Closing my eyes, I sighed and scrubbed a hand over my face. Between my job and being this far from my daughter, I was desperate for some stress relief. Any kind of stress relief. In fact, right about now, nothing sounded better than forgetting the entire world with a cold beer and a hot man. One hot man in particular.

"Don't tell me you've met someone already."

I shivered. Oh, I'd met someone all right. And he was definitely cute. Pity I had no way to reach him.

And I wasn't even in the mood for sex, but sex was better than wallowing in job-related stress or thinking about all the miles between me and anything familiar. Sex was better than killing an evening playing video games in an empty apartment. Sex was better than drinking until I passed out and waking up with a hangover to take with me to work.

And sex with Shane was better than it had been with any other man.

But I didn't have his goddamned number.

Sighing, I set my laptop aside and went into the bedroom. Time to get out of this uniform, grab a shower and think about Shane some more.

Chapter Six

Shane

A couple of weeks had gone by since that scorching night with Eric. I went back to the club a few times, hoping to see him, but he didn't show. Tonight, I promised myself, I'd find someone else. There were other men out there. If one was that good in bed, then others would be too.

But I still had to get through today before that was even an issue, and this morning had an early start. Dressed and ready for work, I sat on my couch with my laptop on my knee, stomach fluttering as I watched my IM program.

Waiting for dconnelly to respond...

Once a month or so, my ex-wife took the kids to stay with my parents for a weekend. Since they were on spring break now, they went to their grandparents' for a few extra days. My mom had e-mailed me last night and said they'd be on this morning, which was Friday morning for me and Thursday night for them.

Initializing connection...

The window shifted to the webcam chat interface, and an animated hourglass did somersaults in the middle of the otherwise blank screen. After a moment, a fuzzy image replaced the hourglass, and as the picture came into focus, I smiled at the sight of my kids vying for space in front of the webcam. Wow, they were growing fast. I still sometimes pictured them in my head as kindergartners. It was hard to remember they were almost out of third grade.

"Hey, guys," I said.

"Hey, Dad," they both said.

Jessica pointed at the screen. "You got a new stripe thing."

"A new stripe thing?"

"On your shirt."

I looked down and realized she meant the rows of awards and medals on my uniform. Chest candy, as some guys called them. "Which one?"

"The one with the big gray stripe in the middle."

"This one?" I pointed at it and looked at the screen.

"Yeah," she said. "It's new."

I chuckled. "Very observant, sweetheart. Just got it a few months ago."

"What's it for?" Jason asked.

"That was for going to Iraq. They finally got around to giving it to me." I smiled. "Enough about me, though. I want to know how you two are doing. Who went first last time?"

"She did," Jason said.

Jessica didn't argue.

"All right," I said. "So what's new, Jason?"

"I'm going camping with Scouts pretty soon." He grinned. "Our pack leader says one of the cabins is haunted."

"Oh, does he?" I said.

He nodded. "Yeah, but I don't believe him."

"You don't? Why not?"

"Because he's always making up stuff like that."

I laughed. He gave me the rundown of his most recent Scout activities, told me about the camping trip planned for the end of the summer and grumbled about how he hoped he didn't get Mrs. Patterson as his fourth grade teacher in September. When he'd finished, he scooted over so his sister could have the camera.

"All right, Jessie," I said. "What about you? What's new?"

She grinned broadly, revealing a gap where she'd recently lost a tooth. "I'm going horseback riding next weekend!"

"Are you?" I smiled. "Bet you're excited about that."

She nodded vigorously. "It's Lily's birthday party. Her parents are taking us all out for the whole day."

"Well, that'll be fun," I said. "All those lessons will pay off."

After she'd told me everything she'd learned in her recent

riding lessons and about everything their grandparents had planned for the weekend, I said, "So, you two have a birthday coming up. Why don't you both write up lists of things you want and have Grandma send it to me?"

"Okay," Jessica said.

"I'll give mine to Grandma tonight," Jason said. "But when are you going to come see us?"

"Yeah, Daddy." Jessica's sad face almost broke my heart. "We miss you."

I forced a smile. "I miss you guys too. I don't know when I'll make it home, but I'm working on it." I hoped they couldn't see me cringing. I hated giving them such ambiguous answers. The truth was, I had already arranged to stay with my parents in December. Katie had agreed to let the kids stay over for a couple of weeks so I could spend Christmas with them. The wild card was the military. I was 95 percent certain my leave would be approved, but the chit wouldn't go through until November. We all planned to keep it quiet and surprise the kids when they came to see their grandparents.

I just didn't want to disappoint them if something fell through. If I could have, I'd have had my folks bring the kids out to Okinawa, but health problems kept them from traveling very far, so I had to go to them.

I chatted with my twins a little longer. Then they took off to get ready for bed, and my mom took their place at the computer.

"Hi, Mom," I said.

"Hi, son," she said with a smile. "How are things?"

I shrugged. "They're all right. The usual. You?"

"About the same. Nothing new since the last time we chatted."

Well, that was good. She and my dad had had enough health problems in the last couple of years, no news was *very* good news.

She glanced off-camera, then looked at me and lowered her voice. "You're still planning on...you know, December?"

I nodded. "The skipper knows I'm planning on taking leave,

so he'll most likely sign off on it unless something comes up."

"Good, good. They'll be happy to see you." She smiled. "We always have our backup plan. If you can't do it in December, we can have a late Christmas in January."

"Sounds good to me." I glanced at the clock at the corner of my screen. "I'd better get going. I have to get to work."

"Okay, honey. You keep in touch, you hear?"

"I will. Love you, Mom."

"I love you too, baby."

We disconnected, and I logged off the instant message program. I put my laptop aside and leaned back on the couch. I loved talking to my kids, but every time I did, I spent the rest of the day in a funk. Much as I liked living on Okinawa, nothing could make me homesick faster than talking to the people I missed. Especially the twins. God, I missed my kids. Sometimes, just talking to them depressed me so much I didn't even want to move.

Didn't have much choice, though. There was no calling in sick in this line of work, so I made myself get up off the couch and head to work.

I guessed I just missed them. I hadn't seen them in almost a year now. After I visited them in December, assuming nothing threw a monkey wrench into that, who knew when I'd see them again?

I trudged into the office. We had a white board just inside the door, which listed meetings and such. According to the board, one of the admirals was coming down from Yokosuka—again—next week, Lieutenant Commander Howell was on leave for ten days, and Captain Warren would be in Sasebo until Thursday.

The lower right quadrant of the board, however, was occupied by one large note:

Welcome Hiroko Amanda Mays
19 April—3:29 am

6 lb, 5 oz
Mom & Baby are Fine

I smiled to myself and kept walking. The message had been up for a couple of days, and Mays and Noriko were probably home from the hospital by now. He'd be out of the office for the next couple of weeks, but I'd have to give him a call later today and see how they were adjusting. Or maybe send him an e-mail. For parents of a newborn, a ringing phone could quickly become the bane of their existence. Katie and I had shut our phones off for hours at a time when the twins were born.

My smile faded. Exhausting as it had been, running both Katie and me ragged month after month, I missed that period. I'd thought it was hell at the time, but I wondered how I'd have changed my tune if I'd known there would be a time when I went long months without seeing them. I always knew there'd be deployments, but back then, I never dreamed my default location would ever be this far from my kids.

I shook my head and continued toward my office. I unlocked the door, tossed my keys on the desk and dropped into my chair.

Once I'd logged on to my computer, I opened my e-mail program and skimmed my in-box for anything that was a priority.

Captain, Captain, Captain, mass department e-mail, Gonzales, Morris, Morris, Gonzales, Captain—

Oh, what a surprise. My ex-wife.

Grumbling to myself, I double-clicked the message.

Shane,

We need to figure out a budget for the summer and the next school year. Jessica is starting band in the fall, and the instrument rentals are pricey. They've both got a few things lined up this summer that need deposits, so let me know if you can help out with that.

Hope all is well,

K.

Band? Since when? What instrument was she playing? When did she even decide she was interested in music?

Thanks for the heads-up before *I talked to the kids, Katie.*

Shaking my head, I started to reply, but before I'd finished typing, another message came through.

BTW, we're taking the kids out of town the first of next month, so I'll be taking them to your parents' the following weekend. Let me know if that works for you.

K.

I scowled. Something told me reservations had been made and Katie had already discussed the matter with my parents. Probably didn't make a difference if it worked for me or not. Great. One extra week between now and when I spoke to the twins again.

I tried not to think about who she meant when she said "we" were taking the kids out of town. I didn't know or care if she was still dating her predivorce boyfriend or if this was someone new. It just bugged the hell out of me that whoever he was, he was spending more time with my kids than I was. Man, this distance sucked.

Shaking my head, I continued with my e-mail.

Katie,

Let me know how much you need, and I'll adjust the monthly deposit.

Switching the dates at the end of the month is fine. Let me know if anything changes.

Also, I was thinking, while they're on summer break, maybe we can work out having them come visit me. I think they'd really enjoy it here.

Shane

What luck. I'd caught her while she was still online, because not three minutes later, while I was going over a lengthy e-mail from the captain, a reply came through.

Shane,

Are you going to come out here and get them? They're too young to fly alone.

K.

I wrote back:

If you can fly with them to Seattle or California, I can take a military flight and pick them up. Will that work?

And in moments, she fired back:

I can't afford to fly across the country, and I really can't take that much time off work. Especially since military flights aren't that reliable, so I'd have to stay with them until you made it. Probably not a good idea until they're older, unless you want to come here and get them.

K.

I released a breath. I wasn't in the mood to argue with her. She would never in a million years prevent me from seeing my children, but she dug her heels in whenever it took any effort on her part to help me do so. God forbid we have to be in the same room for five damned minutes, never mind make her travel a few hours each direction to meet me halfway.

Whatever. I didn't have it in me to fight today.

And I needed coffee. Before I could handle another message from her or anyone else, I fucking needed coffee.

The coffeepot down the hall was our office's answer to a water cooler, so it was no surprise to see a few coworkers milling around with Styrofoam cups in hand and gossip in the air.

As I poured myself a cup, Morris turned to me.

"You hear about Sorenson?" he asked.

Oh, great. Now what? I shook my head.

"Had the cops out at his place last night," Gonzales said. "Guess he and the old lady were duking it out in the parking lot, got a little too loud."

"Lovely," I muttered. "How bad was it?"

Morris glanced down the hall, then shrugged. "He's at work, so they must have settled it or something."

I braced for a snide comment about Sorenson's wife, who Morris probably figured deserved whatever might have happened, but it mercifully didn't come. He must have caught on that I wasn't someone to fuck with today. Even Morris didn't hassle me much when I was in a mood like this.

And really, he was much easier to deal with at work than he was at the bar. Sober, he was abrasive but even-keeled. The dick he was when he drank sort of killed any positive feelings I might have had toward his sober persona. Especially since he could not drink without going off about, among other things, his rampant homophobia. A polite face by day didn't negate being an asshole at night, so even when I wasn't in a mood and he wasn't drunk, I kept him at arm's length.

On a day like this, I kept *everyone* at arm's length, so I bowed out of the conversation and retreated to my office. As the morning wore on, paperwork piled up. The phone rang. The skipper needed this. Commander Morris needed that. Lieutenant Commander Gonzales had papers for me to review and sign. My kids were still a million miles away.

I went through the motions of the day on numb autopilot. I still concentrated on my job—Intel wasn't a good place for daydreaming—but any parts of my mind that weren't needed to safely and effectively work were in another world. Aside from my job and the ever-tightening knot in my gut, I was completely detached.

Maybe I needed to take orders back to the States. At least then I'd be able to see the kids in person more than once a year. Of course, I wasn't up for orders for another two years, and even if I transferred back stateside, I'd be lucky to land within a ten-hour drive of the kids. Katie had moved back to Pittsburgh after the divorce, and the city wasn't exactly spitting distance from any place I might be stationed.

I supposed I couldn't blame her for that. She wanted to be near her family. And to be fair, if I was back in the States, living in the same state as my ex-wife wouldn't be healthy for either of us. Those once-or-twice-a-year encounters to hand off the kids were tense enough.

I sighed and rubbed my eyes. Maybe this was for the better. The kids didn't need to see what their mother and I had become. I doubted they remembered what we were like before—they were barely five when we split up—but they didn't need to see us like this.

The day ground on, and eventually, five o'clock came around.

I was sorely tempted to go out with everyone to the O'Club again tonight but bowed out. There was no point in drinking when I was in a mood like this. All I'd do is get depressed, miss my kids, and curse my ex-wife.

Plus Mays was still on leave. I didn't dare go near a drunk Morris when I was already in a mood and Mays wasn't around to verbally smack that idiot around when his mouth ran off with him. Gonzales and the others would have to babysit Morris tonight and keep him out of trouble, because I was better off anywhere but there, so I made my excuses and left.

As soon as I was home, I stripped out of my uniform and went in to grab a shower. I couldn't think. I couldn't breathe. The world had been suffocating me all damned day, and I just needed to get away from everyone and everything.

Hot water rushed over me, and I shrugged the weight of the day off my shoulders. Tilting my head from side to side to relieve the tension, I wondered if I should go get a massage. There were a few places on the island that were just well-dressed brothels, but I knew of some reputable ones where *massage* just meant *massage*.

Or I could go out to Palace Habu again. See if I could find

an attractive, willing companion for the night.

Maybe Eric.

Goose bumps prickled my skin under the warm water.

Eric. Fuck. Wasn't that a name and a face I'd tried—and failed—to forget? I'd tried my damnedest not to think about him the last few days, but now, I gave up and gave in. I surrendered and let my mind take me to the one place that could relax me and wind me up at the same time.

My cock hardened as my memory took me through everything from the first moment I saw Eric to the last time I'd made him come. My chest wanted to tighten, and my gut wanted to sink with the awareness that I was wallowing in the one and only time I'd ever see him, but I didn't care. I just closed my eyes, closed my fingers around my cock and got lost in that night.

I let my head fall forward. With one arm braced against the wall, I stroked my cock faster, faster, faster. I imagined Eric was right here with me, kneeling on the floor of my shower and stroking and sucking my cock. The way he'd kissed, I had no doubt his mouth was capable of giving the most spectacular blowjobs. I pictured him on top of me, pinning my arms to the pillow as he rode me like I was going to take what he gave me and I was going to *like* it. And, God in heaven, the way he fucked me. Shaking, thrusting, groaning, as if he wanted me to know how in control he was, even when he was as close to falling apart as I was.

My breath caught. My eyes rolled back. Just as my knees buckled, I heard myself groan, and I swore to God I could hear Eric whimpering in my ear, and I could barely keep my hand moving with any semblance of rhythm as my orgasm took over.

Panting and shaking, I touched my forehead to the cool tile. Sparks of electricity still crackled under my skin and through my muscles, and although the earlier tension had melted away, a new tension lingered. A knot coiled in the pit of my stomach, reminding me Eric hadn't actually been here tonight and wouldn't be here anytime soon.

Exhaling sharply, I pushed myself back from the wall and

let the hot water rush over me again. Who was I kidding? I couldn't shake him any more than I stood a chance of having him again. I wanted him so damned bad, not having him just made me want him that much more.

To hell with it. I'd tried and failed to reconnect with him the only way I could, but what was one more try? Besides, if he wasn't at Palace Habu tonight, other men would be, and I needed to get laid.

I turned off the shower, pushed the curtain back, and reached for a towel. There was no point staying home and feeling like hell. At the very least, I could almost always find someone who was attractive and willing at Palace Habu, so maybe I could put a new name and face to all this distraction. If Eric showed up, great. If not, there'd be plenty of other men.

I just hoped he was there.

Chapter Seven

Eric

By the time I left work on Friday night, I was no closer to forgetting about Shane than I was the morning I left his apartment. I'd thought about going to Palace Habu to find him again so I could get him out of my system and out of my mind, but I knew better. Another hit didn't make someone less addicted. If I went back and he was there, and we slept together again, I'd only want more. And more. And more. The only way I was getting him out of my system was to just stop thinking about him, focus on my job and stay the hell away from Palace Habu.

I knew this. I didn't question it. I didn't argue with it.

But it sure as fuck didn't stop me from pushing open that heavy, black-painted door and stepping into the flickering, flashing, fog-saturated club.

The spotlight made me squint, but I quickly stepped out of its beam and found my way to the bar. I flagged down the bartender just like I had the first night, and while he made my drink, I scanned the room and its occupants.

The bartenders were all Japanese except for one, but most of the crowd was American. Everything here was just as I'd left it last time. Blinding strobes and pulsing music. Gorgeous men dancing in the light and making out in the shadows. Jars of Habu sake above the bar.

But Shane wasn't here.

The bartender set my drink in front of me. I pulled a thousand-yen bill out of my wallet and slid it across the bar. In the back of my mind, I actually expected the bartender to refuse it, then gesture across the room at the man who'd already paid for my drink. Ah well. A guy could dream.

After pocketing my change, I picked up my drink. The first sip made me shiver. It was the first rum and Coke I'd had in two weeks, and good God, it took me back to the last one.

Rolling my drink around in my mouth, I scanned the room in search of either Shane or the next distraction. There was no shortage of good-looking guys tonight, that was for damn sure. Some danced together. A few danced by themselves, but judging by the looks they exchanged with other lone wolves, that wouldn't last long. Even through the flickering light and thin fog, the chemistry between some couples was nearly visible to the naked eye. Just watching one couple bantering and touching beside a chest-high table, I swore their crackling connection made the hairs on the back of my neck stand on end as if I were part of that electric equation.

Every time the air pressure in the room changed, I glanced at the door. And every time, I was met with an unfamiliar face, someone coming into the club who wasn't Shane.

Eventually, about the time I was near the bottom of my drink, I stopped looking. It occurred to me that guys would think I was waiting for someone if I kept glancing at the door. And I wasn't waiting for anyone. Though if he showed up, I—

It was a one-night stand, idiot. Let it go.

I flagged down the bartender and slid my empty glass across the bar. While he made my drink, I dug a handful of yen out of my pocket, and when the drink was finished, I handed him a few coins. I still wasn't quite used to the idea of paying six hundred yen for a drink; I had to remind myself each time it was closer to six or seven dollars, not six or seven *hundred* dollars.

Reasonably priced drink in hand, I turned around and leaned against the bar. Shane may not be here, but I was, and he couldn't possibly be the only good-looking man on the island. Might as well have a look around and see if anyone else caught my eye.

My skin prickled. I had the distinct impression someone was looking at me, and slowly turned my head.

From a few barstools over, a toned and tanned guy made

eye contact with me.

My God, he was hot.

I guessed he was a Marine. Some of those guys just had a look about them that was unmistakable. They stood a little straighter, pushed their shoulders back a little more and gave off an air that screamed Devil Dog. I'd probably have suspected most of them of steroid use if I didn't know just how demanding Marine PT was. A lot of Marines were powerfully sculpted from their shoulders and biceps to their six-packs, and this one had on a shirt tight enough to prove he was *no* exception.

He stepped away from the bar and started toward me. Something tightened in the pit of my stomach. He was hot, all right, but didn't stir as much interest as a man like him rightly should have.

Oh. Right. Because he isn't Shane.

I took a drink, silently trying to convince myself that was exactly why I was here—to find someone who wasn't Shane. Or let someone else find me, as it turned out.

He sidled up next to me and rested his elbow on the bar. "Haven't seen you here before."

I shrugged. "Just found out about the place." He didn't need to know how long I'd been on-island. Or that I'd been here once before and sampled what this club had to offer.

He extended his hand. "I'm Glenn."

"Eric," I said as I shook his hand. "You come here often?" It was cheesy, cliché pickup-line conversation, but it got words moving between strangers.

"Sometimes," he said with a shrug. "So what base are you out of?"

Great. The only thing better than small talk and pickup lines was shop talk.

"White Beach. You?"

"Futenma."

His eyes darted away for a split second. Weird. I supposed lying about which base he was attached to was a good cover story, but I couldn't imagine what I'd do with the real information.

Whatever, dude. I sipped my drink. "So you're a Marine, then?"

He nodded. "Yeah, I work in avionics." He shared stories about his job, going into mind-numbing detail about what he did, but I didn't talk about mine. I was here to get away from work, for fuck's sake. But while he went on about avionics and aircraft, I took advantage of being this close to him. So much easier to really look at him when we didn't have ten feet and flashing lights between us.

Glenn was taller than me by a few inches and definitely broader in the shoulders. He was easily stronger than me, and I caught myself thinking I wouldn't mind testing that theory in the bedroom. There were few things hotter than a man who was willing to get rough, and Glenn was certainly built for it. The only question was, was he wired that way? Regardless of size, not everyone was into being rough. Especially not rough by Eric Randall's definition.

I curled my fingers around my glass, both to keep myself cool and to resist the temptation to run my fingers over the grooves between his abs. If he played his cards right, and he was game to go someplace else with me, there'd be time for that later.

I was impatient as hell when I met someone who interested me, but I held back a little. When it came to guys who could easily overpower me, I preferred to feel them out before we went someplace private. Very nearly learned *that* lesson the hard way a few years ago.

But so far, he'd played his cards right, so I was optimistic, even if I wasn't as enthusiastic as I should have been. Ho hum, play games, get laid, move on, repeat next weekend. Didn't even seem worth the effort tonight.

I went to take a drink and realized I was down to ice. I gestured with my empty glass. "Refill?" Nodding at the glass in his hand, I added, "What are you drinking?"

"Orion," he said. "But I can—"

"I've got it." I nodded toward the other side of the room. "You want to see if any booths are available?"

Our eyes met, and he returned the grin with a little more feeling than I could have mustered. As he went to find a booth, I faced the bar and flagged down the bartender.

Mere seconds after I placed the order, Glenn reappeared beside me so suddenly he made me jump. I turned toward him and—

Jumped again.

I could barely breathe but managed to cough out a single word: “Shane?”

He grinned, which made my pulse go berserk. “You remembered my name. Does that mean I made an impression?”

I swallowed, wondering when my mouth had gone dry. “Did you think I’d forget your name after two weeks?”

He laughed. “Well, you never know. Anyway, I kind of hoped you’d be here tonight.” He nodded toward the bar. “Can I buy—”

Glenn stepped out of the crowd and looked at Shane, an unspoken challenge narrowing his eyes.

Shane looked at Glenn and abruptly backed off, stepping away from the bar. “Oh, I’m sorry.” His eyes darted toward me, and he smiled in spite of—holy shit, was that *disappointment* in his eyes? “I didn’t realize you already had company.”

Apparently satisfied Shane wasn’t going to get territorial, the challenge in Glenn’s expression eased. “It’s all right,” he said. “Don’t worry about it.” His biting tone, however, announced it was anything but all right, and Shane would be wise to worry about it.

I ground my teeth. Oh, what a turn-on. The son of a bitch had known me five minutes, he was already possessive, and he wasn’t Shane.

“Well.” Shane took another step back, then smiled halfheartedly at me. “It was good seeing you again.”

“Yeah, good seeing you too.”

Another step and the crowd swallowed him up.

No, no, no, come back. Where are you going? Damn it…

The bartender set our drinks on the bar, and I numbly counted out the yen. As I collected and pocketed my change,

Glenn nodded in the direction Shane had gone.

"You guys know each other?" he asked with an accusing edge.

I shrugged in spite of my annoyance and handed him his drink. "We've run into each other before."

He nodded once and acknowledged my comment with a quiet grunt. Eyes narrow, he looked past me, probably at Shane. Then he looked at me again, and his expression softened. A little. Gesturing toward the opposite side of the room, he said, "There are a few booths open. Want to grab one?"

"Sure." I gave him a watery smile. "Why not?"

We left the bar in search of a booth.

As we made our way through the thick crowd, I surreptitiously glanced around, hoping for a glimpse of Shane. I found him, and I regretted it.

The other guy stood way too close to just be shooting the breeze about something. They were near the speakers, which gave them every excuse to lean in close to be heard. Shane held eye contact with him. Put his hand on the other guy's forearm. Laughed at something meant only for his ears.

Well, at least I got to see him again.

Glenn and I found an empty booth. I gestured for him to go first, then slid in beside him. I slung my arm across the back of the bench but made no move to put it around his shoulders. He glanced at my arm, then raised his eyebrows as a grin spread across his lips. I returned it and winked, hoping he took it as, *Patience. I'm getting there.*

We went back to making small talk and shop talk, but it was stilted and tense now. And all the while, I was off-balance. The whole room had shifted like a bumped chessboard, and all the pieces were out of place. The man I'd come to find had unexpectedly arrived, and his presence tingled at the ends of the hairs standing on the back of my neck.

More than that, Glenn had tipped his hand and revealed a card that would put him firmly out of the running unless he found a way to redeem himself before I found a polite way to bow out of here. Or, rather, he had until I found a way to make a safe exit. If there was one thing I'd learned over the years, it was that a guy who was quick to get territorial was not very quick to let another man leave without a fight. Glenn had had just enough to drink, and been just hostile enough toward Shane, I needed to play it as cool as I could. That was why I let him sit first, so I could leave without needing him to move.

Not that I was intimidated by him—he was bigger and stronger, but law-enforcement training had taken the helpless right out of me—but if this got out of hand, the Japanese police would get called in. Then I'd be involved in an international incident *and* my chain of command would find out I'd been in a gay bar. Not good.

Lifting my glass to my lips, I tried to ignore the heavy, sinking feeling in my chest. That feeling that I really, really didn't want to be here in this club, and that the very thought of taking this evening any further with Glenn simply exhausted me. I swore into my drink. Should've known coming out here tonight was a bad idea.

I set my drink down and rubbed the back of my neck. Even if Glenn hadn't been a little shit earlier, now that I'd crossed paths with Shane, I wasn't sure I had it in me for a one-night stand tonight. It wasn't that the night I spent with Shane was special or any kind of nonsense like that. He just turned me on like no man had in ages. Sex with him was unreal, and fifteen platonic seconds in his presence tonight had been enough to raise the bar impossibly high for every man in this club. What I craved now was the kind of guy who'd slam me up against his front door and suck me off before we even made it into his apartment.

Son of a bitch was a hard act to follow, what could I say?

A hard act to follow who'd showed himself, offered to buy me a drink, then bowed out when Glenn got territorial. And then, of course, went off and found someone else.

And with that, I wasn't in the mood to stay here a minute longer. The one guy I really wanted had his sights set on someone else. Glenn had simultaneously shown himself to be aggressive in a way I didn't find remotely attractive *and* cock-blocked Shane.

Yeah, I was done for the night.

Glenn finished his drink and pushed the empty glass away. “I could go for another. How about you?”

“Actually...” I drained my own drink and set it beside his. “I think I’m going to call it a night.”

“You’re leaving?” He didn’t sound surprised. Well, maybe he did, but the only thing that registered in my ears was irritation.

“Is that a problem?” I asked with twice as much irritation.

Glenn stiffened, then made a sharp gesture. “What the fuck, man?”

Whatever. I didn’t even care if he thought I was an ass at this point. He’d shown the possessive card, and as a result, I couldn’t get past my discomfort at being around him, so I wasn’t about to go someplace where we’d be alone. Besides, while I could be accused of being easy under the right circumstances, I had a low tolerance for bullshit.

Keeping my voice even but firm, I said, “It was nice meeting you, but I think I’m going to go.”

I started to slide out of the booth, but Glenn grabbed my arm.

I froze. Turned. We locked eyes.

“I suppose you think that’s going to win me over?” I asked through gritted teeth.

He blinked, but his hand didn’t move. “Listen, I just think after we’ve—”

“I think you might want to think twice about *that*,” I growled, nodding emphatically at his hand on my arm.

His eyebrows jumped. Then his eyes darted toward his hand, and he wisely pulled it back.

Without breaking eye contact, I straightened my sleeve, silently daring him to even think about trying it again. Evidently, he did have a brain in his head, because he didn’t reach for me again. In fact, he drew back a little.

I got up and shouldered my way out of the club. The door banged shut behind me, muffling the music. Shoving my hands into the pockets of my shorts, I started down the steps.

Well. That sucked.

Now what? I debated my options as I wandered down the stairs and out into the alley. I could always go to another bar. Maybe just go have a few drinks without sex in mind. Show my face in a club or two where the straight guys hung out, just to keep up appearances.

Or I could save that for another night. I had beer at home.

Gate Two Street was choked with taxis, and dozens of people—mostly Americans, and a good many of them drunk as hell—tried to flag them down. Every time I found a cab that wasn't occupied, he was waiting for someone who'd called him. I waited patiently, though. It wasn't like I was in a big rush, and at least I was away from Glenn now.

"I don't suppose I could talk you into splitting cab fare, could I?"

The voice turned my head, and for the second time tonight, that grin almost knocked my knees out from under me. For a moment, I forgot myself and almost grabbed the front of Shane's shirt so I could kiss him, but an instant shy of too late, I remembered all the people around us, any one of whom could work with or for me.

I cleared my throat. "I...sure. Yeah. If you want to."

Shane winked, then shifted his gaze back out to the gridlock of taxis as if to keep anyone from realizing we were talking to each other. "You remember how to get to that cross street? The one where the cab picked us up last time?"

I ran through a mental map in my head. The alley behind us meandered between several buildings, going every which direction, and numerous cross streets and smaller alleys broke off from it, but we hadn't taken any turns until we'd reached the end.

"Yeah, I remember."

"Meet me there in ten." And with that, he was gone.

I stepped back from the curb so I didn't block anyone else's access to a taxi. I glanced at my watch a few times, and when I was sure enough time had passed that I wouldn't catch up with him too soon, I turned and headed down the alley. The layout was exactly as I remembered, and every familiar neon sign or club entrance made my heart beat a little faster. More than once, I wondered if I'd hallucinated that entire exchange.

The alley led me right to the place where we'd picked up a cab last time, but Shane wasn't there. I looked up the street, then down. I glanced at my watch, and it had been almost exactly ten minutes since he'd walked away.

Fuck, was I in the right place? Had I remembered how to get to where I was supposed to meet him? The sleeping storefronts looked as familiar as anything could in a foreign country; hell if I knew if the signs were the same ones I'd seen before. There was a nail salon, and the other usual businesses, but were they the same ones? Shit.

Headlights appeared at the end of the street, and as they approached, the yellow glow of a taxi sign hovered above them. I chewed my lip, wondering if I should flag down this cab and see if Shane showed up.

No. No, I'd wait for him. He must have had something up his sleeve. I couldn't imagine he'd ditched me or gotten lost finding the place he'd told me to meet him.

Then the cab stopped in front of me. The back door opened, and when I leaned down to look in, I shouldn't have been surprised to see Shane looking back in the low light. I supposed I wasn't surprised. The sudden shift in my pulse would have happened even if I'd known from three blocks away that he'd be in that car.

Heart racing, I slid into the cab beside him.

"Ready to get out of here?" he asked with a devilish grin.

"Absolutely."

As the driver accelerated, Shane put his hand on my knee, and the warmth of his palm made me jump.

"I only gave him my address." His thumb traced a single arc along the side of my knee. "I hope that's all right?"

I laid my hand over his. "Fine by me."

Shane said something in Japanese to the driver. I didn't understand it, but I hoped to God it translated to, "Step on it."

Chapter Eight

Shane

Eric and I made it from the cab to my front door, and I couldn't go an inch farther. I grabbed his arm and, just like I had the last time, shoved him up against the door. He gripped the back of my neck in both hands, digging his fingers in and refusing to let me even think about pulling away. I groaned into his kiss; Jesus, he tasted faintly of rum, and that hint of rum tasted even more like that first night together than my beer had. Like the night we'd burned up the sheets, which we'd do again tonight if we ever got to my bedroom.

I put my hands on his shoulders and shoved us apart. Breathing hard, I looked him in the eye and whispered, "Let's get in the house." I fumbled in my pocket for my house key. "Before I end up fucking you right out here."

Eric bit his lip, and judging by the palpable intensity in his eyes, he wasn't far from suggesting I do just that.

Once we were inside, Eric grabbed me and shoved me up against the other side of the door I'd just had him pinned against, and his kiss was desperate and violent and hungry.

"I've been"—he kissed me, dragging his fingers through my hair—"thinking about…this. Since last time. God, Shane…"

"Me too." I dipped my head to kiss his neck. "I don't know what you did last time." I paused to inhale his musky scent, then whispered, "Just fucking do it again tonight."

"With pleasure," he growled.

I raised my head, and he kissed me again. I shouldered myself off the door, pushing him back a step. He held on to the front of my shirt and took another step, pulling me with him. One step and half a dozen kisses at a time, we inched down the hall. My arm brushed the wall. His hip grazed the molding around the bathroom door. We both nearly stumbled, somehow righted ourselves, and when we stumbled again, it was only the lack of condoms and lube within reach that stopped me from just dragging him down right then and there.

Somehow, I guided us into the bedroom. Eric's shirt landed on the floor by the door. Mine fell a few inches shy of the bed. I reached for the front of his shorts, but he grabbed my wrist.

"No," he said, and before I could panic and wonder what I'd done wrong, he added a whispered, "Just fuck me. Now."

I kissed him again, even more desperately this time. Then we pulled apart to get the last of our clothes out of the way.

As I tore the condom wrapper, I looked him up and down. It wasn't like I hadn't memorized every inch of his body last time, but he was just so fucking gorgeous. I'd always loved abs like that, the kind I could bounce a penny off, but looking at Eric's, all I could think of was how his muscles had quivered and contracted when I'd put him on his back and fucked him the second time.

Our eyes met, and damn if his didn't have *do it again* written all over them.

I swore it took me hours to get the condom and lube on. Everything happened in slow motion except the shaking in my hands, and every second I wasn't inside him drove me insane.

Finally, though, everything was in place. The condom was on. Eric was on his hands and knees. I was on my trembling knees behind him.

And…oh God…I was inside him.

I steadied his hips with unsteady hands and pulled out slowly. As I slid my cock into him again, I held my breath, willing myself not to come yet. All week long, I hadn't been able to stop thinking about him, and now he was here. He was here, in my bed, and I was inside him, and I was so fucking turned on I could barely stand it.

Taking slow, smooth strokes, I watched myself disappear into him until I was buried to the hilt. Then I withdrew. Slid in again. Withdrew again. Christ, no one made it this hard for me to hold back. No one. I always came when I was damn good and ready, especially when I'd already come once tonight, but from the first stroke—from the first damned kiss—I was a shiver away from letting go.

Against my will—and my better judgment, if I had any hope of making this last—my hips moved faster. Faster. Still faster.

Eric shuddered and rocked back against me; it was all I could do to keep from coming, especially when he released the sexiest, most helpless moan I'd ever heard.

"Am I hurting you?" I asked through clenched teeth.

"No," he said.

I fucked him harder, my head spinning as I damn near lost it with every thrust. "How about now?"

Eric let his head fall forward, and his shoulders quivered over his trembling arms. "Oh...God..."

He rested his weight on one arm, and I almost whimpered myself as he reached for his own cock. His elbow jerked forward one, two, three times, and every muscle in his back and shoulders tensed. He tightened around me, thrust back against me, and with a throaty groan, he threw his head back and came.

I gripped his hips and gave him everything I had, fucking him deep and hard while his moans and slurred curses drove me on, drove me crazy, drove me right over the edge with him. Every inch of my body ached and tingled as I took one last thrust, then pulled him against me and lost it.

Everything spun and blurred. I couldn't tell my voice from Eric's, but I was certain at least some of the slurred, whispered curses were mine.

Eventually, my vision cleared, and I stopped shaking enough to pull out and take care of the condom. After we'd cleaned up, we both dropped onto our backs onto the bed.

For a while, we were quiet, just staring up at the ceiling and catching our breath. As the dust settled, the coolness of my room set in, so I pulled the sheet up over us, and that was when we both shifted onto our sides to face each other.

"Glad you showed up tonight," he said, grinning.

I ran my hand down his arm. "Likewise. You know, I've

been kicking myself for not getting your number."

"Me too." He propped himself up on one arm and draped the other over my waist. "Any chance I can talk you out of your number before I leave this time?"

I chuckled. "After tonight, you'll be lucky if I don't tattoo it on your arm."

Eric laughed. "I don't think *that* will be necessary. How about if I just put it in my phone and we'll call it good?"

"Works for me." I leaned in and kissed him lightly. "I am so fucking glad you were at the club tonight." Running my fingers through his hair, I said, "And if I may be so forward, I wouldn't mind making a habit of this."

Eric grinned, raising goose bumps along the length of my spine. "Would you, now?"

"Well, if you're...agreeable."

He brushed my lips with his and whispered, "Oh, I am definitely agreeable." Settling back onto the pillow, he said, "And believe me, I didn't think you'd be there, or I wouldn't have given that other asshole the time of day."

I laughed halfheartedly. "He's not someone you want to give the time of day anyway."

"So I discovered. You're familiar with the guy?"

I nodded. "Son of a bitch comes to Palace Habu all the damned time. I guess I'm not his type because he's never said a word to me, but I've heard from plenty of guys that he isn't one to mess with."

"Good to know," Eric muttered. "So who is this guy?"

Shrugging, I said, "Rumor has it he's attached to one of the bases on the north end of the island, and he's been banned from all the clubs up there for drunken behavior, refusing to take no for an answer, and just generally being a dick. No one reports it to his chain of command, of course—"

Eric blew out a breath. "Can't blame them for that."

I nodded again. Regulating asshole behavior in a gay bar was a tricky issue. None of us wanted our own commands finding out we came to places like these, so, short of being socially ostracized, nothing ever really came of it. It was a small world, though, and Okinawa was far, far too small to have a reputation like that. Anyone who'd been on the island any length of time knew Glenn well enough to avoid him.

"Well," I said. "At least now you know to avoid him like the plague."

"Can't say I'm terribly interested in him anymore anyway." He grinned and winked.

"Good." I teased the corner of his mouth with a flick of my tongue. "Now pardon me while I gloat for a moment about getting you into bed after he fucked up."

Eric laughed. "Please. I was ready to get into your bed the second you showed up at the bar."

"Well, damn." I sighed dramatically. "Why didn't you tell me?"

"Because we were rudely interrupted by Jarhead McJackass."

"Oh, right."

"And let me tell you," Eric said, "I ever get called out to deal with that fucker? He isn't going to like me."

Something tightened in my gut. "If you...ever get called out?"

"Yeah. I mean, Eighteenth Security or the JPs would probably handle it if it was near Kadena, but if he fucks with a Navy guy..."

I swallowed. "You're Navy security, then?"

"Yep. CFAO Security out at White Beach."

My mouth went dry. "You're an MA."

And with a single nod, he took us from fooling around to playing with fire.

I cleared my throat. "So, you're enlisted, then."

One eyebrow flicked upward. "Is that...an issue?" Beat. Enlightenment widened his eyes. "You're an officer."

I nodded. It was only now that it dawned on me I'd never even thought to ask him what branch he was in, never mind what rank. Enlisted guys didn't usually pique my interest, and most of the guys who came to Palace Habu were officers anyway, so I never really thought about it.

Fucking another guy couldn't get me in trouble anymore, but getting caught with an enlisted guy? Adios, career.

So much for making a habit of this.

Eric groaned and covered his face with one hand. "*Fuck.*" He pinched the bridge of his nose and exhaled hard. Half a dozen curses came to the tip of my tongue, but before I could bring them to life, he lowered his hand and met my eyes. "So I guess there's no point in exchanging numbers after all, is there?"

I watched my hand drift up and down his waist. "No. Probably not."

There was no probably about it. In theory, we could be friends. I wasn't in his direct chain of command. He didn't answer to me. The only problem was we were gay. Someone saw us hanging out together on a regular basis? There was only one conclusion they'd draw, and that conclusion was both true and a kiss of death for our careers. In a time when the military was downsizing and people were still hostile to DADT's repeal, we were pretty much handing anyone who wanted it an excuse to get rid of us.

But even being friends could be dangerous, and it went deeper than simple fraternization. That could get us both into some trouble, but officers and enlisted men were like two social classes in a strictly separated society. Two classes that did not intermingle. It simply wasn't done. It was an ironclad Navy tradition, one that, when broken, could kill a career. Or two.

It didn't even matter that DADT was a nonissue now. The fact that we were gay was the least of our problems if we kept doing this. If we were younger, things would have been different. If I were a freshly commissioned ensign and he were a seaman straight out of boot camp, we wouldn't have had so much at stake. As it was, we were both too close to retirement to fuck up our careers. Some twenty-one-year-old getting kicked out still had a chance to start a new career. A thirty-five-year-old who pissed away a solid fifteen-plus-year career with an other-than-honorable discharge due to conduct unbecoming a gentleman? Yeah, that would look fucking *spectacular* on a résumé.

I sighed and met his eyes. "No one has to know about tonight. You're already here, we're already in bed, so we might as well finish what we started."

"And after tonight?"

I watched my thumb trace his lower lip. "I think we both know what has to happen after tonight."

"Then I guess we should make tonight count."

"I guess we should."

My ears rang from the gunfire. My mouth was dry and tasted like sand. Cold sweat cooled skin that still burned from the phantom heat of the desert sun.

I opened my eyes.

Bedroom. I was in my bedroom. An all too familiar sense of relief rushed through me, and I exhaled. Another dream. Just another damned dream.

I rubbed my eyes with the heels of my hands and sighed. At least I didn't wake up quite so disoriented anymore. The first few months of postcombat nightmares had me shaking and panicking every damned morning, wondering where the fuck I was until I remembered I was in my own bed. I was much better these days, and if this was the worst PTSD I had—crazy vivid dreams that left me thinking I had sand in my mouth—I'd take it.

I turned my head to look at the alarm clock beside the bed and startled.

Oblivious to the fact that I'd completely forgotten he was even here, Eric was still sound asleep. He was on his stomach, facing away from me, and his hair as disheveled as it could be when it was cut that short.

Goose bumps rose on my back and arms, and I shivered away the chill of my nightmare. I smiled to myself as last night came flooding back.

I still couldn't believe my luck. I'd been at Palace Habu for a good half hour or so when Eric emerged from the crowd and stepped up to the bar. I'd nearly dropped my drink and cut a quick path across the room, hoping I'd get to him before another guy realized such a gorgeous man was among us and moved in ahead of me.

Oh, but I was already too late. Of all people, that fucking jarhead had set his sights on Eric and had already gotten his attention.

I would have backed off the second I realized Eric was there with someone else, but since it was *that* guy, I made an even faster exit to avoid a scene. After they'd moved to a booth on the other side of the room, I wasn't the only one in the club who kept throwing glances toward them. Even while a friend—and occasional booty call—and I chatted over by the deejay, we both kept an eye on Eric just to make sure the Marine didn't get out of line.

Just try it, Jarhead. I dare you.

He tried it, all right, and several of us were on our feet, ready to intervene, but we all stopped dead when Eric shut him down. The stunned Marine released his arm, and Eric stormed out.

I'd probably never know if anyone said anything to the jerk at that point. Maybe they threw him out. Maybe everyone just rolled their eyes and wished he'd find another place to troll.

The object of my interest, however, was on his way out of Palace Habu at that moment, and so was I.

And now, here we were.

Watching him sleep, I sighed. Here we were, and this was the last place in the world we should have been. God damn it, why did the first guy to come along post-DADT with some potential have to be the worst possible choice for me? Every fucking time I found someone who might get my hopes up, the Navy found some way to shoot it down. Deploy me to the Sandbox long enough for my wife to find someone else. Transfer me out of Sasebo right when things with Emiko looked like they might get serious but weren't serious enough for us to get married. Forbid gay relationships so the paranoia drove Paul and me apart, and the secrecy exhausted Gerry and me until we couldn't take it anymore.

And then, right about the time it was okay to be gay, Eric. Eric who was my match in the bedroom, and Eric who was fucking enlisted. Guess it was back to the drawing board. Back to Palace Habu. Groan.

But he was here now, so I slid a little closer and gently rested my hand just below his shoulder blade. He tensed but then relaxed. As I slid closer to him, he rolled onto his side, his back against my chest, and clasped his fingers between mine as I put my arm around him. The heat of his body made me shiver, and when I inhaled the scent of his skin, goose bumps rose along my spine and my arms.

"Morning," I said.

"Is it? I could've sworn we just went to sleep."

"I think we did." I laughed and pressed my lips to the back of his shoulder, grinning when he squirmed and pulled in a breath. "We *were* up pretty late."

"Mmm. It was worth the lost sleep."

"God, I hope so." I deliberately let my unshaven chin brush his shoulder.

"It was. Believe me. It was."

And it was also a good hour before we made it out of bed, grabbed a shower and got dressed. A *very* good hour.

In the kitchen, I handed him a cup of coffee.

I held my own in both hands, waiting until it cooled before I dove in. "So, how do you like Okinawa so far?"

He shrugged. "Haven't had a chance to see much of it."

"Work?"

"Well, that," he said. "But it's just me right now. I don't really know anyone who knows their way around the island."

"So?" I grinned. "That's half the fun of a place like this." I gestured toward the window, as if to indicate everything that existed beyond it. "You go out, get lost and find stuff."

"Yeah, I'm not a huge fan of getting lost."

I chuckled. "Eric, the island is seventy miles long. I think the widest point is like eighteen miles. There's only so lost you can get on a chunk of rock this small."

"Hmm. Okay, good point."

"That, and most of the cool shit, you have to get lost to find it."

"Such as?"

"Some of the castles." I sipped my coffee carefully. It was still a little hot, but I liked it that way, so I drank a little more before I continued. "Some of the best beaches on the island are out in the middle of nowhere. There's shrines, tombs, memorials, shops." I shrugged again. "You just have to get out and find them."

"And if I get lost," he said with a smirk, "I can call you and have you help me find my way back, right?"

We both laughed, but I stopped quickly and so did he.

"Right," he said, dropping his gaze. "I suppose calling you would be a bad idea."

"Well, I mean, we won't get in trouble if you're just lost and asking for directions," I said quietly.

He nodded but said nothing. He probably knew as well as I did that it wasn't so simple. No, a phone call asking for directions wouldn't get us into trouble. It would, however, put us in communication. Which might lead to a longer conversation. Which might lead to getting together just once. Or twice. Or three times.

Can't I have just a little bit of peril?

Eric cleared his throat and gestured at a framed photo on the wall. "Those your kids?"

Thankful for the subject change, I nodded. "Yeah. Jason and Jessica."

"They twins?"

"Yep. They'll be nine soon. Hard to believe."

"Tell me about it." He shook his head, then carefully sipped his coffee. "Mine's graduating next year."

I almost choked on my own coffee. "You have...you have an *eighteen*-year-old?"

"Well, seventeen."

"Are you serious?"

He nodded, chuckling. "I started young, what can I say?"

"Apparently so."

Eric exhaled. "Still, hard to believe that one more year and I'll have a high school graduate." He whistled and shook his head.

"Man, I've got a ways to go before I have to deal with that." I paused. "I can't even imagine what they'll be like as teenagers. They're already hellions."

"With your genes?" Eric laughed. "That doesn't surprise me at all."

"Uh-huh." I raised an eyebrow. "Something tells me yours is a handful too."

"Mine?" He put a hand to his chest and feigned offense. "Please. I'll have you know my kid is the most mild-mannered, well-behaved—"

"Bullshit." I snickered. "No way in hell I'll believe that."

"Okay, you got me. She's definitely her father's daughter." Eric grimaced. "Her poor mother."

At that, my humor faded a little. "She lives in the States?"

He nodded slowly. "Yeah. Still adjusting to that, believe me."

"I know exactly what you mean. Mine live with their mom in Pennsylvania."

"How do you deal with it?" he asked, barely whispering. "Being this far away for so long?"

I rested my hip against the counter and set my coffee cup down. "Same way you deal with anything when you're in the service. One day at a time."

"Amazing how quickly one day at a time adds up to most of your life," he muttered.

"No shit."

Eric was quiet for a moment, drumming his fingers on the counter and staring into his coffee cup. I was about to change the subject to something a little less depressing, but then he suddenly looked me in the eye.

"You know what?" he said. "I don't give a fuck that you're an officer and I'm enlisted."

I blinked. "You...what?"

"Look." He set the cup down and hooked his thumbs in his pockets, holding my gaze with that intensity that had intrigued me the first night. "We're both a million miles from our kids. I'm sure you've had to give up as much of your life as I have. And I'm..." He paused, then shook his head. "I'm tired of it, Shane. As long as no one knows, why can't we do this?"

"Besides the part where this is a small island?" I said. "Tiny commands, tinier gay community. Word is bound to get out."

He gestured around the room. "There's no one here but us. No one knows we're here together. There's no reason anyone needs to find out about it."

I swallowed hard. He was right, but this was the sort of thing that had a bad habit of finding a way to get out. And there was so much at stake.

The distance between us shrank. So did my lungs. As the room spun around me, Eric leaned in, and his gaze only broke away from mine long enough to flick toward my lips.

"As long as no one knows about it, no one can give a shit about what we're doing." His voice hovered between a whisper and growl. "And I don't imagine you're any quicker than I am to tell anyone who cares. Unless you think it's a bad idea?"

"I know it's a bad idea." I slid my hand over his. "But you're right. We've both given up a lot for this life." As his other hand snaked around to my lower back, I said, "And what can I say? You're fucking addictive."

He laughed quietly, shifting his gaze away from mine. A hint of color bloomed in his cheeks, but when he met my eyes again, there wasn't a bit of shyness in his. "As are you. So I don't see why we can't keep doing exactly what we're doing as long as we keep it behind closed doors."

"So," I said. "You're suggesting we just get together and fuck whenever the moment strikes us?"

Shrugging, he grinned. "Put it like that, it sounds even hotter."

I laughed. “I like the way you think.”

Eric kissed me lightly. “Too bad I’ve got absolutely nothing left, or I’d say one more for the road.”

“Well,” I said, “all the more reason for us to get together again, right? Since we didn’t get it all out of our system already.”

“Get it out of our system?” He laughed. “Yeah. That’s gonna happen.”

If it was going to happen, it sure as hell wasn’t happening today. Like Eric, I was completely spent and exhausted, so neither of us even tried to go anywhere near my bedroom again for now. After a pot of coffee between us, I called him a cab.

We double-checked we had each other’s numbers, exchanged one long, last kiss in the safety of my apartment, checked our phones again, and said good-bye.

In my silent, otherwise empty bedroom, I lay back on the rumpled bed and laced my hands behind my head. Staring up at the ceiling, I couldn’t figure out just what I thought of this situation.

Last night, I’d thought the odds were a million to one I’d even see him again. It didn’t occur to me there was a legitimate, nonnegotiable reason I *shouldn’t* see him again.

I wouldn’t get in trouble for being with a man now that DADT had been repealed, but I could certainly cause myself some headache. Getting caught with a man couldn’t officially hurt my career, but it could unofficially ensure I didn’t stand a chance in hell of putting on captain.

But an enlisted Sailor? That could be anything from a letter of reprimand—which would also cost me any chance of making captain—or a dismissal. I could end up at admiral’s mast. He could wind up at captain’s mast. If a higher-up really wanted to make an example of us, we could both face court-martial. This wasn’t something to fuck around with.

Idiot that I was, though, I had his number in my phone. He had mine. We’d both alluded to seeing each other again very soon.

And for that matter, I was lying if I told myself I only

wanted him in bed. Even before he'd told me he was enlisted, he'd piqued my curiosity. He had a vibe about him, a laid-back, relaxed side that completely contradicted his in-your-face aggressiveness in the club. I wanted to know more about him. Trust me not to leave well enough alone. Maybe it was because he was forbidden now, maybe it was because he intrigued me anyway, but I had a feeling I'd be missing out if I didn't also spend time with him between orgasms.

Right or wrong, I wanted to know him.

Chapter Nine

Eric

Oh, the joys of being a watch commander. Even on my day off, my phone wouldn't shut the fuck up.

Someone couldn't find the keys to the training building. Why they called me, I didn't know, because I sure as hell didn't have the keys or know where to find them. Then one of the patrol vehicles wouldn't start, which was somehow my problem. And what I was supposed to do about the malfunctioning air conditioner in the guard shack at Camp Shields, I had no idea.

It's my day off, fuckers. Call your own watch commander.

More than once, I debated having a beer, but I hadn't decided if I was staying in or going out tonight. Of course, I could take a cab, but I rather liked the freedom of driving wherever I wanted and not paying through the nose for the privilege.

So, for the time being, I settled for a soda while I kicked back and played video games. Around quarter after five, right around the time I'd finally figured out how to get past one level that had been driving me crazy, my phone beeped. Again.

I groaned. God, what did they want this time?

It wasn't anyone from work, though.

A text popped up from Shane: *Busy tonight?*

I smiled to myself. Too busy for him? Not a chance. After a week and a half or so of covertly seeing each other, I was lucky I could walk more often than not, but I damn sure had time for him.

I sent back, *No, I'm free. Your place or mine?*

But when he replied, he had something else in mind: *Can you meet me at Katsuren Castle in an hour?*

I stared at the message, furrowing my brow like my phone

or the words on the screen would suddenly explain where he was going with this. Shane must have anticipated my reluctance, because a second text came through: *Trust me.*

This wasn't a good idea. No way in hell. Sleeping together behind closed doors was risky enough. Being seen out in public together was the mother of all bad ideas for us.

Lead me not into temptation, I thought as I sent back a message telling him I'd be there, *for I know the way myself.*

I parked across the street from the castle in the paved lot between a tile-roofed visitor center and a buzzing substation. After I'd rolled up my windows, leaving them open a crack so my car didn't get too hot, I got out.

The back end of the parking lot shared a fence with a small farm. A row of banana trees lined a garden, and along one side of that garden was a cluster of some sort of cacti. How odd, seeing a cactus in a place like this, but there they were—thick, green arms, some with spiny, pineapple-shaped flowers or something on the ends. I'd actually seen them on a few farms as I'd been driving around. I'd have to ask Shane if he knew what the hell they were.

Shane.

This couldn't be a good idea, meeting out in public.

Trust me.

Taking a deep breath and taking him at his word, I started toward the road. On my way to the crosswalk, I looked up at the castle.

No fewer than twenty power lines from the substation sliced across my view of the high gray walls but didn't make the castle any less impressive. Peering over a thick forest and looming above everything from up on top of a hill, Katsuren was more like a fortress than what I would usually imagine a castle to be. There were no towers, no battlements, no real buildings to speak of. It was just a stone wall, but I imagined it was nearly impenetrable in its day.

A sign above the crosswalk read *Katsuren Castle Site—*

200m. Two hundred meters up a hill, of course. At least the heat of the afternoon was starting to ease up. I was in damned good physical condition, thanks to the military, but there was nothing quite like hiking up even a small hill with the tropical sun chewing on the back of your neck and the thick humidity invading your lungs.

The substation's buzzing should have faded behind me, but the farther up the hill I walked, the louder the sound was. In fact, I swore it was coming from the thick copse of trees beside the castle walls. How...weird.

At the top of the hill, with the substation's buzz almost deafening now in spite of the distance, I was in front of the castle instead of looking at it from the side.

The hill rose another twenty feet or so from where I stood now, and the castle stood about two or three stories on top of that. From the far left, a smaller wall angled slightly downward and swept all the way to the right side, revealing the end of a set of wooden stairs that I assumed led all the way to the top. Then the wall curved gently back toward the left and led into a rocky path that ended at my feet.

And somewhere, at the top of the walkway and the stairs and the wall, Shane waited.

Why here? Why now? Why out in public?

And why had I shown up when I knew this couldn't lead to anything good? Or to something really good that was also reckless and stupid and could damage our careers?

Go back, Eric. There is way too much at stake.

We weren't criminals, for God's sake. We were just two men who shouldn't have been fucking, which was why we'd kept it on the down low. No one would know. If they saw us now in civvies, they wouldn't have any reason to suspect anything. Unless they knew one of us, and talked to us, and figured out the difference between our ranks. Christ, we could get in trouble just for hanging out together.

Which raised the question: Just what the fuck was I doing here?

Only one way to find out.

Before my brain could talk my feet out of it, I started up the path toward the stone structure. For whatever reason, plastic had been put down over part of the path and covered with gravel, leaving green plastic pegs poking up between the rocks. I supposed it could have been to give people better footing as the incline steepened, but if so, it didn't work. I damn near lost my balance three times when I stepped on one of the pegs just right, making my foot slip down in between them. Fucking turf was a rolled ankle waiting to happen.

I managed to get from the weird ground to the wooden stairs without falling on my ass. The stairs creaked beneath my feet as I walked past a couple of tourists who'd stopped to take pictures, and I hoped they hadn't noticed my less than graceful battle with the plastic pegs.

The last ten or so steps were the original stone, and they sloped enough to warrant making use of the hand railing someone had installed in recent years.

I climbed the steep stone stairs and looked around the castle. There wasn't much left up here—a chest-high wall encircled a grassy area that must have been the lowest enclosure of the original building. Another steep set of stairs led up to a second enclosure, and above that was another high wall. Some tourists milled around, taking pictures beside the tree in the middle or up against the edge.

It was tempting to go to the edge and look around at the scenery below, but there would be time for that later. For now, the one thing I wanted to see was nowhere in sight, and I needed to find him before my brain caught up with my feet and talked me out of being here.

Normally, every inch of the castle would have fascinated me. I could have spent an hour in each enclosure, checking out the shrines on the second level and marveling at the precision with which the stones had been fitted together to form the walls. On the second level, about thirty evenly spaced stones about two feet across stuck up a few inches from the ground. I assumed they were the remains of the foundation of a building or something, and any other day, I'd have stopped to figure it out.

I walked right past them, throwing only the briefest glance at the foundation and the shrines tucked away in the bushes off to one side.

The stairs leading up to the third enclosure were even steeper than the lower ones. The wall was three or four feet wide and mostly dirt in between the stone interior and exterior, much like insulation between siding and drywall. The dirt was packed down like people had been walking on it, but I took my chances on the stairs and the tricky cobbled path that followed it. Walking on top of the wall was...a bit much.

At least the stairs and cobbles were easier to get across than those stupid plastic pegs down below, and I made it past them all with relative ease. Chuckling to myself, I wondered if the next level had some sort of Indiana Jones booby traps or a shark pit or—

God. More stairs.

Big surprise. At least it was only a small set. Steep, angled sharply because of hundreds of years of shifting and settling, but only ten or twelve steps. Simple enough.

And if you shouldn't be here, you've had ample opportunity to turn around, I told myself. *So if you get in over your head, it's your own damned fault.*

At the top of what I hoped was the last set of stairs, I came to another enclosure. Smaller than the others, grassy like the others, and...

There he was.

My pounding heart had nothing to do with the climb up here. I didn't know why I was surprised to see him. I mean, what did I expect? A giant sign reading *Your Prince Is in Another Castle*?

He certainly wasn't in another castle. His back was to me, giving me time to drink in the sight of him as I started across the enclosure.

The wind tugged at his T-shirt and khaki shorts, and he had his thumbs casually hooked into his pockets. If he looked this good dressed like this, he must have been stunning in his uniform. Most guys looked good in tailored whites, and the very thought of those black boards emphasizing his broad shoulders...

A shiver went down my spine.

It took me a moment to realize he wasn't just standing up here looking over the wall—he was standing *on* the wall.

"Living on the edge?" I said.

He turned around and flashed me that electrifying, toothy grin. "Always."

I stopped beside the wall and looked out at the scenery below us. Damn, we *were* high up. The buildings and cars below us looked like toys, and even with a four-foot-wide wall in front of me, I still had that vertigo that comes with looking over a cliff's edge. Kind of like peering over the side of the flight deck on a carrier. There was a reason I hadn't spent much time on flight decks.

Shane offered his hand. "Come on up."

I looked at him warily. "Are you insane?"

He chuckled. "These walls have been standing since the fourteenth century, and there's a good two feet between where I'm standing and the edge."

"Two feet?" I raised an eyebrow. "And how many feet between the edge and the ground?"

"Relax. There's nothing to worry about." He beckoned with his outstretched hand. "Come on. You'll be fine."

I hesitated, then glanced around the enclosure to make sure no one was around. Once I was certain we were alone, I took his hand.

He helped me up onto the wall, and I craned my neck a little to look over the edge. My God, we were high up. My car looked like a Matchbox car in the parking lot down below, and even the substation looked tiny. Sure didn't sound tiny, though.

"Okay, am I hearing things?" I gestured at the substation. "I swear to God, I can hear the power lines more up here than I could down there."

Shane furrowed his brow and listened. Then he laughed. "Those aren't power lines. Those are cicadas."

"Say, what? Those are...insects?"

He nodded. "They're loud as fuck this time of year."

"So I've gathered." I eyed the trees. Really? *Bugs* were making all that noise? This was one strange island. Turning my attention back to Shane, I said, "So why Katsuren?"

He shrugged. "I just like it up here. The view is incredible."

I couldn't argue with that.

Katsuren kept watch over neatly arranged farms with tidy rows of greenhouses, crops, and perfectly square pastures of black cows. Beyond the fields and fences, houses of every shape and color huddled together between winding highways and shorelines. Huge electricity towers stood at attention along the forested hills, connecting the towns to the substation below us and the power plant in the distance. Beside the power plant, the triplet blades of a wind turbine made lazy circles in the same early evening breeze that played with my shirt and warmed the back of my neck.

The castle was situated on a narrow sliver of land jutting out from Okinawa's west coast into the Pacific Ocean. Fishing boats left white wakes in the otherwise flawless water as they navigated between reefs and concrete tsunami breaks. In the distance, a bridge snaked across the water, connecting the island to a smaller one via a few tiny, possibly man-made islands. From there, another bridge arched over a narrow inlet to yet another small island.

I nodded toward them. "So which islands are those?"

He pointed to the largest. "Off to the right, at the end of the second bridge, is Hamahiga. Not much there, but it's a decent snorkel spot." He gestured to the other larger island. "And it looks like one island, but it's actually Henza, Miyagi, and Ikei Islands. Kind of in a chain."

"There's three islands over there?"

He nodded. "Ikei and Miyagi are worth checking out. Mostly farms and stuff, but there are some great views, tons of real cool-looking tombs, and some awesome beaches." He paused. "There's some amazing snorkeling too, when the jellyfish aren't swarming."

"Good to know," I said quietly.

He said nothing for a moment, then: "We'll have to go drive around Ikei one of these days."

I chewed the inside of my cheek. On my way to and from work every day, I passed that bridge connecting Okinawa to Henza Island. It was just a few clicks away from White Beach, which meant I wasn't the only one in my command who drove past it. Being up here with him on top of Katsuren was risky enough. Being in the same car when a coworker happened past? Not a good idea.

"You know," Shane said after a moment. "They say you used to be able to see Nakagusuku and I think Shuri Castles from here. I suppose you still could if you knew what to look for."

"Really?" I lowered my gaze to the homes and businesses at the base of the hill on which Katsuren sat. "I wonder how many people down there can see us up here."

"Who cares? Not like any of them know who we are, right?"

"Good point."

Footsteps behind us turned both our heads. My heart jumped into my throat. I was certain we'd been busted by both our chains of command or something, but it was just a couple of middle-aged Japanese tourists.

"*Gobenwa*," the man said, smiling and waving at us. "*Good evening.*"

"*Gobenwa*," Shane and I both replied, returning the smile.

Leaving the tourists to check out the walls and the view, Shane turned back around, facing the fields and ocean again. "Relax, they don't have a clue who we are."

"Guess I'm just a little jumpy."

"Understandable," he said with a slight nod. "But the fact is, for all intents and purposes"—he looked at me—"we're alone."

We are. But should we be?

I stared out at the ocean and the farms and the trees and the homes, but all the while, my attention was focused on him. My skin prickled with awareness of him, and uncertainty twisted in my stomach. Finally, I said, "What are we doing up here, Shane?"

"Checking out the view from on top of Katsuren Castle."

I pursed my lips. "You know what I mean."

"I do. And the answer's the same." He glanced over his shoulder, as did I, and the other tourists had left. We really were alone now as he turned to me again. "We're just two guys who came up to look at the castle and happened to strike up a conversation."

Cocking my head, I said, "Where are you going with this?"

"Well, you want to see more of the island, right?"

I nodded.

"And I want to see more of you." He shifted his gaze back out to the farms and islands. "Let me ask you this: How many Americans did you see on your way up here?"

Not that I'd paid much attention to anything except the stairs and my desire to see him, but as I mentally retraced my steps, I realized what few tourists I'd seen down below had been Japanese.

"None, now that you mention it," I said.

"And in the parking lot, did you see any Y plates?"

I looked down at the parking lot. Of course I couldn't see the plates from here, but there were barely any cars at all. I hadn't seen a single Y plate, which was a license plate with a letter *Y* on the far left instead of a kanji symbol, differentiating American-owned from Japanese-owned cars.

"No," I said. "I don't think I saw any."

"Trust me," he said. "Our cars are probably the only Y plates down there. Come up here on a weekend, you might see a handful of Americans. On a weeknight like this? None."

"I'm not following you."

"Right now, we're a few clicks from White Beach. A few more from Kadena or Camp Courtney. The farther we go in any direction from any of the bases, the fewer Y plates we'll see." He looked at me again. "Which means the fewer people who might see us and actually give a fuck about it."

"Are you suggesting we date, just do it as far away from the bases as we can?"

A faint smile played at his lips. "What I'm suggesting is I can show you around the island. Take you to some of the other castles, snorkel spots, hiking, whatever you want to do." He shifted his attention back out to something in the distance. "Like I said, as far as anyone else is concerned, we're just two Americans who bumped into each other and struck up a conversation."

"Unless we're in the same car."

"So we drive separately. Means using twice as much gas, but the island's like seventy miles long. Not like we're driving to another state or anything, you know?"

"True," I said, almost whispering. I let Henza and Hamahiga Islands hold my gaze. Getting together outside of his bedroom or mine was risky. We could get hemmed up for fraternization if we got caught hanging out. If anyone figured out we were sleeping together too, our careers were over. Going out in public meant taking the chance of someone putting two and two together, even if we did say we were two strangers who'd run into each other.

"You really think this is a good idea?" I asked.

"Not at all, if we give a shit about our careers." He turned to me. "And I do care about my career, but this..." He released a long breath. "No matter how many times I tell myself we shouldn't, I just keep coming back to the fact that I want to." He swallowed. "I want you."

The words sent a pleasant shudder right through me. I couldn't deny I wanted him. For that matter, the fact that I'd defied every bit of good sense I had and come up here to meet him at all took the wind out of any attempts I might have made to tell myself I only wanted him in bed. If we dated covertly under the guise of being tourists with the same taste in destinations, then every beach we walked, every trail we hiked, and every monument we explored would be one more strike against my certainty that we were just notches in each other's bedposts.

And my own willingness to even consider this made it clear as day that no matter how much I'd told myself otherwise, I was hooked on him. I was hooked, and I wanted to be.

Shane broke the silence. "We don't have to do this. If you want to keep it to what we've been doing, that's fine with me." He paused. "You can say no."

"I probably should." I stepped across the platonic distance and slid my arm around his waist. "In fact, I know I should."

Shane faced me. "But *are* you saying no?"

I looked around. The whole time we'd been up here, only two other tourists had come up the stairs to this level. The daylight was fading fast, so I doubted many more people would be heading up to the castle today. Anyone below us could probably see us if they cared to look, but I…I didn't care.

"Eric?"

"No," I whispered, drawing him closer. "No, I'm not."

"Good." He touched my face and wrapped his other arm around me.

With just inches between us, I met his eyes, and we just looked at each other for a long moment.

My heart thundered in my ears as I closed my eyes and leaned in. My lower lip brushed his, and he drew back a little. Then he raised his chin, and our lips grazed again, but I was the one to pull back this time. My fingers trembled on his face. Our foreheads touched, and we both just breathed for almost a full minute. On the side of my neck, goose bumps rose in the wake of his gentle fingertips, and my knees shook way too much for someone standing up on top of a wall like this. Finally, I broke the standoff and pulled him all the way into a kiss.

This wasn't like any kiss that had ever happened between us. Prior to this, we'd always been feverish, desperate, hungry. Every touch was rough and demanding, and every kiss was deep and unrelenting. We kissed like it was only a matter of time before someone was in the throes of a spine-tingling, toe-curling orgasm.

This time, it was...different. Oh, the earth-shattering orgasms were inevitable, and I had no doubt we'd be in bed together tonight, but not now. Not yet. For the longest time, only our lips moved together. We barely breathed, barely moved, and it was forever before he gently parted my lips and deepened the kiss to something so slow and sensual it liquefied my knees and spine. Though it wasn't nearly as violent as every kiss before it, this was no less intense. Not even close.

His hand followed the curve of my spine to my lower back, and there he pressed in just enough to pull me against him. His erection brushed mine, and his other hand tightened around the back of my neck as he growled into an even deeper, more passionate kiss. And still, we were miles from our usual desperation.

When I broke the kiss, we were both breathless. Somehow, my hands were on either side of his face and his were on mine. We panted against each other's lips as his thumb drew unsteady arcs across my cheekbone and I trailed my fingertips along his lightly stubbled jaw.

I wasn't afraid someone was watching. For all I knew, everyone from the farms below us to the walls of Nakagusuku watched us now, but I didn't care. If anything, I was afraid of surrendering to something. Afraid we were standing on the brink of a point of no return. I couldn't even say for certain it was fear at all. My hands shook, my heart pounded, but it was the anticipation of the jump, not the fear of the fall.

Eyes still closed, I licked my lips. "Why did you really call me up here?"

He swallowed. "For the same reason you just kissed me."

I pulled back, and our eyes met. If I had any sense at all, if I knew what was good for the career to which I'd devoted half my life, I wouldn't kiss him again. I'd politely pull away, thank him for showing me the view from Katsuren, and I'd go down the steps and the hill to my car and get the fuck out of here. I wouldn't even taunt temptation with another meaningless, no-strings one-night stand that was anything but meaningless.

Deep down, I knew the potential consequences. But standing here on the wall of a fourteenth-century castle with a kiss and a whole lot of carelessness tingling on my lips, watching Shane watch me in the fading daylight, I couldn't even justify the inch of empty space that existed between us.

I curved my hand around the back of his neck.

His lips claimed mine.

And we jumped.

Chapter Ten

Shane

Following Eric from Katsuren to his apartment, I still couldn't believe he'd actually showed up. I'd waited for over an hour, palms sweating, and heart racing, certain he wouldn't show his face in the daylight. I wouldn't have held it against him if he'd wisely insisted we keep this behind closed doors. Or suggested we quit altogether. In fact, I'd fully expected him to, and was surprised as hell when he'd stepped onto the uppermost enclosure of the castle ruins.

But he did show up, and now here I was, parking a block away from his apartment. Walking to his building. Meeting his eyes from across the small garage. Following him upstairs. Biting my lip as he turned the key in the door. Walking into his apartment.

The instant the door clicked shut behind us, there was no turning back. Safely away from anyone who might see us and give a rat's ass, Eric grabbed the front of my shirt and hauled me into a deep, desperate kiss. We both stumbled, trying to hold on to each other and stay upright.

I dipped my head to kiss his neck. Eric groaned, letting his head fall back so I had access to more of his hot flesh. I breathed him in, tasted him, let myself get high off the salt of his skin and the masculine scent that had, since our first night together, been synonymous with spectacular sex.

He gripped the back of my neck, holding me against him like he didn't want me to stop what I was doing.

"God, I'm glad you texted," he groaned, his voice vibrating against my lips. "I've been...all day..." He shivered, pressing his erection against mine. "Thinking about you."

"Have you?" I whispered, dragging my lips across the front

of his throat. “Hopefully the same way I’ve been thinking about you.”

“Naked?”

“Fucking each other until it hurts?”

Eric’s fingers twitched against the back of my neck.

I kissed my way up the side of his neck to the underside of his jaw. “If I’d had a condom with me, and we could’ve gotten away with it”—I let my lips brush his—“I’d have fucked you right up there on Katsuren.”

“So great minds *do* think alike,” he murmured.

“Like I’m ever not thinking about sex with you around.”

“To be fair”—he shoved my shirt up and off—“you’re usually *having* sex when I’m around.”

“Hmm.” I tugged at his belt. “Can’t argue with that, can I?”

“Maybe we should get to that part,” he said.

“In a hurry, are we?”

“And you’re not?”

“Fat chance of that.” I kissed him hard.

Somehow, we made it into his bedroom and out of our clothes without tripping over each other. I’d barely kicked off my briefs when Eric pulled me down onto the bed on top of him, and I gasped when my cock brushed against his.

He wrapped his fingers around both of our cocks and rolled his hips just enough to create a gentle, mind-blowing friction. As he stroked us both with his hand, I couldn’t help moving to complement his motions, and I couldn’t. Fucking. *Breathe.*

I groaned and buried my face against his neck. “Fuck, Eric…”

“Like that?” he asked with a grin in his voice.

“God, yes.” I raised my head and kissed him. My hips moved of their own volition, our bodies falling into some kind of involuntary sync. We kissed, we touched, and more than once I thought I was going to lose it.

“Fuck me.” His fingers loosened, and his hips slowed. “God, please, Shane, fuck me.”

“Condoms?” We’d been here together before, but I was

lucky I could form the word, never mind remember where he kept them.

He gestured in the general direction of the bedside table.

I kissed him once more before pushing myself up off him. “Get on your back.” I stood and gestured for him to move to the edge of the bed.

As I put on the condom, he sat on the edge of the bed and picked up the bottle of lube. He poured some into his hand, put the bottle aside, then pushed my hand out of the way and stroked lube onto my cock. Even through the thin layer of latex, his hand made me dizzy.

I kissed him, and together we sank back onto the bed. I guided myself to him, and he closed his eyes and bit his lip as I pressed against him. As the head of my cock slid inside him, he reached back and grabbed the bedcovers above his head. I slid my hands up his arms. He turned his hands over, and when my palms covered his, we clasped our fingers together. Exhaling, I pushed into him, all the way into him, and we both groaned when I withdrew slowly.

“Fuck...” His back arched.

He hooked his ankles together above the small of my back, and his hips moved with mine.

Like our bodies, our fingers weren’t still. Squeezing. Relaxing. Twitching. As if we both needed to feel as much skin moving across skin as possible.

His fingers tightened between mine, digging into the backs of my hands, and he didn’t let go. Using his grip for leverage, I fucked him harder, and he swore and squirmed beneath me. He screwed his eyes shut, gripped my hands so tight it was painful, and as I slammed my cock into him again and again, he let out a long moan that crescendoed into a strangled, curse-laden cry.

As his orgasm peaked, Eric rocked his hips back, and I was done for. I forced myself as deep as I could, shuddered against him and came.

When the shaking stopped, I withdrew and got rid of the condom. Then we both collapsed into bed together.

We held each other’s gazes. Sweaty and disheveled, he

looked fucking amazing.

"Join me for a shower?" I asked.

He wiped sweat off his brow. "Definitely."

We got out of bed and into the shower. Not surprisingly, we couldn't stop touching each other, but Eric subtly backed off. He avoided my eyes, and his kisses were less than enthusiastic.

"You okay?" I asked.

He exhaled. "Yeah, I'm just..." He bit his lip.

"Having second thoughts?"

Eric swallowed. "Are you sure about this? Seeing each other out in public?"

"Am I sure I want to?" I brushed a few stray drops off his temple. "Or am I sure it's a good idea?"

He shrugged. "Either-or."

"Absolutely, and absolutely not." I cupped his face in both hands and leaned in to kiss him. "But...I just can't get enough of you."

"We could..." He paused, exhaling hard and shaking his head. "We could get in so much trouble."

"Only if we get caught." I kissed his forehead. "The places I want to take you, no one will see us. If they do, they won't give a fuck, and they won't know what's going on between us anyway. Still, if you decide it's more trouble than it's worth, just say the word. We can always go back to just meeting like this."

He grinned. "I assume we'll still meet like this either way?"

I laughed and wrapped my arms around him. "It's certainly an option, yes."

"An option?" He raised an eyebrow. "Only an option?"

"Well," I said with a slight shrug, "I'm not going to twist your arm."

The grin broadened. "Not even if I beg you to?"

I laughed. "God, I love the way you think..."

Chapter Eleven

Eric

I was still a little uncertain about Shane's plan. I had no doubt it would take a while for me to relax into this and accept that we could be seen in public without a giant neon sign appearing over our heads and announcing to the universe that we were sleeping together.

I'd take my chances, though, which was why, in spite of the knots in my stomach, I pulled into the parking lot beside a faded, handpainted sign that read *Nakagusuku Castle Site*.

Shane's car was a few spaces over, parked in the shadow of a tour bus. There were spaces beside his, but irrational nervousness had me choosing a spot on the other side of the gravel lot.

Once I'd parked, I picked up my camera off the passenger seat, put the strap over my head and got out, telling myself I looked every bit the tourist. And I was. I had every intention of taking pictures all over this island, whether I was with Shane or not. I was no professional, but photography was a hobby of mine. And who knew? Maybe I could get through this tour without my equipment getting stolen. Someone jacked my twelve-hundred-dollar camera during my last shipboard deployment. Motherfucker. Anyone laid a hand on this one, there'd be hell to pay.

Camera securely in my hand, I walked across the parking lot. There was an admission fee for this place, so I paid my four hundred yen, took my ticket and map, and started up the steep, paved hill that led to the ruins. On the left side of the pavement was a colorful garden, and the row of trees to my right formed a thick canopy of branches, which provided some shade. I enjoyed that while it lasted; I'd heard Nakagusuku was open air and completely exposed, just like Katsuren. This would probably be the last shade I saw for a while.

As I neared the top, the garden ended, and to my left was a rectangular grassy field. A few tourists clustered here and there in the grass, taking photos of the ruins and a couple of shrines off to one side. The castle itself was up ahead, spanning the width of the narrow hill on which it sat.

And to the right, beside a scale model of the castle in its original glory, was Shane in a baseball cap and sunglasses.

"Going incognito?" I asked as I approached.

He laughed. "Yeah, that's it." He peered at my camera and wrinkled his nose. "Canon?"

"Yeah, so?" Then the yellow lettering on his neck strap caught my eye, and I gave the snobbiest sniff I could muster. "Oh. So you're a Nikon man."

"I am." His lip curled with mock disgust. "I suppose I can be seen with you, even while you're shooting with *that*. Not like anyone will suspect us of being together now."

I laughed in spite of that knot in my stomach.

He winked. "Relax. No one will notice us."

"I'll take your word for it." I still wasn't sure about this, but I followed him to the castle anyway.

Walking together, exchanging playful jabs at each other's cameras in between checking out the centuries-old castle, we passed a small group of Americans on their way down a set of stairs. My blood turned cold and my heart jumped into my throat, but Shane barely missed a beat as he explained some of the history of Nakagusuku. Just as he probably knew they would—and deep down, so did I—the Americans kept right on walking without giving us a second glance.

The more we walked up stairs and paths, through archways and courtyards, the less I worried anyone would notice or care about us. It wasn't like we wore our ranks on our sleeves or anything. Without insignias to incriminate us, we really *were* just two guys hanging out. Eventually, I convinced myself to just relax and enjoy the ruins.

At the base of a small staircase leading up to a stone

archway, Shane knelt and raised his camera. He turned his baseball cap around and looked through the viewfinder.

"Oh, don't you look all gangster now." I flipped his hat up with my finger.

He caught it and threw me a good-natured glare. "Very funny." Chuckling, he fixed his hat, then resumed setting up his shot.

Not long after that, I stopped to get a shot of a vine slithering up the side of the weathered wall. It was kind of nice exploring this place with someone who didn't get impatient when I stopped every few steps to shoot something seemingly insignificant. In fact, he stopped almost as much as I did, focusing on a red hibiscus flower growing beside some stairs or tracking a weird black insect crawling along the top of a warning sign.

Nakagusuku wasn't much different from Katsuren. At least two of Nakagusuku's archways were still intact or had been rebuilt, but otherwise, it was a lot like Katsuren—high walls made from large gray stones fitted together with incredible precision. On one of the top levels, though, unlike Katsuren, there was an archaeological dig in progress. Blue tarps covered a few sections, but in others, aged roof tiles and chunks of pottery stuck out from the carefully excavated soil.

The view from on top of the walls was spectacular. Standing on them like we had at Katsuren, we had a stunning panoramic, unobstructed view of the Pacific, as well as towns and farms down below. It still struck me how big Okinawa really was. It was barely visible on most maps, and yet, standing up on top of a hill like this, looking to the north and the south, I swore the island went on forever in either direction. Maybe it was big enough after all for the two of us to get lost and avoid people who knew us.

Behind the castle was a huge, bizarre structure. It was constructed of gray concrete, not stone like Nakagusuku. It began at the base of the hill below the castle ruins, then stretched all the way up to the top of another, higher hill.

Taking it in from up here, I couldn't put my finger on one

style of construction. The whole thing was connected like one giant complex, but the shapes and styles varied from one area to another. The bottom level, which was closest to us, was flat and rectangular. Beyond that was a section that was probably three stories with a flat roof in most places, but the occasional peaked, tile roof here and there. And as the building continued up the hill, it widened into something asymmetrical, semicircular. The windows, which appeared to be without glass, were asymmetrically sized and arranged. The roof wavered and curved as if the builders couldn't decide how high it should be, or how steep, or how far it should stick out.

And still weirder was this skeletal tower sitting on top of the whole thing. It sat on top of a single-story building and was comprised of rectangular pillars holding up three platforms, each a little smaller than the one before it, kind of like a pagoda. On top of the final platform, eight pillars—three on each side, one on each end—held up a long, peaked roof.

Shane stopped beside me. "Bizarre, isn't it?"

"Uh, yeah. Doesn't look like fourteenth-century construction either, so I'm assuming it's not part of the castle?"

He shook his head, then raised his camera. "It was supposed to be a hotel." He adjusted the focus on his lens, then added, "They built it in the 1970s but never finished it."

"And they've never torn it down?"

"Nope." His camera snapped a couple of times. As I raised my own camera, he said, "The reason they stopped building it was because of a bunch of accidents. The workers insisted the accidents happened because several old tombs were destroyed during construction."

I zoomed in on some graffiti along one of the sides of the hotel. "So, the Okinawan equivalent of building on an Indian burial ground?"

"Basically. No one would continue building it, and they can't get anyone to go in and tear it down." His shutter snapped again. "Plus there's still some tombs next to it that could be damaged, so everyone's just leaving it alone."

"Creepy." Through my lens, I scanned the hotel. I couldn't

decide if it was more eerie when I zoomed in on a shattered window, or when I pulled back and looked at the entire building. Lowering my camera, I said, "I don't suppose we can go wander around in it, can we?"

"Yeah, about that." He shook his head. "It's off-limits. So unless you want to get hemmed up for failure to obey a general order *and* disobeying that order with me..."

I laughed. "Okay, maybe not. Besides, then everyone would know I associate with a Nikon man."

He scowled at me. "Whatever, Canon whore."

I clutched my camera protectively to my chest. "Your jealousy is *so* transparent."

We exchanged playful glares. Then he chuckled and gestured at the hotel again. "Anyway, it's a pity we can't go in there anymore. I went in with a buddy of mine before we knew about the general order, and it's cool as shit."

"Really?"

"Oh, yeah. I mean, it's creepy as all hell, but there's some graffiti in there that's just amazing. Not to mention these huge murals someone painted as spirit wards, plus the altar that a monk set up to appease the spirits."

"An altar?"

"Some monk put up a shrine and altar, and I guess he goes in and prays at it to keep the spirits happy."

"That almost sounds like an urban legend."

"Oh no. I've seen it." He gestured toward the tower at the top. "It's at the base of the tower, right outside one of the entrances."

"You have pictures of it?" I asked. "And the rest of the interior?"

"Hell, yeah. Remind me next time you're over, and I'll show them to you. There's some seriously cool shit in there. Like a real-life haunted house."

I eyed him. "You actually believe it's haunted?"

He shrugged. "I don't know. But it is creepy. I mean, there was a fire at one point, so a bunch of the rooms are burned out. There's broken glass everywhere, busted-up furniture, all sorts of shit. It's just kind of...otherworldly."

"You're not doing much to convince me to obey that general order, you know."

We exchanged glances and both laughed.

From there, we continued through the castle ruins. There was a prayer garden near the rear, and several of the shrines had coins laid on their tiny altars. Since Shane didn't stop to leave any, I assumed that must have been a habit reserved for those who adhered to that religion, and didn't leave anything either.

Just beyond the prayer garden, we stopped to take pictures of a bird that had landed on the corner of the wall. It was a red-breasted blue bird with a black beak, and though they were everywhere on this island, this particular one made for an interesting shot against the stone background.

After we'd each gotten a couple of pictures, the bird flew away, and we continued down the path. The path eventually led us out of the castle and down to a strip of asphalt that, once it crested a hill, connected with the paved road I'd taken to meet Shane earlier. We followed it down to the parking lot, which was now completely deserted except for our cars.

"You have plans for dinner?" Shane asked when we stopped beside my car.

"Not yet." I set my camera on the passenger seat, then rested my forearms on the roof of my car. "Your place or mine?"

"Actually, I was thinking we could go out somewhere."

I stiffened. "Shane, you know we can't take that chance."

He smiled and put up a hand. "The place I have in mind? No one will see us."

I chewed my lip. He was right about Nakagusuku. No one gave two shits about who we were or why we were here. Still, eating dinner together struck me as a little more intimate than wandering around castle ruins.

"We really shouldn't," I said.

"Tell you what," he said. "Meet me there, and if you're not comfortable staying, we won't. You can even text me from outside if you don't want anyone to see us talking."

I considered it for a long moment. Finally, I released a breath and nodded. "Okay, if you're sure no one will see us. Where are we going?"

"You'll want to take a cab. Just give them..." He paused, pursing his lips. After a moment, he pulled a pen and notepad out of his camera bag and set it on my trunk lid. He jotted something down, tore off the page and handed it to me. "Give this to the cab driver."

I looked at it. It was five kanji characters, so of course I had no idea what it meant. I eyed him. "And this means...?"

"It's the name of the restaurant. The driver will know where to go. They all do."

"What's it called in English?"

He shrugged. "It isn't, as far as I know. In Japanese, I think it's the name of the family that runs it, but everyone just calls it the Blue Roof Izakaya. Anyway, take a cab there, and we'll take one back to your place or mine afterward if we feel like it. I don't know about you, but I plan to have a drink or two, and you don't want to fuck with the DUI laws here. The JPs will bust you if you've been standing downwind of a bottle of mouthwash."

"So I've heard," I said, laughing softly. "But you're sure any driver I call will know how to find it?"

"Absolutely. And then when you get there, give the hostess my name."

I smirked. "Will you be wearing a red carnation, or do I need to say a secret password?"

Shane laughed. "Nah, you'll find me."

Our eyes met, and we both smiled, but worry tightened my chest.

More serious now, I held his gaze. "Are you sure about this?" I whispered, as if there was anyone around to hear. "We can stay in tonight, we don't have—"

"Trust me," he said just as quietly. "You'll understand when you get there."

The cab driver took Shane's note and nodded, saying

something Japanese. Presumably he was telling me he knew where to go, because as soon as I was in the backseat, he drove off.

The restaurant was fifteen minutes or so from my place and a few blocks off the main road. It didn't take much to figure out where the Blue Roof part of the nickname came from—the restaurant had the peaked terra cotta tile roof I'd seen on so many buildings around the island, but it had been painted bright glossy blue. I didn't know if I could ever find this place again with a gun to my head, but if I stumbled across it, I'd sure recognize it.

I paid the driver and went inside.

A beautiful Japanese woman stood behind the counter and greeted me in her native tongue as soon as I came in. In English, she said, "How many?"

"I'm meeting someone. Name is Shane."

She cocked her head.

"Um, Connelly?" I said.

She furrowed her brow, then picked up a clipboard from beside the cash register and showed me the list. I scanned it, looking over names written in kanji and a handful in English—*Jesus Christ, Shane, there are other Americans here!*—until I found *Connelly, Shane.* I pointed to it, and she nodded vigorously. She set the clipboard on the counter and gestured for me to come with her. In spite of my uncertainty—I had no doubt I'd be texting Shane from out front within the next five minutes—I followed her.

We stepped through some hanging beads into a narrow, dimly lit hallway, and I realized this was unlike any restaurant I'd ever been in. The usual sounds of chattering voices and clattering dishes provided familiar background noise, but there were no visible tables. Instead, the hallway was lined with wooden doors, and the sounds came from beyond those doors.

A waiter balanced a tray of pint glasses as he opened one of the doors. When he stepped through it, I glanced past him. On the other side was a tiny room with a low table covered with dishes and glasses, and half a dozen people sat around the table on tatami mats instead of chairs.

About halfway down the hall, the hostess stopped in front of one of the doors and tapped twice with her knuckle. Then she gestured for me to take off my shoes, and as I did, she slid the door open.

Beyond the doorway was a smaller version of the room I'd glanced into a moment ago. Shane sat on one side of the table and grinned as I stepped into the room and took a seat across from him.

"See what I mean?" he said, his voice low. "Your entire chain of command and mine could be eating here, and no one would have a clue we were here."

"Yeah, well. I'd rather not think about them being here while we're here, if you don't mind."

He laughed. To the hostess, he said something in Japanese. She bowed, then slid the door shut, sealing us into the tiny room. To me, Shane said, "She'll be back in a minute with some ice water." He slid a laminated spiral-bound menu across the narrow table.

I flipped open the menu. It was a good thing it had pictures, because it was written entirely in Japanese. And even the pictures didn't tell me a whole lot. I recognized the rice, eggs, beef, sushi, chicken—or was that pork?—but some things were...I didn't know what the fuck they were. The sauces and soups were anyone's guess. A few dishes were marked with hot pepper symbols, which I appreciated. I liked spicy food, but damn it, don't blindside me with it.

"So what do you recommend?" I asked.

"You can't go wrong with most of it," he said. "The katsudon is pretty good, and their gyoza rolls are excellent. Not a fan of the yakitori, though."

I eyed him. "For all I know, you just told me the goat brains are pretty good, the octopus rolls are excellent, and you're not a fan of gecko soup."

Shane laughed. "Sorry. Katsudon is a rice bowl with fried pork and a fried egg over it. Gyoza rolls are..." He paused. Then he pulled the menu toward him and flipped to one page. He gestured at a picture of something that looked like a pot sticker. "They usually have meat and stuff in them. And the yakitori" —he turned to the next page—"is kind of like a chicken shish kabob. I usually like yakitori, but this place fucks it up something awful."

"Duly noted." I skimmed the page, then turned to another. Curry, that was something I needed to try while I was on the island. I'd heard Japanese curry was a lot different from Indian. Less spice, more flavor.

This place had a few pasta dishes too, and, my God, they had no shortage of rich-looking desserts. I turned another page and laughed. "They even have pizza here?"

"Oh, yeah. And it's awesome."

"Seriously?"

"Yeah, their pasta is about as good as that beefaroni crap they fed us in boot camp, but—"

I snorted. "Says the officer."

"Hey, we weren't exactly living or dining in luxury."

"Yeah, but somehow I think the conditions were a wee bit better in your 'boot camp' than ours."

Shane chuckled. "Oh, come on. It's not like you went through Marine Basic or anything."

"Well, no. Seeing as I joined the Navy, not the Marine Corps."

"Smart man." He gestured at the menu. "Anyway, their pasta's nothing to write home about, but the pizza on this island? Oh my God, Eric. It's incredible. This place? Not the best. But there's a place up in Nago that makes the most incredible pizza on the planet."

"What's so great about it?" I asked. "I mean, what's different?"

"I couldn't even tell you," he said. "It's just...it's different. You have to try it. But not here."

The door slid open, and our waitress appeared with two glasses of ice water. Before she left, Shane ordered a few things off the menu, and then we were alone again.

After she'd shut the door, I looked at Shane. "I'm assuming

you didn't order some unholy thing that'll make me gag?"

He laughed. "No, of course not. Just gyoza rolls, some katsudon, and some fries."

"Fries? Really going for the authentic Okinawan experience, aren't you?"

"Just ruining fries for you forever."

I stared at him. "How so?"

"These are awesome. You'll never be able to eat McD's fries again."

"Now there's a great loss." I wrinkled my nose. "I don't eat that crap anyway."

"Well, you'll probably like these. Oh, and one of the other perks of this place?" He reached for the end of the table, and from beside the chopsticks and condiments, he picked up a small box with a white button on it. "Waitresses won't come in here unless you page them or they're bringing you something you ordered." He set the box down and winked. "Complete privacy."

"Nice," I said. "Nothing worse than a waiter coming up to ask how everything tastes when you're in the middle of chewing something."

"Exactly."

Five or ten minutes later, the waitress returned with a couple bowls of katsudon, a bowl of french fries, and a plate of gyoza rolls. Shane was right about all three. The fries put to shame anything I'd ever had in the States, and the katsudon was decent. The gyoza rolls weren't bad, but everything I'd eaten so far was salty as hell, so we paged the waitress for more water.

I took a drink. Much better. Now I could eat more. As I took another gyoza roll from the plate, I said, "You've obviously picked up a lot of Japanese since you've lived here."

He gestured with his chopsticks. "Oh, I've lived in Japan off and on for a few years now. And I dated a local national up in Sasebo for almost a year, so believe me, I learned."

"He must have taught you a lot."

"*She* did." He must have read the confusion in my

expression, because he smiled and added a nearly inaudible, "I'm not gay; I'm bi."

"Oh."

Almost whispering, he said, "To be honest, I really haven't dated many guys at all since I've been in the military. Had plenty of one-nighters, but with DADT and all of that..." He shook his head. "Not many relationships."

"Me too. I've had a few relationships since I got divorced, but the secrecy..." It was my turn to trail off. Our eyes met, and the silence took an ever so slightly awkward turn.

Shane cleared his throat. "That why you're divorced? Because you were...you know." Couldn't be too careful in places like this. Never knew which walls had how many ears.

I nodded. "I didn't figure out till a little too late in the game that I was. And I waited a little too long after that to tell her."

"How did she take it?"

"Better than I ever could have expected." I blew out a breath. "I thought she'd be pissed, but..." I trailed off, staring at our food with unfocused eyes for a moment. Then I looked at him. "She said she knew there was something wrong for a long time, and it was killing her that she couldn't do anything about it. When she realized it wasn't her, it was me, it was a huge load off her shoulders." I laughed softly. "Which, of course, made me feel guilty as fuck for putting her through that."

"You're lucky," he said. "Sounds like it ended better than most people would expect."

"It did, definitely," I said. "It could have ended badly, and it very nearly did."

He cocked his head. "How do you mean? I thought you said she took it well."

"She did, but..." I poked at a gyoza roll with my chopsticks as I tried to figure out how to explain what'd happened. "The thing is, we were parents when we were eighteen. We got married when we were nineteen. Twenty-four, and I drop this bomb on her. I mean, we were kids, so what the hell did we know about dealing with something like that? We tried to make it work. You know, for our daughter. I'd only been in the military five years at that point, but I was planning on staying in, so we figured we could stick it out until I retired, and then divorce once we weren't getting moved around all the time." I sighed. "This was exactly what we wanted to avoid—having me PCS to another state or another country, and be this far away from Marie."

"That must have been miserable, though," Shane said with a sympathetic grimace. "Especially if you were planning on staying married for a few years."

"It was. I mean, we both knew nothing could change what I am, so we had an open relationship. We both dated other people and just kept it out of our daughter's sight and didn't rub it in each other's faces."

He blinked. "Wow, seriously? And it worked?"

"For a while. There's only so long you can date someone else and keep going home to the person you're stuck with. We started resenting each other, fighting..." I shook my head. "So we finally just decided we couldn't pretend we weren't miserable, and we divorced."

"How do you and your ex get along?"

"Oh, we get along great now. Honestly, the worst of it was while we had the open relationship. Seeing other people just reminded us of our situation together, and I think we both felt so damned trapped, so we took it out on each other. Now that we've both moved on, we're good friends. I think I talk to her on the webcam almost as much as I talk to my daughter, and to be honest, I don't think I'd have made it through my combat tours without her."

"I envy that," he said quietly. "The relationship you have with your ex, I mean."

"You ever been married?"

He nodded and held up two fingers. "And we weren't nearly as amicable, let me tell you."

"What happened?" I paused. "If you don't mind my asking, I mean."

He looked at the table between us with unfocused eyes. "My first wife and I..." He was quiet for a moment, then waved a hand. "Oh, hell, who knows what happened? We were young, we didn't know how to be married, things fell apart, and here we are. Now, my second wife..." He paused again, folding his hands in front of his glass, and when he spoke, there was a subtle note of bitterness in his voice. "I don't think our marriage was cut out for the military life."

"It wasn't because you're...you know..." I inclined my head.

He shook his head. "Nope. She didn't like being alone." The bitterness was unmistakable this time. "So while I was in Iraq, she found someone to keep her company."

"Oh, ouch."

"Yeah, tell me about it." He shifted a little and reached up to scratch the back of his neck. "She's known since before we got married that I go both ways, so that was a nonissue. She just..." He exhaled, but didn't finish the thought. "On that note, I think I could use something a little stronger to drink."

I laughed quietly. "Good idea."

"And I know just the thing."

I raised my eyebrows. "Oh?"

"You like sake?"

"I haven't tried it."

"What?" He clicked his tongue. "And you've been here how long?"

"Long enough I probably should have had sake by now."

"Yes, exactly." He pressed the button to summon the waitress. "I think I'd rather have awamori tonight, though."

"Awamori?"

"Kind of like sake, except it's served cold. And this shit is strong."

I grinned. "Good. That's the way I like it."

"Yeah, well, make—"

The door opened again. Shane placed the order, and the waitress disappeared, sliding the door shut behind her.

Once we were alone again, he said, "You may like stuff strong, but this shit? Go easy on it."

I raised an eyebrow. "Are you telling a Sailor how to handle his liquor?"

Shane laughed. "You're welcome to pound it like tequila shots, but don't say I didn't warn you." The mischievous sparkle in his eyes may as well have been a dare.

"Hmm," I said. "I think I'll go easy on the awamori."

"Smart man."

The awamori arrived in the form of a bottle, two glasses of ice and a pitcher of water. Shane poured some of the liquor into the glasses, then filled them the rest of the way with water.

"I still think that's sacrilege," I said, watching the water line rising in my glass.

He set the pitcher down. "You're welcome to drink it straight if you'd like, but I'd try it this way first."

"Well, if you're going to take it weak, then..." I picked up the glass and raised it.

He clinked his against mine, and we both drank.

I immediately grimaced, then coughed. "*Jesus*, that shit is strong."

He laughed. "Told you. There's a reason they water it down."

Coughing again, I put the glass on the table. "Yeah, I understand now. My God."

"Like it?"

"Ask me again when my eyes stop watering." I coughed once more, picked up the glass, and took a slightly less ambitious drink. This time, the water tempered the burn a little, and it went down smoother.

We drank for a while, working our way through the various dishes in between putting away glass after glass of awamori. The shit was strong on the palate, and it sure cleared my sinuses, but by the time we'd reached the bottom of the bottle, I didn't feel much.

"Okay, I know I've been a Sailor long enough to have a crazy-high alcohol tolerance." I held up the empty bottle. "But I've had NyQuil kick my ass harder than this."

Shane grinned. "Give it time. It likes to catch up all at once."

"Mm-hmm."

He ordered a second bottle, and we dove into that one along with a second plate of gyoza rolls.

"So you said you went to Iraq?" I said. "When were you over there?

"My first tour was right after everything started there. The second was..." He paused. "Wow, almost five years ago now. Hard to believe it's been that long."

"Time flies once you're out of the Sandbox, doesn't it?"

"God, yeah." He rested his chin on top of his folded hands. "You been over there?"

I nodded. "Did a year in Afghanistan, came home for a year, then did a year in Iraq. Well, technically ten months, since I spent the last two in Kuwait working the supply lines."

Shane cocked his head. "How'd you end up on supply detail?"

"Light duty." I pushed up my T-shirt sleeve and gestured at a scar just above my right elbow. "Busted my arm."

"How the fuck did you manage that?"

"Getting hurt in a war zone? I know, who can imagine." Our eyes met, and we both laughed quietly. I pulled my sleeve back down and reached for the awamori. Shane slid his glass my way, and as I topped them off, I went on. "Kind of fucked up, actually. Ironic as hell, considering why we're over there, but it was all because of an oil slick."

"An oil slick?" He took his drink back and watched me over it as he took a sip.

"Yeah." I sipped the awamori, which wasn't even making my eyes water anymore. "We had a convoy come in that had been damaged by an IED, and we'd stopped it to inspect the damage. You know, make sure there was no unexploded ordnance that could pose a hazard. What no one realized was that some shrapnel had caused a lovely little oil leak, and while the vehicle was stopped, I guess that shrapnel came loose. So did the oil. When they rolled the vehicle out of the way, I was directing the other one into its place, stepped in the slick, and—" I made a sharp downward gesture.

He grinned. "You didn't see an oil slick in the sand?"

"Fuck you. It was nighttime, and we were running low lights."

"Oh, well, that makes sense, then."

I narrowed my eyes. "Are you mocking me?"

"Maybe."

I flipped him off; then we both laughed as I went for my drink. "So what about you? Any battle scars?"

"A few." Shane put his right foot up on the bench beside him and gestured at some jagged white scars below his knee. Each was two or three inches long, and some disappeared behind his knee while others arched over the top.

I cringed. "Shit, what happened?"

"Razor wire." He put his foot down again and rested his arms on the table. "Went right through my cammies and tore the fuck out of my leg. Got my hand too." He held up his right hand, which also had some wicked scars across his palm and wrist.

"What the hell did you do?" I asked. "Try to wear the razor wire?"

He shook his head. "I didn't know they'd strung up some more wire outside our tents. Bit of a lapse in communication between some contractors and my chain of command." He rolled his eyes. "Anyway, we took mortar fire one night, and when me and two other guys in the unit tried to take cover, I found out the hard way they'd strung wire right across the gap between two tents. Spent a week or two on light duty until the stitches came out, but it wasn't exactly Purple Heart material."

"At least yours was in actual combat," I muttered. "I fucking went to war, survived all kinds of firefights and close calls with IEDs, and what do I do?" I gestured at my arm, then picked up my glass to take a drink.

"Well, look on the bright side," he said, his words just slightly slurred. "You could embellish the fuck out of it and make it a story to tell the grandkids."

"Oh, yeah, there you go." I laughed. *Damn, when did I get so light-headed?* "I could tell 'em it happened in Nam. When the

Germans had us surrounded."

Shane snorted. "Damn those Nazis in Vietnam. Get you every fucking time."

I almost choked on my drink. "Guess I was a sitting duck," I slurred. "My desert camouflage fucking stood out in the damn jungle." I paused, suddenly aware of the ridiculous turn the conversation had taken. I peered suspiciously at the glass in my hand. "I think this stuff's kicking in."

"What was your first clue?"

Our eyes met, and we both burst out laughing. Yeah, we were definitely drunk.

"Wow, you're right about this shit." I held up my nearly empty glass. "When it hits you, it *hits* you."

"Yes, yes, it does." He picked up the bottle and topped off his glass with a hell of a lot more awamori than water. "Just means it's doin' its job."

"True facts." I pushed my glass toward him. As he filled it, I looked around the tiny—spinning, when did it start spinning?—room. "Man, do you realize the shit you could get away with in a place like this?"

"No." He slid my glass back toward me and winked. "Never thought of it."

"Was that sarcasm?"

"Maybe."

"I think it was."

He rolled his eyes. "Why do you think we're here, Eric?"

"I thought I was getting cultured." I looked at the glass in my hand. "Well, and shit-faced."

"Yes, you're getting cultured. And shit-faced." Shane swung his legs up onto the seat beside him and, wavering a little, pushed himself to his feet. "But I had other reasons for bringing you here." His gait was unsteady as he came around the table, walking on the tatami-covered seats since there was nowhere else to go, and I almost dropped my glass when I realized he was on his way over to sit beside me.

"You know you didn't have to get me drunk for that, right?" I said.

He eased himself onto the seat beside me and put his arm around my shoulders. "No, but I've never seen you drunk before, so..." He shrugged, but before either of us could speak again, he leaned in and kissed me. His fingers were still damp and cool from holding his glass, and I shivered as they trailed across my cheek.

My head spun, but hell if I knew if it was Shane's kiss or the awamori. Maybe both. Either way, I let myself get lost in him and the alcohol and his kiss, and I didn't give a fuck if my entire chain of command *was* in the next room over.

Shane drew back enough to look me in the eye. "God, Eric, I am so, so..." He ran his fingers through my hair, then laughed. "*Drunk*."

I laughed, touching my forehead to his. "You too, huh? Who'd have thought?"

"All that booze," he slurred. "Can't imagine."

"Thank God for cabs, am I right?"

"Mm-hmm." I kissed him again.

"We should"—he kissed me—"get out of here."

I didn't bother arguing. "Yes. Now."

"Well, in a minute." His hand slid around the back of my neck, and we sank into another long, long kiss. Then...one more. Just like the night we met, it took us so long to pull ourselves apart, the ice had melted in our glasses.

Shane paged the waitress, then went back to the other side of the table. We both dove into the awamori again, though we both went a little heavier on the ice and water than the booze this time.

Settling up the bill was a challenge. We were too drunk, it was too Japanese, and the waitress could've taken us for an extra thousand yen or two and we never would have noticed. Or cared. We'd paid, so that was good enough for me.

Taxis were lined up on the curb outside, and there wasn't an American in sight, so we didn't think twice—probably couldn't have if we'd wanted to—about getting in the same cab. I got in first, and Shane slid in after me. He gave the driver his address, though his Japanese took considerably more effort than usual.

And as soon as the car was in motion, I was in Shane's arms again. In the back of my mind, I worried the driver might say something or be offended, but...God, Shane's kiss. How was I supposed to think about anything else?

All too soon, we stopped. We got out of the car, and I put an arm around Shane's waist just for balance as he counted out the yen for the driver.

The driver took the money and looked up at us, smiling and probably poised to thank us, but then he saw me. His eyes widened, and his smile fell. I couldn't figure out his reaction. He quickly muttered something in Japanese, then left so fast the tires squealed on the pavement.

Shane furrowed his brow and watched the cab go. Then he turned to me, and in the most matter-of-fact tone possible, said, "You know, I think he thought you were a woman."

"What?" I stared at him. "I don't look like a woman."

"No, but you were behind him. He couldn't see you." Shane made a drunken gesture down the road. "Whole time we were back there, he probably thought I was feeling up a girl."

Remembering the look of horror on the driver's face, I put the pieces together. No wonder he hadn't said a word about the two of us making out in the backseat. Any other night, I'd have grumbled about homophobia, but...I was drunk. Like everything else tonight, the man's reaction was funny, and when Shane's eyes met mine, we both collapsed into laughter.

"Great," I said, struggling just to speak through the alcohol and my laughter. "All night I'm worried some fucker will figure out who we are, and this guy mistakes me for a chick."

Shane started to speak but paused. Then he shook his head. "Fuck, I forgot what I was gonna say."

"Probably wasn't that funny."

"Hey, fuck you."

"Isn't that why we're here?"

He slid his arm around my waist. "Yes, it is. Why don't we get upstairs, then?"

"Sounds good to me."

We were too drunk to stand, let alone walk without the other's help, and *way* too drunk to care if anyone saw us leaning on each other on the way up the stairs. Not that it mattered out here. Most of his neighbors were Japanese, and everyone knew service members partied hard. My arm around Shane's shoulders didn't mean we wanted to fuck, it just meant I couldn't fucking walk. As far as they were concerned, anyway.

Somehow, we made it up the stairs and into his apartment. Down the hall. Into his bedroom. We got as far as kicking off our shoes before we just tumbled into bed together, fully clothed.

And that's about the time the second and third bottles of awamori caught up with both of us. Kisses slowed down. Every movement was as slurred as the occasional words we slipped in between kissing. Even our breathing slowed. My body was lethargic, my limbs heavy, and my mind shifted from needing Shane to needing sleep.

"I'm so fucking tired," I murmured.

"You too?" He kissed my forehead. "I can barely keep my eyes open."

"Same here." I rested my head on his shoulder. Shane wrapped his arms around me. I thought he said something. Maybe I did too. Before I could give it too much thought, sleep took over, and I drifted off in his arms.

Chapter Twelve

Shane

Who the fuck installed a sun that bright?

I winced and closed my eyes again, which didn't help me make sense of my surroundings or why I felt like shit. It did ease some of the pulsing between my temples, though. Whatever. It dulled the pain. Good enough for me.

Slowly, I took stock of the rest of my situation. My arm was numb. I was still in my clothes for some reason.

And my head? Jesus fucking Christ. I was certain a pair of battleships had spent the better part of the night playing bumper boats with my skull in the middle.

Good morning, awamori.

At least I'd been just drunk enough I didn't dream. Or if I did, I was drunk enough I didn't remember. Maybe that was why so many guys drank like fish after their tours.

Eric was beside me. His shirt was rumpled, his head was on my shoulder, and he was out cold. He was also on my arm, and I grimaced as I carefully freed that arm.

I opened and closed my hand, wincing at the intense tingle of blood rushing back into my fingers.

He opened his eyes, then covered them and groaned.

"Coffee?" I asked.

"God, yes." He groaned again and rubbed his temples with his fingers. "Why did you make me drink that shit again?"

"Make you?" I laughed. "Oh, come on. I hardly forced it down your throat."

"You might have mentioned it would come back and bite me in the morning."

I shrugged. "You know a hangover is always a risk."

He glared at me, then went back to rubbing his temples.

"To be fair, I did tell you it would catch up with you quickly."

He flipped me the finger but otherwise said nothing.

I laughed and kissed his forehead. "I'll go make coffee."

We put on some clothes and shuffled out to the kitchen, which, like the bedroom, had obnoxiously bright sunlight pouring in through the windows. I drew the curtains to block out as much as I could, and then, squinting and swearing, managed to get some coffee on.

As we sipped our coffee, I said, "What do you think about going snorkeling on your next day off? It's getting to be the perfect weather for it."

He set his cup down. "I suppose I don't need to ask if you know some good places."

"Oh, just a few." I paused. "I mean, as long as you're still down with being out in public somewhere."

He smiled over the rim of his cup and met my eyes. "I'm getting much more comfortable with it, believe me."

"Good." I grinned. "And snorkeling? No one's going to notice us. If they can recognize us facedown in the water, well"—I raised my coffee in a mock toast—"more power to 'em."

Eric laughed. "That would assume they actually went off base once in a while too, wouldn't it?"

"Exactly." I idly ran my thumb up and down the handle of my coffee cup. "I know some good spots. Pretty damn far from any of the bases too."

"Tell me when and where," he said. "I'll be there. I've been dying to snorkel here."

"Can't blame you."

"If it's anything like Hawaii or Guam, you won't be able to keep me out of the water after this. Just so you know."

I grinned again. "Then I guess we'd better stock up on sunscreen, shouldn't we?"

Hangovers, thank God, never lasted too long. The euphoria from a weekend with Eric? Oh, that carried me well into

Monday afternoon. My hips and back didn't ache too much. Maybe that meant my body was getting the hang of having that much sex with someone like him. Which clearly meant we needed to have more.

Eric wouldn't be off until late tonight, so I went with everyone for beers after work. Even Morris couldn't get to me today, so we were safe from brawling tonight. I hoped, anyway. It was always risky taking a good mood anywhere near him. He could make short work of good spirits.

But he'd have to work at it this time. I sat at the end of the bar with Mays and Gonzales, laughing over beers—a Coke for Mays, since he was DD—and a basket of tortilla chips while Morris annoyed some of the other guys a few seats away.

Mays had dark circles under his eyes, and I didn't have to ask why.

"So," I said, "enjoying being a dad?"

"It's awesome," he said. "I'm telling you, though, she has my sleep pattern in a choke hold." He clicked his tongue. "If I'm awake, she puts me to sleep. If I'm asleep, she wakes me up. I think I got more sleep in Iraq."

I laughed. I remembered those days very well. With a pang of sadness, it occurred to me that I'd have given almost anything to be sleep-deprived and running on diaper-changing autopilot again. Beat the hell out of being this far from my kids. But I kept that to myself.

"I feel your pain," I said. "I think mine were working together when they were that age."

He grimaced. "I don't know how you handled two."

"Coffee. Lots and lots and *lots* of coffee."

Mays laughed. "I don't doubt that for a second. Even Noriko's had to break down and have an espresso now and again."

"Not surprising."

"I can't really complain, though," he said, and his smile canceled out the dark circles under his eyes. "I could always go for more sleep, but I wouldn't give up that little girl for the world."

"Aww, aren't you *adorable*?" Gonzales said.

Mays's cheeks colored. "Shut up."

I laughed, but she was right. Mays was so obviously in love with his daughter. Tired as he was, he was probably counting down the minutes before he could drive Gonzales and me back to our apartments and get himself home to be with his baby.

Gonzales elbowed me. "You okay, man?"

"Yeah, of course. Why?"

She shrugged. "Don't know. You just seem really out of it today. More so than lately, I mean."

"I'm fine." I forced a smile. "Just, you know, tired."

Her eyebrow rose as she munched a tortilla chip, and I resisted the urge to draw back from her scrutiny. She was one of those people who could read almost anyone like a damned book. If I looked away from her, she'd see right through me. If I held eye contact, she'd see right through me too.

She washed the chip down with a swallow of beer. Setting her glass down with an emphatic thunk, she said, "So what's her name?"

Mays stopped chewing in midbite, and his eyes darted toward me.

I cleared my throat. "I...um... I beg your pardon?"

"Uh uh, don't even try to deny it." She inclined her head and raised her eyebrows. "I know you better than that, Connelly. Now fess up. What's her name?"

I rolled my eyes. "Her name is A Figment of Your Imagination."

"Bullshit."

"Think what you want," I said with a flippant shrug. "That's all you're getting out of me."

She narrowed her eyes and stabbed a finger at my chest. "Oh, I'll get it out of you eventually. I want a chance to warn the poor girl about what she's getting into."

"Go right ahead," I said, grinning.

"I will. Mark my words."

We exchanged good-natured glares. Then we both laughed.

She pushed herself away from the railing with her hip. “Well, I’m going to get another drink. Anyone want anything?”

“Nope, I’m good,” I said.

“Same here,” Mays said. After she’d gone, he eyed me, and I knew that look.

“Don’t ask,” I said.

“I won’t.” He shifted his gaze away and picked up his soda, and I almost didn’t hear him mutter, “Not here, anyway.”

“Much appreciated,” I said.

It was especially appreciated when, seconds later, the pungent smell of too much booze preceded a heavy arm on my shoulders.

“You guys are awfully quiet down here,” Morris said, half leaning on me. Well, at least he was a happy drunk tonight. “Come on. Join us over there.” He gestured clumsily toward the other side of the bar.

“We’re good, Morris,” Mays said flatly, and he looked even more exhausted now than he had a few minutes ago. “Don’t mind us.”

“Aww, come on.” Morris clapped Mays’s shoulder. “You’re here to drink and hang out. Come drink and hang out!”

“We are.” Mays glared at him.

Morris shrugged and took his arm off me. “Suit yourselves, fuckers.”

As he staggered back toward our other unfortunate coworkers, Mays growled, “I’m going to kill that man one of these days.”

I laughed. “Just tell me when you’re going to.”

“Why?” He chuckled. “Want to watch?”

“Nope. Don’t wanna be a witness.”

“Chickenshit.”

“Yeah, well.” I gestured with my beer. “I’d like to be Captain Chickenshit someday, so...”

Mays threw his head back and laughed. “I am so going to call you that. Just so you know.”

Gonzales dropped onto her barstool. "All right, what did I miss? What's so funny?"

"Oh," Mays said, "Connelly here was just telling me how when he makes captain, he wants us all to call him Captain Chickenshit."

She eyed me, then shrugged and set her fresh beer on the bar. "I can get on board with that."

"You what?" I said. "Fuck you both."

"No, thank you," they said in unison.

After a couple more beers, the three of us went out to Mays's car. Gonzales lived closer to Kadena, so her place was the first stop. We said our good-byes and watched Gonzales go into her apartment.

When the glass door had closed behind her, Mays pulled out of the parking space, and as he started toward the main road again, he said, "Okay, so. Further to her question back at the bar, what's *his* name?"

There wasn't much point in denying it to him. Lowering my gaze and voice, I said, "Eric."

Mays laughed and clapped my shoulder. "So that's why you've been out of it lately. I'll have to buy this guy a beer just for distracting you enough to keep you from decking Morris."

I gave a quiet, unenthusiastic laugh.

"Something wrong?" he asked.

"No, no." I paused. "Not really."

"Not really?" He glanced at me. "What's the deal, man? This guy a minor or something?"

"Hey, fuck you." We both laughed, but my humor didn't last long. "No, he's not a minor."

"What's the problem, then?" He gave a one-shouldered shrug, resting his hand on the wheel as he followed the road toward my place. "With DADT out of the way, who cares if someone finds out?"

"Besides the fact that I'm not out, and I don't want to be?"

He glanced at me again, and suspicion pushed up one eyebrow. "Is that the only problem?"

"Um, well..." If there was anyone in my command I could trust, it was Mays. Still, I hesitated.

"Fuck, dude," Mays said, completely serious now. "What's going on?"

I dropped my gaze. "It's an issue with...rank."

"You doing an admiral or something?" he asked. "I mean, you know that's not why they call him a rear admiral, right?"

Snorting with laughter, I shook my head. "God, no."

"Then...?" He threw me a glance before focusing on the road.

"I...outrank him." I coughed. "By a lot."

His head snapped toward me. "Dude, you're not..." Then he thumped the wheel with his hand and exhaled hard. "He's enlisted, isn't he?"

"Yeah," I said. "He is."

"Fucking Christ." He looked at me with an exasperated expression. "Connelly, for fuck's sake, are you *stupid*?"

"Apparently so."

He shook his head and rolled his eyes. "I'm not even going to waste my breath trying to talk you out of it, but..." He paused for a moment. "Man, the skipper finds out, you are in a *world* of hurt."

"No kidding."

"You do know the admiral is cracking down on any kind of conduct unbecoming, right?"

Pursing my lips, I nodded.

"Which means the skipper's sitting on go to fuck up Morris once he finally gets out of line, and he'll take down anyone else if he has to."

"Yes, I know. But as long as no one knows..."

He scowled. "Well, I won't say a word to anyone, but shit like this has a tendency to make itself known."

I nodded but said nothing. Of course I knew he was right. I'd known from the beginning that Eric and I were playing with fire. The more I saw him, though, the more I caught myself just not giving a fuck. Was it reckless? Gambling with a career to which I'd devoted almost seventeen years of my life? Absolutely.

But more and more, I couldn't bring myself to believe there was anywhere in the world I belonged except with Eric.

Even if that was also the *last* place I belonged.

Chapter Thirteen

Eric

Friday and Saturday nights were never quiet. There was plenty of alcohol and stupid throughout the week, but these were the nights when the alcohol really flowed and the stupid got, well, stupid. Combine those two things with a bunch of bored military guys, and security forces stayed busy as hell.

On Friday night, Colburn and I responded to a call at the hospital on Camp Lester. The Provost Marshal's Office handled most calls on that base, but the person in question was a Sailor, not a Marine, so PMO turned it over to us. They probably had their hands full with their own guys.

Getting called to a hospital was never a good sign. I'd responded to dozens of those calls over the years, and I'd seen it all. Sometimes it meant getting statements about hit-and-run accidents, taking drunk idiots into custody or trying to get a statement out of a shaken domestic-violence victim. I'd arrested parents. I'd turned children over to Protective Services. More times than I could count, I'd arrested service members for alcohol-related incidents after they'd recovered from accidents or alcohol poisoning.

As MA2 Colburn drove us on to Camp Lester and headed toward the hospital, I had no idea what to expect. All we knew so far was that an individual had come in with injuries that didn't match his story, and the corpsman who'd treated him suspected something was wrong enough to warrant calling us in.

We parked outside the Emergency Room entrance and walked inside. As we took off our covers, I turned to the triage nurse and gestured at the badge on my blouse.

"I'm MA1 Randall, CFAO Security, White Beach," I said.

"We got a call about one of our guys?"

He nodded. "I'll have HM3 Hiatt come get you. Just a second."

A moment later, a corpsman in a ponytail and blue scrubs came into the waiting area. "MA1?"

I extended my hand. "MA1 Randall. This is MA2 Colburn."

"HM3 Hiatt." She shook my hand firmly, and as she shook Colburn's, she said, "He's in one of the exam rooms. Come with me."

As we followed her into the back, she said, "His name is Ensign Aiden Lange. I can't give medical details without his consent, but...something about his story just didn't check out."

"Is he lucid?" I asked.

She nodded. "Doesn't appear to be disoriented or under the influence of anything. Totally with it, as near as I can tell. He's just really rattled."

This could get interesting.

She led us to the exam room and tapped on the door. Then she pushed it open. "Ensign Lange? This is MA1 Randall and MA2 Colburn. They'd like to ask you a few questions."

The ensign was just a kid in civvies sitting on the edge of the exam table with a welt on his cheekbone, a bandage above his eye and another mark above his collar. He took one look at us—and most likely the badges on our blouses—and paled.

"I understand you've had a rough night," I said.

He set his jaw and looked anywhere but at me or Colburn. "I don't need the police."

"Understood." I took a seat in the chair beside the door. "And you're not obligated to give a statement. When there's a scuffle or someone comes in looking like they've been in a fight, this sort of thing is standard operating procedure, so we're just doing things by the book." Okay, so that wasn't entirely true, but I didn't want to agitate him any further or encourage him to lash out at the corpsman.

Hiatt shifted her weight beside me. "Should I stay?"

"No, HM3." I smiled at her. "We're fine. Thank you."

She left, and when the door had closed behind her, Ensign

Lange gulped. He gripped the edges of the exam table, probably oblivious to the fact that he'd drawn my attention to the scrape on his arm, not to mention his bloody knuckles.

"Start at the beginning," I said. "Tell us what happened."

Lange eyed us both suspiciously. Then, gripping the edges of the table, he stared at the floor and took a deep breath. "I was at a club on Gate Two Street. Decided I didn't want to stay, so I went to leave, and some drunk guys started fighting right as I was heading out the door." He laughed, but the sound was less humorous and closer to the hysterical sound of someone trying to fake being relaxed. "Fucking Marines, right?"

"So the Marines started fighting," I said. "And what happened next?"

His fake humor instantly vanished, and he once again focused on the floor. "Okay, so I was on my way out. They started pushing and shoving, and I just kind of got caught in the shuffle."

I glanced at his knuckles. "You throw any punches?"

"What?" His head snapped up, and he stared at me incredulously. "Man, I'm not going to fuck up my career—"

"Did you throw any punches?" I asked.

He exhaled. "No. I got shoved around a bit, I lost my balance, and I hit the wall." He gestured at his face. "Split my eyebrow open, so I had a cab bring me here."

Colburn and I exchanged glances. From the furrow of his brow, I guessed he wasn't buying it any more than I was.

To Ensign Lange, I said, "What was the name of the club?"

He stiffened, and his gaze darted even farther away from either of us.

"Ensign?" I asked.

He swallowed. "I don't remember. It was… um…it was Japanese. Sign was written in kanji."

"The clubs on Gate Two Street all have English names," Colburn said. "Can you describe the place?"

"Is that necessary?" Lange snapped, glaring at Colburn.

"We're just trying to get an idea." Colburn showed his palms and kept his voice even. "In case we need to send our guys or have Eighteenth Security check it out."

Lange clenched his jaw. Then he shifted his gaze away, and the slightest drop in his shoulders turned my blood cold. "They all look alike to me after a while. I honestly don't remember which club I was at."

Colburn shifted. "Do you—"

"You said I don't have to give a statement," Lange said sharply. "I'd rather not."

I said nothing for a moment. My gaze flicked from his torn-up knuckles to the mark on his wrist to the scrape on his elbow. From there to the mark on his neck. Up to his darkening cheekbone and his bandaged eyebrow. As pieces fell together in my head, icicles formed along my spine. I curled my fingers around the edge of my notepad. Staying emotionally detached was part of this job, but there were times I couldn't detach myself as much as I should. If this was going where I had a feeling it was going, detachment wasn't an option.

"What happened to your neck, Ensign?" I asked quietly.

"My..." His hand went right to the mark I was referring to. "What do you mean?"

"That's an unusual mark." I injected more calm into my voice. "Especially for someone who just got shoved into a wall."

He chewed his lip and dropped his gaze. "I said I don't want to give a statement."

I turned to Colburn. "MA2, would you mind if I talk to Ensign Lange alone for a few minutes?"

Colburn eyed me. I raised my eyebrows in an unspoken "please," and he nodded.

"I'll meet you out in the waiting room," he said and left.

"I'm not giving a statement," Lange growled.

"I know." I leaned down and set my pen and pad on the floor. Then I sat up and rested my elbows on my knees, clasping my hands loosely between them. "It's just you and me, Ensign. This is completely off the record."

He drew back from me, folding his arms across his chest.

"I need you to tell me what really happened," I said, keeping my voice quiet and gentle. "As long as that's on the floor"—I gestured at my pen and pad—"nothing you say leaves this room."

"You're a cop," he said unsteadily. "If I talk to you…"

"What's your first name, Ensign?"

He gulped. "Aiden."

I extended my hand. "Aiden, I'm Eric. And right now, we're just talking man-to-man. All right?"

He looked at my hand like it was a *habu*, and not a dead one coiled at the bottom of a jar of Habu sake "Why are you doing this?"

I held his gaze. "Because I think something happened that you don't want your chain of command to know about."

"I didn't do anything," he snarled with sudden, shaking rage.

"I didn't say you did," I said quietly, still holding out my hand. "But sometimes things happen, and we're scared of someone finding out because it might tell them more about us than we want them to know."

The ensign damn near came unglued. He didn't say a word, but he squirmed, drawing away from me and making an almost inaudible, choked sound. He'd been nervous since I walked in the door, but he was shaking now, chewing his lip like he was a breath away from tears.

Goddammit, I hated being right sometimes.

"Aiden," I said softly, "I think we have a lot more in common than either of us is letting on, and I think I know why you're scared to say anything about what happened."

He didn't relax. My hand still hovered between us. My shoulder ached, but I didn't pull my arm back.

"I want to help," I said. "I just need you to trust me and tell me what really happened."

He still didn't move.

My heart pounded. Though it meant tipping my hand to a complete stranger, showing cards I also kept close to my vest, I said, "Aiden, tell me what he did to you."

The ensign straightened, his lips parting as he pulled in a sharp breath. "What?"

"You heard me."

His eyes flicked from mine to my hand and back to my eyes again. I knew I was right now, knew it without a doubt from the way he fidgeted. I was surprised I couldn't hear his heart beating a million miles a minute.

Barely whispering, he said, "Off the record?"

"Off the record."

He hesitated, but finally shook my hand.

After he released my hand, I sat back but kept my voice low. "Now, tell me what really happened."

Aiden squirmed, avoiding my eyes. "I was at Palace Habu," he whispered. "Heard about it online, seemed like a good place to—" He cut himself off abruptly, flinching like he thought he'd already said too much.

"It's a good place to meet guys," I said softly. "I know."

He stared at me, eyes wide.

"I've been there," I said. "Go on."

He relaxed a little more. "This guy, he bought me a drink, and we...we were talking. Flirting." Aiden's face colored, which deepened the shade of the bruise on his cheekbone. "But the more we talked, the drunker he seemed, and he ordered us both another round. And, I don't know, he wanted to take things faster than I did."

My blood turned colder with every word.

He went on. "He wanted to go back to his place, but I wasn't sure. So he said we should go to a different club. Said there was one, I don't know, up the street." He gestured as if we were standing on Gate Two Street now and he could indicate the club in question. "It was even farther off the main drag than the Habu, so I figured I could live with that." He shivered and closed his eyes.

A phantom throb marked the part of my arm that jackass Marine had grabbed when I'd tried to leave the club without him a lifetime ago. I shuddered, imagining how things might have happened had I not snarled in his face and stopped just short of threatening the structural integrity of his balls. Ensign Lange didn't strike me as nearly aggressive enough to make someone like that back off, not without some physical force.

My gaze drifted to his shredded knuckles. Barely whispering myself, I said, "What happened next, Aiden?"

He tightened his jaw and spoke through clenched teeth, probably trying to keep himself from losing his composure. "We got outside, and he..." Aiden closed his eyes again and forced out a breath. "I don't remember exactly what happened, but he grabbed me, told me the drinks he'd bought me weren't free, and..." He waved a hand. "I panicked. We fought a bit, and as soon as I got away, I ran like hell." He laughed bitterly. "My dad would be proud if he knew I didn't let a fucker that big overpower me. I think I even busted the guy's lip."

The chill in my veins ran deeper. Aiden wasn't a big guy, but he was no slouch. If someone was big enough to overpower him...

I swallowed. "Do you remember his name?"

Aiden's eyes darted toward the pen and pad that remained on the floor.

"Off the record," I said.

He took a breath. "I think he said it was Glenn."

Fury swelled in my chest, and that phantom throbbing in my arm intensified. Why was I not surprised that son of a bitch had been the one to fuck with Aiden? This was both the problem and the advantage of a tiny island with a tiny military population—the gay community was microscopic, and if one person knew your face, others probably did too. Shane knew Glenn's reputation. I'd experienced it firsthand. Now Aiden had stitches courtesy of the jackass Marine.

Aiden closed his eyes. His Adam's apple jumped. "If my command finds out I was even there, I am so fucked."

"I know," I said. "Believe me, Aiden, I understand. But you're doing the right thing here. By telling me."

"Except this is off the record, and if I name him," he said, speaking quickly now, "I'll have to say what happened. Where I was. My chain of command, I don't want them to—"

"Easy, Aiden." I patted the air with both hands. "Your chain of command isn't going to find out."

"Then…"

"Don't worry about it."

"But how do I explain this?" He gestured at his face.

I thought for a moment. "You do much around the island? Outdoor things?"

He shrugged. "Not really."

"Go hike to Hiji Falls this weekend," I said. "Take some pictures. Post them on Facebook. Make a few offhand comments about the rocks being slick, and you fell and busted your ass."

"Or my face?"

I shrugged. "The rocks are slick, and it's steep. Trust me, it can be done."

He chuckled. "I suppose the guys I work with would buy it if I busted my ass."

"Good," I said.

His humor faded. "What about Glenn?"

"I want you to take a weekend or two off from going to Palace Habu," I said. "Three to be safe. After that, I don't think he'll be a problem."

He raised his uninjured eyebrow. "Why's that?"

I smiled. "He won't be a problem."

I thought he might press for more information, but the ensign just exhaled, rolled his shoulders and then extended his hand.

"Thanks, MA1."

"Anytime, Ensign."

I strolled through the door of Palace Habu, giving the crowd of featureless silhouettes a disinterested scan before continuing toward the bar.

This was my third attempt to find him, and the third time was the charm, because there he was, healing lip and all.

He wasn't such an asshole when he first started chatting someone up, and he was still in his pleasant, charming mode.

Tonight's prey was a young one too. Judging by the shaggy haircut, he wasn't a service member. In fact, he was probably someone's kid, because the drinking age here was twenty, and if this kid was of age, it was by the skin of his teeth.

I scanned the crowd once more, gauging where everyone was, everything that was going on in the club. I hadn't noticed it the first time, but Glenn unsettled the whole place. There was a kind of palpable tension in the room that suggested every man was uneasy, and no amount of booze could settle everyone's nerves. Eyes darted toward Glenn and the kid. Guys paused in their conversations to glance his way. The bartenders, the deejay, the guys trying to flirt with each other—probably half the men in this club kept an eye on the loose cannon and his target. I imagined a few of them wanted to do something about it, but what could anyone do that wouldn't draw the JPs in here and get us all in hot water with our chains of command?

I took a deep breath and started across the room toward him.

Any other guy, I'd have brazenly put my hand on his elbow or his waist, but this was a drunk, volatile Marine. Unexpected physical contact was only a good idea if I wanted to wind up lying on the floor and spitting out my teeth.

Instead, I went from the front and sidled up to him.

"Glenn?" I said with a huge grin. "I *thought* I recognized you."

He looked at me and did a double take. His expression darkened, but before he could snarl something at me, I beat him to the punch.

"You know, we really got off on the wrong foot last time." I winked and laid a hand on his forearm, leaning in just right to put my shoulder between him and the kid. "I wondered if I could buy you a drink, and maybe we could try again?"

"Um, excuse me?" The kid shoved my arm. "Could you be a little more rude? He's talking to me."

"You know, you look a little young for this place." I narrowed my eyes. "Why don't you go see if the bartender can mix up a Shirley Temple for you?"

He looked at Glenn, lips parted and eyes wide. Glenn just shrugged.

The kid rolled his eyes and stalked off.

Be pissed all you want, kid. I just did you a bigger favor than you can imagine.

Turning my attention back to Glenn, I smiled. "So, about that drink?"

He eyed me suspiciously, but then shrugged. "I'll take an Orion."

"Why don't you go find us a booth, then?" I nodded toward the other side of the room, pretending my skin didn't crawl with both nerves and disgust. "I'll get our drinks."

At that, he relaxed, and his suspicious look turned into a slimy grin.

As soon as he'd gone, I flagged down a bartender. "Orion and a Coke." No alcohol for me this time.

Drinks in hand, I moved to the booth where Glenn waited, his arm slung across the back of the bench, just waiting to coil around my shoulders like a goddamned python.

I slid into the booth, and it took everything I had not to shudder or visibly cringe at the thought of him wrapping that snakelike arm around me. Fortunately, he didn't.

He took a long drink. "So," he said, breathing beer fumes in my face, "we did get off on the wrong foot last time, didn't we?"

"We did." I put a hand on his knee and leaned in as close as my already queasy stomach would allow me to. "I wanted to apologize for that."

"Well, I'm less concerned with apologizing," he said, running his hand up my arm. "I'm more interested in seeing if you're willing to make up for it. Especially after you chased off my friend over there."

"Your friend?" I laughed. "He's a kid. Seems like you'd prefer a man, wouldn't you?"

He chuckled and shrugged with one shoulder. "If he can get in this place, he's man enough for me."

The shudder almost came out, and I had to remind myself

to stay focused. I put my arm around his wide shoulders and moved a little closer. "Before we go any further, there *is* something I want to know."

"Oh?" His hand slid up my thigh, and it took everything I had not to snatch his wrist away or squirm right out of my own skin. "And what's that?"

I raised my chin and leaned in until my lips were almost touching his ear. "How much do you value your career, Devil Dog?"

He drew back and met my eyes. "What?"

"You've been in the Corps awhile, haven't you?"

"What the—"

"You want to make a scene?" I snarled. "Because I assure you, I can make a bigger one."

He blinked, his jaw going slack, and I had him where I wanted him.

I inclined my head and narrowed my eyes. "I have eyes and ears all over Gate Two Street, Glenn. And in this club. You set foot in this part of town, I will know about it."

He laughed. "You think you're some kind of mob boss or something, fuckhead?"

"No." I kept my expression and voice even. "I'm some fuckhead who doesn't want to see some idiot Marine fucking around like every ass is his for the taking." I paused. "And I've got people watching."

He looked past me, and his posture stiffened a little more. I didn't have to look to know a few guys had thrown glances our way.

"One guy calls me," I growled, "and I promise you I will make sure PMO, the Eighteenth, the MAs, none of them get anywhere near your ass before the JPs do. And I will make sure the JPs hold you until you're UA. You know they can do that, don't you? How do you think an unauthorized absence would go over with your command, especially tied to an international incident?"

He gulped.

"And that's if I'm feeling generous," I said. "Do *not* fuck with me, Marine. Do not fuck with anyone else in this bar or any other bar around any base on this island. Do you know where I'm attached or even which branch of service I'm in? What I do?"

He laughed. "You told me you're at White Beach, genius."

"You told me you're at Futenma." I raised an eyebrow. "And we both know *that* isn't true." Something flickered across his expression, and it was close enough to fear to satisfy me. I leaned in closer and went on, "So I'll ask you again, do you know where I'm attached or what I do?"

"I...no, I don't."

I grinned. "Then you have no idea who I know or what I can do. So might I suggest you take your happy Devil Dog ass back up to the base you came from, keep your head down and your dick in your pants, and just lay low until your tour here is over. Do I make myself clear?"

His Adam's apple bobbed.

"I asked you a question," I snapped.

He glared at me. "Motherfucker..."

"Call me whatever you want," I said. "But if I ever see you on Gate Two Street again, or I hear of you laying a hand on someone who's wisely decided he doesn't want to sleep with you, I will fucking end your career and make sure the only job you ever stand a chance of holding involves paper hats and fry grease." I narrowed my eyes. "Are we clear?"

He scanned the crowd again, and I hoped a few more guys had turned to check on us just then.

"Are we *clear*, Devil Dog?" I snarled.

"Yes," he threw back. "We're clear."

"Good." I started to slide out of the booth. "And by the way, that kid you were fucking with?" I gestured toward where I'd interrupted the two of them. "That was a colonel's son."

It was hard to tell in the low, flickering light, but I was pretty sure Glenn blanched.

I stood and beckoned for him to get up too. Avoiding my eyes, probably thinking of about four hundred ways to break me in half, he slid out of the booth.

I nodded sharply at the door, and if the man had a tail, it

would have been between his legs as he lumbered through the crowd—which got out of his way—and got the fuck out of Palace Habu.

The door closed behind him, and all the air left my lungs at once. I dropped onto the bench in the booth, closed my eyes and just took a few slow, deep breaths. It was done. It was over.

A hand on my shoulder startled me, but when I looked up, I smiled.

"Mind if I sit?" Shane asked.

I scooted over, and he sat beside me, wrapping his arm around my shoulders.

"Remind me never to get on your bad side," he said, grinning. "I'm surprised he didn't piss himself."

I laughed. "Come on, I'm not *that* scary." I kissed him lightly. "Thanks for keeping watch."

"You really think I'd let you near that asshole without me supervising?"

"Supervising?" I scoffed and picked up my untouched Coke. "Please. I just needed a little backup in case things got out of hand."

"Whatever helps you sleep at night." He kissed my cheek and murmured in my ear, just loud enough for me to hear him over the music, "And I think every man in this bar was a little turned on watching you make that jackass your bitch."

I laughed. "I wouldn't go that far."

"Trust me." He let his lower lip brush my skin. "Everyone in the room noticed."

"Doesn't mean—" I sucked in a breath through my teeth as he kissed the side of my neck. "Doesn't mean they were turned on."

"Maybe, maybe not." He nipped my earlobe. "But I was."

"Let's get out of here."

Chapter Fourteen

Shane

"Oh my *God.*" Eric dropped onto his back beside me, panting and soaked with sweat.

Breathing hard, I wiped my brow and grinned at him. "I'll take that as a compliment."

He laughed. "Oh, it was. Believe me."

"Good. Give me a few minutes, and we'll do it again."

"You're gonna kill me before this night's over," he said with a hint of a slur in his voice.

"Should've thought of that before you went all badass cop with me in the room."

He looked at me, grinning. "I didn't realize that kind of thing turned you on."

"Neither did I." I ran a fingertip down the center of his chest. "But apparently it does, so keep that in mind."

"I'll make sure to have you come along next time I do any ops." He winked. "So you think he'll come back and mess with anyone?"

I snickered. "I think you put the fear of God into him. I'd be surprised if he left his base between now and whenever he transfers."

"Good." He slipped his hand into mine. "And all joking aside, thanks for being there. It was good to know I had backup."

"Looked like you had it under control."

"Yeah," he said. "But it's a little easier to go into something like that knowing someone has my back."

"You know if he'd even tried to fuck with you," I whispered, reaching up to touch his face, "I'd have fucked his world up."

Eric smiled. Then he sighed. "It's too bad the kid I talked to the other night didn't have a wingman."

"I meant to ask you," I said. "What happened with that?" Eric had been gnashing his teeth and seeing red since that night, focusing entirely on either kicking Glenn's ass or scaring the shit out of him, and he hadn't given me the whole story. Just that Glenn messed with some kid, and Eric was going to rain hell upon him. When that man was on a mission, he fucking *focused.*

Eric lay back on the pillows, lacing his hands behind his head. "We got a call last weekend. Some kid was at Lester. Said he got caught in the shuffle when some drunk Marines got into it over on Gate Two Street, but the corpsman didn't think his story checked out. So she called us in." He ran a hand through his short, sweaty hair, leaving it slightly spiked. "It took me a while, but I got it out of him that he'd actually been at Palace Habu and had a run-in with Glenn."

"Oh, shit," I said.

"Yeah. I promised I'd keep it on the down low," he said. "I didn't take an official statement, and I said I wouldn't notify his chain of command. And"—he met my eyes, and I could only imagine the intense, determined look he'd given that kid—"I promised him I'd take care of it."

"Good," I said. "And I assume his chain won't ask questions?"

Eric shrugged. "They might. He had some visible injuries, and we had to at least document we'd been there to talk to him. I just kept the actual facts to myself and gave him a cover story to tell anyone who asked about the marks." He laughed quietly. "Told him to tell people he'd busted his ass up at Hiji Falls."

My breath caught in my throat. A memory from early last week flicked through my mind. My coworkers and I had been at a meeting with the department on the floor above us, and one of the ensigns had an impressive bruise on the side of his face along with a few stitches in his eyebrow.

Ever the helpful one, Morris had said, *"Man, that is one hell of a shiner, Ensign."*

"Wow," Gonzales had said. *"He's right. I don't even know if I want to see the other guy."*

At that, Ensign Lange had paled. *"What...the other guy?"*

"Yeah." Gonzales gestured at his face. *"The one who messed you up? Please tell me you beat the holy hell out of him."*

"Oh." The ensign had laughed and gestured dismissively, which only drew my attention to his scraped up knuckles. *"Went hiking over the weekend. Fucked myself up on the rocks up at Hiji Falls."*

I'd been up to Hiji myself and nearly fallen on the rocks, so I hadn't thought much of it at the time. But now...

I gulped. "What was his name?"

"Hmm?"

"The kid," I said. "What was his name?"

"Lange. Aiden Lange."

I closed my eyes. "Oh, fuck..."

"What?" Eric asked. "What's wrong?"

"Ensign Lange, he..." I lowered my voice even though there was no one else around. "Eric, I work with him."

Eric's eyes widened. "You do?"

I nodded. "Not directly. But he's in my department. Unless there's another kid by the same name with a stitched-up eyebrow who's telling people he busted his ass at Hiji Falls."

Eric shifted his gaze to the ceiling. "Wow. Small world."

"And an even smaller island," I said.

"No kidding." He turned onto his side, facing me. "Then maybe we should take this as a sign we need to be extra careful." Sliding his hand over mine on my chest, he added, "Extra discreet."

"We're being careful and discreet," I said, turning my hand over beneath his. "Let's just take this as a hint to really watch our backs and be careful, but I don't see it as a sign we need to stop."

"Stop?" Eric grinned. "Who said anything about stopping?"

I laughed to mask the sigh of relief. "Good. We'd better not be stopping."

"We aren't. Not if I have anything to say about it." He watched his thumb trace the side of my hand. "Does make me realize how amazingly small this place really is, though."

"No shit. Gets a little claustrophobic sometimes."

"Yeah, it does."

I absently ran my fingers through his hair. "You know, maybe we need to get *off* this island for a little while."

He furrowed his brow. "And go where, exactly? Up to the mainland?"

I shook my head. "I was thinking somewhere a little more local. And less populated."

"I'm listening."

"There's this island off the coast," I said. "Komaka. It's tiny. Seriously, you can walk around it in about five or ten minutes."

Eric blinked. "I believe those are called rocks, Shane, not islands."

I laughed. "Oh, it's decent sized. Mostly sand, but it's got some rocks on it. They even built a restroom on it a few years ago. Anyway, it's about two miles off shore, fifteen minutes by boat, and has some amazing snorkeling." I met his eyes and trailed my fingers along the shaved side of his head. "Maybe we can take off. Camp there for a night. Get away from this place for a little while."

"You don't think that's a little conspicuous?"

"There's never any Americans there. Especially not in the middle of the week."

"Hmm." He pursed his lips. "Well, maybe next time I have a couple of days off during the week..."

"You bring the beer," I said with a grin, "I'll pack the tent."

He returned the grin and slid closer to me. "Who brings the condoms and lube?"

"Hmm," I said, shivering when he bent to kiss my neck. "How about we both bring some?"

"Extra prepared," he murmured beneath my jaw. "I like this plan. Sign me up."

"Consider yourself signed up."

"Excellent." He pressed his hips against mine. "And

consider *your*self signed up for another round of everything you did a few minutes ago."

"Bring it on."

Chapter Fifteen

Eric

Small world or not, our clandestine method of dating turned out to be the perfect excuse to explore the island. Just as Shane predicted, we rarely saw any Americans, especially as we drove farther and farther from the bases. There wasn't a Y plate in sight when we went up to Cape Hedo, the cliffs at the north end of the island. No one spoke a lick of English when we checked out the castle ruins south of Naha, and I didn't see a single American as we chanced being in the same car and drove around Henza, Ikei, Miyagi, and Hamahiga Islands. After a couple of excursions, I relaxed.

And so much for my cousin's summary of this place. Okinawa was fucking stunning. The areas immediately surrounding the bases were moderately westernized, but once we were ten or fifteen clicks from Kadena in any direction, the number of signs written in English decreased significantly. In some of the smaller villages, we were lucky to find anyone who spoke English, so I was more than a little thankful for Shane's ability to speak enough Japanese to get us by. I picked up words and phrases as we went, but he was almost fluent.

And he was right about being out in public together—even when we did run into Americans, no one batted an eye at the two of us. They didn't know who we were, never mind what our ranks were, and two American men talking to each other wasn't terribly unusual. In a place where you don't speak the common language, it's almost a given you'll start talking to anyone who speaks yours. If we bumped into someone one of us knew, which happened on rare occasions, we just acted, as always, like Shane and I had only *just* met and struck up a conversation.

Not that anyone questioned us or even really noticed. Standing in the turquoise glow of the Churaumi Aquarium's enormous shark tank, I couldn't imagine anyone bothered giving any thought to the two guys standing a few inches apart, watching the stingrays dart between massive manta rays and whale sharks. At the Japanese Navy Underground Headquarters, as far as anyone else was concerned, we were just a couple of World War II buffs comparing notes on the Battle of Okinawa. And there wasn't an American in sight to give a rat's ass about us while we wandered through Shuri Castle or along the walls of Nakijin Castle.

Still, we didn't dare show any affection in public. Even when we were deep in the forest hiking to Hiji Falls, or soaking up the sun and scenery on some remote beach we'd probably never find again, we didn't risk more than the occasional exchanged look or a brief stolen kiss now and then. It was tempting—oh God, was it ever—to make out on the cliffs of Manzamo while the sun sank into the East China Sea, or strip off our clothes and fuck in the moonlight on a deserted strip of white sand, but we held back. There was always time for that when we made it back to the privacy of our respective apartments.

I had never experienced such incredible snorkeling in my life either. I swore Shane knew all the amazing places around the island. Either that or there was no such thing as a bad snorkel spot here. Whatever the case, he took me to all kinds of secluded areas where the wildlife were colorful and fearless. And dangerous. I swore there wasn't a creature on or around this island that couldn't kill or dismember us. Even the snails were deadly.

And finally, we both had a few days off in the middle of the week so we could go check out that tiny island he'd been talking about.

So, here we were, way down on the southeastern coast, standing on a dock while Shane made arrangements with the boat owner to take us out to Komaka Island.

It was a flawless day for snorkeling—the sky was clear, the seas were calm, and while it wasn't unbearably warm, it was hot enough to make the water nearly irresistible. Perfect. Absolutely perfect.

One thing that struck me as odd, though, and had every time we'd been snorkeling, was the lack of seagulls on Okinawa. After a few years in San Diego, it was hard to reconcile a marina, the sounds of boat engines, and the smell of salt and diesel fumes with complete radio silence from those winged white rats.

While Shane and the owner discussed everything, I looked out across the water at the island. Thanks to my camera's zoom lens, I was able to get a pretty good look at it from here. It was probably three or four miles away, but it didn't look quite like what Shane had described. A thin belt of golden sand encircled it, but it was definitely more island than beach. Even from here, I could make out some buildings and other signs of civilization, and while it was certainly a small island, it was hardly something we could walk all the way around in five minutes like he insisted we could.

I lowered my camera. "Thought you said this place was tiny and uninhabited."

He glanced up from counting out yen. "It is."

"Looks like more than one building to me."

Shane turned. "No, that's Kudaka, not Komaka." He pointed about fifteen degrees to the south. "*That* is Komaka Island."

I stood corrected. Maybe two miles off shore, the island was little more than a large rock with a few smaller rocks jutting out into the water on one side and, on the south side, a sandy beach that made up about half of the island. Through my zoom lens, I was able to make out the one and only building, which was a tiny, gray peaked roof peering over the thick bushes, but otherwise, Komaka was just sand, rocks and vegetation. And just as Shane predicted, as near as I could tell from here, there was no one on the island. The beach was deserted, and no boats bobbed in the water beside it.

"Oh," was all I said.

"Told you it was tiny."

"Yeah, you were right." I lowered my camera and glanced at him. "And there isn't a single vending machine over there?"

He laughed. "Well, all there was last time I was out there was the restroom, but hey, you never know."

Shane finished settling up with the boat owner, and we took our gear, a cooler and a couple of backpacks to the boat launch.

He glanced at his watch. "We've got twenty minutes before the boat leaves. You want to put on your wet suit here or wait until we get out there?" He nodded toward the island.

"Might as well do it now," I said. "As long as we're just sitting here."

"Go ahead. I'll keep an eye on our stuff."

Not that any of it was going anywhere. We could probably leave our stuff there all day—cameras, wallets and all—and no one would touch any of it.

I left Shane by the boat ramp and went to the restroom across the gravel parking lot to change clothes. Wet suits weren't entirely necessary here, but I preferred to wear one, as did Shane. The water was warm enough, we didn't really need more than a pair of swimming trunks, but it minimized the amount of skin exposed to the tropical sun. That, and there were box jellyfish around here. I wasn't terribly keen on getting stung by one of those critters or any of the other things out there with stingers, so I opted to cover up. It wasn't even a full wet suit, just a half suit: it covered my torso and extended to my knees and elbows but left my lower legs and my forearms exposed. Anything more than that was too restrictive for my taste. Gloves kept my hands from getting scraped up or stung, and either fins or scuba booties—depending on the current—kept my feet covered. If I couldn't keep my forearms or calves away from something's stinger, I supposed I deserved to get stung.

When I came back, Shane picked up his wet suit and headed in to change clothes. As he walked past me, he did a down-up with his eyes, then grinned at me. I was suddenly glad he'd had the forethought to bring along more than just beer, food and snorkel gear. I still wasn't so sure about fooling around somewhere outside our bedrooms, but it would get dark eventually. And with the looks we'd just exchanged and how well he always wore his wet suit, it was a good thing we had condoms and lube with us *just* in case.

While I waited for him, I sat on a weathered old bench at a nearby picnic table to put sunscreen on my exposed skin. The tropical sun bit hard, a lesson I'd learned very well in both Hawaii and Guam, and I wasn't spending another weekend sick and miserable because I hadn't put on enough sunscreen. Once I'd put on enough to seal out the sun, I capped the bottle, dropped it into my backpack and glanced up just in time to see Shane on his way back from changing clothes.

God. I couldn't imagine anything Shane could wear that wouldn't look good, but painted-on black Lycra was fucking glorious on him. The material clung to him, showing off every groove and contour of his muscles. It didn't matter how many times I'd seen him in that wet suit, I was always ready to peel it right off him. This time was *no* exception.

I suppressed a shiver and shifted my gaze back to the water.

Shane sat beside me, his arm brushing mine. Gesturing at the boat, he said, "You're not going to get seasick, are you?"

"Fuck you." I glared at him. "I've probably spent more of my career on the water than you have." I elbowed him back. "You have *your* sea legs, *Sir*?"

"Watch yourself, Petty Officer," he said with what didn't even aspire to be a stern look. "Or you'll be swimming to Komaka."

I shrugged. "Go ahead and try it. I go in, you're going in with me."

We tried to exchange menacing looks, but both burst out laughing instead.

A few minutes later, an elderly bronze-skinned local in a pointed straw hat gestured for us to come down the ramp. We loaded our gear onto the boat and sat with our backs to the bow while the old man untied the lines from the dock. He barked an order at another younger man, who jumped from the dock into the boat and busily went about coiling lines. They pushed off, and we were underway.

The boat bounced across the rolling waves, and Okinawa gradually shrank behind us. I rested my elbow on the side and turned so I could see our destination. Though it had to be my senses screwing with me, I was sure Komaka got smaller as we approached. Or maybe the closer we got to the island, the more I realized just how tiny it was in the first place. If I had to guess, I'd have said the island was maybe two hundred meters from end to end.

About fifteen minutes after we'd left the dock, the old man cut the engine. He and the younger man used oars to guide the boat as close to the shore as they could get. The tide was partway out, so the boat scraped bottom with ten feet or so left between us and dry land.

Shane and I picked up our gear, shouldering our backpacks and snorkel bags. I stepped out first, Shane followed, and the old man handed him our cooler. We each carried one end of the cooler and, stepping carefully to avoid falling on our asses, waded through the shin-deep water to the beach.

Once we were on the dry sand, Shane stopped. He and the younger man exchanged a few words in Japanese, and a moment later, the men in the boat were pushing off.

I stared at them. "They're just...leaving us here?"

He nodded as the boat's outboard motor fired up again. "Usually, they stick around, but they've seen me enough times they know I don't need a babysitter."

"I don't know," I said. "I would think they'd know you well enough to—"

"Very funny." He shot me a playful glare. "Anyway, they'll be back around two tomorrow to pick us up. But until then"—he gestured around the island—"the whole place is ours."

"What about other people?" I asked. "I would assume we're not the only ones who know about this place."

Shane put a hand on the small of my back. "Trust me, the

only time you see anyone else out here is on Sundays, and I have never seen another American out here unless I've brought them myself." He kissed my cheek. "In the middle of the week? I doubt we'll see another soul here until the guys come back to get us."

I let my gaze drift up the beach, then back down again. Up over the vegetation-blanketed rocks. And across the water to Okinawa, which looked like it was even farther away than it was.

The whole island. No one here but us. Sure, Komaka was just a tiny speck on a map, but for now, it was ours. Only ours. It was like having an entire world to ourselves.

We put our stuff on the beach well above the tide line. I supposed we should have brought a couple of beach chairs, but oh well. They would've been that much more shit to carry off the boat and through the water. We had towels and a blanket to sleep on in the tent, and I didn't imagine we would be spending much time out of the water anyway. Throwing a glance at Shane in that skintight Lycra, I figured if we did spend much time on shore, beach chairs wouldn't be part of the equation anyway.

Goose bumps rose on my bare arms. I leaned down to put my wallet and keys into my backpack, and casually checked to make sure that, yes, we had plenty of condoms and lube with us.

I was still a bit uncertain, though. Everything about him was a turn-on, but we were still out in the open. This beach was completely exposed, right out in the open where everyone and his mother—or commanding officer—could see us. I could see miles of coastline, both on Okinawa and Kudaka, from here, which meant people on Okinawa and Kudaka could see us too. With binoculars or a telephoto lens, anyway. Or from a plane. Or a boat.

Still, at least we had what we needed in case the mood struck us.

I glanced at Shane as he pulled on his black scuba gloves. He looked up, met my eyes and grinned.

Today's forecast calls for a 95 percent chance of the mood striking and a 5 percent chance of nerves.

He fastened the strap on the back of his glove. "Ready to get in the water?"

"Absolutely." *That or a cold shower.* I dug my gloves, mask, underwater camera, snorkel and fins out of my bag. "Let's roll." I could pay attention to my attraction to Shane later. For now, I wanted to see if he was blowing smoke when he said this was one of the most amazing snorkel spots in the region.

We got into the swimming-pool-warm water, and I knew the instant I submerged my face and mask that he was right about this place. This was going to be a spectacular day of snorkeling. Nothing promises a great swim like getting in the water and finding oneself face-to-face with dozens of colorful fish. We didn't have to seek out the animals; they were right there waiting for us.

Some of the fish scattered, but others stuck around, watching us curiously. I suspected other swimmers fed them, encouraging them to come up to people. Pity we hadn't brought any food for them. Though, knowing Shane, he'd probably try to feed his finger to something with sharp teeth before the day was over. After snorkeling with him a few times, I was truly mystified that the man still had ten fingers.

Since Komaka was out in the open water instead of sheltered like some of the coves and inlets where we'd snorkeled before, the current was substantially stronger. With our fins on, though, we didn't have too much trouble swimming against it.

The water was six to eight feet deep in places, but some of the rocks and parts of the reef were big enough they almost broke the surface. We swam between the rocks, checking out the sea urchins, anemones, coral and fish that made their home here. Yellow, black and white angelfish nibbled at some unseen food source on the rocks. Electric-blue fish that were anywhere from an inch long to the length of my finger darted into crevices and under outcroppings, watching us warily. Larger fish, some as long as my forearm, kept a careful distance but didn't scurry away. I hadn't even seen some of these critters before. Some were dull gray. Some were speckled to camouflage them against the sandy sea floor. Others ranged from fluorescent yellow to deep purple, with all kinds of patterns in between.

The sea floor was mostly rippled sand instead of some of the rockier areas where we'd swum before. There were clusters of rocks of varying sizes, but if we needed to put a foot down in one of the shallower areas, we didn't have to worry too much about landing on a stonefish, which was yet another creature existing here specifically to make snorkeling dangerous. They were nearly impossible to see in some places but wouldn't blend into this smooth, white sand.

Humans, one. Stonefish, zero.

This time.

Shane tapped my arm. When I turned my head, he gestured down at the sea floor. I looked where he'd indicated. A thick belt of white-speckled brown wove between the rocks. I was about to lift my head out of the water to ask him what it was, but then it slithered into a crevice and turned around. When its head poked out, staring up at us with huge, round eyes and opening its jaws to reveal its sharp teeth, I realized it was a moray eel. A pretty good-sized one too. Easily four feet in length, with a mouth that could seriously fuck up someone's hand.

Shane started taking off his glove, and I eyed him. He looked at me, grinning around his snorkel. Jesus. Even underwater and through our diving masks, his devilish eyes did crazy things to me.

He gestured at the camera in my hand. I gave him a thumbs-up. Then he took a deep breath and dove down toward the eel. It balked, but when he waved his glove near the crevice, the eel lunged for it before recoiling into its hiding place. Again it snapped and recoiled.

After a few seconds of teasing the irritated creature, Shane swam up. He surfaced and cleared his snorkel. With his face underwater again, he gestured at the camera, gave a thumbs-up, and raised his eyebrows under his mask, an unspoken *did you get a good picture?*

I nodded and returned the thumbs-up. He came back with this thumb and forefinger in a circle, then pulled his glove back on. Crazy SOB.

I popped my head out of the water and glanced back at the beach to see how far we'd gone. We both did that whenever we snorkeled—every few minutes, we'd double-check just to make sure the current hadn't carried us too far from shore. Satisfied we were close enough, I ducked back under the water.

We left the eel to its hiding place, though it watched us warily as we swam past it. A school of tiny yellow fish caught our attention, and we followed it between some rocks, around another and behind a jagged reef. The sea floor dropped a few feet here, and in the deeper water, we found bigger fish that were no more afraid of us than the ones closer to shore.

I was about to look up to orient myself to the shore again, but Shane broke the surface first. He came back down and gave another "okay" gesture, so I continued swimming.

On one side of the reef, we found dozens of enormous, menacing-looking sea urchins. These weren't colorful little pincushion urchins that could sit in the palm of a gloved hand. Their thin, black spines were easily eight to ten inches long. We'd seen them before whenever we'd snorkeled, but this was the first time we were able to get up close and personal with them. Not that I wanted to get up close and personal with such a thing, but Shane—surprise, surprise—did.

The body was like a black golf ball with these weird little blue, black and orange buds sticking out between the bases of the spines. Maybe my inner nerd was showing, but I swore the buds looked like the Eye of Sauron or something. Strange things.

And, naturally, Shane liked to play with them. He held his hand less than an inch from the end of one urchin's spines, and—

Oh, my God, that was creepy as fuck. The spines near his hand *moved*. Not because the motion of his hand had disturbed the water. This was a deliberate motion, several spines moving so they pointed directly at his palm. As far as I knew, sea urchins weren't sentient creatures, but one way or another, this one responded to him. When he moved his hand again, the fucking spines followed like the damned thing was tracking him.

So. *Weird.*

He gestured for me to do the same. Creepy as it was, I couldn't resist. I grabbed on to a rock to brace myself so the current wouldn't make me get too intimately acquainted with the urchin. Then I held my free hand over the ends of the spines, and just as they had with Shane, they moved, bunching together to concentrate their pointy efforts on my palm in case I came any closer. And the little blue-and-orange, evil eye-bud thing? It moved too.

I glanced at Shane. He grinned around his snorkel again, and I just shook my head. I'd have laughed, but I'd learned on my first excursion with Shane that laughing was a quick and easy way to spit out one's snorkel. Nothing quite like swimming with a comedian.

A flash of silver caught my eye, and I turned my head.

The long, slender fish cruising just below the surface made my heart skip. It was facing away from me, but its shape was almost unmistakable. I knew there were barracuda out here, and I'd heard even the smaller ones—this one was maybe three feet long—could be dangerously aggressive.

With a sweep of its tail, its whole body turned, revealing its head in profile, and I relaxed. A little. The fish had a thin snout, kind of like a crocodile, instead of the more blunt, salmon-like head of a barracuda. Just a gar, then. They could be aggressive as all hell, too, but to my knowledge, weren't quite as dangerous as barracuda.

I tapped Shane's shoulder. When he took his attention from the creepy Sauron urchin and looked my way, I pointed toward the gar. He turned, then nodded to acknowledge he'd seen it before we both swam in the opposite direction. Better to just stay out of its way. Even Shane didn't mess with things like that, which made me even more inclined to keep an eye on it. Well, when I wasn't playing with another sea urchin. Which I only did because Shane suggested I should try it. Not because I actually found it amusing or anything.

Eventually, the creepy urchin novelty wore off, the gar swam away, and my arms and legs were getting tired. I tapped Shane's shoulder and gestured toward the shore. He nodded, and we both swam back to the beach.

The tide had gone out a little more, so some of the rocks we'd swum between were now exposed. I sat on one, tugged off my mask and snorkel and hung them on my elbow so I could take off my fins.

Shane sat beside me. "What'd I tell you?" he asked. "This place is incredible."

"You're right." I set one fin on the rock and reached for the other. "But must you always mess with the dangerous creatures?"

Shane laughed as he peeled off his glove. "Morays aren't dangerous. I mean, as long as I keep my hands out of their mouths."

I reached toward him and wiggled my fingers in his face. "That is a good way to get a hand in its mouth, Shane."

He snapped his teeth, narrowly missing my hand, and laughed when I drew it back. "Yes, and that's why I was waving my glove at it, not my actual fingers."

"Okay, but if you'd pissed it off enough, and it had bitten you, you'd have been in a world of hurt."

He shrugged and ran his fingers through his wet, disheveled hair. "Which is why I didn't let it bite me."

I stood, picking up my fins, and eyed him. "You do know those things don't let go, right?"

"No, they don't." He picked up his gear and stood too. "Have to be pried off."

"Just so you know," I said over my shoulder as I started toward the shore, "if it had bitten you, you'd have worn it home."

"What?" He scoffed. "You wouldn't even try to take it off?"

"Nope." I glanced back. "Figure it would be a good lesson for you."

"Hey, at least I didn't mess with the gar."

"Well, maybe there's hope for you yet."

We both laughed and continued across the rocks to the hot sand. We dropped our wet gear beside the cooler. I pulled my sunglasses, a beach towel and the bottle of sunscreen out of my backpack. I laid the towel on the sand and sat on it to put some more sunscreen on my arms and legs.

Duly screened against the sun, I handed the bottle off to Shane and lay back on my towel. Sunglasses on, I lounged with my fingers laced together behind my head. Ah, this was paradise.

"Dude, Okinawa is a fucking shit-hole."

Yeah, okay. Whatever, dude.

"Feel like eating anything yet?" Shane asked.

"Nah, I'm good for now. I might get back in the water in a little bit anyway." I paused and sat up. "Should probably drink something, though."

"Good idea." He took a couple of water bottles from the cooler and handed me one.

Funny thing about snorkeling-I never knew how thirsty I was until I took that first sip of water. One taste of something other than seawater, and I finished off three-quarters of the bottle before I came up for air. Much better, especially since it rinsed out most of the taste of the ocean.

Once I'd finished it completely, I handed the empty water bottle back to Shane, and he dropped it into the cooler with his own.

I lay back on the towel again. Shane stayed upright and reached back to unzip his wet suit. He stripped partway, letting the upper half of his suit hang around his waist, and sat on a towel beside mine. He rested his forearms on his knees and looked out at the water. And me? I had the perfect view and the dark glasses to hide the fact that I was staring.

Stray droplets of water sparkled in the sun on the ends of his hair, the back of his neck, and along his arm. Even when they were relaxed, his muscles were well-defined, just begging me to run my fingers along the grooves and contours. And the slight bow of his back as he leaned forward reminded me of how he looked when I—

Easy there, Randall. I cleared my throat and shifted my gaze away before I stared too long and my wet suit gave me away. Too late for that, I realized, and casually sat up again so he wouldn't notice.

Oblivious to my thoughts about him, he looked at me. His gaze drifted down my arm, and a hint of a smirk pulled up the corner of his mouth. "You don't have to keep that thing on, you know."

I raised an eyebrow. "Are you suggesting I should take it off?"

He shrugged with one shoulder. "Well, I was just suggesting you didn't have to leave it all the way on." He gestured at his own suit around his waist. "But, I mean, if you want to take it all off, don't let me stop you."

"Ah-ha. I knew it." I looked at him over my sunglasses. "You're just trying to get me out of my clothes."

"Maybe I am." He leaned toward me, resting his hand behind me on the towel. "What are you going to do about it?"

I leaned closer so our lips almost touched. "Who said I wanted to do anything about it?"

"Just checking." His other hand brushed the side of my face, and the resulting shiver made me pull in a sharp breath, which drew our lips together.

His hand went from my face to my neck, then down the front of my suit, and my abs contracted under his touch. "I don't know if I've ever mentioned this," he murmured, "but you drive me insane when you wear this thing."

"You don't look so bad in one yourself."

His lips curved into a grin. "Should I put it back on, then?"

"Oh no. Don't do that." I slid my hand over his shoulder and down his arm. His skin was hot to the touch, which made me even more aware of the layer of Lycra separating his palm from my abs. "In fact, maybe I'm overdressed."

"I agree."

We separated, and I sat up on my knees.

“Need a hand?” he asked.

“I’m not going to turn it away.”

”Didn’t figure you would.”

Shane knelt behind me. He unzipped the back of my wet suit. The sun’s heat met my newly exposed skin, but only for a second before he put his arms around me. His skin touched mine, and his lips brushed the side of my neck. I bit my lip and tilted my head back so he could explore more of my neck. We both made a halfhearted effort to get my suit over my shoulders and down my arms, but he was too interested in kissing behind my ear, and I was too distracted by his lips on my skin.

I groaned softly. “Do you have any idea how uncomfortable a hard-on is in a wet suit?”

“Oh, I think I have a pretty good idea.” Shane’s hands slid over my hips, and he pulled me back against him so I could feel how aroused he was. “Ever had sex on the beach?”

I licked my lips. “Ask me again in an hour, and I’ll say yes.”

“An hour?” His quiet laugh cooled my skin. “Oh, Eric, you’ll be lucky if I get through the next few minutes without being inside you.”

“Then it’s a good thing we brought condoms, isn’t it?”

“Yes, it is.” He nipped my earlobe. “Why don’t you get out of that suit, and I’ll get a condom on?” He kissed the base of my neck and added, “Because I am so goddamned desperate to fuck you right now...”

Words. Lost on me. The best I could do was a nod, and he got the message.

We both got up and peeled off our wet suits, careful to keep sand off the towel and our hands. Whatever inhibitions I might have had were gone from the moment he’d kissed my neck, and I didn’t know the meaning of nerves now. We were as out in the open and exposed as we could be, but there was no one else here. A broad expanse of water separated us from anyone who might give a damn about us, and with every touch, I lost my ability to give a damn about the consequences. I wanted him so bad I couldn’t see straight now, and every move we made took us closer to the gratification of that first stroke.

My mouth watered as Shane stroked lube onto the condom. His hand stopped, and he took and held a deep breath like he needed a moment just to calm himself down. Then, slowly, he exhaled, and our eyes met. With a nod, he indicated the towel I'd been sitting on a moment before.

"On my knees?" I asked.

He nodded again. I thought he'd have some witty or dirty comment, but maybe he was as tongue-tied as I was just then.

I got on my hands and knees. When the sand shifted behind me, I closed my eyes, and Shane's hand materialized on my side. With lubed fingers, he teased my entrance, and the coolness as well as the contact and anticipation made me light-headed.

His fingers lifted away, and a second later, his cock took their place.

"I guess now," he said, almost growling as he pressed into me, "you can say you've had sex on the beach."

I supposed he was right, but at the moment, I couldn't say anything. I couldn't think. I was lucky I could breathe as he pushed deeper inside me. As much as he liked to tease me until I was begging him to fuck me hard, he didn't this time. His first few strokes were slow and easy, but once he was moving comfortably with no friction or resistance, he didn't hold back.

"Like that?" he asked, his voice taut.

"*Ooh*, yeah. God, Shane, don't...don't stop."

"Why would I stop?" He groaned softly. "You feel too fucking good to stop."

I screwed my eyes shut and clawed at the towel beneath me. I didn't want to come yet, not until I was inside him, but the way he fucked me felt too damned good.

To hell with it. I'd get my chance to fuck him. Right here, right now, on this beach with Shane driving his cock into me so hard my eyes watered, I *had* to come.

I shifted my weight to one arm, and I had just enough presence of mind make sure there was no sand on my hand before I reached down to stroke my cock.

"Oh...God..." The words came out as a moan, and Shane

must have liked that because he gripped my hips tighter and thrust harder.

"Jesus Christ, you feel amazing," he said, probably through clenched teeth. "And you look...oh, my God, Eric..."

"Fuck me harder." I almost choked on the words, but before I could repeat them in case he hadn't heard, he slammed his cock deep inside me, and all that left my lips was a soft, helpless moan. My arm shook too much to hold me up, and I dropped onto my forearm. Still stroking my cock with my other hand, I rocked back against him, desperate for everything he could give me.

Shane groaned, slamming into me again and again, and every time I tried to inhale, he knocked the air right out of my lungs. The world spun around me. The sand shifted under me whenever I tried to move with him. Then my eyes rolled back. Electricity shot up my spine. My rhythm fell apart, but I kept stroking anyway, even as I cried out a string of curses, then whimpered, then shattered. I managed a few final strokes before the touch of my semen-slicked palm was too intense, and when I stopped my hand, I shuddered once more and released my breath.

Seconds later, with a roar that people on Okinawa and Kudaka probably heard, Shane pulled my hips against him and forced himself as deep as he could go. Then he slumped over me, and when his lips touched the back of my shoulder, I was stunned that my skin didn't sizzle.

"Jesus, Eric," he said, pausing to kiss the base of my neck. "This is what happens when..." He paused again, panting from exertion. "When you wear that damned suit."

I laughed between gasps for air. "Not the first time you've seen it."

"No." He kissed just beneath my hairline. "Just this time, I could finally do something about it." He straightened up and pulled out.

I wiped my hand on one side of the towel, then dropped onto my back, half on the towel, half on the scorching hot sand. He took the condom off and put it aside so we wouldn't forget to get rid of it properly. Then he came down to kiss me, and I wrapped my arms around him. The sand burned my skin, but I didn't care. Shane and I just held on to each other and kissed like there was no earthly reason not to. We both trembled, both panted, and for the longest time, the only sounds in the world were our uneven breaths and the tide lapping at the island around us.

After some undefined stretch of time had passed, Shane pushed himself up. Resting his weight on one arm, he touched my face with his free hand. His skin was sweaty and sun-kissed, and his hair was still damp as I combed my fingers through it.

This couldn't be wrong. Out of uniform, away from the rest of the world, we were just two men, and I'd never been drawn so strongly to another man. Never.

But the rest of the world still existed, and we'd have to put on our uniforms again, and there were reasons why we couldn't do this. Why we shouldn't.

And, pulling him down to kiss me again, I just didn't care.

Chapter Sixteen

Shane

Nightfall found Eric and me sitting in our swim trunks on towels in the sand in front of our tent, beers in hand, looking out at the island across the water. The air was still heavy with the day's heat, but it was perfectly comfortable. The gentle breeze whispered across my shoulders and teased the ends of my hair. Which, of course, made me realize I needed to get to the Exchange and get a haircut before I was completely out of regs.

"Almost seems like we wouldn't need a tent out here," Eric said. "Weather's perfect for sleeping under the stars."

"Yeah," I said. "Problem is that really big star that likes to show up in the morning. You want to wake up with a sunburn, be my guest, but..."

"On second thought..."

I laughed. "That's what I thought."

He chuckled. For a long moment, we just stared out at the island we'd left behind. A few lights dotted the landscape, which was solid black against a starry background, and the whole island seemed as still and quiet as this one. Eric rested his forearms on his knees and held his beer bottle between both hands. "You know what kind of blew my mind when I got to Okinawa?"

"What's that?" I asked.

"How big the island really is." He laughed softly. "Looking at it on a map, I guess I thought it would be more like..."

"Like this one?" I gestured at the sand below us.

"Something like that, yeah." He kept his gaze fixed on the distant landmass. "Still just amazes me, I guess. It's huge and it's small at the same time."

"Tiny enough to be suffocating," I said, staring in the same direction, "big enough to get lost when you need to."

"Exactly."

We both fell silent.

"You know," Eric said after a while, "if we're going to start getting into metaphors and that kind of shit, we really ought to have a joint or something to pass around."

I almost choked on my beer. "You got one with you, MA1?"

"Afraid not." Sighing, he shook his head. "They keep that shit under lock and key at the precinct."

"Bastards."

We glanced at each other and both laughed.

"Man, sometimes I really wish we could," he said, chuckling. "You'd think with everything the military puts us through, it would be a fair trade."

"Agreed." I gestured with my beer bottle. "They haven't taken away the booze, though."

He raised his own to his lips. "They'll have to pry it from this Sailor's cold, dead hands."

"I'll drink to that."

We clinked the necks of our bottles together and each took a long drink.

Down the beach, the tide continued lapping at the sand. The occasional plane cut a lazy arc across the sky overhead. On the bigger island, an occasional lone car meandered along one of the dark roads. The soft sounds and dark, barely interrupted night were almost hypnotic, and I hadn't even realized how long it had been since we'd spoken until Eric broke the silence.

"Listen, um," he said, "my daughter's coming to the island soon. For a few weeks right after school lets out."

I absently played with the label on my beer bottle. "So we probably won't see much of each other while she's here, then."

"Well, not necessarily. The thing is, I've kind of made it a point to let her meet guys I'm dating."

I looked at him in the darkness. "Even if it might not, you know, last beyond the end of your tour?"

He nodded. "Honestly, I think it's better that way. A lot of parents don't introduce their kids to people unless it's getting serious, but I think that can backfire a bit. Because then, if a kid's introduced to someone, they're going to assume it is getting serious, and if it doesn't work out? Yeah, not good."

"Huh. Never thought of it that way."

He shrugged. "Her mother's done the same thing. Once Marie was old enough to understand dating and things like that, we started introducing her to people. Not one-night stands or anything like that, but someone who was..." He hesitated, then turned to me. "Someone who might be in the picture for a while, even if not permanently."

I swallowed. "Interesting way of approaching things."

"It's worked so far. We've both found it's easier for her to accept when we split up with someone if she doesn't have the expectation that we're going to be together forever." He held my gaze. "If it's not too weird for you, I'd love to have you meet her."

"Sure, yeah," I said. "I'd definitely like to meet her."

He smiled, but it faded. "We'll still have to keep things sort of on the down low," he said. "No eating dinner in a restaurant on base or anything."

"Right, right, of course. Well, maybe we can all go snorkeling or something." I made a sweeping gesture at the beach with my beer bottle. "We can bring her here for a day."

"I think she'd like that," he said, and though I couldn't see it, his smile made it into his voice.

"I can't say I've had much opportunity to introduce my kids to anyone." I bit my tongue to keep from adding, *they barely see me, never mind anyone I've dated since the divorce*. "I mean, they know. That I date both men and women, that is. I can say a lot about my ex-wife, but she's always treated it as completely normal that I'm bisexual. So the kids have always understood there's nothing wrong with it."

"You know," he said. "It's pretty sad that our kids get it, but our commands probably wouldn't."

"Such is the military."

"Yeah. Such is the military." He paused for a minute or two. "So what are you going to do when you get out?"

"Don't know yet," I said. "Depends on when I decide to retire, which depends on if I make captain."

"So, assuming you get out at twenty..." He turned to me, the lift of his eyebrows barely visible in the low light.

"I've looked at a few options. Department of Defense contractor, maybe." I paused. "Man, I keep thinking I've got years and years to think about it, but retirement is coming up fast."

"Yeah, I know what you mean," he said. "Amazing how retirement goes from being a million years in the future to something you actually have to start thinking about."

I laughed. "No kidding. So what about you?"

Eric shrugged. "Probably stay in law enforcement. I like being a cop, so..."

"Seems like a solid career path."

"It's always in demand, that's for sure," he said, laughing softly. "And I finished my degree a few months ago, which will make it easier to move up in rank in a police force."

"You...have your degree?"

He nodded slowly, gaze fixed on Okinawa.

"Have you ever... I mean, have you considered—"

"Getting my commission?"

"Ycah."

Another nod. He lowered his gaze, probably focusing on the beer bottle between his hands. "I've thought about it a lot." He paused, and then turned toward me. "Especially recently."

"Is that right?"

"Yeah. Either LDO or OCS." He took a long swallow of beer. "If I put in for LDO, I could put on ensign within a year. If I go to OCS, it could be sooner, but..."

I exhaled. Officer Candidate School may have been a faster route than limited duty officer for him to put on rank, but he stood a good chance of getting transferred elsewhere after he finished.

"Well, whatever's the best thing for your career."

"It wouldn't solve all our problems," he said. "There's still the possibility of getting nailed for fraternization while I'm a junior officer."

"I know," I said. "It would help, though."

"True. It would be a less severe reprimand if we got caught then versus now."

"There is that." I paused. "You're not making the decision based on us, are you?"

He was quiet for much too long for me to believe the answer was no. He twisted away from me and, I guessed, pushed his beer into the sand, because when he faced the island again, his hands were empty. After a long moment, he shook his head. "I don't know what I'm basing this decision on. I really don't."

"Eric," I said. "This is a two-decade-long career. We're...who knows what?"

"I know," he said. "And part of me says I shouldn't make any career decisions based on this." His whisper was barely audible over the gently lapping waves below us. "But then, I'm already gambling with it." He turned his head toward me. "Seems like I could do worse than making a decision that'll further my career and could save it."

"That's true," I said. "Which begs the same question we've had to ask ourselves over and over from day one."

"Is what we're doing worth it?"

"I think so." I paused. "Is it?"

Eric was still and silent for a moment. I couldn't see his features, couldn't make out anything except the vague outline of his face, but I imagined his eyes were as intense as they always were.

"I think it's worth it," he said after a moment. "What do you think?"

The ambitious, dedicated, career-oriented side of me who'd worked through four years of college and a decade and a half in the Navy knew damn well this wasn't worth what I was risking. The side of me who'd spent way too much time with Eric, and who'd been alone far too long before that, disagreed.

I turned away long enough to twist my beer bottle into the sand. With my hands free, I faced him again and reached for the side of his neck. "I don't know," I said, leaning closer. "All I know is that I want you." I barely grazed his lips with mine. "I probably want you more than I should. I just don't care."

"Neither do I." He cupped the back of my neck and kissed me.

The kiss went on. Deepened. Still went on. We wrapped our arms around each other and moved closer, letting skin touch skin as we kissed tenderly, lazily.

Eric lay back, drawing me down with him, and we landed softly on the towel. I leaned down and kissed his neck. His skin was still salty from the ocean, but the faintest hints of his familiar scent teased goose bumps to life on my back and arms.

My chin grazed his collarbone, and he shivered, digging his fingers into my shoulders. When he squirmed beneath me, his erection brushed mine through our shorts.

"Oh God..." He whimpered softly. "Tell me we still have condoms."

"Of course we do." I raised my head and kissed him. "You're not tired from that last go-around, then? Or the last swim?"

"Are you?"

"Not even close."

"Good." He kissed me and ground his hips against mine. "Neither am I."

We took off our swim trunks, and then Eric handed me a condom. I couldn't get it on fast enough, and thank God he had the presence of mind to put some lube in his hand so it was ready to stroke onto my cock the second the condom was in place.

Once I was on my back, Eric straddled me, and I held his hip in one hand and my cock in the other as he lowered himself onto me. Biting my lip, I arched my back, the sand shifting beneath the towel. Christ, he felt amazing.

"This count as sex on the beach?" he asked.

"Close enough," I said. "It's sex with you; that's all I care about."

"Ditto." He came down to kiss me, and I wrapped my arms around him.

Sex on the beach, sex on the moon, I didn't give a fuck. I

was deep inside him, our bodies moving together like they were made for this, and it just didn't get any better than this.

"Fuck..." He pushed himself up on his arms and rode me faster. The wind tried to carry away his whispered curses, but then he threw his head back and groaned, and I swore his voice carried for miles. Let everyone hear him. I didn't care. Let them hear both of us.

I gripped his arms and screwed my eyes shut, thrusting up into him, my hips moving in sync with his, and I thought I heard myself begging him not to stop, or maybe it was him, because I could barely catch my breath at all, never mind speak, and my whole body shook and tingled and—

"Oh God, Oh God, *fuck*..." I grabbed his hips and pulled him down onto my cock, and both our voices echoed into the stillness of the night as I came, and he came, and we both shuddered together.

Eric slumped over me. He panted, but that didn't stop him from finding my lips with his and trying to kiss. Though my limbs were heavy, my body already getting lethargic after such a powerful orgasm, I wrapped my arms around him and returned his gentle, breathless kiss.

"I have to say," he whispered, letting our lips brush, "coming out to this island? *Awesome* idea."

"Hmm." I touched his face and raised my head to kiss him. "You know? I think I'm inclined to agree."

When Eric and I stepped off the boat, I hoped the owner took my slight stumble onto the dock as a lack of sea legs. No Navy man would want to admit to being unsteady on the waves, but at least that would mean the guy didn't catch on to my lingering unsteadiness from having sex with Eric.

After we'd carried everything up the boat ramp, we both loaded our gear into the trunks of our cars. I slammed the lid and looked at Eric.

"Want to grab something to eat?"

"Definitely," he said. "You know any places near here, or

should we head back up north?"

"There's a little town not far from here. Great place for soba." *And staying out a little longer than we probably should, but I just don't fucking care.*

He seemed to chew on the idea for a moment. "And this is someplace where people won't see us?"

"Just the locals, who won't care one way or the other."

Another moment of mulling it over. Then he nodded. "Okay, yeah. I'll follow you."

My car groaned all the way up the steep hill from the dock to the highway. Eric's probably did too. These little piece-of-shit cars were not made for some of the hills and mountains on Okinawa.

At the top of the hill, a right turn would have taken us back up north to Kadena and White Beach, but I turned left, and Eric followed.

This was one of the more rural areas of Okinawa. Truthfully, almost anything outside Naha, Nago, or the areas immediately surrounding the main bases qualified as rural. Down below us, small fishing boats lined concrete docks beside heaps of drying fishnets, and as the highway wound up into the hills, small houses dotted the heavily forested terrain between farms and clusters of concrete, turtle-shell-shaped tombs. Farther inland, three white wind turbines towered over the hillside, carving lazily spinning shadows over sugarcane fields, banana trees and dragonfruit farms.

It was hard to believe one of the bloodiest battles of World War II's Pacific Theatre had occurred here. Most of this area, even more so than the northern half of the island, had been razed. The plants had grown back, the buildings had been reconstructed, and if I didn't know the history, I never would have guessed a battle, never mind a decisive and destructive one like that, had occurred here.

Thirty minutes or so after we left the boat launch, I pulled into a mostly empty parking lot beside two rows of shops. I hadn't been down to Itoman in a while and had been meaning to come here anyway. I wasn't at all worried about anyone seeing us here; this was another place where the only Americans I'd ever seen were the ones I'd brought with me.

We wandered past the shops in search of a place to eat.

Across the street from one shop, an elderly Japanese woman sold small bouquets of flowers from a tiny wooden booth. People purchased the bouquets, then disappeared up a wide concrete path that led into a park.

Eric nodded toward it. "What's going on over there?"

"That's the Himeyuri Peace Memorial," I said. "Want to check it out?"

"Sure, why not?"

I dug out three hundred yen and handed it to the woman selling flowers. She gave us each a small arrangement, and Eric and I started up the path.

"So, what's the deal with the flowers?" he asked.

"You'll see."

The path wound past several small monuments and shrines, most of which were inscribed in kanji. One placard was written in English, detailing what had happened here and the purpose of the peace park, but we didn't stop to read it. Having been here twice before, I'd concluded that the memorial had a greater impact if someone saw it first, *then* learned the significance behind it.

At the end of the path was a concrete monument. It was inscribed with kanji that I didn't understand and stood behind the wide mouth of a cavern entrance that went straight down into the earth. The cavern entrance was probably ten or twelve feet across, encircled by a few stone shrines and a waist-high fence. And in front of the fence was a black granite altar on which dozens of flower arrangements like the ones we carried had been laid.

Eric and I were, like most people gathered around the memorial, silent. We approached the altar, and I put my flowers on top of the others. Eric followed suit, both of us making sure we'd placed ours facing the same direction as the rest.

Then we stepped back so others could add theirs.

I gave Eric a minute or two to absorb the somberness of the

memorial. There weren't a lot of people here today—the first time I came, the flowers were piled three feet high—but it wasn't deserted. Some people spoke amongst themselves in hushed tones. Some read the kanji with grim expressions. An elderly Japanese man closed his eyes, rested his elbows on the railing, and bowed his head behind clasped hands.

Without being able to read or understand Japanese, it was impossible to discern what exactly this was all about from the memorial alone. Still, the solemn atmosphere had a palpable thrum to it, that distinct sense that *something* had happened here.

Eric turned to me, and when he spoke, kept his voice low. "What exactly is this?"

I gestured toward the cave. "The cave was used as a makeshift hospital by the Japanese army during World War II. They conscripted a couple hundred Okinawan high school students, made them work down there in the most unbelievable conditions, and then when the Americans closed in? Shoved the kids out into the line of fire."

Eric blinked. "Are...you serious?"

I nodded. "Killed most of them. I think twenty or so out of over two hundred survived. It was unbelievably horrific."

"Yeah, sounds like it." He turned toward the memorial again, eyes wide, and I thought he whispered, "Jesus..."

Then, just as I did when I came here the first time, he shifted his gaze from the cave to the people standing around us. He looked from one person to the next, his posture stiffening a little more as he undoubtedly realized we were the only Americans in sight.

He swallowed. "Um, should we, you know, be here?"

"Yeah, it's fine. As long as we're respectful, people have no problem with us being here." I pursed my lips. "In fact, it irritates the hell out of me that you never see any Americans here. Ask around on base, and I guarantee most of them have never even heard of the place." Rolling my eyes, I added, "Live on a major World War II site, don't even bother to visit the battlefields or anything."

"Does that surprise you?" he said softly but with a note of sarcasm. "Most people can barely be persuaded to leave base. Forget coming all the way down here for a little bit of history."

"No shit," I muttered. I gestured to the left, toward a tile-roofed building with glass double doors between a pair of terra cotta Shi Shi dogs. "There's a visitor center and museum up there if you want to check it out. It's fascinating."

He glanced at it, then looked at me. "You want to?"

I shook my head. "I've already been through it twice. More than enough, believe me." I shuddered. "But if you want to..."

He looked at it again, chewing his lip, probably weighing his desire to go through it against his desire to stick together.

I nudged him gently with my elbow. "Go ahead. It only takes a half hour or so to go through it."

Turning to me, he said, "You don't mind?"

"Not at all. It's worth going through." I paused, then added, "*Once*."

He shrugged. "Sure, I'll check it out. What's the admission charge?"

"It's not much. Maybe five hundred yen. Do you have enough on you?"

"Oh, yeah, I have plenty."

"All right." I gestured back down the path that had brought us up here. "I'll meet you back at the shop we passed. The one with all the Shi Shi dogs in the window."

While he went into the museum, I returned to the safety of the twin rows of shops. I'd been meaning to come down here and get some souvenirs, T-shirts and Japanese candy for my kids anyway, so that was something I could take care of while he checked out Himeyuri.

I wasn't kidding when I told him twice was more than enough. The only other museum that had ever had a similar effect on me was the Holocaust Museum in DC. What had happened here was significantly smaller in scale, of course, but both museums left me off-balance and in dire need of a drink.

And I was off-balance enough today without an emotional sucker punch on top of it.

I shook my head and kept walking. I went into one of the shops in search of things to send to the kids. Looking at T-shirts, I realized I needed to ask Katie what size they wore now. No point in buying any clothes for them until I knew, so T-shirts would have to wait.

Shi Shi dogs were always a winner with the kids. I'd sent them countless pairs of the dog statues that guarded every gate and doorway on Okinawa, and the twins always begged me to send more. Fortunately, the statues came in every possible shape and size, from an inch tall to waist high—which was a little big to ship home—and in everything from terra cotta to glazed ceramic. So I perused the shelves of Shi Shis, my mind only half focused on picking out a couple of pairs for Jason and Jessica.

After I'd found some, I moved on to another shelf, where I picked up a box of shortbread cookies. I absently held it up like I was reading the back of it. I could read some kanji but not enough to understand everything written on the label. Even if I were completely fluent, though, my mind wasn't on the arrangement of Japanese characters describing the contents of the box. All I could think about was Eric. And I was thinking about him like I had no business thinking about him.

A knot tightened in my gut.

You're asking for it, Connelly.

I was. I really was.

Eric had been right to hesitate over going out together like this, but maybe not for the reason he thought. We avoided Americans, kept it all platonic in public and had cover stories at the ready in case we bumped into someone we knew. We had the stealth thing down pat.

But time together meant conversations. Conversations meant finding out all the little things we had in common, like photography, a love of history and the same taste in wine. Little things in common meant more to talk about, which meant more conversations. Even when we snorkeled and could only communicate with gestures, we were undeniably together. We didn't just stay close and keep an eye on each other in the name of safety while we each did our own thing. If I found something cool like an eel or an octopus, I didn't have to get his attention from ten, twenty, thirty feet away, because he was right there beside me.

So we had similar interests. We were friends. Daytime friends and nighttime lovers, as the old country song said.

Well, except I caught myself wondering if day and night were starting to bleed together. The friendly banter continued after the sun went down, and it followed us into the bedroom. The intimacy of the night showed itself in daylight with the occasional look, the banter that was dangerously close to flirting, and those moments when I *almost* forgot myself and touched him.

And that intimacy had followed us to Komaka Island yesterday, which was what had me off-balance and half out of my mind. Sure, we'd fucked on the beach, and it was pure lust that had driven us, but last night? No, that wasn't just lust.

We didn't even make it into the water this morning. We'd had every intention of another round of snorkeling before the boat came to get us. When we'd put our wet suits back on, we meant to go back in the water but didn't get that far. A light kiss became a longer one, and we sank back onto our beach towels and kissed for the better part of a lazy, sensual hour like we wanted nothing more than to just touch and taste each other. That was until we moved back into our tent, stripped out of our wet suits again and slowly, gently, tenderly fucked each other blind.

"*Samosen?*" *Excuse me?* A woman's voice startled me back into the present.

I looked up from the box in my hand. The woman cocked her head, and I wondered how long she'd been standing there trying to get my attention. I cleared my throat. "I, um…*gomenasai*, I…" Then I just smiled and waved a hand. "*Daijobu. Arigato.*" *I'm fine. Thank you.*

She gave me a politely skeptical look but then bowed and left me to my distraction. After she'd gone, I exhaled hard and rubbed the back of my neck.

Jesus, what was wrong with me?

Right. Like I didn't know exactly what was wrong.

Forcing Eric out of my mind, I tucked the box of cookies under my arm and continued looking for things to send home.

About thirty minutes after we separated at the memorial, Eric walked into the shop. He looked about as shell-shocked as I felt after going through that museum.

"Man," he said. "I thought the Underground Headquarters was a headfuck."

"Yeah, there's nothing quite like standing right there where it happened and finding out how bad it really was."

"No shit," he said quietly.

Eric was a history buff like me, but he wasn't just a facts-and-figures man. Dates and statistics were interesting to a point, but Eric was one of those people who actually grasped the magnitude of things. At the Underground Headquarters, when he stood in a small room that had deep pockmarks in all the walls, he'd paled when he read the clumsily translated placard: *Wall Riddled With a Hand-Grenade When Committed Suicide*. But then, we'd both been to war zones. Guys who'd been to the Sandbox either compartmentalized everything and refused to emotionally connect with things like this, or they understood it on a profound, too-close-to-home level. I empathized with the former—there was only so much room in a man's head for the things we'd seen—but I related to the latter. And Eric fell very firmly into that category.

Like I needed another reason to be addicted to the man.

As we wandered through the shop, finding souvenirs for our kids, I kept stealing glances at him. After Komaka Island and the way I'd been so distracted while he wasn't here, I was even more hard-pressed to pretend that things between us were the same as they'd been in the beginning. Back when we actually convinced ourselves we could be lovers at night and friends during the day.

A knot of apprehension twisted in my gut. There probably wasn't an American within five miles of us right now, but I was irrationally certain someone would see the way I looked at him.

Or that, whenever we exchanged glances, electricity would visibly arc between us and give us away.

Shaking my head, I focused on browsing through Okinawa souvenirs. And glancing at Eric. And browsing through—glancing at Eric.

No one knows, I told myself. *No one will know unless we tell them.*

As long as no one asked, I wouldn't tell. No one would ask, because no one knew. No one knew about the secret excursions, the passionate nights behind closed doors or the fact that my feelings for him were starting to run much deeper than they had any right to. No one knew.

But I did.

Chapter Seventeen

Eric

Pacing outside baggage claim at Naha International, I glanced at the clock above the reader board.

2257.

My daughter's flight had been delayed a few times, but it was due to land any minute. Then I just had to wait for Marie to deplane, pick up her luggage and come through the glass double doors dividing the waiting area from baggage claim.

A sparse crowd milled around the terminal, everyone throwing glances at the reader boards and baggage claim. This was probably the heaviest concentration of Americans I'd ever seen off base. Most Americans flying commercially came in on either this flight or the next one, so friends, family and sponsors actually left the safety of their bases and ventured into Naha to pick people up.

Normally, I'd have had her take a military flight to save money, but she needed to be back in the States by a certain date to start a summer internship, and military flights were about as reliable as doomsday predictions.

I glanced at my watch for the hundredth time, then looked up at the list of incoming flights. Still another fifteen minutes before the plane landed.

I wandered over to the fish tank. From here, I could still see the doors but at least had some sea creatures to hold my attention so I'd stop staring at the clock.

A moray eel stuck its head out of a crevice, opening and closing its jaws as the other fish swam past. It was probably twice the size of the ones I'd seen while out snorkeling, but if we ran into something like that out in the water, I had no doubt Shane would be waving his glove in its face. I chuckled to myself.

The ten-foot-cubed tank held my attention for a while. The fish were cool to watch but not nearly as fun as when I was actually swimming with them. I wondered if we'd ever see an eel that big. So far, we'd seen a few decent-sized ones, but the fucker in this aquarium looked like he could nip someone's arm off with minimal effort. Especially if someone like Shane gave him the opportunity.

A voice came over the loudspeaker. Though I didn't understand much of what she said, the flight number caught my attention. People started moving toward the double doors, and my heart beat a little faster. The plane must have been unloading now, so I left the fish to their tank and joined everyone else by the doors.

Moments later, on the other side, passengers started coming down the ramp, looking exhausted and dragging wheeled carry-on suitcases behind them. I fidgeted, shifting my weight and willing myself to be patient, as one person after the other appeared.

Then, after a seemingly endless line of unfamiliar faces, my daughter came into view. I smiled and waved at her, and she waved back.

While she waited for her bag, I inched toward the door. She picked everything up, started toward the door, but had to pause to let some people ahead of her wrangle a couple of large bags through the door. As she patiently waited, I just stared at her. My God, she looked more like her mother every time I saw her. She even wore her blonde hair in a messy ponytail like Sara often did. When had my kid turned into an adult, for crying out loud?

The people in front of her finally got out of the way, and she hurried past them.

"Hi, Daddy!" Marie squealed. She dropped her bags and threw her arms around me, almost knocking me backward.

"Hey, kiddo." I closed my eyes and held on to her for a moment. I hadn't expected to get choked up just greeting her off the plane, but...damn.

When I was sure I could keep my composure, I loosened my embrace. "So, how was your flight?"

She groaned. "*Long.*"

"Uh, yeah. What did you expect?"

"Nothing less." She picked up her bag. "I'm so sick of airports. Let's get out of here."

"Good idea." I paused. "Do you have a T-shirt on under that sweatshirt?"

"Yeah, why?"

"You might want to take off the sweatshirt before we leave, or you're going to melt."

She raised an eyebrow. "It's eleven at night. Isn't it?"

"It is, but this is Okinawa." I gestured over my shoulder with my thumb. "It's about eighty degrees out right now, and the humidity's unreal. Trust me."

She shrugged and set her bag down. She took off her sweatshirt, tied it around her waist, and we headed out. As soon as we stepped outside, she coughed.

"Oh my God," she sputtered. "It *is* humid."

I laughed. "You'll get used to it."

In the parking garage, after we'd put her luggage in the trunk, she started toward the right side of the car, just like I did when I arrived.

"Other side," I said.

"What?" She looked in the car. "Oh, right. I forgot."

We both got in on the correct sides. After I'd paid for the parking space, I followed the confusing-as-hell curving road out of the airport to the highway.

"So aside from long," I said as we continued into Naha, "how was your trip?"

"Well, the in-flight movies were torture."

I snorted. "Let me guess. They weren't Cannes or Sundance material?"

She wrinkled her nose. "They wouldn't have shown those films in the Porta-Potties at Sundance or Cannes."

"Snob."

"Yeah. What of it?"

I laughed. "Nothing at all."

"So, while I'm here," she said, grinning, "do I get to meet your mysterious boyfriend?"

My cheeks burned, though I wasn't quite sure why. "Yes, you do. In fact, we're going snorkeling with him this weekend, assuming you're up for it."

"Up for it? Of course I am."

"Yeah, well," I said. "Let's see how jet-lagged you are before we throw you in the water."

"As long as I at least get to meet this guy."

"So you can approve of him?"

"Damn right."

I chuckled. "Well, I'll tell him to be on his best behavior. God forbid he doesn't get the Marie Randall Seal of Approval."

"Well, if he doesn't," she said with an apologetic shrug, "we'll just have to hide the body and never speak of him again."

"Did you bring a shovel?"

"They wouldn't let me put it in my carry-on."

We exchanged glances and both cracked up.

I patted her leg. "Good to have you here, kid."

"Do you actually know where we're going?"

"I beg your pardon?" I threw Marie a glare, then shifted my attention back to Highway 58.

"It's a valid question, Dad."

"Okay, I've never been there myself," I said. "But Shane gave me directions, and he's been there plenty of times."

"You've been to Uncle Brett's house plenty of times," she said. "And your directions still got me lost."

"Not my fault you weren't paying attention."

"Says the man who used a sign the size of a walnut as a landmark."

I laughed. "Whatever. We'll find this place. If not, I'll call him."

"Okay, I'll take your word for it."

The highway followed the west coast of Okinawa from Naha up to Nago, the other major city, and then, if we were inclined to keep following it, on to Cape Hedo, the northernmost point of the island.

To our left, the East China Sea was bright blue and sparkling. The swells were a little high today for snorkeling, and there were a few whitecaps, but Shane had said the place we were going was completely sheltered.

"Only way you'll find big waves there," he'd said over the phone last night, "is if you go during a typhoon."

There was sure as hell no reason to worry about a typhoon right now. A gentle wind ruffled the palm, banana and banyan trees, and colorful kanji-inscribed banners fluttered above shops and restaurants. There wasn't a cloud in the sky, and the Okinawan sun was intense. Marie and I both had on sunglasses, and it wasn't to look cool.

Once we'd passed through Nago, Marie picked up the printed e-mail in which Shane had given us directions.

"After Nago, you'll pass an inlet on your left," she read. "Look for a stoplight with a Family Mart on the left and a blue sign overhead that says Kouri Island. Turn left." She lowered the paper. "Okay, I've seen about four billion Family Marts in the last half mile. How the hell is that a landmark? That's like telling someone to turn at the palm tree." She gestured outside at the twin rows of palm trees on either side of the highway.

"Yeah, but there's a sign for Kouri Island," I said. "You don't see those every ten feet."

"Mm-hmm." She sounded dubious, and I couldn't help chuckling.

I drove through a small town just after Nago. As the town faded behind us, a broad expanse of calm, sheltered water glittered in the sun to our left. Unlike the open ocean we'd seen for miles, the water was glass smooth.

"This must be the inlet he was talking about," I said. "Look for a...stoplight and Family Mart?"

"So he says."

Up ahead, a stoplight came into view, and there was a blue sign overhead. We'd seen several of those along the way, usually announcing in both English and Japanese that a particular town or road was coming up. Among the points noted on the sign was Kouri Island.

"See?" I gestured at the sign. "He didn't lead us astray."

"Not yet," she said. "There's still plenty of directions on—oh, hey, there's the Family Mart."

"So it is." I put on my turn signal and went left at the light and the Family Mart. "Now what?"

"Now it says to drive for eight clicks—what the hell is a click?"

I laughed. "Kilometer. Don't judge him. He's military. Anyway, go on."

"Okay, so eight 'clicks' until you reach a stop sign. Turn left."

"Any mention of a Family Mart?"

"No, Dad. No mention of a Family Mart."

This was truly the countryside of Okinawa. Sugarcane fields sprawled over hills and valleys. Farmers—from young to very, very old—hunched over wheelbarrows and shovels, their faces shielded from the sun by pointed straw hats. An elderly man on a bicycle that was probably as old as he was peddled up a hill like he was unaware of the huge bundles of sugarcane stacked on the back of the bike.

After roughly eight kilometers, we came to the stop sign in question. I turned left, and the road curved between a cluster of banana trees and palms.

"He says to turn right at the sign for Kouri Island," she said. "Then take the long bridge across to Kouri, make the first right, and pull into the first parking lot on the right."

"Simple enough."

We crested the hill, and both the bridge and the island came into view.

Marie leaned forward, staring at the gorgeous view. "Wow. I can see why we're swimming here."

"No kidding," I said, glancing at the water as much as I

could without running off the road.

The bridge was almost perfectly straight, held up on pylons above the turquoise water and leading to a strip of white sand and a couple of concrete breakwaters at the edge of a heavily forested island. The entire island was maybe a kilometer end to end and looked virtually uninhabited aside from a small resort, a couple of tiny buildings and some tombs tucked between a field or two and the thick forest.

Following Shane's directions, I turned at the end of the bridge, then pulled into a parking lot that was part grass, part crumbling concrete, and part sand. Shane's car was nosed up to a cement barrier dividing the lot from the beach, so I took the space beside it.

As we unloaded the car, footsteps turned my head, and my heart skipped as Shane came around the corner. He already had on his wet suit, which never failed to throw my pulse out of whack, and though I couldn't see his eyes through his sunglasses, his grin threw my balance off just like it always did.

"So I didn't get you too lost?" he asked.

"No, you didn't get us lost." I gestured at Marie. "Shane, this is my daughter, Marie. Marie, Shane."

"Nice to meet you," he said as they shook hands.

"You too." She smiled. "I was starting to wonder if you were just Dad's imaginary friend."

Shane laughed. "No, I'm plenty real." He nodded toward our gear. "You guys need a hand with all of this?"

"I think we've got most of it." I hoisted a backpack onto my shoulder. "Though if you can grab the two chairs, that would help."

"No problem."

He picked up the folded beach chairs and also took the umbrellas. Marie and I picked up as much as we could carry and followed him to the beach.

"Nice going, Dad," she said under her breath.

"What?"

"He's hot."

"*Marie.*"

"I'm just saying..."

From the corner of my mouth, I said, "Stop ogling my boyfriend."

"Not my fault you like hot guys."

I glared at her.

"What?" She shrugged. "It's not like he's my stepdad."

"Uh-huh."

She snickered and adjusted her snorkel bag on her shoulder. We followed Shane to the beach and set up our chairs, cooler and umbrellas beside his.

Marie looked around. "Is it safe to just leave all this stuff here while we're swimming?"

"Oh, hell yeah," Shane said. "You could leave your wallet out in plain sight around here, and no one would touch it."

"Guess this isn't exactly New York City," she said quietly. "But I'll pass on leaving my wallet out."

"Smart girl," I said.

Shane smirked. "She gets that from her mother, then?"

"Oh, very funny," I said.

Marie laughed. "God, you two are *so* cut out for each other."

Chuckling, I rolled my eyes. "Great. Glad you approve."

Once we'd set everything up, put on wet suits and had our gear ready to go, we hit the water.

Shane was right about Kouri Island. The visibility was unreal. Unlike Komaka Island, Kouri was fully sheltered from the open ocean, with virtually no waves to speak of, and all three of us navigated the gentle current with ease.

Aside from the massive concrete pylons beneath the bridge, the area was mostly sand and underwater vegetation rather than rocks and reefs. Still, there was plenty of interesting sea life. Out in the open water, colorful tropical fish eyed us warily while crabs—hermit and otherwise—skittered along miniature dunes and darted down into holes between sea cucumbers and sea stars.

In the slightly deeper water near the first pylon, we found a large sea anemone occupied by black-and-orange clownfish.

They were aggressive little fuckers too. When Marie and I swam in to get a closer look, a few of them lunged at us, bonking into our masks and nipping at our gloves. Naturally, Shane couldn't resist playing with them. Funny, none of us knew clownfish could bite, but apparently they could. Of course, the bite was toothless and painless, but it made Shane laugh, which is never a good idea with a snorkel. Personally, I thought the mouthful of salt water served him right for pissing off the clownfish in the first place.

Once Shane had finished coughing and clearing his snorkel, we moved on to the bridge pylon. Out here, the water was a good fifteen feet deep, and the pylon was about ten-by-twenty feet of solid concrete that was covered with those huge black sea urchins, colorful branches of coral and some shellfish I couldn't identify. A pair of lionfish, one of which was almost as big as a medium-sized cat, swam amongst the urchins' spines.

And at the bottom of the pylon, huddled between a few chunks of broken concrete, was an octopus, which was cool as hell. That was something we didn't encounter often, and had it not been quite so far down, and had one of the rather poisonous lionfish not been swimming just above it, even I might have gone down for a closer look.

As it was, the current was stronger out here than it was elsewhere. With that many urchins and the pair of lionfish hanging around, we decided not to stay by the pylon too much longer.

We swam on, riding the current until we reached a shallower, calmer area.

As we explored, I threw occasional glances in Marie's direction. She was a strong swimmer and had a good head on her shoulders, so I wasn't worried about her doing something stupid or not being able to handle the current. Anything could happen, though. I preferred to err on the side of keeping an eye on her just in case.

As we swam past a broad expanse of lazily waving sea grass, I looked at her as I'd done a hundred times already. She cruised along, checking out the scenery and searching for sea life, and—

My heart skipped.

Rippling between her fins was a three-foot-long ribbon of alternating black-and-white bands, and there was no mistaking that distinctive pattern.

A sea snake.

Intellectually, I knew they weren't aggressive creatures like the habu on land, but they were highly venomous, which meant, aggressive or not, that one was *way* too close to my kid.

Movement caught my eye, and when I turned, I realized Shane was swimming toward Marie.

And he was taking off his glove.

My throat tightened. *Shane, my God, if you tease that thing when it's that close to her...*

While I watched, Shane fell in behind her and approached slowly. She was completely oblivious to him. Diving masks meant limited peripheral vision, so she wouldn't have seen him coming.

He swam up beside her, staying a few feet to her right. Then, he held out his glove, keeping it a foot or so below the surface, and slowly waved it back and forth.

The snake went from a long ribbon to something like a messy figure eight or an ampersand. When it straightened again, it dipped downward and cut through the water toward Shane.

The snake approached Shane warily, but kept its distance. Then, apparently realizing the man was crazy, it swam off in a different direction and slipped into the tall sea grass.

Away from Shane. Even farther away from Marie.

I exhaled.

Maybe there was an advantage to the man's fearlessness around dangerous animals.

We continued swimming. Eventually, we all got out of the water and went back to where we'd set up our stuff on the beach. We dropped our gear unceremoniously in the sand and sank into our chairs.

"That was some amazing snorkeling." Marie poured some

sunscreen into her hand. "I think this place is going to ruin me for swimming anywhere else."

"You ain't kiddin'," Shane said.

I chuckled. "Yeah, assuming something doesn't kill any of us."

"I know, right?" Marie slathered sunscreen on her arm. "Is *everything* on this island poisonous?"

"Everything except the spiders and the bats," Shane said.

"The spiders aren't?" She glanced at him.

He shook his head. "You'd think they would be. They're huge, though. Motherfuckers are—" He stopped abruptly and looked at me with a sheepish expression. "Sorry."

"Oh, I don't fucking care," Marie said with a dismissive gesture.

"Marie." I gave her a disapproving look over my sunglasses.

"Whatever, Dad. I learned most of it from you."

"And the rest from your mother, I'm sure."

"That and rap music." She put the back of her hand to her forehead and sighed dramatically. "All those curse words. Rap music has stolen my innocence, Daddy."

I tried to keep a somewhat stern face, but when Shane muffled a laugh, I couldn't help it.

"Anyway," he said, still chuckling, "the spiders here are huge, but they won't hurt you. Unlike the fish, snails, snakes..." He waved a hand. "Pretty much everything."

"Sort of like that sea snake that was following you around," I said.

Marie glanced up, and when she looked at me, she jumped like she hadn't realized I'd been talking to her. "What sea snake?"

"The one that was between your fins," Shane said.

She pursed her lips and shook her head. "Yeah, whatever."

"He's not kidding," I said. "I was ready to choke him because I thought he was coming over to play with the damned thing."

Shane sniffed. "Oh, come on. I'm crazy, but you didn't

really think I'd get something to bite her, did you?"

"Well, no," I said. "But I have to admit, it would have been nice to be able to read your mind when you started chasing after it and taking your glove off like you always do when you're going to harass something."

"Wait, wait, wait." Marie capped the sunscreen and tossed it on top of a snorkel bag. "You guys aren't kidding?"

We both shook our heads.

"It wouldn't have bothered you," Shane said. "I was just concerned you'd turn around and see it, then panic, scare it and wind up bitten."

"Panic?" She raised an eyebrow. "Do I really strike you as a girl who's afraid of snakes?"

He laughed. "Not in the least. But they're a little disconcerting when they're between your fins. Even I've about jumped out of my skin when I've seen one following me like that."

"Wimp," she muttered. "So you scared it off. Damn it, Shane. What if I'd wanted to play with it?"

I gave an exasperated sigh and rolled my eyes. "Jesus Christ. I knew it would be dangerous to introduce you two."

Shane shrugged. "Well, at least I didn't tease the octopus. Those things are poisonous too."

"Octopus?" Marie sat up. "What octopus?"

He pointed at the bridge. "Up against the second pylon. We pointed it out to you."

She furrowed her brow. "You pointed out the lionfish."

"No, I was pointing out the octopus," I said. "If you needed me to point out a lionfish, then it's no wonder you didn't see the octopus."

"Ha-ha, very funny."

"It's probably still out there." Shane took a drink and set his water bottle in the sand. "They don't move around much."

"Show me, then." Marie picked up her mask and snorkel.

"All right." He grabbed his own gear and looked at me. "You coming?"

I eyed him. "Are you planning on pestering the poor

creature?"

"Define pestering," Marie said.

I groaned. "Oh God. No way am I letting you two go out there by yourselves."

I picked up my gear.

Laughter dragged me out of a sound sleep.

Apparently oblivious to me, Shane and Marie continued with their conversation.

"No, Cronenberg completely owns Lynch," Marie said.

"Pfft." Shane laughed. "Not a chance."

"So if I go look online," she said, throwing him a challenging look, "After I go verify that Cronenberg had the balls to film *eXistenZ* and *Crash*, I won't go look under Lynch's filmography and see crap heaps like *Mulholland Drive* and *Dune*?"

"Hey. Hey. We don't speak of *Mulholland Drive*."

"We do when you're trying to call Lynch a better director than Cronenberg."

I blinked a few times, lifting my head off Shane's shoulder to stretch a kink out of my neck. "What are you two going on about?"

"Hey, you decided to join us." Shane ran his fingers through my hair.

"What can I say?" I rubbed my eyes. "I was tired from keeping up with the two of you all damned day."

"You're just old." Marie playfully nudged me with her elbow. "Come on, Dad, I'm the one who's jet-lagged, and you were out cold before the opening credits finished." She gestured at the TV, where end-credits scrolled up the screen.

I chuckled. "Well, it sounds like you two did just fine on your own."

"We did," Shane said. "But I'm disappointed you haven't properly indoctrinated your child into the world of David Lynch. She seems to have this delusion that he's inferior to Cronenberg."

I blinked. Looked at her. Back to him. "Who is inferior to who?"

Shane rolled his eyes.

Marie groaned and let her face fall into her hand. "Dad. God."

"Sorry, baby," I said with a tired shrug. "You know I'm not the film snob you are."

"Yeah, that's obvious."

Shane laughed.

Shaking my head, I said, "I don't know how the two of you even pick movies based on their directors. I couldn't begin to tell you who directed this one." I gestured at the TV.

"That's because you fell asleep before it started," he said. "Do you even know what movie we were watching?"

I furrowed my brow but drew a blank. "Now that you mention it, no."

Marie released an exasperated sigh. "Dad, we need to get *Crash* and *eXistenZ* so you can watch them and explain to your boyfriend how awesome they are."

"Um. Okay…"

Shane nudged me. "Just make sure you pick up some Lynch for a palate cleanser."

I laughed. Patting his leg, I said, "You know, if I'd known you were into films like this, I'd have warned you my kid is working on getting into film school."

Shane's eyebrows jumped. To Marie, he said, "Is that right? Doing what?"

"I don't know yet. I kind of want to try everything. Directing, screenwriting, maybe some pyrotechnics."

"Pyrotechnics?" Shane and I said in unison.

Shane laughed. "Wow. Here I thought you were a bona fide film connoisseur, if one with questionable taste, and now you're talking about blowing things up."

"Well," she said with a shrug. "There are films out there that could arguably be improved by a few explosions."

He cocked his head. "Such as?"

Marie smirked and looked him right in the eye. “Anything by David Lynch.”

Chapter Eighteen

Shane

After two solid days of showing Eric's daughter as many sights as we could without collapsing from sheer exhaustion, the three of us decided to kick back at his place for the evening.

"So, you're going to film school?" I asked Marie as we made dinner in Eric's kitchen.

She nodded. "Hopefully. I'm trying to get a scholarship to NYU, but I'd be fine with Vancouver Film School too."

"Ambitious," I said with a nod. To Eric, I said, "And you and her mom are on board with this?"

"Absolutely," he said. "It's what she wants to do. She's had her eye on Hollywood since she was a kid, so..."

"And you know what he got me for my fifteenth birthday?" Marie asked.

I shook my head.

She grinned from ear to ear. "He took me to the Sundance Film Festival."

My jaw dropped, and I looked at Eric. "Are you serious?"

"Are you kidding?" He laughed. "She'd been talking about how bad she wanted to go for like three years. Seemed like a no-brainer."

To Marie, I said, "So how was it?"

"Oh." She clasped her hands over her heart and sighed. "It was *amazing*." Then she giggled behind her hand. "Especially when Dad got all starstruck over Robert Redford."

"What?" Eric threw her a horrified look, but the color in his cheeks gave him away. "I most certainly did not."

"Yes, you did." She turned to me. "Redford walks out of a restaurant, and Dad was about this close to being a squealy fangirl."

"Uh-huh," Eric said. "This from the girl who turned into a stuttering mess when someone said some director or another was in a building the next block over."

I laughed. "You know, most teenage girls get starry-eyed over actors, not directors."

"Yeah," Eric said. "But most teenage girls don't have a DVD collection where almost every movie has subtitles." He paused. "And you should see the movies she and her friends have made in school. Some of them are absolutely hilarious."

"Is that right?" I asked.

Marie giggled. "Dad, you remember the one we made with zombies attacking Grandma's house?"

Eric laughed. "How could I forget?"

To me, she said, "Dad actually helped us choreograph the battle scenes and roped a few guys from the ship into volunteering to play the zombies."

"God." Eric shook his head. "You would not believe how much beer I had to buy after that."

"Oh, whatever." She waved a hand. "It was totally worth it, and you know it."

"Yeah, it was," he said. "That was a fun weekend. What about the romantic-comedy spoof?"

Marie laughed. "God, that was so ridiculous."

Eric looked at me. "She had her mother and me for one scene—"

"That's dedicated parenting," she said matter-of-factly. "Two divorced parents willing to act together in a romcom for their kid's school project."

I chuckled. "You really did that?"

"Yep," he said. "Her friends thought it would work because things would naturally be awkward between Sara and me."

"Uh-huh." Marie glared at her father. "So much for that. Damn you two for getting along."

He shrugged. "I never said we were the greatest actors in the world. Hey, did you guys ever finish that sci-fi thing you were working on?"

She shook her head. "Not yet. The SFX budget is a

bit…ambitious."

"Hmm." Eric pursed his lips. "Well, let me know if you need help with it." Then he threw her a pointed look. "Within reason. You're not getting Michael Bay's pyrotechnics budget."

"Damn it," she said.

"Sorry, honey," he said, chuckling. "I'm in the Navy. Not exactly made of money."

"But *Daddy*." She stomped her foot and folded her arms across her chest. "How am I supposed to knock Hollywood's socks off with a Navy SFX budget?"

"Sorry, princess," he said, and they both laughed.

I rested my hands on the counter. "Guess you'll just have to fall back on things like dialogue and plot to make a good movie."

She shifted her weight and sighed dramatically. "Oh, if I must."

"You must," Eric said. "Hey, you should show Shane some of the videos. You have them on your computer, right?"

"Yeah, I do." She looked at me. "Do you want to see them?"

"Heck yeah," I said. "I'm curious now."

"Okay, I'll go get my laptop." She left the kitchen.

Eric put his hands on my waist. "You know, it's a real shame the two of you don't get along."

"No kidding." I kissed him. "So does that mean you'll keep me around a little longer?"

"Oh, I suppose I could be persuaded," he said with a smile.

"I certainly hope so."

He grinned, then leaned in and kissed me again.

"Oh, Jesus." Marie's voice turned both our heads. "I leave you kids alone for five seconds, and you're all kissy-face."

Eric and I separated, both laughing.

"Whatever," he said. "Now fire up the movie so he can see what we were talking about."

"On it." She grinned. "Here, let's start with Mom and Dad trying to be awkward…"

Later that evening, after we'd eaten dinner and watched several of Marie's videos—which were *quite* impressive—we went into the living room to play some video games. I sat on one end of the couch. Eric lounged against me, his feet up on the other armrest.

Marie sat on the floor, leaning against the middle of the couch. Glancing up at us, she said, "So, isn't the whole point of a Wii to be more active while playing video games?"

"Sure." Eric concentrated on holding up his controller, aiming at the dartboard on the screen. He snapped his wrist forward, and the animated character threw his dart, which *just* missed the ring around the bull's-eye. "We're being active. Sort of."

"Uh-huh." I pulled a Dorito out of the bag on Eric's chest. "Active compared to, say, just staring at the TV."

"See?" Eric "threw" another dart. "Could be worse."

Marie clicked her tongue. "You two are such a horrible influence."

"What are you going to do about it?" Eric asked. "Tell your mom on me?"

"Maybe I will."

"Fine." He pulled a chip out of the bag "Then as punishment, she'll make me sell my car, which means—"

"Okay, okay." She put her hands up. "I won't tell Mom."

"I knew you'd see things my way."

"Whatever." She elbowed his leg. "Now quit hogging the chips, you two."

She reached for the bag, but Eric snatched it up and held it out of her reach.

"Nope, these are for adults."

Marie snorted. "Oh, right. You let me drink beer, but I can't eat Doritos?"

I laughed. "You let her drink beer?"

"I've let her *try* it," he said, lowering the bag so she could grab a handful of chips to refill the bowl sitting beside her. "Somehow, I don't think she'll be making a habit of it."

"Ugh." Marie wrinkled her nose. "Not a chance. Okay, whose turn is it?" She picked up a chip and crunched on it.

"I think it's Shane's turn, isn't it?" Eric looked at the screen. "Yep, all yours." He slid the wrist strap off and handed me the controller.

I took my turn, then passed the controller to Marie. It was easier when we each had one, but we'd burned through the batteries on the other two, so this was the best we could do until they finished charging for the hundredth time.

As we played, Marie and Eric teased each other, but I couldn't bring myself to throw in as many comments as I usually did.

For the last few days, as we'd spent more and more time together, a knot had slowly formed beneath my ribs. It wasn't that I was jealous of the attention Eric showed his daughter. Far from it. And I didn't feel like a third wheel at all; the three of us got along so well it was almost frightening.

But something bugged me, and I couldn't put my finger on it.

"Oh, hell yeah!" Marie held up her controller triumphantly as the dart landed square on the bull's-eye. "You're going *down*, old men."

"*Au contraire*, kiddo," Eric said. "Enjoy it while it lasts, because you're toast."

"Whatever, we'll—hey! That's cheating!" She smacked his leg, and he laughed. As she tried to focus on her throw again, he nudged the back of her head with his foot. "Shane, would you keep your man in line, please?"

I laughed. "I think you're overestimating my ability to keep him in line about as much as you're overestimating your ability to beat us 'old guys'."

She glared at me over her shoulder.

"Looks like you're outnumbered," Eric said, and I didn't have to look to know he had that devilish grin on his face.

Marie rolled her eyes. Turning back to the game, she muttered, "When you least expect it, Dad, I'm getting you back."

"Yeah," Eric said, "we'll see about that."

I had to give the girl credit. She had me convinced she'd let it go, that she'd forgotten about her dad trying to sabotage her game. Apparently she was just lying in wait, though, because several dozen throws later, when Eric was four points from beating us both, she made her move.

He raised the controller, furrowing his brow and focusing on the screen, and just when he made his throw, she smacked his leg, this time closed-fisted.

"Ow!" He sat up, putting his hand on his shin. "What the hell was—"

"Ha! You lose."

He stared at the screen, slack-jawed. The dart had hit the eighteen instead of the four, which pushed his score over the line and cost him the game. "Oh, now that's just playing dirty."

She batted her eyes at him. "Well, I did learn from the best."

He looked at me. "You see this abuse I take?"

I held up my hand, rubbing my thumb and forefinger together. "And this is the world's tiniest violin—"

"Oh, fuck you." He laughed and rolled his eyes.

"Daddy!" She scoffed, putting a hand over her mouth. "You shouldn't swear like that around me."

"Right, like you've never heard it before," he said.

She gave an indignant sniff. "You're going to warp my fragile little—"

Eric and I both burst out laughing.

"You know what?" she said. "Fuck you both."

Eric glared at her.

She put up her hands. "What? You say it, don't you?"

I patted his shoulder. "Father of the Year, right here."

Eric snorted. "Yeah, that'll be the day."

"No kidding." Marie chuckled as she stood and picked up her empty glass. "I'm going to get another drink before we start the next game."

As soon as she was gone, Eric sat up and put his hand on my arm. "Hey, you all right? You've been kind of quiet all evening."

I forced a smile. "I'm fine. Why?"

His eyebrows knitted together. "You sure?"

"Yeah." I leaned in and kissed him gently. "I probably should get going, though. *Some* of us have to work tomorrow."

He grinned. "And some of us get to sleep in and slack off for a few more days."

"Very funny." I kissed him again. "But seriously, I should get out of here."

He touched my face, and his brow furrowed a little. "You sure you're all right?"

I nodded. "I'm fine."

He eyed me skeptically but let it go, and we both got up just as Marie came back into the room.

"Well," I said. "You two have fun."

"Aww, you're leaving already?" she said.

"Yeah, I have to work in the morning." I gestured at her father. "Do me a favor and make sure you beat him soundly on every game tonight."

She touched her hand to her forehead in a mock salute. "I so will."

Eric snorted. "Yeah. We'll see about that."

"Bring it on, old man."

"Hey!" Eric and I both said.

She laughed. "Hey, if the shoe fits..."

"Yeah, yeah, whatever," I said.

I gave her a quick good-bye hug. Then Eric showed me to the front door.

"You guys have plans tomorrow?" I asked.

He nodded. "I'm taking her up to Nakijin Castle, and then, I don't know, probably check out the Pineapple Park in Nago while we're up there."

"If you do go to the park, grab another bottle of that pineapple wine." I winked. "We can drink it when we have a night to ourselves."

Eric grinned and wrapped his arms around me. "I will

definitely make sure to stop by, then."

"Good." I kissed him lightly. "You could always grab some of the pineapple sake too."

"Pineapple sake?" He raised an eyebrow. "You trying to get me drunk or something?"

I shrugged. "Well, you are kind of fun when you're drunk."

"So are you." He kissed me, drawing it out for a moment.

When I broke the kiss, I glanced toward the living room before meeting his eyes again. "I guess I should let you get back to your game."

His amusement faded, and his earlier concern crept back into his expression. "You sure you'll be all right tonight?"

I ran my fingers through his hair. "Eric. I'm fine." Cupping his face in both hands, I said, "Now go enjoy your evening with your daughter, and we'll catch up on spending time together this weekend."

He smirked. "Is 'spending time together' a euphemism?"

"You're damn right it is."

"Good." He pulled me to him and kissed me. We both started to pull away, hesitated and sank into a longer kiss.

After a moment, I drew back, and our eyes met. Like that kiss, the eye contact lingered, and I caught myself drawing in a breath like I was about to speak, but I wasn't sure what I'd thought to say.

Finally, Eric cleared his throat and dropped his gaze. "Anyway. I guess Marie and I will see you tomorrow night?" His eyebrows rose.

I smiled. "Of course."

He kissed me once more, briefly this time, and after we exchanged one last lingering look, I left.

As I drove, I couldn't stop thinking about the way Eric and his daughter interacted. Admittedly, something about what I felt was jealousy, but not in the sense that I wanted to get territorial or that I was looking forward to Marie leaving so I could have Eric to myself. Not even close. I would never have dreamed of wanting to get between a parent and child.

But there was something. Something I couldn't put my finger on. A knot that tightened as the two of them carried on with their rapid-fire banter and easy conversation. A heavy feeling that sank a little deeper when Eric ribbed Marie about her taste in boys, or they both teased each other about their respective bad habits behind the wheel, or he deadpanned a few cutthroat suggestions for methods of eliminating competition for the varsity softball team next year.

About halfway home from Eric's apartment, as I sat at a red light, a piece fell into place, and I suddenly understood what it was about them that threw me.

I envied them.

They bantered. They had the same sense of humor, enjoyed the same video games, and knew exactly how to playfully jab at each other. They *knew* each other.

And, with that heavy, sinking feeling in my gut, I realized I didn't know my kids like that. If I was honest with myself, I didn't know them at all. I saw them so rarely it was like interacting with my nieces and nephews, not my own children. After watching Eric with his daughter, I couldn't help realizing the twins were strangers to me. I loved them more than life itself, but I didn't *know* them.

That needed to change, and while I didn't relish the thought, I may have had an idea about how to make that change.

I shut the front door behind me and leaned against it. All the way here after that stoplight epiphany, I'd told myself what I needed to do, but now that I was home, nerves threatened to close in on me.

No, I can do this. It's long overdue.

I pushed myself off the door and crossed the living room to the couch. I picked up my laptop, opened it and rested it on my knee.

While my computer powered up, I glanced at my watch. It

was a little after eight o'clock here, which meant it was seven in the morning in Pennsylvania. Knowing my ex-wife, she'd be up by now. She usually got up early to take care of e-mails and such while the kids were still asleep.

Heart thundering, I opened up the IM program I used to talk to my kids when they were at my parents' house. I pulled up the Add User function and, after a long moment of hesitation, entered my ex-wife's e-mail address.

My finger hovered over the button, and the cursor hovered over Send. Holding my breath, I pushed the button, and as soon as the pop-up window disappeared, panic rushed through me. Fuck, what was I doing?

Too late. No turning back.

I refreshed my e-mail in-box. Again. Then I read a news site, checked a couple of blogs I liked to read, and checked a few I hadn't looked at it in months, just to give myself something to do. When I refreshed my in-box again, there was nothing. Five minutes later, still nothing.

Sighing, I wondered why I'd even bothered. I couldn't imagine she wanted to talk to me. Some exes had a wall of ice between them, but Katie and I were on opposite sides of a damned glacier. It was bad enough having such a rift between me and someone I used to love, but my kids were on the other side with her. It had hurt to lose my connection with my first wife when we bitterly went our separate ways, but at least we were able to walk away and be done with it. Katie and I had no choice but to be part of each other's lives. It was like being handcuffed to someone when all I wanted to do was get the fuck away from her.

The fact was, the only way I'd ever have a relationship with my kids was to find a way to mend fences with her.

Obviously, that wasn't happening today, though. Exhaling hard, I minimized the IM window and opened up my browser again to screw off for a little while.

Then my e-mail pinged. I flipped to my in-box, and my heart skipped.

Katie Connelly has accepted your add request.

I maximized the IM window again, and sure enough, her name showed under Available Contacts. Ignoring my nerves, I sent a video chat request.

Waiting for K_Connelly to respond...

I chewed the inside of my cheek, wondering if this was a mistake.

Connecting...

My heart beat faster.

The video window popped up.

Initializing video connection...

And all at once, she was there. The picture was grainy, but it was definitely her. Her dark hair fell over her shoulders, and her ever-present red coffee cup was in her hand. She didn't have her makeup on yet, since it was still early, but I always thought she was prettier without it anyway. This was how she looked in the morning, and I hadn't seen her like this in...in far too long. Since the days when she could turn me on with an e-mail and I'd never heard her tell me she had someone else to e-mail like that.

God, Katie, how did we get here?

"Hey," I said with a nervous smile.

"Hey." Katie smiled back, though it didn't extend beyond her lips, and her tone was guarded. "The... um... the kids aren't up yet, so if—"

"Actually, I wanted to talk to you."

She blinked. "Oh." Her posture stiffened, and, though it was hard to tell with the digitized image, I thought a hint of fear flickered across her face. She gulped and set her jaw like she was steeling herself. "What's going on? Is everything okay?"

"Yeah, everything's fine. I mean, I..." I paused, trying to find the words, and I couldn't help noticing she'd relaxed a little. With a pang of guilt, I realized her expression a moment ago had been the same one she'd had when I broke the news to her that I was going to Iraq for the second time. I took a breath. "Listen, I think we need to put our past behind us."

She narrowed her eyes a little. "Why now?"

"You and I can barely have a conversation and I..." I

exhaled hard. "Look, I barely know the kids. And the longer we keep a wall between you and me, the longer we'll be keeping a wall between me and the kids."

"I have *never* kept them from you," she snapped.

I put up a hand and shook my head. "No, you haven't. It's both of us."

"What do you mean?"

"We don't get along," I said. "Which puts them in a bad position anyway, but it also makes it harder for me to get in touch with them. You don't want to talk to me, I don't want to talk to you, and the end result is that I don't get to talk to the kids." I swallowed hard. "You're my only connection to them, Katie. And for that matter, this has gone on long enough, don't you think?"

"You're the one who refuses to let it go," she said coldly.

I avoided her eyes. She had a point. Nodding, I said, "You're right. Maybe we need to talk this through, then. Put it behind us."

"What is there to talk about?" she asked. "If you want to talk to the kids more, fine. But, really, what is there for us to talk about? It's *over*, Shane. We're done."

"I know it is. I'm not suggesting we get back together or anything like that. Just, you know, maybe find some middle ground? Be civil?"

She looked away but said nothing.

"I'd suggest getting counseling like we should have back then," I said. "But from here, this is all we have." I chewed my lip. Then, struggling to keep my voice even, I went on. "There's something I want to know. And you don't have to answer, but I hope you will."

She faced me again, raising her eyebrows, but still didn't speak.

I hesitated, then finally said, probably *just* loud enough for the microphone to pick it up, "Why did you do it?"

Katie flinched. "Shane..."

"You don't have to answer," I repeated softly. "I'm just...it's been eating at me for the last four years." I chewed the inside of my cheek. "I mean, was it something I did? Did you—"

"No," she said quickly. "No, it—well, I guess in a way, but it"—she released a sharp, frustrated breath—"it wasn't your fault."

I furrowed my brow and inclined my head, silently asking her to continue.

She didn't speak for a long moment, eyes closed and hands folded in front of her lips. Finally, she said, "Do you really want to know?"

I forced my voice to stay steady. "Yes."

She set her shoulders back, and I half expected a defensive expression and a hard edge to her voice. But then her shoulders dropped. A second later, so did her gaze. And finally, she spoke.

"When you were just at sea, it wasn't as bad. It was a separation, and it wasn't fun, but I knew going into this that you'd be gone sometimes." She bit her lip. "But when you went to Iraq, I was so scared, and after a while, I resented you for putting me through it. I know, I know, it's selfish, but..." She trailed off, shaking her head and looking at something off-camera before she turned to me again. "God, Shane, I never thought you'd be gone for an entire year, and knowing you were getting shot at instead of just being on a ship, I was scared to death. And then when you went over there the second time..."

I forced back the lump that tried to rise in my throat. "Tell me."

She brushed a strand of hair out of her face with a trembling hand. When she spoke again, her voice shook, and she spoke quickly, like she couldn't stop now that she'd started. "I just, I hated you for it. I was basically a single mom, and I was always terrified someone was going to call and tell me I was a widow." She wiped her eyes and cleared her throat. "I jumped every time the phone rang. I can't tell you how many times I almost had a panic attack just watching the news. And the kids, God, the kids. They kept asking when you'd be home, and I wanted to tell them you'd be home soon, but I was afraid you wouldn't, and then they'd never forgive me for lying to them about you. I guess I just needed someone who was here and who wasn't..." She bit her lip.

"Who wasn't, what?"

She batted an unseen tear from her cheek. "During both years you were over there, I had nightmares every night. About going to the base to pick you up when you came home, but when you were supposed to step off the plane, they brought—" Her voice cracked, and she covered her mouth with shaking fingers. Then she took a breath and whispered, "They brought out a casket with a flag over it instead."

I winced.

Katie went on. "And then I started hearing about guys doing third and even fourth tours, and I was hanging by a thread just trying to get through the second. I know it sounds so wrong and selfish, but I resented you, and I hated you, and I just needed someone I didn't have dreams about losing."

My heart dropped. "My God, why didn't you tell me before?"

"What difference would it have made?" A hint of bitterness crept into her wavering voice. "You were over there. What the hell could you have done?"

I shifted my gaze away from her. There were few things in this world I hated more than that helpless feeling of being thousands of miles away when someone needed me. And in Iraq, there wouldn't have been anything I could have done for her, especially if the very fact that I was over there was the problem.

"I'm sorry," she whispered. "I'm sorry, that was out of line."

"No, it wasn't." A lump rose in my throat, but I forced it back. "I am so sorry, Katie."

"You don't need to be. I'm the one who cheated." She chewed her lip and dropped her gaze. After a long moment, she looked at me again. "I'm sorry, Shane. For...everything that happened. I never set out to hurt you, I just..." She looked away and made a sharp, frustrated gesture.

"I know you didn't, honey," I said softly. "And I'm sorry I put you through that."

"It's not your fault," she whispered. "We both knew what the military life meant."

"I don't think either of us thought I'd ever be gone for a year for a combat deployment, never mind two of them." My voice threatened to crack, but I managed to add, "It was hell for me too."

"I know it was, which is why I feel even worse for what I did." From thousands of miles away, she met my eyes. "You were a good husband, Shane, and you deserved better than what I did to you."

"You deserved better than a life that gave you nightmares," I said. "Neither of us signed up for that."

"No." She dropped her gaze and sniffed sharply. "But I signed up to be a military wife. I knew that was a possibility, and I..." She wiped her eyes again and looked at me. "I'm sorry."

"So am I," I said. "We should've sat down and talked about this a long time ago."

"Do you think it would have changed anything?"

"Do you mean, would we have stayed together?"

She nodded.

"I don't know," I said. "Maybe, maybe not. But if nothing else, I think we could have walked away on better terms. The kids deserved better than what we gave them, and quite frankly, so did we."

"Yeah," she said so softly I barely heard her.

"We can't change any of that now," I said. "But if I try to do things differently in the future, can you meet me halfway?"

Katie dropped her gaze but nodded. "I can do that. And, the kids..." Her eyes met mine again. "How often do you want to talk to them?"

"As often as I can." I shrugged. "With the time differences and our work schedules, it probably won't be more than a couple times a week. Just, you know, if you see me online, you can always ping me."

"Okay." She released a breath. "Okay, yeah, I can do that. And maybe..." She folded her arms on the desk and shifted her weight. "Maybe they can come see you."

I grimaced. "They're awfully young to be flying that far on their own."

"Well..." She hesitated. "I could fly part of the way with them, and then you can meet me halfway. Seattle, or Tokyo, or wherever you usually change planes."

"You...wouldn't mind flying that far with them?"

Katie chewed her lip. "I might need a little help for the plane ticket, but I think they need to spend more time with you, so..." She trailed off again and shrugged.

"Thank you," I whispered.

She looked at something off-camera, and when she turned to me again, she said, "Sounds like the kids are getting up. You want me to go tell them you're on the line?"

I sat up. "Would you?"

She smiled. "Give me a minute. I'll go get them."

"Thanks, Katie."

"You're welcome." With that, she got up and stepped out of the frame.

While she went to get the kids, I leaned back against the couch cushions and looked up at the ceiling. A tremendous weight had pressed down on my shoulders since the day I found out she was cheating, and it slid off now. Sure, there were feelings that wouldn't disappear overnight, but the grudge had been the worst of it. The grudge, and that question that had been eating at me since I'd learned about the affair. Why?

Guilt tugged at my gut. I'd been so angry and hurt that she'd cheated, I'd never considered the reasons she'd just given. I'd worried incessantly about her and the kids every day I spent in that godforsaken sandpit, but I never imagined the fear and loneliness would drive her into another man's arms. Her reasons didn't make it right, but I...I understood.

I stared at the screen where she'd looked back at me a moment ago. After all this time, after seeing her face-to-face like this, I didn't see her as the bitch who'd cheated on me. Oh, I'd had no shortage of angry names for her. Whore, mostly. But now I couldn't look at her that way. When I'd looked at her on my computer screen, I hadn't seen my cheating whore of an ex-wife. She was just...Katie. She was human. Deployments weren't easy for anyone. Combat deployments were hell. Who was I to judge her if she'd buckled?

Nothing could ever take us back to what we were before I left on that deployment. We'd both moved on now. Our marriage was over. Contacting her tonight, I'd hoped to bury the hatchet enough to function as parents, but now I had an inkling of hope that maybe we could do better than just gritting our teeth and tolerating each other.

Movement on the screen caught my eye, and I couldn't help grinning as my kids vied for space on the desk chair.

"Hey, Dad," Jason said. "What time is it there?"

I chuckled. The kids were fascinated with the time differences. "It's"—I made an exaggerated gesture of looking at my watch—"well past your bedtime."

Jessica laughed, revealing two gaps. "Is it tomorrow there?"

"Not quite," I said. "Couple more hours. And when did you lose two more teeth, missy?"

She leaned forward to show off the missing teeth and edge her brother farther out of the frame. As they fought for screen time and she told me all about how she'd lost her tooth at recess last week, I just smiled.

Maybe there was hope for this family yet.

Chapter Nineteen

Eric

On Wednesday afternoon, I took Marie into Naha to visit Kokusai Street.

Shane didn't join us this time. He had to work anyway, but from what I'd heard, this was one of the few places off base that Americans actually visited. We didn't dare show our faces together in a place like this, so he'd catch up with us at my place for dinner tonight.

According to Shane, Kokusai was touristy as all hell but a great place to buy souvenirs, not to mention local produce. As much as he avoided all the places where Americans gathered, even he liked the food and atmosphere that Kokusai offered, so he encouraged me to take my daughter to check it out.

And here we were.

Kokusai Street was an odd blend of the Japan with which I was familiar and a casual, touristy atmosphere. The sidewalks were teeming with people, but it wasn't shoulder to shoulder like Tokyo or dangerously, rudely crowded like New York. Some people strolled; some people walked like they had somewhere to be.

I'd heard Kokusai Street was home to numerous street festivals and a busy nightlife, and even on a lazy afternoon like this, it had the relaxed but upbeat atmosphere that must really come alive when the sun went down or a festival rolled through. A blend of traditional Okinawan music, Japanese pop and American pop came from speakers in shops and restaurants, adding an ever-changing background to the sounds of cars and voices. People wore flip-flops and sunglasses, drank from coconuts and ate chunks of pineapple off bamboo skewers. Palm trees spaced a few feet apart along the sidewalk offered a little bit of shade here and there from the blazing tropical sun.

We were in the heart of Naha, the closest thing the island had to a bustling metropolis, but Okinawa had virtually no pollution, so aside from the exhaust of the occasional passing car, the air was clean and fresh. Instead of smog and garbage, Kokusai Street smelled like curry, coffee, steak and garlic.

Colorful banners flapped in the warm wind, and dozens of colorful signs—mostly in kanji, some in English—lined the various buildings, most of which weren't more than three or four stories high. It was daytime, so there weren't a lot of neon lights or brightly lit displays, but I didn't imagine this place ever aspired to produce the flickering sensory overload of Tokyo or Hong Kong. It wasn't necessarily more subdued than places like that, but considerably less electrified.

"Didn't you tell me Okinawa was a total dump?" Marie threw me a look, then made an emphatic gesture at our surroundings.

"That's what I was told. Completely Americanized too."

Marie looked at a sign outside one of the shops. It was nothing but kanji and a few cartoon images. "All Americanized. Right. Okay."

"My sentiments exactly."

Most of the shops definitely catered to tourists. I couldn't begin to count the number of T-shirts, key chains, stickers, stuffed animals and whatever else someone thought to put Okinawa-themed slogans on. Then there were the more specialized things, like Okinawan shortbread cookies and these weird purple cookies made from *beni imo*, a bright-purple sweet potato that grew here.

Every possible size and style of Shi Shi dog imaginable could be found here, from ceramic to terra cotta to carved jade. Some were hand-glazed in the traditional style; others were molded plastic painted in bright colors or shaped into silly poses.

And, of course, almost every store sold Habu sake, that lovely amber liquor that came in a huge jar with an openmouthed snake coiled at the bottom.

"Oh my God." Marie stared at a display of Habu sake. "Is that...is that a *snake*?"

"Sure is," I said. "It's Habu sake."

"Sake?" Her eyebrows shot up above the frames of her oversized sunglasses. "You mean people drink that?"

"Sure," I said, trying not to smirk. "Just like tequila with a worm in it."

"Tell me they don't actually eat the snake."

"God, I hope not." I chuckled. "No, it's supposed to add some sort of medicinal properties to the sake, but you don't actually eat it."

"I would hope not. Eww." She shuddered. "Looks just like the jars of dead animals in my biology teacher's classroom."

"Oh, they do not." I gestured at the jars. "These have pretty lids and crap on them."

Marie shot me a pointed look. "So if I put a pretty lid and a nice little bow on one of Mr. Haggerty's pig fetuses, you'll drink it?"

I laughed. "No, but that's formaldehyde. Totally different."

"Totally different? It looks exactly the same!" She wrinkled her nose. "Tell me you haven't tried this stuff."

I shook my head. "No, not yet. Too expensive."

The wrinkles in her nose deepened. "But you'd try it if it wasn't too expensive?"

"Hey," I said with a shrug. "When in Rome."

A block or so later, while I looked at some T-shirts, Marie snickered.

"Hey, Dad," she said. "Think you can put your money where your mouth is about the Habu sake?"

"Hmm?"

She gestured at a sign that read *Habu Sake Sample* above a very appetizing image of a striking habu. "You said you'd try it if it wasn't too expensive." She made an after-you gesture into the shop.

"So I did," I said. "Guess I'd better."

"Well, unless you want me posting all over Facebook that

you wimped out."

"God forbid the people of Facebook think I'm a wimp." I laughed, and we walked into the shop. At that point, I realized I'd been spoiled having Shane around; he spoke enough Japanese to make communication with the locals a breeze. The shopkeeper's English was shaky but beat the hell out of my embarrassingly tiny Japanese vocabulary. Still, through some gesturing and a lot of apologizing on both our parts for our mutual lack of understanding, I conveyed to her that I wanted to sample some of the Habu sake.

She took a jar out from behind the counter, and I tried not to notice the snake still in it. When she brought out a tiny plastic cup, I shifted my gaze away before she started pouring so I didn't have to think about the fact that I'd be drinking something that had been marinating a snake for God only knew how long.

I picked up a smaller jar off a shelf beside the counter. The label was almost entirely in kanji, but one word was written in English: *Awamori.*

Oh God.

Not that I was planning to have nearly as much of this as I'd had with Shane at the Izakaya, but holy hell, I remembered that headache.

The shopkeeper finished pouring the sample cup and set the jar aside. She took the cup in both hands and held it out to me, bowing as she offered it.

I returned the bow and took the cup from her with a murmured, "*Arigato.*" *Thank you.*

Then I looked at the faintly amber-tinted liquid in the cup in my hand.

Awamori. We meet again.

"Come on, Dad," Marie taunted. "You can handle it, can't you?"

"Of course I can." And, hoping I wouldn't regret it, I threw it back. It was faintly herbal, almost sour, but the alien flavors paled in comparison to the sinus-clearing burn of the alcohol.

"Holy..." I coughed and grimaced. "Wow. That is strong."

Marie and the shopkeeper laughed.

"Wimp," Marie said.

"Oh, whatever." I coughed again.

The shopkeeper looked at Marie and gestured at the jar. "You try?" To me, she added, "*Daijobu*?" Basically, "*Is it okay?*"

Marie looked at me, eyebrows up.

"I thought it grossed you out," I said.

"Yeah, but it didn't kill you, so..." Her eyebrows rose a little more.

I chewed my lip. Her mother and I had always let her try things—wine, beer, even some Scotch—in order to keep them from becoming forbidden fruit. She didn't like most of it, fortunately, and usually turned up her nose if we offered her any. Which was exactly what we'd hoped for.

So what was a little taste of Habu sake? Judging by the aftertaste that was still making my eyes water, she wouldn't be coming back for more.

Finally, I looked at the shopkeeper and held my thumb and forefinger about a half an inch apart. "*Skoshi.*" *A little bit.*

"*Skoshi.*" She nodded and poured a tiny bit of the Habu sake into another cup.

"If you can handle this stuff," I said, giving Marie a pointed look, "I may have to talk to your mother about what you've been doing after school."

She rolled her eyes. "Whatever. I just want to taste it."

I laughed and shrugged. "Your funeral."

Alarm flickered across her expression, and I just grinned. She threw a wary look toward the cup as the shopkeeper held it out in both hands. "Um..."

"Too late now." I nodded toward the cup in the woman's outstretched hands.

Marie hesitated, then bowed to the shopkeeper and carefully took the cup. She held it for a moment, staring into it. I was about to tease her about chickening out, but she took a deep breath and, just as I had, threw it back.

She downed it one swallow and immediately coughed. Shaking her head, she said, "Oh, wow. That's..." Another cough.

When she looked at me, her eyes were watering, and the shopkeeper and I both laughed.

The shopkeeper tried to encourage me to buy a jar of Habu sake, but I declined. From what I'd heard, it was illegal for us to export the stuff, and I sure as hell wasn't drinking an entire jar in three years. That, and the price tag made my eyes water almost as much as the awamori itself. The smallest bottles with the tiniest snakes were over a hundred bucks. The more impressive ones with the three- to five-foot snakes were easily over five or six hundred dollars. The stuff would have been cool to put on display, but not that cool.

After sampling a few of the shop's shortbread cookies to get the taste out of our mouths, Marie and I left to continue our exploration of Kokusai Street.

Just beyond one intersection, where a Starbucks faced a couple of sleek, trendy clothing stores and some Japanese restaurants, a wide, cobbled path broke off from the sidewalk and led into the marketplace. This was one of the areas Kokusai was famous for. It was a combination farmer's market, fish market, and flea market, with shops and semipermanent booths selling everything from pineapple slices to ceramic sake flasks.

Marie and I both took off our sunglasses and hooked them in our collars. High above us, stretched between arched red-metal bars, a canopy of opaque, white plastic filtered the sunlight, illuminating everything comfortably without making everyone squint or shade their eyes. The heat of the day still infiltrated this area, reminding us we were still more or less outdoors, but a few of the shops had air conditioning, which offered refreshing gusts of cooler air.

One of the produce vendors had baskets full of pineapple, star fruit, mangoes, papayas, bananas and...what the hell was that?

I picked up one of the bizarre fruits. It was about the size of a softball, mostly a deep pink with a little bit of green, and looked like the love child of a mango and an artichoke.

Marie tilted up the label on the box so she could read it.

"Dragonfruit?" She leaned a little closer, eyeing the strange fruit like it might come to life and explain itself.

"Oh, *this* is a dragonfruit?" I turned it in my hand. "Huh. I've been wondering what they looked like."

"I was going to ask if you'd ever eaten one," she said. "But I'm guessing not."

"Not that I'm aware of, anyway."

"Hey, we should buy one."

I shrugged. "Hell, why not?"

She peered at the box of fruit. "How do you tell if they're, like, ripe?"

"You're asking me?"

She sniffed. "You're the dad. You're supposed to know this shit."

I raised an eyebrow.

"Stuff." Her cheeks colored. "You're supposed to know this *stuff*."

I tried to scowl but failed miserably. "Jesus, Marie. You sound like you were raised around a bunch of Sailors or something."

"Funny, that."

I looked around in search of a shopkeeper to ask how to pick out a dragonfruit, but a refrigerated case caught my eye. Amidst the slices of star fruit, pineapple, and God knew what else, there was a handwritten sign that read *Dragonfruit—¥200/slice.*

"I've got a better idea." I set the one in my hand back in the box. "Why don't we get a couple of slices and see if we like them before we drop eight hundred yen on a whole one?"

"Sounds good to me."

With some pointing and gesturing and no shortage of apologizing for being an idiot English speaker, I asked the shopkeeper for two slices of dragonfruit. He understood me better than I understood him, but we figured it out, and I handed over the yen.

Dragonfruit in hand, Marie and I stepped aside so we were out of other people's way.

I regarded mine cautiously as I brought it up to my mouth, but before I took a bite, I looked at my daughter. She looked at me over her own slice, silently daring me to go first. I lowered mine a little. "Hey, I dove into the Habu sake first. Your turn."

"Something tells me this will taste better, but, okay." She took a bite. There was no immediate disgusted reaction, but her brow furrowed. "I swear to God, I've tasted this before."

That was enough of an endorsement for me, so I took a bite myself. She was right; it was definitely familiar. I stared at the fruit. "It tastes like...I can't put my finger on it." Sweet but not terribly so. Even the soft but not mushy texture—particularly with the abundance of tiny seeds—was familiar. "I have a feeling I'm going to feel like a total idiot for not figuring this out faster."

"Mm-hmm." Marie took another bite. She chewed it slowly, her brow still furrowed above unfocused eyes. Then she snapped her fingers. "Kiwi! It tastes like kiwi fruit."

"Yes, that's it." I chuckled. "And I do feel like an idiot for not figuring it out."

She shrugged. "Eh, whatever. It's good, though."

With the mystery of the dragonfruit solved, we discarded the rinds and kept walking down the cobbled thoroughfare.

The fish market made itself known well before we got to it. At least that gave us time to adjust to the smell, so when curiosity dragged us through the double glass doors, the odor wasn't too overpowering.

We both stopped and looked around. This wasn't the grocery store seafood section we were both used to in the States. We were accustomed to neatly packed and wrapped filets, crabs and shellfish stacked on top of pristine white piles of ice. Here, row upon row of counters, cases and coolers displayed whole fish of every variety, live crabs, live snails the size of my fist, and slimy, tentacled things I wasn't quite sure I wanted to identify.

"Oh my God." Marie put a hand over her mouth and recoiled from a case of brightly colored fish. "Didn't we see some of those when we were snorkeling?"

"Yeah, I think we did. Though they were a little more"—I moved my hand like it was a fish swimming past—"active."

She made a gagging sound. "Okay, I think I've seen enough of the fish market. If we keep looking around here, I'm afraid I'm going to find Nemo."

I laughed. "Good call. Let's get out of here."

Back on the other side of the glass doors, the air was warmer but not quite so ripe with the scent of seafood. The farther we walked, the less I could smell the fish market. Thank God for that.

We found a shop that specialized in handblown Ryukyu glass. It was expensive as hell, but I'd already accumulated a few pieces myself. The glassware was simply too cool not to buy.

The trademark style of Ryukyu glass was a two-tone—yellow on top, orange on the bottom—highball glass. The bottom third or so had an odd crackled look, which was another distinguishing trait of the island's glasswork. Of course there were numerous other styles and colors, but the crackled look was a recurring theme, and every shop that sold this stuff, including the one Marie and I browsed, had the orange-and-yellow highball glasses.

This particular shop was extremely narrow. It seemed like it was designed to make customers hold their breath and walk as carefully as possible to avoid tempting the you-break-it-you-buy-it rules. When my elbow brushed a shelf, I jumped, preparing to catch whatever glass I was sure I'd just knocked over, and in doing so, almost knocked a very expensive vase onto the concrete floor. It wasn't the most dignified moment of my life, and I was thankful my daughter, who walked ahead of me, missed it. I could almost hear my wallet pleading with me to *get out, get out, for the love of God, get out.*

Marie had no problem navigating through the jungle of glass, though.

"Hey, you think Mom would like something like that?" She pointed at a decanter made of glass. It was clear up on top and a deep cobalt blue on the bottom, with a narrow, slightly curving neck.

"Hmm, I think she would," I said, moving carefully toward her so I could get a better look. "We'd probably have to ship it home, though. No way in hell this will fit in your suitcase once we wrap it enough to keep it from shattering."

"Can I get it for her?" she asked.

"Let me see if I have enough yen," I said. "If not, I'll come back another day and pick it up for you when I have more."

"They don't take Visa?"

I laughed as I took my wallet out of my back pocket. "Honey, Visa's everywhere you want to be unless you want to be on Okinawa." I glanced up at the decanter. "How much is it?"

She craned her neck. "Seven thousand yen. Is that a lot?"

"Nah, it's about seventy or eighty bucks." I pulled a ten-thousand-yen bill out of my wallet and handed it to her. "You go ahead and pay for it. I'll wait for you outside." I gestured—carefully!—at the glass around us. "Another minute in here, I'm going to break something, I know it."

She laughed. "Okay, I'll be out in a minute. Thanks, Dad."

I got the hell out of the minefield of glass and released my breath when I'd made it into the safety of the cobbled walkway.

As I waited outside for Marie, a couple of familiar faces emerged from the crowd. It took a second to register, since they weren't in uniform, but then I realized it was Grant and Diego.

"Hey, MA1." Grant extended his hand.

"Hey, guys," I said, shaking their hands in turn. "You know, I think you're the first Americans we've seen here all day."

"We?" Diego looked past me. Then his eyes widened. "Oh, damn, dude. You tappin' that?"

I blinked. "I…beg your pardon?"

"The blonde chick," he said. "Are you—"

"That's my *daughter*," I growled. "Remember, I said I was taking leave because my kid was in town?"

"Oh. Right." Diego coughed into his fist, and he at least had the decency to look sheepish. "So, you're enjoying your leave?"

"I'm not at work," I said. "Of course I'm enjoying my leave. Am I missing any excitement?"

"Not really." Grant shrugged.

"Except we had some guys from one of the ships get into some trouble with the JPs," Diego said. "Dipshits got drunk, and the JPs brought them in."

I rolled my eyes. "Oh, there's a shock." Whenever a ship was in port here, just like anywhere, at least some trouble could be expected. Sailors and booze were always a fantastic combo.

"Anyway, we should get out of here," Grant said. "See you at work when you get back."

"Yeah, don't remind me," I said, chuckling.

They turned to go but hadn't quite made it into the crowd and out of earshot before Grant looked at Diego and said, "See, man? I told you he wasn't gay."

I chewed the inside of my cheek. So the rumors were going around. I tried to tell myself the rumors about me being gay didn't mean they'd connect me to Shane. I knew how this worked, though. Once the bug was in everyone's ear that I might be gay, they'd notice anytime they saw me engage another man.

You're asking for it, Randall. You know you are.

Marie came out, shopping bag in hand, and we walked back out to Kokusai Street.

"This place is so cool," she said, looking around the semicrowded sidewalk.

"Kokusai Street?" I asked. "Or the island in general?"

"The whole place. You're so lucky you get to live here." Before I could reply, her smile fell, and her shoulders sank a little.

I cocked my head. "You okay?"

Her head snapped toward me, like she hadn't expected me to notice her sudden change in demeanor. "What? Yeah, I'm fine."

"You sure?"

Marie swallowed hard and dropped her gaze. "Just kind of sucks having you this far away." She looked at me again. "You get to live in a cool place like this, and I'm, you know, back home."

"I can understand that. Have you been doing okay with it? I mean, with me being this far away?"

"I don't know." She shrugged. "It's better than when you were in Iraq or Afghanistan."

"Except I wasn't over there quite as long."

"Yeah, but no one's shooting at you this time."

"True," I whispered.

She said nothing for a moment. "Are you going back over there after this?" There was a note of fear in her voice that made my chest ache.

"I don't think so, baby," I said. "IA tours are pretty much volunteer-only right now, and most of the troops in Iraq have been yanked anyway. Anything's possible, but I'm not worried."

"Good," she said softly. "Mom will be glad to hear that too."

"I figured she knew," I said. "But if she's still worried about it..."

"She hasn't said anything about it for a while, but..." She trailed off. "You know, every time the news said someone had been killed over there, for like the next day or two, Mom would panic if her phone rang. She was sure it would be Grandma calling to say something had happened to you."

I blew out a breath. "I'm sorry you guys had to go through that. Combat deployments suck for everyone involved."

"Yeah, they do."

We walked in silence for a while, and when I glanced at her a few times, she looked around like she was only halfheartedly taking in the exotic scenery.

Between a souvenir shop and a tropical-themed snack bar, I stopped, and so did she. I turned to her. "Is that the only thing that's bothering you?"

She pursed her lips and looked at something down the sidewalk. Something that wasn't me. "I..." She ran a hand through her hair. "It's just hard, you know? I get used to you being in the same state, and they move you to California. I figure out how to deal with you being at sea for six months, and they send you into a war zone for a year. And now"—she made a sharp, sweeping gesture with one hand, indicating our surroundings—"you're here for the next three years."

I sighed. "God, I'm sorry, baby. The military life isn't easy."

She laughed bitterly. "Yeah, I hadn't noticed. I mean, when you were in California, at least I could call you."

"I know. Believe me, not being able to talk to you or anyone else while I'm here sucks." I swallowed. "Is there anything I can do to make this easier? I mean, these are the cards we've been dealt, but..."

"There isn't much you can do," she said. "It's just frustrating. I miss you, Dad."

I put my arms around her and hugged her tight. "I miss you too, kiddo. But you know you can always e-mail me, and I try to be online as much as I can so we can talk that way. It's not much, but I'll do what I can."

She pulled back and quickly wiped her eyes before she looked up at me. "Are you going to be home for my graduation next year?"

I smiled. "I'll go UA and kayak home if I have to, but I'm not missing your graduation."

She grinned. "Like you could kayak that far."

"What?" I scoffed. "Are you suggesting I couldn't?"

"Not at your age, no."

"Hey!"

We both laughed, and I hugged her again.

"Come on," I said, releasing her. "Let's see what's up this way."

We continued up the sidewalk until we reached the end of the street. Then we crossed over and started back down the other side. Along the way, we picked up a couple of Shi Shi dogs for her, an Okinawa baseball cap and a box of some to-die-for pastries that we'd probably wind up finishing off in the car before we even got home.

A lot of things like pastries and cookies were in packages written entirely in Japanese, and we couldn't quite identify what some of them were. I knew the bright purple tarts were made from the beni imo, and we soon figured out that anything green had a tea-like taste to it, but there were plenty of other colors and flavors we couldn't identify.

At one point, I tried to get a shopkeeper to explain what something was made from, but I didn't know enough Japanese, and she didn't know enough English. We just looked at each other, her expression as blank as mine undoubtedly was. I searched for the right phrase, but just couldn't figure out how to ask. I bought the mystery cookies anyway; the samples were amazing, so to hell with what they were actually made out of.

On the way out of the shop, I said, "This is one of those times it would be really handy to have Shane around."

"Uh-huh. And I'm sure that's the only reason you want him around, right?"

I cleared my throat. "Well, I mean, I do enjoy his company."

"Is that what kids are calling it these days?"

Heat rushed into my face. "Do you have conversations like this with your mother?"

She shrugged. "Sometimes. But she usually doesn't pretend she doesn't have feelings for someone."

"What are you talking about?" I gestured in the direction the shopkeeper had gone. "Just because I could use Shane's help translating doesn't mean I'm hopelessly in love with him or something."

"Doesn't mean you aren't either." She paused. "What *is* the gay equivalent of pussy-whipped, anyway?"

"*Marie!*" I stared at her, slack-jawed. "What the hell?"

She laughed and shrugged. "Hey, I'm just saying, Dad. I mean, come on. You are so head-over-heels for this guy..."

"What?" I gestured dismissively. "Look, I like the guy, and..." *And what, Randall? I don't think about him constantly? I'm not knowingly gambling with my career because I want him? I haven't noticed a hundred times over that being with him makes more sense than it has with any other man? Bullshit.*

Marie snickered. "You're blushing, by the way."

"Am I?" I couldn't help laughing self-consciously.

"Yes, you are." She tilted her head. "Are you and Shane, like, serious?"

I avoided her eyes. "I don't know, to be honest." I swallowed hard. "The thing is, though, we could both get in a lot of trouble for seeing each other, so..." I trailed off, shaking my head.

"I thought all that DADT crap was repealed."

"It was," I said. "But it's not that... It's not that simple. To make a long story short, we still have to be careful."

"But you're dating him anyway."

"Yes."

"But you're not in love with him."

I can't be. "No, I'm not." *Not even if I want to be.*

She eyed me skeptically. I thought she'd press the issue, but instead she clicked her tongue and said, "What *is* it with you and Mom?"

"What do you mean?"

"You guys are seriously like magnets for people you shouldn't date."

"Since when? Your mom's dated good guys, hasn't she?"

"Well, yeah, but they're almost always wrong for her. I mean, Drew wanted kids and Mom won't have anymore, so that was a deal-breaker. Then Adam was awesome but gambled too much, and Mom didn't want to support his ass." Marie shook her head. "Every time she meets a guy, we pretty much make bets on when he's going to come out with some fatal flaw."

"Come out?" I raised an eyebrow.

Her cheeks colored. "That's not what I meant."

I chuckled. "I know what you meant. But, I guess that's just one of the joys of dating. Great people come along, and they bring along reasons why you end up having to go your separate ways."

She groaned. "Oh God. Is that what I have to look forward to? I thought this crap was supposed to get easier after high school."

I laughed. "Sweetheart, I hate to break it to you, but high school never ends."

"Ugh, so I've heard." More serious now, she said, "So what are you guys going to do? Not tell anyone you're dating until after your...whatever it was goes through?"

"My LDO package? Yeah, I guess." I sighed. "We're just

seeing where things go for now."

She smiled. "Well, I hope he sticks around. I like him."

"Do you?" I smirked. "You know, I kind of like him too."

"Kind of, my ass," she muttered.

"You cuss like that around your mother?"

She gave a flippant shrug. "Sometimes."

I shot her a somewhat-stern look, then laughed. "Why don't we go grab some food?" I gestured up the street. "There's a *yakiniku* place a few blocks that way that's supposed to be good."

Marie eyed me. "A yaki-what, now?"

"Yakiniku. Basically, it's a buffet of raw meat, and you cook it on a gas grill at your table."

"Sounds interesting," she said with a shrug. "If we're really good, do they let us do our own dishes too?"

"Smart-ass."

"I just take after my old man."

"Hey, I'm not *that* old."

"Keep telling yourself that, Dad. Keep telling yourself that."

Chapter Twenty

Shane

The day Marie left Okinawa, I couldn't get away from the office fast enough. As soon as the day was over, I texted Eric to let him know I was on my way home. We hadn't spent a night together while Marie was in town, but that wasn't the only reason I was eager to see him.

While I was certainly looking forward to some one-on-one time, I had a feeling we wouldn't be doing much tonight. Not with the way he'd looked like he was barely keeping it together when we had dinner with Marie last night. Like Mays wore his baby-related fatigue on his sleeve, Eric couldn't hide—and probably didn't even try to hide—how he felt about Marie going back to the States. He'd taken her to the airport this morning. I thought he might want to be alone tonight, but when I'd texted him earlier, he still wanted to come over.

And having quietly broken down myself on more than a few flights back to this side of the world after visiting my kids, I was worried about him.

I had been home only a few minutes, not even long enough to strip out of my uniform, when he rang the doorbell. When I answered, everything about him confirmed what I thought—that he was having a hell of a time with the fact that his daughter had gone home. His eyes were as tired as Mays's had been lately, and his usually set-back shoulders slumped under an unseen weight.

"I can't promise a lot of exciting company tonight," he said quietly as I shut the door behind us. "It's...been a long day."

"I can imagine." I kissed him gently. "How are you doing?"

He shrugged like it took every bit of energy he had left. "Okay. She landed safely in Tokyo a few hours ago, so..." He trailed off. I supposed he meant to say he felt better after she'd had a safe flight, that he was less worried, but he probably couldn't convince himself of that any more than he could convince me. Like any parent, I had no doubt he was concerned and certainly relieved to hear one flight had been uneventful, but that wasn't what pressed down on his shoulders.

He shook himself to life. "I'll be all right. Don't...don't worry about me."

Yeah. That was going to happen. "You want something to drink?"

"No, I'm fine. Thanks."

We went into the living room and sat on my couch. He covered up his mood with the kind of small talk that he usually preferred to skip. Bullshitting about work. Halfheartedly trying to figure out what we wanted to eat tonight. Suggesting we spend a weekend out at the Keramas, the outlying islands southwest of Okinawa where we'd been meaning to go snorkeling.

He probably thought he was playing his cards close to his chest, but he'd tipped his hand several times. Quickly changing the subject when the conversation started to involve Marie. The unenthusiastic monotone that subtly wavered once in a while. Watching his wringing hands instead of making eye contact like he always did. I wondered if he knew I could tell when his smiles were forced. Just laughing softly at a smart-ass comment seemed to require everything he had.

And the charade continued until, about an hour after he showed up, his phone beeped.

Eric pulled out the phone and looked at the screen. Then he closed his eyes, sighed and tossed it unceremoniously on the coffee table.

"What's wrong?" I asked.

"Marie was just letting me know she's getting on her plane in Narita." He chewed his thumbnail and stared off into space.

"Eric?" I put a hand between his shoulders. "You okay?"

He leaned forward and rested his elbows on his knees. Clasping his hands together, he closed his eyes and pressed his thumbs into the bridge of his nose.

I didn't say anything. I...wasn't sure what to say.

Finally, Eric spoke, but he didn't look up.

"We shouldn't have to be parents in two-week increments," he whispered. "Our kids deserve so much better than that."

"So do we," I said, gently rubbing the back of his neck.

"But this is what we signed up for." His tone was distinctly tinged with bitterness. "Selling our souls to Uncle Fucking Sam so we can get shot at and miss our kids more than we see them."

I nodded. "It sucks. Believe me, I know."

His lips tightened. When he unclasped his fingers, his hands shook. "God, this is just..." His shoulders quivered, and he slid his hand down over his eyes. "Fuck..."

I put my arm around him and rested my other hand on his forearm.

Barely whispering and nowhere near steady, he said, "How the fuck am I supposed to be this far from her for three years?"

I put my arms around him and let him rest his head against my shoulder. Stroking his hair, I didn't speak. I wasn't sure what I could say, what kind of comfort I could offer. Closing my eyes, I just tried not to break down right along with him.

His free hand found mine on his forearm, and I turned mine over to lace our fingers together. After a moment, he sat up and wiped his eyes but didn't let go of my hand.

He exhaled sharply. "I'm sorry. I guess I just...really miss her right now."

"Don't apologize for missing your kid, Eric. Believe me, I know exactly what it's like."

Sighing he leaned back against the couch cushion. Watching his thumb trace circles on the inside of my wrist, he said, "You know, this is exactly why Sara and I put off getting divorced. Even if we had to be miserable together, at least then I could be there for Marie."

"So you'd be miserable either way," I said. "Either miserably married, or this far from Marie."

"There are days when I really wonder which is worse." He rubbed his forehead with two fingers and took a deep, uneven breath. "I fucking enlisted so Sara and I could give Marie a better life. I mean, we were both waiting tables, working insane shifts for next to nothing, could barely afford a one-bedroom apartment. So we figured the Navy would mean more stability. Job security, steady income, health insurance. And it did, but…" He sniffed, then cleared his throat. "God, between shipboard deployments and combat tours, I've completely missed five years of my daughter's life. Probably a hell of a lot more if you count work-ups, sea trials and all of that shit. Now I'm over here for three." He looked at me. "By the time I'm back in the States and out of the Navy, she'll be two years into college."

"I know what you mean." I absently ran my fingers through his short hair. "I haven't lived on the same continent as my kids since they were three."

Eric wiped his eyes again. "Kind of makes you wonder what the point is, doesn't it? We do this to give our kids better lives, and…" He waved a hand. "And all I can think is that when this is all said and done, she's either going to be a stranger to me, or she's going to resent me for being gone all these years."

"After watching the two of you together," I said, "I doubt it. I really do."

"Yeah," he said bitterly. "We'll see."

"You're doing the best you can for your daughter, Eric." I stroked his hair. "It's not like you walked out on her. It's hard for both of you, but I've seen the way you two interact. She adores you. I only wish I had the kind of relationship with my kids that you have with yours." I paused. "Actually, it's because of you and Marie I might have the chance of a better relationship with mine."

He looked at me. "What do you mean?"

I chewed the inside of my cheek. "The other night, after I left, I spent some time talking to my ex. Smoothing things out." I laughed softly. "Should've done that a few years ago, but better late than never, right?"

"Yeah, I guess so." Confusion still deepened the crevices between his eyebrows.

I clasped his hand between mine and raised it to my lips. "The thing is, after being around the two of you, I realized..." I paused, swallowing hard. It hurt and shamed me to even admit it. "I realized I don't even *know* my kids. They're...they're pretty much complete strangers to me, and it's not just because of the distance." I kissed the backs of his fingers and met his eyes. "The kind of father-daughter relationship you have with Marie, *that's* what I want with my kids, and I'm nowhere near it yet."

Eric dropped his gaze.

"What you guys have is a hell of a lot better than you think," I said. "And I think it's admirable you've managed to maintain that even when you've been gone for a quarter of her life."

He tensed. Exhaling slowly, he rubbed his temples. "A quarter. Jesus."

I squeezed his shoulder. "Don't beat yourself up, Eric." I kept my voice as gentle as my hand. "The alternative would have been more years of waiting tables, working stupidly long hours and struggling to make ends meet. You did what you could to provide for her, even if it meant making some sacrifices."

"Sacrifices. God, isn't that the truth?" He sighed. "Sorry to be such a downer tonight."

I kissed his cheek. "Don't be. You know I understand where you're coming from. My kids come to see me, you can bet I'll be a fucking wreck after they leave."

"Well, if you are"—he looked at me and offered a smile—"I'll return the favor."

"Good to know." I smiled and put my arm around him.

He exhaled hard. "Anyway, I...guess it's just bothering me. I really can't promise much tonight."

I ran my fingers through his hair. "Do you really think I'm going to hold it against you if you're not in the mood tonight?"

He laughed softly. "Well, I mean, I'm here, so..."

"So?" I shrugged. "Doesn't mean either of us is obligated to put out."

"Good to know," he said. "But if you don't want me to stay, just say so.

I touched his face. Leaning in slowly, I whispered, "I don't want you going anywhere unless you want to." Our lips met before he could respond.

I only meant for a brief kiss, just quick, light contact, but when I started to pull away, Eric curved his hand around the back of my neck. I relaxed against him, wrapped my arms around him.

What had started as a gentle, reassuring kiss turned into something hungrier. He teased my lips apart with the tip of his tongue, and when I slid my tongue past his, he pulled me closer. He kept one hand on my neck while his other alternated between touching my face and sliding up and down my arm.

His hand drifted from my shoulder to my chest, and his fingers curled around the front of my shirt. Still holding on tight to my shirt and the back of my neck, he broke the kiss.

Our foreheads touched.

"So you want to stay?" I asked.

"What do you think?" And he kissed me again.

Chapter Twenty-One

Eric

I wasn't in the mood. Not even close. But after a day of alternately worrying myself sick and wallowing in misery, I wasn't about to turn down something that felt good. And this felt good. Really good. Shane's kiss unwound tension and built its own. I wanted him, I needed him, and he wasn't holding back any more than I was.

And when I pulled back and let myself look him up and down, seeing him in his uniform for the first time since I'd known him, I couldn't help being turned on. God, he looked amazing.

Tom Cruise in *Top Gun* didn't wear that uniform nearly as well as Shane. Not that I cared for Tom Cruise all that much anyway, but even he looked good in that uniform. Hell, most men did. And Shane? Shane had a body *made* for officer whites. His narrow waist was spectacular in snug white, and the gold-striped black shoulder boards made his shoulders look just a little broader. It was just as well I already knew his rank, because I was so distracted by the way his uniform fit him, I barely noticed all the gleaming insignias and colorful chest candy.

I rested my hands on his waist. "You're taking a chance with this uniform. Just so you know."

"Am I?"

"Mm-hmm. Might get dirty, being thrown on the floor and all. Or, you know"—I grabbed his belt loops and pulled him toward me—"ripped."

"Well, I wouldn't want it getting ripped." He kissed me and, as he did, pried my fingers off his belt loops. Then he put my hands behind my back and held them there. "I'll just have to make sure your hands aren't anywhere they can tear my uniform."

He kissed me again, harder this time. With my hands restrained, I couldn't put them on him like I wanted to, but I was acutely aware of everywhere else we touched. His insignias pressing into my chest through my shirt. His cock against my own erection. Every release of breath whispering across my skin and every inhalation taking the air right out of my lungs.

As it always was, Shane's kiss was undeniably *him*, from the way the tip of his tongue slid under mine to his soft groan thrumming against my lips.

When I broke the kiss, we looked at each other, both panting. Then I let my gaze slide downward, taking in the way his white shirt sat *just* right on his broad chest and shoulders.

"God, you are so fucking hot in that uniform," I said.

"Hmm, you're right. I am a little hot in it." He kissed me and barely broke away enough to add, "Maybe I should take it off."

"Take it off?" I freed my hand and slid it over the front of his pants. Tilting his head back, Shane closed his eyes and gasped, and I leaned down to kiss his neck as I whispered, "What's your hurry?"

"I thought you were in a hurry."

"I was." I raised my head and met his eyes. "But now I want to take my time."

"When have we ever taken our time?"

"It's worth a try." I stroked him through his clothes. "Don't you think?"

Shane bit his lip and groaned.

I grinned. "I thought you'd be agreeable."

He licked his lips. "You know, this is probably the very definition of conduct unbecoming a gentleman."

I laughed and kissed beneath his jaw. "Well, then it's a good thing I've never claimed to be a gentleman, isn't it?"

"Very good thing. You wouldn't be nearly as much fun if you were."

"Then maybe we should take our ungentlemanly conduct in

the other room?"

Moving in to kiss me again, he growled, "I fucking love the way you think."

We left a trail of sandals and dress shoes from his living room to his bedroom door. Fully dressed, shirts half-unbuttoned, we tumbled into bed together. Shane pinned me on my back and kissed me in that desperate, hungry way that always drove me insane.

At one point, we abandoned trying to get clothes off. We'd opened most of the buttons, but now we just ran our hands all over each other. Over clothes, under them, through hair, down backs, it didn't matter.

In spite of my desperation, I found enough presence of mind to unbuckle his belt and unzip his pants. He unbuttoned and unzipped my shorts, and we both managed to push our clothes far enough over our hips to get them somewhat out of the way. Then he pressed his cock against mine, and the heat, the friction, the sheer closeness of him, drove a moan from my lips. I wanted to get undressed and find a condom, but now I couldn't remember how to do anything except press against him and let the warmth of his body intoxicate me.

The insignias on his disheveled shirt rattled every time he moved. It was all I could do not to grab—and potentially destroy—that shirt.

Destroyed or not, it needed to get the fuck out of the way, so I grabbed the lapels and shoved his shirt over his shoulders. He shook his hand free from the sleeve, then threw his shirt to the floor with a thud and a rattle. We both dragged his T-shirt over his head, and I tossed it aside. When my hands met his bare skin, we both sucked in hisses of breath before sinking into another feverish, demanding kiss.

Shane pulled back enough to roll onto his back, and I went with him. Now that I was on top, we both struggled to get my shirt off, but between kissing and grabbing on to each other, we didn't make much progress.

"Fuck," he whispered between kisses. "Jesus, we need to get…to get all these damned clothes…"

"Good idea." I kissed him quickly, then made myself sit up and shrug off my shirt. We separated, tore off the last of our clothes, and when we came together again in a breathless kiss, there was nothing but skin against skin.

I bent to kiss his neck, and he tilted his head both to give me access and so he could return the favor. His skin was warm and salty, and his lips and stubble brushed the side of my neck at the same time. When we sank down to the bed, landing softly on Shane's back, his cock brushed mine so deliciously, I released a shuddering, curse-laden breath against his ear. Shane slid his hand down my back, stopping just above my ass and pressing down with his palm at the same time he raised his hips.

"Oh…God…" I groaned, nearly sinking my teeth into his neck.

"Like that?"

"Yes," I murmured just below his ear. "But I want to fuck you,"

Shane nipped my shoulder. "I've been dying for you to fuck me for the last few nights."

I raised my head. "Well, then—" I kissed him. Hard, violent, eager.

He raised his hips again, letting his cock brush past mine. When he did it again, I moved to complement the motion, and we fell into a slow, smooth rhythm. We picked up speed, moving faster and with more urgency, more desperation. Every kiss was more intense than the last as our bodies moved together with more fervor. The need for release escalated with every brush of hot skin or cool breath.

I pushed myself up so I could see him, and the second our eyes locked, a shiver ran from the back of my neck all the way down to my toes.

Sex wasn't what I needed tonight. It was Shane. Just Shane. Against me, inside me, kissing me, fucking me; I didn't care as long as he was here with me, and that realization just made me want him that much more. God *damn*, I wanted to be inside him, deep inside him, forcing myself as deep as he would take me while he begged for more, and the very thought brought me closer to losing control. I couldn't bring myself to stop, not even to get a condom and fuck him like I so desperately needed to. I couldn't stop. Not yet. Just a little more of this. A little longer. A little—

Shane broke the kiss with a gasp, and his entire body seized beneath mine, and I couldn't take it another second. Closing my eyes, I buried my face against his neck and came with him.

I collapsed against him. He stroked my hair and the back of my neck with a shaking hand, and I kissed his damp skin. The room spun around us. My heart pounded in my ears. Every orgasm I ever had in his presence was powerful and breathtaking, but never failed to surprise me.

Long after the dust had settled, we didn't move or speak. I rested my head on Shane's chest. His arm was draped around my shoulders, and I probably could have drifted off to sleep if not for the inexplicable tightness in my stomach.

"Not in the mood" wasn't usually in my vocabulary, but tonight? Sex had been the last thing on my mind. I just didn't have the energy to even think about it.

When he'd kissed me, though, everything had changed. I didn't care if I had the energy. One kiss, and I went from not feeling like sex to needing Shane's touch so bad it hurt.

And now? Now I just wasn't sure what to make of anything.

This was unlike anything I'd ever experienced. I'd had amazing sex before Shane, but something about this was different. Not just the sex. *This.* Even my most serious relationships weren't in the same ballpark, and I wasn't sure why.

Sara and I had been a couple of horny teenagers stumbling through a clumsy attempt at a relationship before a positive pregnancy test and a couple of rings turned us into spouses. It took much too long, but we eventually figured out the lack of passion and the uncomfortable awkwardness had nothing to do with inexperience or anything like that. After my marriage ended, my relationships with men were more intense, both emotionally and sexually. I'd been infatuated with Lee. I'd had butterflies over Jon. I'd spent many nights lying awake at night thinking about Sven.

But this? This was new.

Yeah, my body had decided to get on board after he'd kissed me, and I'd been as horny as I ever was with him, but that deep, palpable need for him wasn't what I was used to. That I could still want him and need him like that, even when I was stressed and distracted, that was unusual.

I'd needed him like he was the only thing right in my life tonight.

"What is *the gay equivalent of pussy-whipped, anyway?"*

No, it wasn't that. So what if I'd found some stress relief with him? So what if being away from Shane was painful, and even being *with* him was painful?

Well, maybe painful wasn't the right word. Being with him was intense, almost to the point of discomfort, but that discomfort stemmed from a need to get even closer to him. I could never get close enough to him, even when we were tangled up together, and yet just being in the same room sometimes seemed too close.

"You are so head over heels for this guy..."

It was like when we were in the same room, I was constantly on the verge of either bursting into flames or falling to pieces.

"But you're not in love with him."

No, I wasn't.

I gulped. Was I?

Shane's voice broke the silence. "Something wrong?"

"Hmm?" I looked up at him. *God, you're beautiful.* "What? No, not at all. Why?"

He trailed his fingers along the shaved side of my head. "You seem...tense."

"Just thinking, I guess." I hoped he didn't notice me cringing. *Please don't ask what I'm thinking about. Please don't ask.*

Evidently satisfied I wasn't going to elaborate, Shane didn't push the issue.

I draped my arm over his chest, and I was sure he had to hear my heart pounding just then. The chessboard had been bumped again, but the pieces weren't necessarily out of place. The board had shifted. The pieces had moved. The game had changed.

Shane put his hand over mine on his chest, and I closed my eyes as my heart shifted into overdrive.

So this was what falling for someone felt like.

Chapter Twenty-Two

Shane

At my desk one Friday afternoon, I tapped a pen on the side of my keyboard and tried to focus. There was no rational reason why I should have been more worried today than any other day that someone would figure out I was seeing an enlisted man. We'd been discreet from the start. I hadn't said a word to anyone but Mays, and I had no doubt I could trust him.

It wasn't just today, though. Lately, I'd just felt…conspicuous. Like someone would take one look at me and see every one of my sins written in big red letters.

Since the day Marie flew back to the States a couple—maybe three?—weeks ago, Eric and I had been inseparable. More so than usual, anyway. More insatiable than usual too, for that matter. I couldn't put my finger on what had changed, but I was either counting down the minutes until we were together or trying to bargain with the clock to slow down and give us just a few more minutes before we separated. These days, I wondered how I functioned at all, what with all the sleep I *wasn't* getting.

I glanced at my watch. Work was nearly over. I hadn't planned on joining everyone at the O'Club tonight, but now I caught myself reconsidering. Eric had to work for a few more hours, so maybe I could kill a little time. And a nice cold beer or two did sound pretty good.

I decided I'd go with my coworkers after all.

When I walked into the Officers' Club with Mays and Gonzales, I immediately regretted coming here.

"Hey, man." Morris clapped my shoulder, and the smell of alcohol made me cringe as much as his presence did. "Thought you weren't coming out tonight?"

Great. He'd been drinking alone, and he'd started early. That was never a good sign. I would have loved to leave at this point and just go have a beer at home before Eric came over, but knowing Morris was already here and already a mess, there wasn't much I could do. If I left, we'd all leave, and if he had another alcohol-related incident after we'd taken off, we could be reprimanded for knowingly leaving him on his own in that condition. And the only thing worse than hanging out with him while he was like this was trying to convince him he needed to stop or that he couldn't drive.

I sent up a silent prayer for the serenity not to kill Morris, then followed the others into the lounge, where we found seats beside the bar. There weren't many barstools left, so Gonzales and Morris sat while Mays and I leaned against the bar. After a day behind a desk, I didn't mind standing.

When my beer arrived, I took a long drink. Ah, Orion. I couldn't help grinning to myself. I'd been drinking this stuff since I first came to Japan several years ago, but now it always reminded me of the night I met Eric. The taste that was in my mouth the first time I'd laid eyes on him.

Even if I did have someone here to sour the taste on my tongue with his obnoxious, alcohol-fueled attitude.

"I was right about that new fucking ensign," Morris slurred. "Queerer than a goddamned three-dollar bill."

"Right," Mays grumbled. "So I suppose that wife and kid back in the States are just a cover story?"

"Must be." Morris made an exaggerated, flippant gesture, almost smacking Gonzales in the process. "The way that fag was strutting around and acting like a fairy at the Dragon Club the other night—"

"Oh, for fuck's sake," I muttered. "That doesn't mean he's gay. If you caught him with another guy's dick in his mouth, then you might be on to something."

Gonzales snickered over the rim of her beer and looked at Morris. "Maybe you should offer your own."

"Fuck you," Morris growled. "I'm not offering my dick to any dude."

"Eh," she said with a shrug. "Even if you did, the data would be inconclusive. If Lange turned him down, he might still be gay. He'd just have, you know, standards."

"Whatever, bitch."

Mays scowled. I half expected him to flip his lid, but he just rubbed the bridge of his nose and grumbled something I didn't catch.

"So what if Lange is gay, anyway?" Gonzales said. "It's allowed now, you know."

"I'm not joking." Mays shot each of them a warning look that was even icier than usual, thanks to his lack of sleep. "Get started on DADT, *any* of you"—he threw the same look at me—"and I swear to God…"

Gonzales opened her mouth to say something, but Mays glared at her, and she went for her drink instead.

"I am so fucking serious right now," Mays muttered. "I am sleep-deprived, my patience is shot, and I'm this close to strangling the first person who kills my goddamned buzz."

I was right there with him. Long day. Long week. Exhaustion from one long, *long* night. Those nights with Eric were worth it and then some, but they did admittedly shorten my fuse during the day. I was so not in the mood for Morris's crap.

And he wasn't in the mood to quit either.

He put his drink down and sneered at both of us. "Man, as much as you two defend fucking gays, how do we know *you're* not?"

"Jesus. Really?" Mays put his hands up and stepped back from the bar. "I'm going to the damned head." He stormed off, probably just needing a minute to cool himself off before he went to blows. Another minute or two in Morris's presence, I'd probably need to do the same.

Morris laughed. "I'll bet he is. Motherfucking fag."

Anger burned in my chest, and I fought to keep my temper in check. "This is getting old, Morris. Can we just have a couple of drinks without you starting in on this shit?" I gestured in the direction Mays had gone. "He's here for a break from his kid.

We're all trying to wind down from work. Is this really necessary every damned time?"

"Says the man who seems thrilled as fuck that they're letting gays in—"

"God, Morris." Gonzales glared at him. "All joking aside, give it a rest, all right?"

"Fucking queers need to give it a rest," he muttered. "You all make it sound like it's no big deal, but guys have to share showers and berthings with other guys."

I laughed. "What does that have to do with you? Even if you go back to a ship, you'd have a damned stateroom."

"Don't matter," he slurred. "There's boys in the fleet that don't want to take showers with them."

"They'll get over it," Gonzales muttered into her glass.

"Easy for you to say." He slammed his glass down. "You ever tried to take a shower when—"

"You know," I said through gritted teeth, "with as hung up as you are about gays, I can't help wondering if there's something we should know about *you*."

And the son of a bitch snapped.

He flew toward me, and I had just enough time to think "oh, *fuck*" before his fist came out of nowhere and connected with my jaw. I stumbled back, and he was off-balance, so he went with me, and we both went down. The edge of a table bit into my back and collapsed under our combined weight.

Shouts erupted all around us. Morris drew his fist back again, but when he let fly, my reflexes beat his alcohol-dulled coordination, and he missed my face. I grabbed his wrist to keep him from trying again, and a second later, Mays and Gonzales hauled him off me. Morris tried to take a swing at her, but Mays shoved him up against the bar.

"Goddammit, Morris," Mays shouted in his face. "What the *fuck* is your damage?"

"I'm no fucking queer," Morris slurred.

"So the fuck what?" Mays snarled. "Jesus Christ, you've been asking for that for months. Now calm the fuck down, Commander, or I will *calm* you down."

While Mays tried to get Morris to settle down, Gonzales offered her hand. I clasped my hand around her forearm, and she helped me to my feet. She kept a firm hand on my shoulder, and I had no doubt it was as much to keep me from lunging at Morris as it was to help me find my balance. “You okay?”

I dabbed the corner of my mouth with two fingers and wasn’t surprised when they came back bloody. Aside from that, a cut inside my cheek and a few places on my back that would certainly be bruised, though, I was no worse for the wear. “Yeah, I’m fine.”

At Mays’s direction, Morris took a seat and wisely didn’t move. I was too wound up to sit, so I just leaned against the bar and tapped the leg of a barstool with my foot.

The club manager elbowed his way through the gathered crowd. Red-faced and fuming, he snarled, “What the hell is going on here?”

None of us spoke. One of the bartenders explained, in Japanese, what she’d seen. I didn’t understand everything she said, but caught enough to gather she didn’t think anyone except Morris had thrown a punch.

The manager barked an order at her. Then, to us, he said, “All of you, sit tight. Eighteenth Security is on its way.”

I shuddered. All four of us were getting cuffed, of that I had no doubt. That was how these things worked—anyone who laid a hand on anyone during a scuffle was arrested until things were sorted out. At least it was the Air Force. If they called Navy security, I’d be as fucked as Morris. Eric was the watch commander tonight. Shit, we’d both be screwed.

Beside me, Mays muttered something under his breath. He flipped his phone open and speed-dialed someone. For a moment, I thought he’d called the CO, but when the person on the other end answered, he spoke Japanese. I figured it was his wife, especially when he said, “*Ie ni kaetara setsumei shite.*” *When I come home, I’ll explain.*

After he’d hung up, he looked at me. “*Navy no keisatsu o yondara, oretachi yarrareta.*” *If they call Navy security, you’re fucked.*

"*Wakaru yo.*" *I know.*

Morris and Gonzales shot us both puzzled glances. Neither of them spoke much Japanese, so I wasn't concerned about them understanding what we'd said.

The four of us stayed quiet after that. A waitress brought me a bag of ice to put on my jaw. I gingerly pressed it to the side of my face and absently tongued the cut on the inside of my cheek, trying not to look as nervous as I was. All four of us would be arrested, but Morris would take the fall for the fight. That much I wasn't concerned about.

I just hoped to God the Air Force handled it.

About ten minutes after everything went down, four Airmen walked into the club, all of them dressed in the usual desert camouflage and wearing the black gun belts that set cops apart from other Airmen. A sergeant led the pack, and he stopped dead when he saw Morris.

He rolled his eyes. "Fucking Christ. You *again*?"

Oh God. That's not a good sign.

To the manager, the sergeant said, "How many were involved?"

"Four." The manager gestured at each of us in turn.

"Everyone who went hands-on," he said, "read them their rights, cuff them, and take them to the precinct."

I swallowed.

The sergeant looked at Morris, then me, then Morris again. Finally, he said to the junior Airmen, "Don't bother getting statements. I'm calling the Navy over to sort their own fuckers out this time."

My blood turned cold. I looked at Mays. He grimaced sympathetically.

Yarrareta.

I'm fucked.

Chapter Twenty-Three

Eric

"Oh, thank God," I said as the waitress appeared with our food. "I am fucking starving."

Diego laughed. "You know that means your phone is going to ring, right?"

I glared at him. "Shut. The fuck. *Up*."

Grant and Colburn both laughed.

Diego, Grant, Colburn and I sat around a table at the Enlisted Club on Camp Shields. Diego and Grant had been standing the gate, and Colburn had responded with me to a call for a traffic accident in base housing. It was one of those days when we hadn't even been able to think about food for several long hours, but things had finally settled down enough for us to grab a bite to eat.

I reached for the ketchup. Before my fingers had even landed on the bottle, my radio crackled to life.

"Whiskey Charlie, White Beach."

I exhaled sharply. "*Really?* Are you fucking kidding me?"

Diego laughed. "So much for dinner, am I right?"

"Always when I'm trying to fucking eat." I swore and picked up the radio. To the guys, I muttered, "I'm almost afraid to ask." Then I pressed the button and said, "Go ahead."

"Whiskey Charlie, be advised: Assault with minor injuries and property damage at the Kadena O'Club. Meet with Eighteenth Security for turnover."

Resting my elbows on the table, I pinched the bridge of my nose and tried not to groan.

There was no sending another patrol for this one. A watch commander was pretty much mandatory.

"Show me responding," I said.

All three guys struggled to keep from snickering.

"Very funny." I pushed my chair back and stood. "Colburn, I need you on this one."

"What?" His eyes widened. "Why me?"

I shot him a look. If he knew what was good for him, he heard loud and clear, *Because a first class just told you your ass is coming with me.*

He muffled a cough. "Right. Let's roll."

We had the waitress box up our food to go, then hurried out to the patrol vehicle.

"You mind driving?" I asked. "If I don't eat, I'm liable to deck someone."

"Not a problem." He took the keys from me. "I can eat and drive."

In the ten minutes or so it took for us to get from Camp Shields to the Eighteenth Security precinct on Kadena, I managed to inhale half my sandwich and most of the fries. At least that was enough to stave off the wicked headache that had been brewing between my temples, and with any luck would keep me from killing whoever's shenanigans had taken me away from my relaxing dinner.

Colburn pulled up in front of the precinct and parked. "Let's go see who beat who up."

"Probably a bunch of drunks getting an early start on the evening," I said. "They're lucky I've eaten, or I might've kicked their asses myself."

He laughed. "I'd pay to see that."

Chuckling, I pulled open the door to the Eighteenth Security precinct. We stepped inside and out of the sweltering heat.

An Airman at the front desk looked up as we took off our covers.

"MA1 Randall, CFAO Security," I said. "We got a call you're holding on to some of our guys."

He gestured over his shoulder. "Yeah. Victim, assailant, two witnesses who went hands-on. We've got 'em separated so they don't kill each other." He started down the hall, and Colburn and I followed.

"What happened?" I asked.

He shrugged. "Couple of officers had too many beers at the O'Club. Someone threw a punch." He waved a hand, leaving it to me to add up the rest of the situation.

"Great." Glancing at Colburn, I added, "This is why they shouldn't let officers drink."

He laughed.

To the Airman, I said, "Any injuries?"

"Nothing serious," he said. "Just needed a couple of ice packs, and they're all good. Well, except the one. Fucker doesn't shut his mouth, he's going to have an ice pack *in* it."

"Can't imagine how the fight got started, then," Colburn muttered.

"That's how it always starts," I said. "Booze, blab, brawl. Morons."

The Airman laughed. "Pretty much. Anyway, they're in holding cells now. Total of four individuals in custody, and our guys took voluntary statements from witnesses at the O'Club."

"And they've all been read their rights?"

"Yes," he said. "They're all being cooperative. One's pretty intoxicated, but the other three are lucid. They won't be driving for an hour or two, but..." He trailed off.

"Well," I said, "let's let the drunk one sober up a bit before we talk to him."

The Airman nodded. He pulled open the door of the first holding cell, and I stepped in ahead of Colburn.

In an instant, my blood turned to ice and my lungs to lead. Shane and I locked eyes, and the panic was as palpable in his expression as the chill running down my spine. The ice pack against his jaw killed any hope I might've had that he was just a witness.

He cursed and shifted his gaze away.

Oh, fuck. This isn't good.

I cleared my throat and turned to Colburn. "You know, you

could use the experience. Why don't you take this case?"

He blinked. "What?"

"Take their statements." I gestured at Shane, then the room across the hall where his assailant was penned up. "I'll be here if you need help, but you could use the experience."

"Uh, okay." He glanced at Shane and the Airman, then looked at me. "Can I talk to you outside?"

"Sure." Anything to get me out of this room before someone caught on that I was sleeping with Shane.

We stepped out into the hall.

"MA1, are you sure I should be handling this?" he asked. "I'm not questioning your judgment, but..." He hesitated, his eyes darting toward the door again. "I'm not sure I'm comfortable handling this."

"You know the procedures for taking statements in cases like this." *Please, man. Don't let me down here.* "Just take your time, have them each walk you through what happened. If you need a hand, I'll be right outside, so—"

"Outside?" He stared at me. "You're not even going to stay in there and look over my shoulder?"

I gulped. *Fuck, Colburn, don't make me explain myself here.* "This isn't an interrogation. You're not trying to drag a confession out of anyone. You're just getting the facts from everyone in their own words. They've already been read their rights, so just run them through that once more to be sure, and then have them walk you through what happened. The only way you're ever going to get this kind of experience is to just do it." I gestured toward the door. "You'll be fine."

He eyed me skeptically. Then he dropped his gaze and nodded. "All right. If you think this is a good idea."

"If it was anyone else"—*I'd be so colossally screwed you can't even imagine*—"I wouldn't. But I know you can do this."

He gnawed his lower lip and shifted his weight.

"Just ask them what happened," I said. "Get clarification if anything doesn't make sense. You're not the judge and jury here; you're just finding out what happened."

"All right," he said. "You're the boss."

I clapped his shoulder. "You'll be fine. It's not as bad as you think."

He took a deep breath. "Okay. On it."

Colburn took everyone's statements, and as soon as he was done, I read them over. Thankfully, he'd done a flawless job. The statements from Shane, Commander Mays and Lieutenant Commander Gonzales all lined up perfectly. Commander Morris, the alleged assailant, didn't disagree with them, especially the more he sobered up.

I looked up from the statements. "Nicely done, MA2."

He smiled. "Thanks."

I owe you so big, kid. Seriously.

"So what do we do with them?" he asked.

I hesitated. Watch commander or not, I couldn't be the one to give the order. Not in this situation. "Well, based on the statements you took, what do you think should happen?"

He swallowed. "Uh, well, Morris should be turned over to his chain of command, and we should let the other three go." He raised his eyebrows, silently asking if that was the right answer.

I turned to the sergeant and gestured at Colburn. "You heard him."

I waited by the precinct's front door as the two commanders and lieutenant commander were released. My stomach twisted and turned, and as the three of them walked out, I avoided Shane's eyes. A moment later, Colburn came out with Commander Morris in handcuffs, and I gritted my teeth as we led him out to our patrol vehicle.

I made an excuse about wanting to look over the paperwork one last time and let Colburn drive us back to White Beach.

And we hadn't even made it off Kadena before our passenger opened his damned mouth. Gays in the military, women in the military, the kinder, gentler, pussy military; he just didn't quit. I ground my teeth even harder and tried to ignore him, but when he started ranting about Shane, my patience frayed *fast.*

"He had it coming," Morris slurred. "Motherfucker thinks

queers belong in the military. Just what we need. Guys showering with gay guys, fucking pansy-ass pussies out on the fucking battlefield. That son of a bitch thinks I'm a queer? I'll bet good money he—"

"With all due respect, Sir," I growled over my shoulder, "shut the fuck up."

His teeth snapped shut.

Colburn's eyes widened, and he glanced at me. Keeping his voice so quiet I could barely hear him, he said, "You okay, MA1?"

"I'm fine," I said, probably more tersely than I needed to. "Ready to turn him over to his chain of command, that's for sure."

Colburn shot me a puzzled look but let it go. He probably wondered why I was at my wit's end with this guy. I'd only been in the man's presence for ten or fifteen minutes by this point, while Colburn had had to question the drunk idiot.

Neither of them needed to know my reasons. They also didn't need to know how tempting it was to tell Colburn to pull over so I could show him what a "pansy-ass pussy" a gay man could be. I wasn't a fighter, but damn if he hadn't fucked my world up in ways he couldn't possibly imagine. He was lucky for what little restraint I had.

The twenty-minute drive to White Beach felt like it took hours, but eventually, we made it. I put in the call to his commanding officer—that much I could handle, since I was merely relaying a message rather than giving the order or making the decision—and had some other MAs babysit him.

It had been a slow week, so word about the brawling officers spread quickly. Rumors flew, and, of course, Chief caught wind of it. He pulled me aside and had me brief him on what really happened.

"Now, I'm a little confused about something, MA1." He looked up at me from his chair behind his desk. "Help me out here." He held up the statements. "I see Colburn's handwriting and signature on everything. Looks to me like he took the statements for all four suspects."

"Yes, Chief." I forced back my nerves. "The case was cut and dry. No one disputed what happened, so it was a good opportunity for MA2 Colburn to get some experience."

"You mean to tell me," Chief said, "that when you responded to a call involving officers whose paygrades are so high above yours you're lucky you didn't get altitude sickness just being in the same room, you dumped it off on a second-class petty officer?"

I swallowed. "Yes, Chief."

He slammed the reports down on his desk. "Why in the *fuck* would you pull a stunt like that?"

"He is a completely competent MA," I said. "He's a rock-solid patrolman, we don't get cases like this very often, and he needed the experience."

"He needed *supervised* experience," Chief shouted. "Not you leaving him alone to take statements from an assault victim and his assailant. From goddamned *officers*, MA1."

I put up my hands. "I reviewed the statements, Chief. They were correct and clear, and the assailant was read his rights by the Eighteenth and by MA2 Colburn. Colburn knows the procedures for taking statements, and he handled it—"

"Listen here, MA1," the chief said. "This isn't a traffic accident. You don't just pawn this shit off on junior, Sailor."

I gulped. "I understand, Chief. But I was there in case he had questions, if—"

"You are the watch commander," he snapped. "There's a situation involving officers and goddamned criminal charges, you step up and fucking *handle* it." He gestured sharply. "And handling it doesn't mean leaving it in the hands of a kid who barely knows his own ass from a radar gun. Am I understood?"

"Yes, Chief," I said quietly.

"If I find anything out of place in your investigation," he snarled. "If I find a goddamned typo on one of those reports, anything a fucking watch commander should have handled and corrected before it went on paper, I will make sure your ass is sent to captain's mast. If you value your watch commander qual, not to mention your third chevron, you will step up and behave as a first class and a goddamned watch commander, not pawn shit off on your junior fucking Sailors. Am I clear?"

I swallowed. "Yes, Chief."

"Am I *clear*, MA1?"

"*Yes*, Chief."

"Good. Now get the fuck out of my office."

I went out into the hall. Leaning against the wall, I groaned and rubbed my temples. This was bad. This was real bad. I'd dodged one bullet, yes, but quite possibly put myself in the path of another. Colburn was a good cop. I'd triple-checked his work today, and I was confident he hadn't fucked anything up. Even if he had, though, I couldn't have corrected him. Anything I did or said—if I so much as corrected a typo or told him to move a comma—would have tainted the entire investigation. My hands were tied, and I'd taken the least dangerous route for my career and Shane's.

Eyewitnesses all confirmed the verbal dispute was between Shane and Commander Morris, but Morris had thrown the first and only punch. Gonzales and Mays had neutralized him without excessive force. Everything was cut and dry, and I had a feeling Morris wouldn't argue once he'd sobered up.

That idiot's career was probably over. If I didn't navigate this minefield the right way, Shane's career and mine might be over too. Or mine could go down in flames while I kept my mouth shut for Shane's sake. Not that I'd get kicked out for handling this case badly, but if I went to mast and the skipper decided to strip me of a rank and make an example out of me? If he found a reason to call it dereliction of duty? Then I was fucked. I'd been in sixteen years, so I was past high-year tenure for a second class. If I was busted down a rank, I'd be discharged. Good-bye retirement, hello unemployment.

And if anyone found out why I'd pawned the case off on a younger, less-experienced cop, retirements would be the least of our worries. Shane and I could both kiss honorable discharges good-bye.

Fuck, Randall. What are you doing?

I ran a hand through my hair. It wasn't like Shane and another officer would get into fisticuffs on a regular basis. This was likely a fluke. A one-time thing.

But what if he got into a fender bender? Witnessed one? Witnessed a fight between a couple of drunk officers? Had something stolen from his car?

Bumping into each other on base was one thing. We could salute each other, act like we didn't know each other out of uniform and move on.

Just showing up today could have gotten us both in deep shit. If I had so much as spoken to him, and someone subsequently found out about our relationship, the entire investigation would have been compromised, and we'd both be court-martialed so fast our heads would spin. The guy who punched Shane probably wouldn't be in as much trouble as we would be.

Even now, if someone found out, we'd be fucked. And if someone got any more curious than Chief about my hesitation to get involved...

I exhaled.

Then I took my phone off my belt. Shifting uncomfortably, I debated doing this now or doing it later. No. It had to be now. It had to be now, before I lost my nerve.

I sent Shane a text: *Blue Roof Izakaya tonight?*

I stared into my beer. Every time someone walked past on the other side of the closed door, my heart thudded in time with their footsteps until they'd gone far enough for me to be sure they weren't Shane. For the first time since we'd met, I didn't want to see him. I didn't want to do this, but what choice did I have?

The door slid open, and a waitress gestured for Shane to go in. He asked her to bring him an Orion beer, toed off his shoes and joined me in the room. He kissed me lightly, then sat across from me.

Once we were alone, I muffled a cough. "How's your jaw?"

He touched it gingerly, then moved it from side to side. "It's been better."

I avoided his eyes. I had no idea what to say. Well, I knew what I needed to say, but I wasn't ready to go there yet. God, this wasn't like me. I was used to cutting to the chase and skipping the small talk, but this was one point B that I was in no hurry to reach.

Finally meeting his eyes, I struggled to work up the nerve.

I wish I could tell you I love you.

Shane reached across the table and put his hand over mine. "Look, I'm sorry you had to be in that position today. I've kind of worried for a while that things would get out of hand with Morris, but that..." He trailed off, shaking his head. "I'm sorry, Eric."

"It's not your fault. But..." I took a deep breath. As much as it hurt, and probably stung him too, I slid my hand out from under his. Folding my arms on the edge of the table, I made myself look at him. "I think it might have been too close a call."

"What do you mean?" The hint of panic in his voice made me flinch.

I swallowed. "My chief is threatening me with mast if anything about this investigation is off."

He exhaled hard and raked a hand through his hair. "God, I'm so sorry."

I shrugged halfheartedly. "It's done. We can't change it. But if anyone asks questions..."

"I know," he said with a nod. "Do you think they will?"

"I don't know. I mean, they're questioning how I handled it today, but as far as us..." My heart sank. I knew where I had to take this, and it killed me to think about it, but I couldn't keep putting it off. I wrapped both hands around my glass and stared into the shallow reserve of beer left in the bottom. "We can't do this. I need..." I trailed off, closing my eyes for a long moment. *I need you so bad it hurts.* Then I made myself look him in the eye again but couldn't quite keep my voice even. "I need this to be the last time we see each other."

His lips parted. "Eric, we—"

"We *can't* do this." I swallowed hard. *God, I want to. I can't even tell you, Shane.* My throat ached, and it was all I could do to keep my voice from breaking. "Today was... We can't risk a closer call next time."

"Think about it," he said. "What happened today, what are the odds of it happening again?"

"What were the odds of it happening in the first place?"

"Considering Morris and I won't be working together after this, I don't think we have to worry about it happening again."

"And what if you get into a fender bender on base?" I shook my head. "If I'm called to a scene, and I refuse to take a statement from you again, people are going to ask questions. I don't know how to answer those questions, Shane."

He winced and looked away, but didn't speak.

"We both have too much on the line. We can't take this risk." *No matter how much I love you.* "It's not fair, but this is what we signed up for." As I reached into my pocket and pulled out a few coins, I added, "There's nothing we can do about it. You know that as well as I do." I dropped a few hundred yen beside my glass. "This will cover my bill. I...I need to go." I got up and started for the door.

"Eric."

I turned and looked back at him.

"Have you considered this might be worth what we're risking for it?" he asked.

I dropped my gaze. Forcing back emotion, I avoided his eyes as I said, "Yes, I have." I put my hand on the door and, just before I slid it open, added, "But that was before today."

And before I could think of another reason to stay, I left.

Chapter Twenty-Four

Shane & Eric

The door closed behind Eric with a hollow thud.

I sat back against the wall and closed my eyes. My jaw still throbbed relentlessly, keeping today's fiasco at the forefront of my mind, just in case there was any chance I might try to think of anything else. I could blame Morris for all of this until I was blue in the face, but I knew better than to get involved with an enlisted man.

Morris had bruised my face, but this? This was all Eric and me.

The door opened, and my heart jumped. For a split second, I thought Eric had come back, but it was the waitress bringing the beer I'd ordered earlier.

She handed me my beer, then slid the door shut again.

Alone again, I didn't take a drink. I rested my elbow on the table and pressed the glass against my jaw. The cold lessened some of the throbbing, but I was far from getting anything I could call relief.

I knew why Eric left. I understood. I wanted to be pissed at him for leaving, but the only anger I could muster was directed at the military regulations that made our relationship criminal. I supposed I knew deep down that this couldn't last, but my God, it hurt to watch him go.

I lowered the glass and took a long swallow of beer. As soon as the cool liquid met my palate, my eyes stung.

I wished to God I hadn't ordered Orion.

All the way home, I couldn't stop thinking about Shane.

I stared out the window of my taxicab. I couldn't read any

of the signs, and they wouldn't have made any more sense if they'd all been in English. Bright lights and colors ran together. Kanji and English alike blurred.

Wiping my eyes, I shifted my gaze away from the scenery. I wrung my hands in my lap.

The taxi pulled up in front of my apartment, and I numbly counted out the fare. After he'd given me my change, I trudged up the stairs, my feet heavy like they were encased in concrete.

We knew this could happen. We knew from the start this was a bad idea.

I was supposed to be worried about getting caught, Shane, but I've been too busy falling in love with you, and look at us now.

My stomach twisted. My head throbbed. I knew I'd made a colossal mistake, but I couldn't say if the mistake was the beginning or the end of the relationship. There was no other choice. I had to end it. We couldn't keep doing this. But if it was the right thing to do, then why did it feel so damned wrong to walk away?

After Eric left, I stayed at the Blue Roof Izakaya for...I couldn't say. A half hour? Maybe an hour? I wasn't sure and didn't really give a fuck. When I was finally sure I could trust my knees to stay under me, I paid my tab and left.

The cab dropped me at the foot of my apartment. I wasn't nearly drunk enough yet, so I pulled a beer out of the refrigerator and went out onto my balcony for some air.

I rested my hands on the railing and stared out at the night. The beer I'd brought out with me stayed untouched and unopened beside me.

This couldn't possibly be the way things ended with us. Not when in six, nine, twelve months, Eric could be an officer.

Or...not.

Closing my eyes, I let my head fall forward and exhaled. It shouldn't have hurt like this. We hadn't even been dating that long, and I supposed we both knew it couldn't last forever. But my God, the only split that had been painful like this was when Katie and I broke up after my combat deployment. And this was different. I didn't feel betrayed or like Eric had lied to me. I didn't wonder how much of the last few months had been real and how much he'd faked. No, it was all real. Of that I had no doubt. It was real, and so was this deep sense that everything was suddenly wrong in the world.

God, Eric, you just don't know how much I love you.

Or maybe he did. And maybe that was why he knew we couldn't continue.

I am so, so sorry, Shane.

With an unopened beer on the railing beside me, I stood on my balcony and stared out into the night.

You did the right thing. You were just stupid to wait until you got this attached.

My own thoughts made me wince. It was the right thing. There was nothing else I could have done. Nothing else we could do.

I pulled out my phone and scrolled to Shane's name.

Edit contact.

Delete contact.

Are you sure you want to permanently delete 'Shane' from your contacts?

My thumb hovered over the button.

It was over. The long overdue ending had come and gone.

Are you sure you want to permanently delete 'Shane' from your contacts?

Well, Eric. Are you?

Cursing to myself, I pressed the Cancel button and shoved my phone into my pocket. I couldn't do it. Not tonight, at least. I just...I wasn't ready for that. I'd regretted not getting his number when I first met him, and I couldn't quite bring myself to delete it just yet.

Splitting with my last boyfriend hadn't hurt like this. Not even close. That breakup had been just as inevitable, but deep down, he and I had both known we weren't playing for keeps. With Shane, I...I couldn't make sense of it. I couldn't even begin to dull the sting with reassurances to myself that this was for the best.

How much was I willing to give up for this career? I'd already lost time I could never replace with my daughter. I'd spent almost two years in the blazing-hot desert with bullets and mortars flying over my head, and at least three combined years at sea.

For the sake of my career, was I really willing to give up the love of my life?

The thought made me flinch.

The love of my life.

He was. Of course he was. Who was I kidding?

But I'd signed the contract. I'd sworn to defend this country with my life and obey, on penalty of court-martial, the Uniform Code of Military Justice. Hell, I'd pledged to uphold the UCMJ when other Sailors violated it. I'd agreed to it knowing full well what constituted conduct unbecoming a gentleman, but meeting a man like Shane had never been part of the deal.

This wasn't right. The Navy had already taken enough from me.

But what else could I do?

Chapter Twenty-Five

Shane

On Monday, everyone at work kept their distance. Gonzales came into my office to see how I was doing, but she figured out quickly that I wasn't in the mood to be social. I let her believe it had to do with what happened with Morris.

With Mays, I was a bit more candid.

"Sorry you and Gonzales had to get involved," I said.

Mays shrugged. "I wasn't going to let him beat your ass."

I laughed dryly. "You don't think I could have taken him?"

He chuckled. "Well, probably. But then you'd be in trouble, so..." He shrugged again. "So how did things go with security? I mean, since..."

I kept my voice low. "The MA2 handled everything. Eric kept his own name off everything, didn't talk to any of us."

Nodding, Mays said, "Smart move on his part."

"Yeah." I blew out a breath. "At least one of us was thinking that night. I—" I stopped abruptly when my desk phone rang. I scowled at the extension that lit up. "That's the skipper." I picked up the handset. "Yes, sir?"

"I'd like to see you in my office. At your earliest convenience, please."

My heart quickened. That was the captain's code for "Get your ass in my office *now.*"

"Yes, sir. I'll be right there." I hung up and stood.

Mays stood too. "Boss wants to see you?"

"Yep. This should be fun."

He clapped my shoulder as we walked out of my office. "Relax. You didn't do anything wrong. He probably just wants to hear your story."

"Thanks," I said quietly.

At the end of the hall, he went left to go back to his own office, and I went right to go see the captain.

Steeling myself, I knocked.

Captain Warren opened the door. "Commander."

I swallowed. "You wanted to see me, Sir?"

"Have a seat." He gestured at the chair in front of his desk as he went around to sit in his own chair.

I sat, trying not to look as nervous as I was.

He leaned back, his desk chair squeaking in the otherwise silent office. "So what exactly happened the other night?"

I kept my eyes down. "Commander Morris was drunk. I'd had a little bit myself, but I..." I rubbed the back of my neck. "He has a tendency to run off at the mouth when he's drunk. I let it get under my skin, and I said something that admittedly provoked him. Then..." I trailed off, making a sharp gesture at the bruise on my face before resting my hands in my lap.

He steepled his fingers below his chin. "So you're aware of Morris's drinking problem."

"Yes, sir. That's...that's why we go with him. It's either that, or he drinks alone, and we're all concerned about him getting a DUI."

He nodded slowly. "The admiral isn't going to be pleased about this situation."

"I know, sir." I folded my hands in my lap to keep from wringing them.

"That said, I'm going to recommend that you not receive any kind of reprimand," he said. "From everything I read in the statements and after speaking with security, it sounds like Commander Morris did all the attacking." His expression softened a little, and he laughed. "Men like him, makes you wonder why they don't raise the drinking age to forty. But then I suppose that would mean mutiny from the enlisted ranks."

I forced out a laugh and nearly choked on it. A prickle of panic spiked up the length of my spine, as if the mere mention of the word *enlisted* would give away that I had been sleeping with MA1 Randall.

The captain didn't notice, though. He dismissed me, and I went back to my office.

Staring out my office window, I gritted my teeth.

I couldn't ask Eric to risk his career for me, but I also couldn't walk away as easily as he apparently could. What was at stake didn't change what I felt for him. I couldn't help it. I loved him.

A day passed.

Two.

Three.

A week.

Another.

Morris was long gone. Our after-work beers—*no* Orion for me—were less frequent now that we had no one to babysit. More pleasant now too, for the same reason. I had a hell of a time mustering any enthusiasm for the beer, the food or the company, though, so more often than not, I didn't bother going.

Tonight, I needed it. Beat the fuck out of staying home, drinking alone and being depressed, after all. It was probably just as well I was roped into being DD. Drinking was probably the last thing I needed to be doing.

Gonzales elbowed me. "Man, what is wrong with you lately? You miss your brawling buddy or something?"

I forced a laugh and picked up my Coke. "Yeah, something like that."

She eyed me. "You get dumped or something?"

I shot her a glare, and she tensed.

"Oh." She cleared her throat, and her cheeks colored. "Sorry, I thought...you said you weren't..."

"It's okay." I took a drink, and when I glanced at Mays, his inquisitive expression raised my hackles. It was all I could do to keep my irritation out of my voice as I said, "I'm not seeing anyone now. Let's just leave it at that."

The question lingered on his face, but he didn't push it. Neither did Gonzales.

At home that night, I lay back on my long-since-cooled sheets, staring up at the ceiling like I had the morning I'd finally gotten Eric's number. Hadn't I known then that this was a bad idea? I couldn't have foreseen exactly how things would go down, but even then, I had to have known the end was inevitable. I didn't think it would hurt like this, but if I was honest, the end no more surprised me than did the tears stinging my eyes.

I wiped my eyes and took a deep breath. This hurt, this sucked, but the more I thought about it, the more it made sense. Eric was right. This was how it had to be. It would take time to get over it, but I had to make peace with it and move on. No matter how we felt about each other, we couldn't be together. We'd signed the contract. We'd agreed to the rules. Such was life in the military.

The next day at work, I felt a little better. Some time, some distance, some objectivity, it all conspired to help me inch closer to accepting that no matter how much it hurt to be away from him, this was how it had to be.

Then, around the time my day was winding to a close, my text message alert went off. I pulled my phone out of my pocket, and my heart jumped into my throat when I saw the name: *Eric.*

Chapter Twenty-Six

Eric

Okinawa wasn't the same without Shane.

Alone on the highest wall of Katsuren Castle, surveying the panoramic view that had once been foreign, it was all I could do to keep my vision clear enough to take in all the places that were now familiar.

Across the water, at the other end of the long, meandering bridge, was Henza Island, where Shane had cracked me up by swearing at a slow sugarcane truck that wouldn't get out of the way. Then Miyagi Island, where we'd pulled over to get a picture of a vending machine standing between a pair of tombs. Ikei Island, where I'd caught him giving me a look that left me weak in the knees, and he'd whispered a promise that had me tingling and fidgeting until we made it into bed hours later.

Eyes stinging, I shifted my gaze in a different direction, but it didn't matter. Every inch of this place had Shane's name on it now. If I could have seen Nakagusuku from here like people once could, I'd have seen the two of us walking along the walls, bantering about Nikons and Canons and the haunted hotel. And all around, there was the turquoise water where he'd teased moray eels, sea urchins and puffer fish. And the roads that had taken us to distant, discreet places where we could pretend we were just a couple of guys taking in the sights.

Okinawa wasn't the same without Shane, and neither was I.

I pulled my phone out of my pocket to check the time and also to see if Shane had replied to my text. He hadn't, and it had been an hour since I'd sent it. I stared at my phone, wondering if sending that message had been a good idea or if I was just pouring salt in my own wounds. Being here alone was bad enough when every minute wasn't a reminder that he probably wasn't coming.

He hadn't responded to my text, and I doubted he would.

I pocketed my phone and looked out at the scenery again. The cicadas were noisy as always, electrifying the air with their deafening buzzing, but my heartbeat drowned out all but the most enthusiastic among them. Could I blame him if he didn't come? After I'd rattled off all the reasons we couldn't be together and then walked away from him? Every reason he had to stay away from me was a reason I'd handed to him.

"I need this to be the last time we see each other."

I flinched at the echo of my own words. Maybe that had been the right thing to do, but for the last two weeks, the thought that kept me up all night, every night, was that we shouldn't have been apart. This wasn't right. It couldn't be. It didn't fucking make sense.

More than once, I'd thought about going to Palace Habu to find someone else, but I'd only be kidding myself if I said I was searching the crowd for any face but Shane's. I didn't want another man. I wanted him. And I stayed the fuck away from the club because I was afraid he'd be there with someone else.

Over the electric buzzing of cicadas, a faint scuff made it to my ears. Then another. Slowly, with my heart thundering in my chest, I turned around.

Shane came around the top of the stairs, and from across the grassy enclosure, our eyes met. I didn't breathe as he came across the enclosure, grass hissing past his shoes.

A few feet shy of the wall on which I stood, he stopped. He hooked his thumbs in the belt loops on his khaki shorts but didn't look even remotely casual or relaxed.

"I'm assuming you wanted to talk?" His tone was flat, his expression blank, betraying absolutely nothing to let me gauge if he was hurt, angry, numb, apathetic.

"Yeah." I chewed my lip. *God, where do I start?*

He glanced over his shoulder. Then he looked at me again and shifted his weight. "We shouldn't be here."

"We shouldn't have been here the first time."

Shane looked away, shifting his gaze out toward the ocean.

"No one else is going to come up here," I said.

"I know, but..." He exhaled hard, still avoiding my eyes.

"But you came anyway."

He finally looked at me again. "Yeah, I did."

We held each other's gazes, each waiting for the other to say...something. Anything. Since I'd initiated this, I needed to say it, but damn if I could remember any of the words that had replayed in my mind all the way up here from the parking lot. Hoping for the best, I took a deep breath and spoke.

"Look, about what I said at the Izakaya, I'm sorry. You were right." I swallowed. "This is worth the risk."

"Eric, think about what you're saying."

I stared at him. "I thought you said—"

"I know what I said." Shane's tone was gentle, but firm. "And watching you walk away that night hurt like hell." He cleared his throat. When he spoke this time, his tone wavered. "Just like I know it's going to hurt like hell to walk away from you tonight."

My heart dropped. "Shane..."

"Between us, we've invested over thirty years in the Navy," he said. "What happened the other day could have cost us both everything we've worked for. We both have kids to look after, and we have civilian careers to think about after we retire. I..." He exhaled, then shook his head. "I don't see how we could do this."

I swallowed. "My LDO should go through in a few months. We just have to keep this on the down low until it does."

He exhaled. "And you know as well as I do, that still won't solve everything. I'll still outrank you. We could still get in trouble."

"A hell of a lot less trouble than we can get into now."

He pursed his lips. "And if the package isn't approved?"

"Then...I..." I ran a hand through my hair before making a sharp, frustrated gesture. "I don't know. If it doesn't, I'll try again."

"And then what?" He gave an apologetic shrug. "We wait

another six to nine months until it's denied again?"

"If it's what we have to do. I know we'd be risking a lot, but..." I dropped my gaze and bit my lip, not sure how to finish the sentence.

"Eric?"

I made myself look him in the eye. "There's a lot at stake here, but I think this is worth it." I willed my voice to stay steady as I whispered, "I think you're worth it."

"And if something happens again?"

"Honestly?" I forced myself to hold his gaze. "They can take my damned retirement."

"That's easy to say now," he said. "But what about Marie? My kids? Our careers after the Navy? It's just...it's not that simple."

"Shane, I"—I shook my head—"I'm sorry. That's all I can say."

"So am I." He took a step back. "But we can't do this." Another step. "You know we can't. I think it's better if we just let it go."

With that, he turned to leave.

"Shane, wait."

He stopped and turned around.

"Look, I know full well what we'd be risking," I said, speaking quickly now. "That night, I was scared, all right? Everything with the assault case, it freaked me out. But ever since I walked out of the Izakaya, I haven't been thinking about my career or getting court-martialed or anything."

He inclined his head, his eyes asking the unspoken question.

I hooked my thumbs in my belt loops in a feeble attempt to look less tense than I was. "I've only been thinking that walking away was a huge mistake."

"But how can we do this? We've already had one close call. We'll still have to keep it on the down low, and my God, you know as well as I do how exhausting that can be." Shane paused, shifting his gaze toward the ocean again. "I put you in a situation where you had to choose whether to risk your career or both of our careers." He faced me. "I can't do that to you again. If that MA2 had fucked up..." He shook his head. "I can't ask you to put yourself in that position for me again."

I wanted to look him in the eye, but for the first time since I'd met him, his eyes were too intense. Or maybe I was just too afraid of what I needed to say. Of what he'd say once I finally forced out the words.

Hoping for the best, I made myself speak. "I have already put so much shit on the line for the Navy." My voice tried to crack, but I kept going. "I've been shot at. I've had mortars fired at me. I've been closer than I care to think about to more than one IED." I paused, struggling to keep my emotions in check. "I've missed out on a quarter of my daughter's life, and now I've been moved thousands of miles away from her." Though I wanted to look anywhere but right at him, I made myself meet his eyes. "The Navy has taken so damned much from me. I'm not ready to let it have the one time I have ever really been in love with someone."

Shane's lips parted. "What?"

I dropped my gaze to the ages-old stones at my feet. I'd never in my life been reduced to this, to fearing eye contact like a terrified kid, but I was so, so afraid he'd turn and walk away.

Relief rushed right through me as he took a couple of tentative steps forward. "And what happens if something like the other night happens again? I know I put you in a bad position, and I don't want to do that to you again."

With a cautious grin, I said, "Well, you could start by not antagonizing another officer until he punches you."

We both laughed softly.

Then I went on. "I don't know what will happen. I don't know what will happen with any of this. The only thing I'm sure of is that I want to be with you, even if we have to continue keeping it a secret until we retire."

He avoided my eyes again.

"Look," I said. "Even if we can't date, I don't want to lose you as a friend."

"I don't think we can be friends, though." Taking a deep

breath, Shane looked at me. “Not now that I know you feel the same way I do.”

My heart leaped into my throat. “You do?”

“Yes,” he said softly. “I do.”

He stepped closer again, this time stopping a foot or so from the wall. Our eyes met.

Then he put his hand up. I reached for his, and we clasped hands around each other’s forearms. I helped him up onto the wall, and in an instant, we were face-to-face. Inches apart. Almost too close.

The intensity in his gaze bordered on too much, and I broke eye contact. “Shane, I’m sorry. About that night.”

“Me too.” With two fingertips, he raised my chin. Our eyes met again.

“I love you,” he whispered.

“I love you too.”

Stroking my face, Shane held my gaze for a moment. Then he laughed at something and looked out at the distant water.

“What?” I asked.

“I guess...” He chuckled again and gave me a sheepish look. “I guess I’m just really not good at doing what I should when it comes to you.”

And he kissed me.

Chapter Twenty-Seven

Shane

Clothes on the floor and arms around each other, we sank into Eric's bed.

It didn't matter if this was right or wrong anymore. It just *was*, and it needed to be. All the way up to the castle, I'd asked myself what the hell I was thinking, and all the way here I'd wondered how the fuck I'd lasted this long without him.

With Eric under me and his arms around me, with his mouth against mine and his breath rushing across my skin, I was simultaneously about to lose my mind and closer to sane than I'd been in recent memory. My pulse was out of control, blood surging through my veins as my heart pounded with nerves and relief and anticipation.

We shouldn't do this.

We have to do this.

We can't do this.

We need to do this.

"God, I've missed this," he said, panting between kisses.

"I've missed you," I said and kissed him hungrily. Neither of us spoke. My head spun, my body tingled, and if not for the gasps and moans he brought out of me, I probably wouldn't have even bothered breathing.

Eric broke the kiss. "Holy hell, I want you."

"Likewise." I pressed my cock against his. "I want you to fuck me, Eric."

"With pleasure," he growled. "Let me get a condom."

We pulled apart enough for him to reach for the condoms he kept next to the bed, and we didn't waste any time. I rolled onto my back, Eric put on the condom and lube, and then he positioned himself over me again. We both released ragged breaths as he guided himself to me, and we both moaned as he pushed in. He was slow at first, careful, and it took all I had not to beg him to force himself all the way in. I wanted every inch of him, and I didn't care if it hurt.

After a few cautious strokes, though, he picked up speed. Not much, not his usual fast and furious pace, but oh God, it felt amazing.

I looked up at him, and, eyes locked, both of us panting, we moved together. Slowly, smoothly, like we'd done this enough times to perfect it, like it had been perfect from the beginning, like it didn't matter when we'd gotten it right because it was perfect *right now*.

I touched his face with an unsteady hand. I still couldn't quite believe he was here, that *we* were here. A million memories flashed through my mind—Eric riding me on the beach of Komaka, his back arching off my apartment door while I sucked him off the first night, the way we'd fucked each other senseless the night he put Glenn in his place—and every one of them added up to everything about *this* moment making perfect sense. Going our separate ways was an ending that didn't fit, a conclusion that didn't match the facts. This was right. This was how it needed to be.

I slid my hand behind his neck and raised my head off the pillow as I pulled him down to me. "God, I love you," I said.

"I love you too," he said and kissed me. Even as he moved faster, he still kissed me, both of us breathing hard as he went from slow and easy to the kind of hungry, forceful rhythm that always drove me insane.

Eric raised himself up on his arms, and he fucked me hard and fast, driving the air right out of my lungs. His bed creaked and groaned beneath us, and I didn't give a damn if anyone heard us. Not his neighbors, not his chain of command, not my chain of command. Fuck them all. I needed him.

"Oh...fuck..." He let his head fall forward, his lips pulled tight across his teeth and his eyes screwed shut.

Abruptly, he stopped. He withdrew, and before I could find enough air to protest, his mouth was around my cock. I shivered so violently, I damn near sat upright. Propping myself up on my elbows, I stared down at him, my lips parted and my breath barely moving. He swallowed me slowly, an inch at a time, almost deep-throating before rising again.

He stroked the shaft with one hand and teased the head of my cock with his lips and tongue. Going from being fucked to being at the mercy of his hand and mouth was beyond intense, beyond incredible, and there was no way I'd last. Not when he knew just how hard and fast to stroke and just when and where to swirl his tongue.

"Oh God..." I rested my hand in his hair and let my head fall back. "Oh God, Eric, I'm gonna...oh fuck..."

I collapsed back onto the bed, and everything turned white. My whole body seized with the force of my orgasm, and there was nothing I could do but lie back and ride every last, incredible, spine-melting wave. By the time my vision cleared, Eric was over me again, and when he kissed me with salt on his tongue, I was almost certain I was about to come again. Christ, this man turned me on like no other. I grabbed his shoulder and the back of his neck, lifting my head off the pillow in search of more of his kiss.

He pulled away, though. Confusion mingled with panic for a few seconds before I realized what he was doing. As soon as he opened the lube bottle, I couldn't help whimpering softly. *God, yes...*

He put on some more lube, then set the bottle aside and guided himself to me again. With the aftershocks of my orgasm still crackling along the length of my spine, I could barely stand it as he pressed into me. He moved slowly, gently, but holy fuck, the sensation of his cock sliding into me was so damn intense.

Holding my gaze, he kept fucking me slowly, and I rocked my hips just enough to complement his smooth, fluid strokes.

Then he closed his eyes and furrowed his brow, digging his teeth into his lower lip. Though he moved slowly, every muscle in his body quivered, from his abs to his shoulders, and the cords on his neck stood out.

I rocked my hips back a little more. Eric groaned, the creases between his eyebrows deepening, and he fucked me just a little harder, a little faster.

His eyes flew open. His lips parted in a soundless cry. Finally, he groaned, forcing his cock all the way inside me and shuddering.

"Holy... Oh my God..." The cords stood out from his neck. He screwed his eyes shut, and his lips pulled tight across his teeth. Eric threw his head back, thrust all the way inside me, withdrew a little and tried to force himself even deeper.

His forehead touched my collarbone as his shoulders rose and fell with deep, uneven breaths. Withdrawing just as slowly as he'd pushed in, Eric groaned softly.

He pushed himself up on shaking arms.

"I love you, Shane," he whispered.

"I love you too." I touched his face and kissed him gently.

"I don't expect this to be easy," he said. "I just think you were right. That it'll be worth it."

"Yeah, it will." I caressed his face, wondering how the hell I'd made it the last couple of weeks without touching him. "We'll find a way to make it work. Even if we do have to keep it quiet."

"I don't care if we have to keep it quiet until we retire." He kissed me gently. "I just don't want to lose you again."

"You won't." I wrapped my arms around him and drew him down to me. "I'm not going anywhere."

Epilogue

Eric

About a year later

My heart beat a little faster as my plane slowly descended over Okinawa. The familiar island was mostly shrouded in darkness, but I knew Naha well enough to make out a few signs and buildings that had become landmarks.

It was strange, looking at Okinawa from the air like this again. Last time, I'd been dreading arriving at this shit-hole of an island, but my God, how things had changed. If I was honest with myself, I'd missed this place. Going back to the States had resulted in some serious culture shock. Driving on the right again wasn't too difficult, but I was accustomed to Okinawa. The exceptionally polite people. The language I barely understood. The climate, the architecture, everything. By the beginning of my second week of leave, I was chomping at the bit to get back to this side of the world.

Well, aside from leaving Marie, that was. Parting ways at the airport this morning—yesterday? Whenever it was—hadn't been easy, but since we knew we'd see each other again soon, it wasn't as bad as the last couple of times.

That kid was about to find out the true meaning of jet lag. When she came back from her graduation trip to London, Marie was stopping in to Pennsylvania to meet with Shane's ex-wife and pick up the twins. Then all three of the kids would make the trip to Okinawa to spend some time with us.

But for the next month or so, I had Shane to myself.

I closed the window shade and leaned back against the headrest. My heart fluttered at the thought of seeing Shane in the next twenty minutes or so. After three weeks apart, we'd be lucky if we made it back to my apartment tonight.

The secrecy had gotten old. I wouldn't deny that. I'd been keeping boyfriends a secret for the better part of my career, and the irony that I could be openly gay but not with *this* boyfriend was not lost on me. Still, no matter how much the secrecy sucked, it was better than the alternative. I'd rather have Shane in secret than not have him at all.

The plane touched down, and as soon as it stopped beside the gate, I pulled out my cell phone.

Plane's on the ground, I wrote. *See you shortly.*

About the time the flight attendants opened the door to let us off, my phone beeped.

Shane's message said simply: *E12.*

I pocketed my phone and shouldered my bag. E12 was the parking space where he waited for me. We didn't dare meet up in the baggage claim area. Way too out in the open, especially since it would take all the restraint I possessed not to make sure everyone in the room knew I was in love with him.

Once I'd collected my bags, I hurried toward the parking garage across the street. The first thick, humid breath of Okinawa made me shiver. I was really here. I was finally back. My Japanese vocabulary could fit on a license plate, but I'd never felt more at home than I did on this island.

God, I'd missed this place.

I stepped into the parking lot and followed the signs through the lettered sections.

A.

I walked faster.

B.

My heart beat faster.

C.

Come on, come on...

D.

Almost. Almost. God, Shane, why couldn't you have parked closer? There's like four million empty spaces—

E.

And there was Shane's car. As I crossed the small expanse of pavement, he got out of the car, and his grin almost knocked my knees out from under me.

I was finally here. We were face-to-face. In a few minutes, we could touch. And I could tell him what else I had on my mind, because I could barely keep it to myself a moment longer.

"How was your trip?" he asked, opening the trunk.

"Great." I hoisted my bag into the trunk. "Long-ass flights, but it was good to be home for a while."

"And now you're the father of a high school graduate." He clicked his tongue. "Getting old, Randall."

"Fuck you."

"Don't mind if you do." He shot me a toothy grin.

I laughed. "Well, we'd better get out of here, then, shouldn't we?"

"We should."

I started toward the left side.

"You driving?" he asked, chuckling.

I stopped in my tracks, looked at the car, then shook my head and laughed. "Forgot what country I was in."

"Happens every time," he said. "I do the same thing."

"Well, yeah, but that's just senility, isn't it?"

"Very funny."

Laughing, I went around to get in on the passenger side.

He slid into the driver's seat and looked at me. "Think this is private enough?"

"Quite honestly," I said, leaning across the console, "I couldn't care less if it is."

My lips met his, and electricity crackled all down the length of my spine. His fingers combed through my hair—suddenly I was glad I'd let it grow out a little while I was on leave—and his tongue teased my lips apart.

Some footsteps punctuated the grinding of suitcase wheels on pavement, but even as they passed behind the car, I didn't give a fuck. It had been three long weeks, and so what if anyone saw us? So what, because—

I broke the kiss abruptly. "My paperwork went through."

Shane blinked, probably as startled by the broken kiss as

what I'd said. "What? It..." Then his eyes widened, and his lips parted. "Are you serious?"

Smiling, I nodded. "My LDO paperwork went through. In a few months, I'll be an officer."

"It...really? It finally..." He laughed and shook his head, then pulled me to him again. "*Finally.*"

I held him close and kissed him.

He touched his forehead to mine.

"I love you," I whispered.

"I love you too." He smiled in the low light. "And pretty soon, we won't have to keep it a secret anymore."

I returned the smile, then leaned in and kissed him again. There would still be the need for discretion. Politics being what they were, our relationship could damage our chances at promotions. But once I put on ensign, once I was no longer enlisted, we were a step closer to a relationship that wouldn't get us kicked out. He was a senior officer, I'd be a junior officer, but since we weren't in the same chain of command, the risk of getting in trouble—and the punishment if we did—wasn't as severe.

But even if it hadn't gone through, if I'd retired three years from now as an enlisted Sailor, I just didn't care. I'd keep this a secret forever if I had to.

Shane and I were in love.

And no one could take that away from us.

About the Author

L.A. Witt is an abnormal M/M romance writer who, after three years in Okinawa, Japan, relocated to Omaha, Nebraska, in late 2011. She lives there with her husband, two cats, and a buck-toothed turtle named Sheldon. In between writing smutty books full of smutty smuttiness, she continues her tireless pursuit of her archnemesis, erotica author Lauren Gallagher.

The virgin isn't the only one with something to lose...

The Closer You Get

© 2011 L.A. Witt

Self-described manwhore Kieran Frost is loving the single life. Two years after moving to Seattle, he still has his friends with benefits, Rhett and Ethan, plus a never-ending supply of gorgeous, available men wandering through the bar where he works. A relationship? Spare him the drama and heartbreak. He's got no complaints about his unattached lifestyle.

When Rhett's daughter introduces him to newly-out-of-the-closet Alex Corbin, Kieran's interest perks up. After all, the quiet ones are always the freaks in bed. But Alex isn't just shy and reserved. He's a virgin in every sense of the word, having never even kissed anyone else.

Kieran is no one's teacher, and his first instinct is to run like hell in the other direction. But his conscience won't let him throw the naïve kid to the wolves for someone else to take advantage of. The plan is to introduce Alex to his own sexuality, pull him out of his shell, then go their separate ways.

It's the perfect, foolproof plan...assuming no one falls in love.

Warning: This sequel to The Distance Between Us *contains a curious virgin, a shameless slut, a trip to a sex shop, and one stubborn heart. Oh, and a dildo.*

Available now in ebook and print from Samhain Publishing.

CPSIA information can be obtained at www.ICGtesting.com
Printed in the USA
BVOW04s0424210415

396951BV00001B/15/P